Colin Wilson is one  popular writers at wo— 1931, and left school working in a wool v factory and a coffee was published in 19 acclaim and was an immediate bestseller. Since then he has written many books on philosophy, the occult, crime and sexual deviance, plus a host of successful novels which have won him an international reputation. His work has been translated into Spanish, French, Swedish, Dutch, Japanese, German, Italian, Portuguese, Danish, Norwegian, Finnish and Hebrew.

By the same author

COLIN WILSON

The World of Violence

Grafton
An Imprint of HarperCollinsPublishers

Grafton
An Imprint of HarperCollins*Publishers*
77–85 Fulham Palace Road,
Hammersmith, London W6 8JB

Published by Grafton 1991
9 8 7 6 5 4 3 2 1

First published in Great Britain by
Victor Gollancz Ltd 1963

ISBN 0 586 21049 0

Set in Times

Printed in Great Britain by
HarperCollinsManufacturing Glasgow

For Jean and Harry
and the boys in the back room
at the Wolfe

Acknowledgements

I wish to thank ex-Superintendent Bill Mallet of the Cornwall police, and Keith Perks of the St Austell Pistol Club, for help and advice. Perhaps this is also the place to acknowledge a debt of gratitude to my friend Tristram Carlyon, who was killed in Africa last year; it was in his shooting gallery at Tregrehan that the first ideas of this book came to me. I also wish to thank Susan Bramble, for invaluable editorial assistance, and Mr J. B. Priestley for permission to quote passages from his *Postscripts*.

PART ONE

The Outer Dark

1

My father believed that any intelligent child can be moulded into a prodigy if his parents make the effort when he is young enough. Being himself a fine musician, and a superlative performer on the violoncello, he dreamed of turning me into a young Mozart, and my training on the piano began when I was three years old. He had great hopes for me, because I could sing in key at the age of two.

He was not mistaken. I became a prodigy – but unfortunately of the wrong kind. This was the fault of Uncle Nick Dawson, who discovered that my talents lay in the direction of mathematics. I must begin by writing about Uncle Nick. And the most important fact about him was that he was insane.

No one knew about this, although my mother suspected. My grandfather had died of delirium tremens at the age of forty, and there is a tradition in the family that his uncle (my father's great-uncle) was either Jack the Ripper or Peter the Painter (the leader of the Sidney Street Gang). My father's Uncle Sam (of whom I shall write later) was definitely peculiar, but had a talent for making money, so that the family never tried to have him certified. But Uncle Nick had once spent a year in a mental home, after he declared that he was a bird and jumped off the roof. (Luckily a neighbour's pigeon-house broke his fall; but Uncle Nick fractured his shin-bone, and walked for the rest of his life with a limp.)

Uncle Nick had been out of the mental home for many years when I first knew him. Although he was taciturn and secretive, he seemed sane enough. He had inherited a little money, and lived alone in a rented room, close to our house.

Uncle Nick was a big man with a bird's-nest beard and a completely bald head. He had a habit of muttering to himself under his breath, but as he was known to be a mathematician, it was assumed that he was probably doing calculations. Before I was born, he had attended a church that called itself 'The Church of the Third Zion', and was known to be writing a book about morals. This church had apparently been formed by a man who called himself Gaylord Mumford, and believed that men can be redeemed by living exclusively on a diet of cabbages and boiled stinging-nettles. Uncle Nick became his chief disciple and close friend – until, one day, the Reverend Mumford disappeared with all the money he had been able to coax out of his female converts, and was later caught and sent to prison. After this, Uncle Nick became morose, stopped going to church, and gave it out that he was writing a book. The family felt that he had made a fool of himself, and tactfully avoided all reference to religion in his presence. It was suspected – but not known for certain – that the Reverend Mumford had gone off with a large sum belonging to Uncle Nick; so for a time he was treated with the tactful respect due to someone recently bereaved

Uncle Nick had been trained as an engineer, and continued to make a hobby of mathematics, even when his main interest was in writing his book on morals. Whenever he got tired of his own room he would come over to our house, seat himself at the table without ceremony, and absorb himself in a book or a sheet of figures. Frequently he produced a pencil or slide-rule and muttered calculations.

I came home from school one afternoon – I must have been about four and a half at the time – and found him sitting at the table, sipping from a pint mug of tea, and making calculations on a sheet of paper. My mother was sitting opposite, reading a newspaper. I sat down and ate bread and jam. Uncle Nick muttered: 'Twenty-five times twenty-nine.' I said: 'Seven hundred and twenty-five.' Uncle Nick ignored me and took out his slide-rule. My mother glanced at the paper, and saw that he wrote down 725. She said: 'Hugh was right, then?' Uncle Nick muttered: 'What?' and went on writing. But my mother never liked his bad manners, and persisted. Finally, Uncle Nick looked up irritably, and listened while she explained that I had multiplied the figures in my head. He glared at me, and said: 'Seventeen times nineteen.' I thought for a moment, then said: 'Three hundred and twenty-three.' At this he blinked and said: 'Astonishing.' My mother thought I was showing how well I'd learnt my school work, and said vaguely: 'They only taught us as far as the twelve times table when I was at school.' Uncle Nick said: 'How did you do it, boy?' I had to think about this for a moment, then explained that I had multiplied seventeen by ten, doubled it, and subtracted seventeen. Uncle Nick laid down his pencil and pushed the sheet of paper away from him. I noticed the curious, feverish gleam in his eyes, but wasn't alarmed. (After all, most grown-ups were a little mad.) He tried me with a few simple problems in algebra; one of them, I remember, was: 'The head of a fish is nine inches long; the tail is as long as the head and half the body; the body is as long as the head and tail together.' This seemed very simple to me; as he said each phrase, a picture of the fish came into my mind, and almost as soon as he had finished speaking I said: 'The tail is twenty-seven inches, the body thirty-six.'

By this time, even my mother was startled. She began muttering: 'Nine inches – head as long as tail and twice the body . . .' wearing an expression of exaggerated bewilderment that I believe she had developed as a defence against being asked to think. (She is a small, plump woman with exceptionally large blue eyes, and is definitely the vaguest woman I have ever known.) Finally, she asked Uncle Nick: 'What does it all mean?'

'I'll tell you,' Uncle Nick said, fixing her with his feverish stare; 'it probably means that your son could be another Einstein.'

'Who's Einstein?' asked mother. I was glad she had asked. I wanted to know too.

'Another Newton, Gauss, Riemann!' shouted Uncle Nick, his eyes bulging.

Mother asked mildly: 'You mean he's good at figures?'

Uncle Nick ignored her. He suddenly smiled at me, and beckoned to me:

'Come here, Hugh. We'll try you with one or two more little sums.'

I disliked the smile more than the insane stare, and refused to get up. He finally persuaded me with the help of a bar of chocolate, and I went and sat on his lap. An hour later, when my father came home, he was already teaching me the elements of Euclid, and setting me simple problems in geometry.

At first, my father was delighted to be told that I was a mathematical prodigy. He thought that if I could be precocious in mathematics, then the chances were that I could also be a musical prodigy. I think he had visions of me playing at a recital in the town hall at the age of six, then going on a lucrative tour of Europe, playing his compositions to enthusiastic audiences who would hail this unique partnership of father and son. (My father was a successful solicitor and a very bad and academic composer; but he believed that there was a conspiracy of professional musicians to prevent his works being performed.) Uncle Nick was tactful enough not to shatter this illusion immediately. It was many months before he broke it to my father that, if I had the seeds of mathematical genius, nothing was less likely than that I should also have the makings of a great musician. (He pointed out that no mathematician or musician in history has shown genius in both subjects, although it is a fact that most mathematicians enjoy music.) My father took it badly – very badly indeed – but by this time I had already been thoroughly injected with the virus of mathematics. Nothing could have saved me.

I began spending an hour – sometimes hours – every day with Uncle Nick, usually in our house, but occasionally in his own room. I liked figures. They amused me. They gave me a certain sense of power. I liked to be able to tell people how many gallons of water were used in our town every day, how many hours everyone sleeps in a lifetime, how long it would take to cover Mount Everest with the cigarette stubs thrown away every week in London. Uncle Nick was an excellent teacher. He took care not to bore me with too many theories; instead, we went through books of puzzles, and invented puzzles to try to baffle one another.

I often wonder if Uncle Nick went permanently insane as a consequence of becoming my teacher. I now believe that, like my father, he harboured extraordinary ideas about me. But while my father was mainly interested in using me to gain money and fame, Uncle Nick was more interested in power. I never learned much about his relations with the Reverend Mumford, but I believe that they had once discussed the idea of going to America and starting a city that would be inhabited solely by members of the Church of the Third Zion, and that would revere them both as prophets and teachers. It may be that some such idea now revived in him, and that he began to think of me as his St Paul.

One day I went in to see him on my way home from school. That afternoon we had had our first history lesson, and the teacher had shown us pictures of sabre-toothed tigers and of mastodons. It was explained to us that the men of those days had almost no chance of protecting themselves against such monsters. How, in that case, had it come about that the monsters were now dead, while we were sitting comfortably in a classroom? The teacher had a sense of suspense; she told us that she would tell us the answer in our next history lesson.

I walked home with a school-friend, and we discussed the problem excitedly, and finally, as we approached the house where Uncle Nick lodged, I decided that I would go and ask him. He knew everything – of that I was sure. And it seemed intolerable to be asked to wait another week to learn more about this fascinating world of jungles and prehistoric monsters. So I left my friend and went up to see him.

He looked pleased to see me. But as soon as I started asking him about history, he looked grave. Finally, he placed a hand on my head, stared into my face, and said:

'I didn't mean to talk to you about these things until you were a bit older. But I think you'd better have the truth from me before your teachers poison your mind with lies.'

I found this confusing but exciting, and made myself comfortable on the settee. Uncle Nick looked upset and distracted. He walked up and down the room, running his hand over his huge bald forehead, then combing his tangled mat of a beard with his fingers, and contemplatively picking his nose. Then he began to talk, in a rambling, choked voice, so that I had to concentrate hard to make any sense of it. But finally I gathered that we were talking about astronomy. After ten minutes or so, I interrupted cautiously to explain that I found him difficult

14

to follow. He drew a deep breath, came over to the settee, and began talking to me about a scientist with a Russian name. This I also found hard to follow. But he ended by pointing his finger at me, leaning closer, and saying ominously: 'They found him dead at the foot of a cliff. It was supposed to be suicide, but no one ever explained why there were three shoes by the body.' My hair tingled; I asked breathlessly: 'You mean . . .?' He nodded. 'I do.' Suddenly he turned, rushed to the door, and flung it open. A woman who was entering the room next door gaped at him. He glared at her, muttered something, and slammed the door. 'You see!' he said. I didn't, but I nodded. Uncle Nick sat down beside me, stared at the floor, and ran his fingers through his beard. Finally, he said:

'Go on home, boy. Come back tomorrow. I'll explain it all then. But listen. I want you to promise me that you won't mention this to anybody – not even your parents. Do you promise?'

I nodded, but asked him why.

'I can't tell you that. But if you tell anybody, you might never see me again.'

I was duly impressed, and ran home. I didn't feel much temptation to tell anybody. To begin with, I didn't know what I wasn't supposed to tell. Anyway, I was used to the weird standards of adult values, and how they were liable to make mountains out of mole-hills.

But the next afternoon I called in again on my way home from school. This time, Uncle Nick was more matter-of-fact. Perhaps he had decided that the mystification was hardly necessary for a six-year-old boy. He began by explaining to me that almost everything I was taught at school was false – or rather, such an ingenious mixture of fact and falsehood that only a genius could unravel it. For example, we had been taught that the

15

earth revolved around the sun . . . Here I interrupted him to say that we hadn't yet been taught anything about the earth. They were too busy teaching us to read and write to bother about geography. So Uncle Nick took a deep breath, and gave me a brief sketch of astronomy from the Greeks onward. I must admit that he was an excellent teacher, with a natural gift for making things interesting. He spent so long on this – and I interrupted him so many times to ask questions – that I had to run home for supper, and the great secret was still unrevealed. But the next evening I was back again. I had gone into the geography classroom, looked at the globe, and asked the teacher some elementary questions, so I now had proof that Uncle Nick's account of current ideas was accurate. When I told Uncle Nick about this, he looked excited, then grave – and then told me to sit down. He then explained to me the truth about our earth, which sounded to me plausible enough. It was that the earth is not a simple globe, like an orange, but is a whole series of globes, one inside another, so that its structure resembles that of an onion. At both poles – the North and South – there are immense holes, fifty miles across, leading into the interior. These holes run right through the centre of the globe, so that, in theory, you could stick an enormous pole right through the earth, from North to South.

I found this idea delightful and enthralling. I wanted to ask a thousand questions – but there was no need, because Uncle Nick talked so fast that I had difficulty in distinguishing all his words. The outer shell of the earth, he explained, was five miles thick, and this applied to all the inner shells. The diameter of the earth is, of course, about eight thousand miles, and since each of the inner worlds was five miles thick, with an atmosphere five miles high, this meant that there are no less than forty inner

16

worlds. All the inner worlds are lighted by their own sun, which is embedded in the 'sky' (that is to say, in the shell of the world above). This is why scientists discover that the temperature rises as one penetrates underground; they imagine that this is because the earth is still hot inside, but the truth is simply that it contains several suns.

Our own sun, he explained, is not, as astronomers believe, ninety-two million miles from the earth, but a mere ten; and it is not millions of miles in diameter, but only two. God made the sun to light the world, so it stands to reason that he would place it fairly near the world. The sun revolves round the earth, just as the ancient astronomers thought it did; Galileo was mistaken.

I cannot go into the fantasies of Uncle Nick at length; it would take five hundred pages. They went on for over a year, although my regular lessons in mathematics also continued. Every night, before I left, he would make me solemnly swear not to reveal his teachings to anyone else, in case his enemies heard of it and tried to murder him. All this I also believed implicitly. It was obvious to me that his claim to know more than any man in the world was justified; I only had to ask him a question, on any subject, to prove it. I once read a story in a comic paper about Frankenstein, and asked him about it. The result was a terrifying lecture on the reanimation of dead bodies, the manufacture of Frankenstein monsters, and endowing statues with life. It was during this lecture that he began to refer to his 'master'. I gathered that his master was a man of enormous wisdom who had initiated him into the great secrets. Unfortunately, he had been murdered by the 'enemies'. But he told me how this master had discovered a statue, five hundred feet tall, buried in the sand of the Sahara desert. This was the

17

famous Golem of Hebrew legend. The master had reanimated this statue, and had ordered it to help him excavate a lost city buried under the sand. Unfortunately, the statue had dug a little too enthusiastically, and had fallen through the earth's shell into the next world. This disturbance of the divine order had been punished by death – the 'enemies' were, in some obscure way, the instruments of revenge.

It is now obvious to me that, if Uncle Nick had not been insane, he would have made a fine imaginative writer of the Rider Haggard type. I still cannot understand why he told me all this, and how far he believed it himself. I am sure that he believed his theory of several earths inside one another – but how far did he believe his fantasies about his 'master', which were obviously developed on the spur of the moment when I asked him about Frankenstein?

One thing that became apparent to me as my lessons continued was his monomania. He once said: 'I can smash any man who argues with me. I know more about any subject than any professor, even if he is an expert in it.' This seemed to me a modest enough statement of the truth. I asked him why he allowed the world to continue in its ignorance, and he explained that the 'enemies' thought him dead, and that he was not strong enough yet to risk letting them know he was still alive. One day he would be strong enough to challenge them openly – with my help. But this might not be for many years.

It is a pity that there is not space here to write in detail about Uncle Nick's ideas; they formed an astonishing and complex system. I once asked him what happened to the sea round the holes; he replied that it poured into the Northern hole in a great waterfall, and then fell straight through the earth like the water from a tap, emerging at the South hole. These holes had never been discovered because they were concealed by a thick mist due to spray – this was why Admiral Byrd had not seen the Northern hole when he flew over the pole. Ships that ventured too close were swept in and never seen again, although in one instance – the *Marie Celeste* – the ship had fallen right through the world, shaking out all the passengers *en route*, but being otherwise unharmed. The ten lost tribes of Israel had found their way through the outer shell into the next world, and were still there in comfort. They had descended through a secret tunnel underneath the great pyramid, which still exists (although it is now concealed) – and left the story of their descent in a secret code on the walls of one of the hidden chambers.

Sometimes, when I asked Uncle Nick a question, he would tell me that I would have to wait until the next day for the answer – giving me the impression that he had to consult some secret 'master' to ask permission to reveal it. And usually, the next day, he would give me a detailed answer explaining, for example, what the inhabitants of the next shell looked like (they were eight feet tall and wore pale-blue clothes; they were also far more beautiful than human beings, and knew everything about our history). He also told me that the Aurora Borealis is the reflection of the sun of this inner world on the mist above the Northern hole.

It might seem that all these stories were no more harmful than the *Arabian Nights*; this is partly true. But it should be remembered that Uncle Nick never stopped warning me that we were guarding a dangerous secret. At school, when the teacher told us about the earth and the sun, I had difficulty in restraining myself from telling her the 'truth'.

I actually took one small boy into my confidence about some of the lesser secrets, swearing him to silence; this helped to relieve the strain. Uncle Nick made me feel that we had tremendous work to do. A child naturally feels 'insignificant'; the world has been going on for a long time before he comes on the scene, and he feels less important than a gnat. But here was I, at the age of seven, feeling that it would be my task, one day, to change the whole outlook of the human race. This was an awful secret to carry around. I suppose I didn't believe in it completely – a part of me always felt it was a game – but even to believe in it partly was quite a mental burden for a child. A child is still half in the womb; he likes warmth and enclosure and curling up in a ball in bed; the world is a nuisance; it is pleasant to escape from it. The world goes on whether you are asleep or awake. But I already felt responsible to the future; I was like a prince who is schooled from the age of five to the idea of becoming king. Only my task was more difficult because I had none of the prince's privileges; I had to live as though I was in the secret service, concealing my identity.

I do not know what would have happened if this had gone on much longer, and how far Uncle Nick could have involved me in his fantasy. The basic passivity of a seven-year-old prevented me from taking it too seriously, yet it coloured my world and my outlook. One day, it stopped abruptly.

We had been away for a few days, staying with an aunt who lived near Beachy Head. I remember that my aunt commented unfavourably on my dislike of the country-side and preoccupation with mathematics. They had taken me for walks along the cliffs; I tried to persuade them to go on without me and collect me on the way back; I wanted to work out a problem in the theory of numbers. Irritably, they dragged me along behind them, and I showed my boredom by refusing to find any interest in the views. (This was not affectation; nature aroused no response in me.) They took me along to a nearby farm, expecting me to be fascinated by the cows and pigs; my uncle even hinted that he might arrange for me to spend a day helping the farmer. I loathed the place; I disliked the messy farmyard with its great pats of steaming cow-dung and stink of pigs and stupid, pointless hens. There was something about the futility of animal life that frightened me. I escaped to a quiet spot under a hedge and read Diophantus's arithmetic; an hour later they found me, after a search, and there was another scene. Finally, my uncle had a workshop with a lathe and various other tools for carpentry or metal-work. He kept trying to induce me to take an interest in it; it was the joy of his life and he wanted to see me share it. He made me stand watching while he turned me a spinning-top on his lathe; but I had never been interested in toys; I accepted it politely, hid it at the bottom of a case, and forgot about it. On my last evening, there was a kind of showdown; my father took me into the front room and explained to me that I was an ungrateful little wretch who had consistently rejected the kindness offered by my aunt and uncle. He talked about their hospitality as if we had the option of paying for it in cash or gratitude, and implied that I was now heavily in debt. He told me that I should at least make a gesture and apologize to my aunt and uncle. I was not sure what I was supposed to apologize about; but I always took the line of least resistance, and agreed to say I was sorry. So I went into the living-room, where my aunt and uncle were already looking benevo-lent and prepared to forgive, and said I was sorry. They asked me what for. I said I was sorry I hadn't enjoyed myself. This touched off a new argument, and I had to do a lot more apologizing, and they ended by being nice to me and giving me a long lecture on the importance of being 'normal' and making people like me. They seemed to feel that mathematics was on the same level as chronic

21

alcoholism or an unhealthy interest in sex; I didn't argue, but I went off to bed feeling worried; they had given me the impression that I would grow up with a curved spine, round shoulders and a myopia that would end in blindness. Later, my mother and father talked in bed – assuming I was asleep – and I heard them agreeing that Uncle Nick's influence had been thoroughly bad, and that they would have to find some excuse for keeping me away from him.

This proved unnecessary. When we got back, I took the first opportunity to hurry off to Uncle Nick's lodgings; his landlady answered the door – she was a gaunt old lady who was less bad-tempered than she appeared – and looked grave when she saw me. She told me to go back home and tell my father that Uncle Nick was in hospital. I asked what was wrong with him, but she wouldn't answer; she finally turned me round and pushed me towards the gate, then banged the door. I ran home and delivered the message; father immediately set out to find out what was wrong. He came back looking upset, and whispered to my mother in the kitchen. All that they would tell me was that Uncle Nick was ill, and would be in hospital for a long time. (I heard my mother say: 'It's the answer to our prayer.') It took me nearly a week to find out the truth, and I did this by piecing together hints and rumours that I heard at school (two of my schoolfriends lived near Uncle Nick), and by trying to trap my mother into telling me the whole story. In the end she gave way – she always did – and admitted that the 'hospital' to which Uncle Nick had been taken was the lunatic asylum.

It is an odd story, and I am still not sure of the details. It seems – fantastic as this sounds – that Uncle Nick's insanity was somehow induced by the insanity of the woman who lived in the next room. This old lady was some kind of relative of Uncle Nick's landlady; I often saw her on the stairs, and she seemed harmless and sweet and very withered, with the vague manners of the deaf. Apparently she had occasioned disquiet when she began to wander into the rooms of the other lodgers at odd hours of the day and night; Uncle Nick had woken up on two occasions to find her looking down at him and smiling oddly. She would then laugh crazily and go away. I wonder whether Uncle Nick thought that she was an agent of the 'enemy'. (She was the woman whom he had surprised outside the door on the day when he first took me into his confidence about the structure of the earth.) A few days later she went completely insane; she wandered out in the early hours of the morning, dressed in her nightgown, and carrying a tray of jam-tarts that she'd found on the kitchen table. She walked half a mile or so, to one of the main streets, and began accosting workmen and offering them tarts, explaining that, from then on, she would be there every morning to distribute food. It was all harmless enough; two policemen escorted her home, and later in the day an ambulance called to take her to the mental home.

When Uncle Nick was told about this, he became very quiet, and locked himself in his room. Towards evening he apparently called at our house, but found no one at home; the next-door neighbour spoke to him, and noticed that he seemed tense with suppressed excitement. He returned home, packed a few clothes in a case, and wrapped up a number of books in a brown-paper parcel; then, when the rest of the lodgers were at supper, he sneaked out of the house, and walked down to the nearest bus-stop. His parcel and case were heavy, and he put them on the pavement and joined a short queue. At this point, a small black dog approached the parcel of books, sniffed it, then raised its hind leg and soaked it. Uncle

23

Nick went wild with excitement; he ran at the dog and tried to beat it with his stick; it ran away and he followed it, shouting and swearing. Up to this point, no one thought there was anything strange about his behaviour, and a few people were smiling. A small boy now approached the parcel of books, and bent over it. Unck Nick turned and saw him, and immediately rushed back, still shouting. Then, to everyone's surprise and indignation, he began hitting the small boy with his stick. The boy was also taken by surprise and fell down, and Uncle Nick might have done some damage with the stick (I remember the stick – it was heavy and knobbly) if several men had not jumped on him and pulled him away. It was now Uncle Nick's turn to be in danger; the people were not aware that they were dealing with a lunatic; they thought he was simply a bad-tempered elderly gentleman who should be taught a lesson, and one woman began hitting him with an umbrella while an angry man (perhaps the boy's father) twisted his arm, and another kicked his legs from underneath him. A policeman saw the fight and interrupted; but as soon as the people drew back, Uncle Nick sprang to his feet and rushed away, shouting curses in a queer, throaty voice ('like an angry dog', someone said). He did not go far; twenty yards from the bus-stop there was a children's recreation ground, which was closed; its swings, roundabouts, and the rest were chained up. Uncle Nick clambered to the top of the slide – ignoring the boards that had been placed on it to prevent children climbing up – and stood astride the top, swinging his cane and daring anyone to come and get him. A crowd gathered; but no one liked the look of the stick. They couldn't understand what he was shouting – with his talk about 'enemies' – but his language was so bad that it was agreed that something had to be done. The efforts of the policeman to persuade him to come down

24

were unavailing; but after half an hour or so an ambulance arrived, and two muscular attendants climbed out, one of them carrying a strait-jacket. They started ascending the slide from opposite sides; Uncle Nick crouched, waiting. But he had the advantage, since the boards that covered it were smooth. As one of the men got close to the top, Uncle Nick leapt at him and sent him spinning with a blow of the stick; he lost his own balance and fell off the slide, but picked himself up and rushed into the crowd, swinging the stick. There was panic; everyone scattered, and Uncle Nick set off running like a hare, with the attendants after him. However, his stomach was large and his wind short; they caught him, tied him expertly in the strait-jacket, and bundled him into the ambulance. And Uncle Nick spent the remaining eight years of his life in the mental home. I never saw him again, although my mother and father both went to visit him. Apparently the excitement was followed by some kind of attack that made him foam at the mouth; when this passed off, he became very dull, and could not be persuaded to speak. Two years later he could be trusted in a ward with other patients, but continued to be dull, almost moronic. His interest in mathematics vanished completely.

What happened to his intellect? I have often wondered. Can it be wiped away as cleanly as chalk off a blackboard? Can the mind collapse like a city in an earthquake, so that structures that have taken years to build crash down like granite blocks; and is the collapse of a cultivated mind a far greater catastrophe than that of an ignoramus?

At all events, Uncle Nick's catastrophe was complete; it was total mental bankruptcy that seemed to involve every idea he possessed; his mental level at the time of his death was that of a four-year-old child.

It is difficult for me to describe in detail my reaction to

the news of his insanity. First of all, there was the irrational school-boy reaction of pleasure which is one of the mysteries of human psychology. A child will feel pleasure at almost any catastrophe, even the death of all his family in a fire. I have even observed traces of it in myself as an adult. This is partly because he would rather have *anything* happen than nothing at all; he likes to feel that life is moving. But where Uncle Nick was concerned, I had lost a friend and an ally, a man who asked very little of me and who very seldom bored me. So my next reaction was despair; I was afraid that my father might make another attempt to turn me into a musician. Then, later still, came horror. They all said that Uncle Nick was insane – but had he not warned me that his enemies might engineer something like this? Perhaps it was my duty to try to set him free.

And what about the 'secret doctrine' of the hollowness of the earth? Should I keep it to myself? Supposing – and this really frightened me – supposing the 'enemies' knew that I knew about it; might they not try to murder me? It took about a week for this thought to occur to me, but when it did it frightened me so much that I had to tell somebody about it. I had no wish to speak to my father; he seemed completely unsympathetic. My mother was too vague to be much comfort. I ended by telling the geography mistress at school. She was not one of my teachers – I was still too young for geography – but I had talked to her on two or three occasions since the day I went into the geography classroom to look at the globe. One afternoon, about a week after Uncle Nick's outbreak, I wandered into her classroom after school and pretended to look at the globe. She glanced up from marking a pile of papers, and said: 'Hello Hugh. What do you want?' I plunged immediately:

'Do you think the world might have a big hole at the North Pole?'

She asked cautiously: 'What kind of a hole?'

'A great big hole that the sea flows into?'

I was trembling as I asked the question. It was the first time I had broken the stern prohibitions of Uncle Nick. I half expected strange little demons with red eyes to leap from out of the floor and silence me on the spot. Miss Bloomfield noticed my agitation, and said casually:

'It's a fairly old idea. Several of the ancient geographers believed it.'

I was astounded. Miss Bloomfield told me to wait for her and went out; a few minutes later she came back with a volume of Poe's tales from the school library. She showed me a picture of a ship about to plunge over a tremendous abyss of water – it was an illustration to *MS Found in a Bottle* – and told me that Poe had borrowed the idea from Strabo or some other geographer. She handed me the volume and said: 'Take it home and read it.' I took it and walked out of the classroom in a daze. She called me back as I reached the door, and asked me where I'd heard the idea. I told her everything, from the beginning – the 'enemies', the 'master' in the desert, the animated statue. She listened without interrupting me, nodding, and occasionally smiling. When I had finished, she only remarked:

'Your uncle sounds a remarkable man.'

'But is it *true*?' I asked.

'Oh no. It's pure imagination.'

'You mean it's *all* lies?'

'I don't suppose he meant to tell lies. Mad people usually believe everything they say.'

'Are you sure he was mad?'

'Oh yes. Of course. He's in an asylum now, isn't he?'

This seemed unanswerable. Yet I could not believe it.

After all, if Uncle Nick had been telling lies she might also be telling lies. However, her easy manner had me half convinced. She took it all so casually. I walked home with Poe's tales, and spent the evening picking my way through *MS Found in a Bottle*. It was hard work; I had learned to read only the year before, and although I felt at home with a page of figures or symbols, Poe's language baffled me. But I persisted, and finished the story before I fell asleep. I was still puzzled. After all, Poe was writing fiction; he knew it was not true. But Miss Bloomfield was asking me to believe that Uncle Nick had been insane all the time he had been telling me about the hollow earth. I could imagine telling elaborate lies – but I could not imagine telling lies and not knowing you were telling lies. It seemed as obviously self-contradictory as saying that black is white. I decided that I had several more questions to ask Miss Bloomfield the next day.

I did not realize it, but Miss Bloomfield's casualness had been assumed. She was probably the most level-headed teacher in the school, and she had seen immediately that there would be no point in getting excited about my peculiar ideas. If I was confused, then excitement on her part would only make things worse. Her attitude was right. It is a pity that she hadn't enough basic confidence in it to keep the whole thing to herself.

Unfortunately, she felt that she had to pass it on to the headmistress, a Miss Gulliver. And Miss Gulliver was horrified, and immediately wrote a letter to my parents. This arrived the next day after I had left for school. At mid-morning, I was called out of class and told to go to the headmistress's study. There, I was startled to find my father waiting. He and the headmistress looked so serious that I immediately assumed that I was going to be punished – although I had no idea why. Then Miss

Bloomfield came in, and smiled uncomfortably at me, and I understood.

They made me sit down, and the headmistress settled a cushion behind me as though I was an invalid. My father sat in a hard chair, looking very uncomfortable and embarrassed, and when I caught his eye he glowered at me. Miss Gulliver said soothingly:

'Now, Hugh, I want you to tell us everything about your Uncle Nick, and everything that he's ever told you, and everything he's ever done to you.'

(Apparently the story about the hollow earth struck them as so sinister that they assumed Uncle Nick's motives to be of the very worst. I can see now that this episode probably formed a little oasis of excitement in the headmistress's daily routine, so that her reaction was to inflate it as much as possible. I think that she almost hoped that Uncle Nick had been sexually assaulting me for the past two years.)

I told the whole story again; but this time it was more satisfying from my viewpoint, because Miss Gulliver kept interrupting with gasps of excitement and horror; my father simply looked grave and uncomfortable. When I had finished, he asked me awkwardly if Uncle Nick had ever touched me or fondled me; I said no, wondering what he was getting at. (In fact, I had always kept my distance from Uncle Nick because I disliked the smell of tobacco on his breath.) This seemed to cheer them a little, but Miss Gulliver kept repeating: 'Why? Why did he do it?' Miss Bloomfield shrugged and said: 'What does it matter? It hasn't done any harm.' Miss Gulliver glared at her. 'How do you know? This child may be affected for life.' She then explained to me in the most solemn and emphatic way that everything Uncle Nick had ever told me had been wickedly untrue, and that I must disbelieve every word he had ever spoken. I asked her whether there was anything wrong with the idea that the world was hollow, and she had to admit, though reluctantly, that it was not actually a wicked idea, just a mistaken one. There was still one point that I wanted clearing up. I asked her if she was quite sure that the world wasn't hollow. This seemed to me a reasonable question, for Uncle Nick had spent a lot of time explaining to me that people take too many things on trust, without bothering to probe them. Miss Gulliver stared at my father, shook her head slowly, and said: 'You see. It may be too late.'

Miss Bloomfield said irritably: 'I think perhaps you're making a little too much out of this.'

'Are we?' Miss Gulliver said. She looked at my father, and repeated solemnly: 'Are we?' My father wriggled his shoulders and said: 'I don't know whether any harm has been done.' Miss Gulliver interrupted:

'No harm! The boy has been in the hands of a madman for two years, and you say no harm has been done! Why, he might have been murdered!'

I was a little confused. I asked:

'You mean by the enemies?'

She threw up her hands, and gave a sort of groan. Then she came and sat on the arm of my chair, and repeated slowly that everything Uncle Nick had ever told me was wicked lies, and I must forget it. I asked: 'But what about the mathematics?' My father and Miss Gulliver looked at one another blankly. I had forgotten to mention to Miss Bloomfield that Uncle Nick had taught me mathematics.

'What kind of thing did he teach you?' she asked me.

'All kinds of things,' I said vaguely. 'Arithmetical progressions and sequences and binomials and imaginary numbers . . .'

'Imaginary numbers!' Miss Gulliver shrieked.

'Like the square root of minus one,' I explained. But neither Miss Bloomfield nor Miss Gulliver nor my father knew any mathematics. All three immediately jumped to the conclusion that Uncle Nick had also been teaching me his own insane form of mathematics.

'This is most difficult,' Miss Gulliver said. 'I don't know quite what to advise.' She ended by telling me that Uncle Nick's mathematics was almost certainly as untrustworthy as his geography, and that I had better disbelieve everything until they could make a thorough investigation. Miss Bloomfield demurred; she said she thought this was probably unnecessary, but Miss Gulliver snapped at her and suggested acidly that perhaps she and my father should now be left to handle the situation. Miss Bloomfield shrugged and went out. Miss Gulliver repeated several times: 'I've never had a case like this before,' as if I had a dangerous and contagious disease. She had me rather alarmed by this time. I was relieved when they finally sent me back to my classroom.

In the mid-morning break I stayed in the classroom and looked through Lancelot Hogben's *Mathematics for the Million*, which Uncle Nick had given me a fortnight before he was taken away. Sure enough, there was the section on imaginary numbers. It was in black and white. So Miss Gulliver *had* been lying when she said that this was an invention of Uncle Nick's. I had a bad quarter of an hour wondering if Miss Gulliver was one of the agents of 'the enemy'. Luckily, Miss Bloomfield came looking for me, and found me reading Hogben; I showed her the passage on imaginary numbers, and she asked me if she might borrow the book. I presume she showed it to the headmistress, but I have no idea of what happened, for she returned the book to me a few hours later, saying merely: 'That seems rather advanced for you.' But for some reason my panic had disappeared by this time.

31

Nothing more happened for several days, except that my father asked me why I had never told him about Uncle Nick's 'hollow earth', and did not seem to understand when I said that I had been sworn to secrecy. He explained that he was my father, and Uncle Nick was only a distant relative, so that I had no right to make such a promise. This did not convince me, though I said nothing. But it increased my feeling of distrust for my father and Miss Gulliver.

Uncle Nick's effects had to be moved out of his room so that it could be re-let. His landlady was unwilling to store them, so she asked my father to collect them. It was a big job, for Uncle Nick had hundreds of books. They had to be collected in a van, and were taken down to our basement one day when I was at school. I was not told about this; but on returning home from school I noticed a small jade statuette of an athlete on our living-room shelf; I knew it belonged to Uncle Nick, and began looking around for the rest of his things. When I found that the door to the coal-cellar had been locked, I guessed they were down there. I showed no curiosity. A week later I returned from school and found the house empty, my mother being at the shops. I knew another way into the coal-cellar, through a grating on the far side. It was a tight squeeze, but I managed it. The cellar was large; coal and coke were kept on one side, and sacks of potatoes, cooking-apples, and jars of preserve on the other. Most of the books had been packed into an enormous old trunk, and the remainder piled on top of it. I switched on the light, and went carefully through the books. The ones on top of the trunk were boring volumes of theology and biblical commentary; I piled them on the floor, and looked inside. These were the ones I wanted to see; I had often looked at them on Uncle Nick's shelves, but had been afraid to ask to look at them. There was a volume called: *Did Atlantis Exist?* another called *Hörbiger's World Ice Theory*, and finally, near the bottom of the trunk, the one I wanted, *The Hollow Earth* by Paul Jackson Caine.

While I was still searching through the trunk I heard my mother come in, and had a momentary panic. Then it struck me that she was unlikely to disturb me, and that even if she came down for potatoes I could probably hide myself behind the coal. So I went on searching, until I had selected a dozen volumes that I wanted to read. I replaced the others carefully, and carried my books over to the grating. I pushed them outside, then wriggled through. The problem was getting them into the house. But I overcame this by hiding most of them inside the tool-shed, and taking the one I wanted most – *The Hollow Earth* – under my coat. I even remembered to wipe the coal off my face with a handkerchief damped with spittle before I went into the house.

Up in my bedroom, I opened Caine's volume. Immediately, the hair stirred on my head. The frontispiece was a finely reproduced coloured diagram, showing the earth exactly as Uncle Nick had described it to me. It took me some time to discover that there were a great many differences between Caine's Hollow Earth and Uncle Nick's – Uncle Nick had an altogether richer imagination than Caine – but the essentials were there: the holes at the North and South poles, with the sea pouring through in a cataract, the various shells.

A great deal of Caine's language was incomprehensible to me at the age of seven; he writes a pseudo-scientific jargon full of circumlocutions and Latin phrases. But the pictures were plain enough. I imagine that Caine must have had the book privately printed in America, and spent a great deal of money on it; it was beautifully produced, bound in green leather, with highly attractive

33

colour-plates that were supposed to be based on sketches that Caine had made in the various 'inner worlds'. These showed strange trees and animals, and all had beautiful misty effects of dawn or sunset. A particularly impressive one showed a ship about to be swept into the Northern hole, and the interior sun glowing through the heavy mist over the gulf. I would sometimes stare at this picture for hours, until I could imagine whole worlds behind it; it always left me feeling remote from the real world, breathing an atmosphere of mystery and nostalgia.

For some weeks I found it very hard to resist the temptation to show Caine's book to my father and the headmistress. Only the conviction that it would be immediately confiscated prevented me. For it was obvious to me that everything Uncle Nick had ever told me was true. Uncle Nick might have been a liar, but who could doubt a book full of coloured plates, bound in green leather? Therefore Uncle Nick was not mad; his enemies had succeeded in silencing him. But what could I do about it? Only adults regard martyrdom as sensible; at the age of seven, my sense of self-preservation was so strong that it never entered my head to defend Uncle Nick openly or try to convince my parents that the earth was hollow. I read the book in my bedroom, and carefully hid it in the bottom of my 'toy-cupboard' when I had finished.

Some time later – I cannot remember how long – I had another surprise. I had read, or tried to read, the other volumes I had borrowed from the cellar. Some excited me – like the volume on Atlantis; some were completely bewildering, like Hörbiger's explanation of the world-ice theory (which insists that the moon is covered with a sheet of ice hundreds of feet thick). I decided to return the unwanted books to the cellar and investigate further. One afternoon, when my mother was out, I wriggled through the grating again and looked through the chest. Then I heard my mother arriving home. For some reason or other I thought she was coming into the cellar, so I grabbed the first volume that came to hand and clambered out. And in fact, when I went into the house a few minutes later, the cellar door was open and my mother was down there getting potatoes for supper.

I took my find upstairs, and was disappointed to find that it looked a bore. I have now forgotten its exact title, but it was written by a man called Garvin, and the title was something like *The Vision of Zogosh*. It was a small book – little more than a pamphlet – and very tattered. I started to read it, and was pleased to find that it was written in a clear, unpretentious style that I could follow without difficulty. The author began by explaining that he had been 'psychic' ever since the age of two, and he described various examples of second sight, mediumship, and so on. This fascinated me. I knew about ghosts, of course – they were a favourite subject of conversation among my friends – but had never taken them any more seriously than fairies. But somehow Garvin's account sounded like sober truth. I remember that he described how he saw his father's funeral some weeks before it actually occurred, and while his father was still in perfect health; he also saw blood on the hooves of the horse that was later to bolt and trample his father to death.

I was a slow reader, and read only about half the book before I went to sleep. The next day at school I remember going around the playground asking the boys if they had ever seen a ghost, and managed to collect a few old family heirlooms of ghost stories that failed to excite me.

As soon as I got home I locked the bedroom door and took up Garvin. Then came the shock. Halfway through the book, Garvin explains how he had his first lessons in astronomy, and was terrified by the idea of infinite spaces.

35

The thought that the universe had to *end somewhere*, and yet that the end was somehow contrary to human laws of thought, struck him as absurd. He went around asking people what lay beyond the stars, and no one could answer; most of them said: 'What does it matter?' Young Garvin started to pray every night for enlightenment. And then, one day in his late teens, the vision came; there was a distant music that kept disturbing him at his work; in the evening it became louder, and his bedroom filled with a greenish light. Then an angelic-looking man appeared, clothed in some kind of glowing transparent veil. Garvin's attention was drawn to this appearance when his clock stopped. The 'angel' told Garvin that he had been selected to give the world a great message – the truth about 'infinite space'. This, apparently, was stunningly simple. Space is not infinite. We are actually living on the *inner* surface of the earth, and the sun, moon and stars are all inside the earth. The world is, indeed, round, as the astronomers claim – but it is round in a concave way, not a convex way, and all life inhabits this concave shell. If the atmosphere were not so opaque we should be able to see right across it to the countries on the other side. And what is *outside* our earth? Nothing. This is obviously the answer to the riddle; we cannot imagine an infinity of somethingness; but it is as easy to imagine an infinity of nothingness as a thimbleful of nothingness.

As a special privilege, the angel took Garvin on a brief voyage out into space. For a few seconds the atmosphere was made transparent – and it was just as the angel had said. There, right opposite him, was the outline of Europe, just as on a map.

There was a great deal more in Garvin's book – long descriptions of the odd movements of the sun, which is half light and half dark, and explanations of how the moon and the planets are really illusions, reflections. All this I have forgotten.

But what shattered me was the convincingness of Garvin's account of his vision. His earlier talk about second sight had me fully convinced because he wrote in a pedestrian, rather dull manner, giving all kinds of details of name, place, and date, as a child does in telling a story. His remarks about his terror at the idea of infinite space made me feel the same terror as if the floor had suddenly opened under my feet. It was impossible to doubt his 'vision'.

But if Garvin was right, what of Uncle Nick's concentric spheres? And why had Uncle Nick never mentioned Garvin to me, since he possessed the book and must have read it?

This had me completely baffled. I now no longer bothered my head about the opinions of my parents or the headmistress – they were obviously pathetic dupes. But what of Garvin?

I was so upset by this that I actually broached the subject of visiting Uncle Nick to my parents. They refused flatly, feeling that a lunatic asylum was no place for a young boy – that it might give me nightmares. But I wanted to ask Uncle Nick about Garvin, for I now doubted Uncle Nick's theory of the earth, and wanted to know whether he had lied deliberately, or was simply unaware of Garvin's amazing disclosures. Garvin convinced me in a way that Uncle Nick never had, simply by appealing to a genuine sense of mystery. Uncle Nick's theories were very plausible, but they were neither supported nor refuted by the world I saw about me. Garvin made me aware that the world about us is not to be trusted. It tells us that everything is simple, straightforward, and it has the plausibility of a clever conjurer or a confidence trickster. But it cannot answer the question:

Where does it all end? Does it go on for ever – and ever and ever and ever? If it does, then there is room for millions of worlds – so many millions that our own world must be exactly duplicated somewhere among them. Somewhere among them, there is another me – another Hugh Greene – looking out towards our earth and asking: Does it go on for ever?

The thought staggered me. And the implications were driven home when I went downstairs for my bedtime cocoa. My father had a friend in for a game of dominoes, and they were arguing about politics as they played, and about whether Hitler would dare to start a war. At first I paid no attention to them; then their raised voices broke my train of thought, and I started to listen. It was a relief after the voyage through nothingness. My mind felt at home again.

They were both convinced, and both sounded convincing. My father was certain that Hitler would never dare to start a war because Britain had never yet been defeated in a war, while his friend declared that the invasion of the Saar proved the contrary. They grew warm; both drew examples from history. (They were both readers of history and political memoirs, and they sounded to me as learned as two dons.)

After half an hour they paused to draw breath, and I stared from one to the other and thought: Who is right? Then I thought: But time will soon prove which of the two of them is right. And then my mind went back to my problem about infinite space and the concave earth, and I felt spiritually dizzy, for I suddenly realized that there is no way of establishing the rightness of a theory of what lies behind the stars.

My father noticed me and told me it was time to go to bed. I asked if I might ask a question. Father said no; his friend looked interested and said *he* would like to hear it

38

anyway. So I asked them: What does infinity mean? At this, they both looked disappointed, and my father growled: 'It means never coming to an end.'

'I know that,' I said. 'But if space doesn't come to an end what *does* it do?'

To my surprise, his friend merely said: 'Ah, that's a question nobody can answer, lad. You'd better ask your teacher at school tomorrow.' (This was another way of telling me to go to bed and forget it.)

My father added: 'Why worry about what's out there, anyway? We've got to live down here, so it doesn't matter to us, does it?'

I was sent off to bed. I lay awake, now angry with them instead of frightened about infinite space. After all, if nothing matters but what is here on the surface of the earth, then what does mathematics matter? Or the Copernican theory of the planets? Or ninety per cent of science? And if the depths of space are unimportant, then how about the remote past? Why should my father take an interest in history if he preferred to stick to the present?

I dwell on this at length because I believe that this was the first night of my life when I *thought for myself*. Uncle Nick had taught me to think – after a fashion. But it was a kind of thought that did not matter, that touched no living nerves. All right, the earth was hollow; and the square root of four is two; and the French word for God is *Dieu*. This kind of knowledge is part of a ritual, like breathing; it may be important, but it is meant to be taken for granted. But the idea of infinite space came closer to me; it was like a betrayal by someone you love and trust. The thought that came to me – obscurely and instinctively – was: 'The world is a clever illusion.' A confidence trickster might lie convincingly and circumstantially, and his lies stand the test of immediate inquiry;

but pursue them far enough, and they are seen to have no foundation. I began to feel that our world is a plausible lie; but pose the question of infinity, and it stands exposed as an impossibility.

That night, as I lay awake, something happened to me, something as decisive as catching smallpox. I felt suddenly that I *had* to know what is true. It was a feeling of total revolt. This is too complicated to explain, but its meaning will emerge as I go on.

I must mention now a circumstance that perhaps sounds absurd – or almost meaningless – but which has been of central importance to me since I was very small. It is this: I have never liked human beings. I do not mean that I felt a Swiftian hatred for them. This was something different; an obscure discomfort, as if mixing with people was like sitting in a dentist's chair having one's teeth drilled. As a small child, and well into my early twenties, I could not even go into a shop to buy a pencil without overcoming a certain revulsion. This was not shyness or a sense of inferiority, but a feeling that human relations are somehow absurd. I have never been able to watch two people talking about the weather without a deep feeling of wonderment; I watch them closely, expecting to see their faces crumble suddenly into horrible grief.

I suppose this is partly because human relations offend my sense of economy. I learned to think mathematically at the age of six; when I had a spare moment, I worked at some problem, such as Fermat's question of a formula that will generate prime numbers. I therefore feel astonished at the amount of thought-energy that most human beings seem to waste as a matter of course. It is rather as if someone should say to a long-distance hiker: 'Well, I'm going to take my morning walk now,' and then proceed to walk around in a three-foot circle, explaining that when he has done this five thousand times he has walked the equivalent of five miles.

I certainly inherited this part of my temperament from my father's Uncle Sam, and I must write about Uncle Sam at this point.

Uncle Sam abruptly retreated from the world one day, locked himself up in an attic room, and refused to see anyone for several months. This happened when I was four years of age, so I have no early memories of Uncle Sam. He was the richest member of our family – he owned a lumber business and had a great deal of money invested. My Aunt Bertha, his second wife, was a plump, cheerful woman who did not seem to be in the least worried by his eccentricities. When people asked her why Uncle Sam had retreated, she would say, 'He doesn't like noise,' as if this explained everything.

But the oddest part of it was that Uncle Sam's attic room was dark; two workmen bricked up the window, under his instructions, and a carpenter made a new door twice as thick as the old one, and with a sliding hatch near the bottom, through which he could take food. He stayed in his attic for twenty years, until his death, and refused to see any of the family. There was no talk of having him certified, for everyone in the family expected to benefit in his will. When he had been in the room a few months, he allowed Aunt Bertha in to tidy up, but never saw anyone else.

As it happened, I was the first person to see Uncle Sam (except, of course, Aunt Bertha) after his 'retreat'. This happened about four years later – when I was nine. This was at the beginning of the war. I was in the habit of spending whole evenings with Aunt Bertha; she liked my company, let me listen to the radio, and made me cakes and tarts. One day there was a power-cut just as she was about to take Uncle Sam's supper upstairs, so I preceded her with a lighted candle. From behind the locked door, Uncle Sam called: 'Who's that with you?' Aunt Bertha told him, and he opened the door and invited me in. He stood there, blinking in the candlelight, wearing a long grey nightshirt. His hair and beard were astounding – he looked like an old biblical prophet. (In fact, he allowed Aunt Bertha to trim them every six months or so; but to me, it looked as if they had been uncut for years.) He peered at me, then said: 'Come in, boy.' I looked at Aunt Bertha; she seemed so pleased that I was reassured. 'Put the supper down there, Bertha. You cån go.' 'What about the candle?' she protested. As if to answer her, the light at the bottom of the stairs came on, although the room itself remained in darkness. So she went and left me alone with him. I disliked the room, and had no reason to like Uncle Sam. He smelt of sweat and unwashed clothes; there was a full chamber pot under the bed. Since there was no window, there was no way for air to circulate, and every smell of the last four years seemed to have left its traces in the room, including all the meals he had eaten.

I cannot remember how long I stayed, or what we talked about, except that he asked me a few questions about my mother and father. He sat at a table, eating his meal, and finally asked me to go down and fetch him a bottle of beer. I went, glad to escape. 'Take the candle,' he said. He was still eating, and I asked him if he would not need it to see his food. He said briefly: 'No.' This puzzled me so much that I stopped at the door, and asked him: 'Why don't you get a light, uncle?'

'Because I prefer to live in the dark.'

'But why?'

'Because, boy, darkness is man's natural element.'

I wanted to ask him what he meant by 'element', but

42

he told me to hurry and send up his beer. So I went downstairs again, and Aunt Bertha took up the beer.

Later, I asked Aunt Bertha about elements. Evidently Uncle Sam had said the same kind of thing to her, because she explained that water is the fish's element, and air is the bird's. This failed to satisfy me. I objected that a fish dies in the air, and a bird dies if it is held under water, but a man doesn't die when he's not in the dark. Aunt Bertha just said: 'You'd better ask him next time you see him.' I didn't because I was not interested, although I saw Uncle Sam fairly frequently after that. I learned the truth ten years later, after his death. He left me money – as I shall tell – and a document, which is in front of me now. It consists of forty handwritten pages, and is headed: 'Letter to my Nephew Hugh.' I am going to quote the relevant pages, because they seem to me important enough to cite at length. The early pages tell the story of his first marriage, his years in India, and his first business successes. By the time he was forty, in 1925, he was a member of the boards of two large companies. He writes:

'The ease with which I made my first ten thousand pounds convinced me that destiny was reserving for me some role of cardinal importance. One day, however, an incident occurred that changed my whole outlook . . .

'I was on my way to a board meeting, and was confident that I could persuade the other directors to follow my advice and buy up Cardew's business before the news of his impending bankruptcy circulated in the trade. I remember feeling pleasurable anticipation as I travelled across London by tube – the congratulations, and the comments: "Dawson's done it again." It was a hot morning in spring, and the train was crowded, but I felt cheerful and full of optimism; I even decided to take Mildred to the Savoy for supper. I cannot now recall the train of thought that then occurred to me; but I remember pushing my way through the crowd on the platform, and suddenly being overwhelmed by a feeling that struck me as abruptly as a heart attack. *It was a sudden and violent hatred for all my fellow human beings.* As I stood there, surrounded by pressing bodies, loathing and contempt rose in me until I felt as if I were drowning. I looked at their faces, and they seemed alien monsters, beings of clay and corruption. It is true that I could have restrained this hatred; but it seemed to me that I had glimpsed some great truth, and I had no right to turn away. My body felt drained of strength; I got up to the street with difficulty, and wondered why fate had waited so many years to play this trick on me. It was really like a denouement in a play. As I walked through the streets, all the stupidity and pettiness of humankind were present to my mind. I recalled the *saeva indignatio* of Swift, but this seemed inadequate. I felt as if I had been transported into a city of gigantic and hairy spiders, who perspired rottenness. I began to think how sweet the earth would be if freed of all animal life, and realized that, if I were God, I would destroy all life on this planet. It has occurred to me since that my vision was a kind of religious revelation.

'I attended my board meeting, but I found myself unable to utter a word. Loathing made me incapable of speech. But force of habit made me scrawl on a sheet of paper: "Cardew going bankrupt; suggest we move in quickly," and pass it to the chairman, then I hurried out of the room.

'I expected that the feeling would slowly pass away, and as I went home I tried to look into myself and discover how it had come about. It was as sudden as the bursting of a boil; but how had I failed to notice the boil earlier? I am still unable to explain this, except to say that *I have always been unusually sensitive to the idea of violence.* [My italics.]

'I was mistaken; it did not pass. I had always been fairly fond of my wife, although I had ceased to respond to her on a physical level since she had put on weight. But when I arrived home I found that she had become wholly repulsive to me. All her faults seemed magnified; her voice threw me into a rage; the sight of her face made me feel sick; the thought of ever having embraced her convulsed me with nausea. I realized that I had to escape immediately. I pleaded that I felt ill, refused to go to bed, and hurried out of the house, saying that I was going to see a doctor. Instead, I took the first train to Scotland and stupefied myself on the journey by drinking a bottle of gin – an unusual indulgence for me, for I have always been very nearly a teetotaller. I remembered a deserted cottage on the coast of Ayrshire that I had seen when shooting grouse . . . From there, I cabled Mildred that I had been called away on a business trip and would be back in a fortnight.

'The strange state of mind persisted, but I now suspected it was pathological. Instead of disappearing, my hatred seemed to increase. It vanished only when I could be alone and forget human beings. Even the local tradesman who delivered food seemed to me a kind of monstrous vegetable, a walking fungus, wholly alien. I felt as if I had been transported from some more civilized planet on to a strange world, full of creatures.

'. . . When I returned to London, a month later, it was to discover that Mildred had left me and returned to Horatio [her previous husband]. I was not sorry. I allowed her to divorce me on the grounds of desertion.

'It was some time before I was able to rationalize my strange malady. No doubt it had some physico-cerebral origin. But it was clear to me that I had stumbled upon an apocalyptic vision of human life that was totally *useless* to me as a living man. As a painter, I might have made use of it in depicting human beings as monsters. But as a family man, it was like a weight around my neck. There were times when I felt as if I had been branded by the Lord. (For although I have never regarded myself as a religious man, I have never been able to accept the ruthless economy of the atheist, and forgo the convenience of a universal scapegoat.)

'My business losses in 1929 occupied my mind for the next three years. Although I now felt a stranger among human beings, I no longer experienced acute discomfort when in their presence. I had lost all real interest in money, but I treated business as a game, and played it with some success in the early thirties, accumulating enough money to insure against starvation in case another "attack" should make human society completely intolerable to me. In 1932 Bertha became my cook. She had escaped from two unfortunate marriages, and showed no tendency to ask questions or to try to impose her personality on me. I was so impressed by her independence of mind that I finally proposed marriage to her, and immediately settled half my fortune on her in case I should again feel the need to "retreat". I was even able to explain to her, in guarded terms, the nature of my occasional attacks; she said she understood perfectly, because her brother had suffered from jaundice. She has been an excellent wife, and as I write this I feel nothing but affection for her.

'And yet I was never unaware of a basic uneasiness in these days, and in 1936 a certain moral exhaustion warned me that I would shortly pay the price of another collapse of vital force and motivation. Since my physical health was also delicate, I dreaded this event. I discovered that a smell of grass or privet had the power to soothe me, and Bertha made a habit of placing boxes filled with both in my bedroom. I believe that it was some association of childhood with the smell that helped to hold back the rising tide of sickness in me.

'One morning in 1936 I accompanied Bertha to church. Dr McNab, the well-known Scottish nonconformist, was preaching. He was a widely travelled man and, aware, perhaps, of the number of businessmen in his congregation, took occasion to express harsh criticism of President Roosevelt's New Deal. All at once a strange excitement came over me, for I saw in a flash the origin of my troubles. The political new deals may or may not be effectual; but the new deal for which all men wait is an alteration in God's relations towards man. This idea so excited me that I stood up halfway through the sermon and hurried outside. It was a fine autumn morning, and I sat on a stone in the churchyard and pursued my revelation. Now for the first time I understood my attacks of hatred for human beings. They are all more or less contented slaves. Certain malcontent intellectuals have taught the workers to feel dissatisfaction with their employers. But it seems to have struck no one that human beings are *grossly exploited by God*. We are expected to bear misfortune, to learn from experience (like obedient schoolchildren), to offer thanksgiving for benefits received; our role is in every way that of the slave and the sycophant. We are entrapped in the body, which we carry around like a suit of armour weighing a ton, and we have to endure with patience its stupidities and enfeeblements. The days pass quickly, devoted to eating, defecating, reproducing, and combating the irony of fate. No Egyptian slave suffered more continuous indignity under the lash of his overseer than man suffers constantly under the mismanaged government of God. (You understand, Hugh, that I use the word "God" as a

47

convenience to describe what the Ancients would have called Fate or The Gods, and what certain modern writers have preferred to call Life.)

'Once this became clear to me, I trembled with excitement. I experienced the astonishment that has fallen upon all thinkers when their greatest ideas have occurred to them; I understood the feelings of Newton discovering the law of gravity, of Darwin recognizing natural selection, of Karl Marx apprehending the principle of class war. Perhaps the last parallel is closest to my own case. My excitement was so great that I could not bear to wait for my wife; instead, I made my way home alone. As I walked among the Sunday-morning crowds, I now understood what had happened to me on that other morning ten years earlier, in the St Paul's underground station. These people were loathsome to me because they were slaves, and accepting them as fellows made me loathsome to myself. And yet, it seemed to me, other revolutionary thinkers had succeeded in changing the state of mankind. Was it not possible that my revelation was a sign that new changes were about to occur in man's relation to his destiny?

'As the day wore on, however, my excitement vanished, for I recognized that my analogy was a false one. Marx depended on the physical discomfort of the workers to provide the explosive power of revolution; the only precondition was to direct the attention of the workers to the employers, and propagate the idea of underprivilege. But God had concealed himself so carefully that man's agony can discover no direction or object. I had frequently been struck by the absurd logic of criminals who claim that their crimes have been an attempt to get their revenge on "society".

'In spite of my perplexity, two facts were clear to me. One, that I strongly objected to being an exploited human

48

being, a slave of God or chance; two, that most people have no such objection. Besides, how could I call upon human beings to revolt against an entity that I myself recognized to be an abstraction?

'This much was clear. It then became apparent to me that I could do no more than make my individual protest, that all the higher powers within me pointed to this aim. If I could not call on the rest of the human race to protest with me, I could at least have a one-man strike.

'The rest of the story you know. I moved into the attic and had the window bricked up. I preferred darkness, recognizing that it was important to keep my mind concentrated on its object. Besides, I had no desire to bring my mind into contact with the stupidities and half-measures that make up the literature of the human race.

'I had been in the room three days when it came to me that only one other man in human history had felt impelled to act in the same way, as an intercessor for all mankind. In that moment, I began to shiver uncontrollably with fear and joy.

'At first, I had an idea that, if I concentrated hard enough on the grievances of mankind, the Great Employer might try negotiation with me, might deign to treat me as a spokesman of the human race and reveal himself to me. After a few months, I recognized that this was unlikely, and contented myself with recognizing that my protest was unique in the history of the human race and that, like Christ, I also had made an attempt to treat directly with God on behalf of my fellow human insects.

'I cannot honestly advise you to do the same, unless you feel strongly so inclined. But I have observed in you signs of a kind of perception similar to my own. Do not try to force this; but in the event of your wishing to retire into solitude, I have made provision in my will, which is in the hands of Mr Pollard of Lake and Pollard . . .'

There followed a sub-heading: 'Summary of my religion and philosophy', which occupied some twenty pages. The deterioration of the handwriting indicated that it had been written some time later. I shall not quote it because it seems to me that his attitude has already been explained clearly enough in the section quoted already. Only one phrase strikes me as immediately important, and this is part of a sentence that is only half decipherable; the phrase is: 'What is the *logical response* to being alive?'

There is only one thing to add. Aunt Bertha told me that, two days before he died, Uncle Sam went into a kind of trance; he refused to eat, and stared in front of him with a strange, fixed expression. But Aunt Bertha told me that she thought it was an expression of joy. A few hours before he died, he drew her attention by tugging at her dress (she was asleep in an armchair beside the bed) and indicated that he wanted a pencil. But when she handed it to him, his hand shook so that he could hardly write. Finally, after several efforts, he managed to scrawl: 'I saw it.' He then dropped back, looking exhausted, and died quietly an hour or so later. The paper disappeared after the funeral.

This puzzled me. If Uncle Sam had written: 'I saw Him,' it might have made sense; he had spent twenty years waiting for a vision of God; but Aunt Bertha was quite definite about it; the final pronoun had been 'it'. I still have no idea of what he meant, although I suppose it is remotely possible that he was referring to some vision of the purpose of human life. Whatever it was that he saw, it had the effect of Aquinas's final vision; it robbed him of the desire to go on living.

If I have spent too much time writing about Uncle Nick and Uncle Sam, I apologize; but it seems to me that I cannot explain myself without explaining them. What it amounts to is this: that at an early age I came into contact with two men who were absolutely certain they were right and the rest of the world wrong. I had no way of judging their sanity; but from then on, I could never believe that an idea is right just because everyone accepts it.

But before leaving this problem of belief, I must mention one more relative, my Aunt Dinah. Aunt Dinah was not actually an aunt; she was some kind of relation of my mother's. She was also a spiritualist, and it was through her that I had, at about the age of ten, a brief spiritualist phase.

Aunt Dinah was not liked by my father's family; she was considered vulgar. She talked with a broad Yorkshire accent, and the shape of her front teeth and protruding lips made her shoot out little globules of spit as she talked. She had a very large bosom and a man's walk. She was not married to the man who was known as 'Uncle Tod', for she had a husband somewhere. She seldom came to our house, but my mother sometimes went to see her, and spent the evening drinking hot rum and lemon juice; I occasionally went along on summer evenings and played in the backyard or the street while they talked.

One day I was left alone with Aunt Dinah, and the conversation somehow got on to the subject of religion. I think I must have said that I was not interested in the subject, because she began to argue with me. Finally, I explained my idea that we can never be sure that anything is true except mathematical propositions, and told her about Uncle Nick and the hollow earth. (By this time I had come to accept that Uncle Nick was simply insane.) I argued that all the statements made by human beings might be lies or delusions, and that even the laws of physics and chemistry are open to doubt; they might be just 'rules' that apply in our part of the universe and nowhere else.

Aunt Dinah got rather excited at this, and said that it was a disgrace that my father should bring me up as an atheist. (She immediately put the blame on father.) Then she told me that she *knew* her beliefs were true. I challenged her to prove this to me. She said 'All right,' and went out of the room to fetch a book. When she came back, she told me that she herself had been a 'doubter' in her teens, but that the following story had completely convinced her. I have forgotten the title of the book, but I think it was issued by the Society for Psychical Research or by someone connected with it.

The story was about a certain Lord Tyrone, who was brought up by a guardian. He and his sister were taught that the scriptures are not divine revelations from God, and that religion is only the reasonable pursuit of virtue. (I believe this doctrine is called Deism.) Later on the guardian died, and their teachers tried to convert them to ordinary Christianity, but they could not be convinced. The brother and sister were very fond of one another, and one day made a bargain: that the first to die should appear to the other, and tell the other whether 'revealed' religion is really true or not. Some years later the sister – then married – was asleep beside her husband, when she woke up to find Lord Tyrone beside the bed. He told her that he had just died, and had come to keep their agreement, and tell her that Deism is false, and revealed religion the only true one. He made a number of other prophecies, including that her husband would die shortly, and that she would marry again and be very unhappy. She asked him how she could believe that he was real, and not just a dream; he asked her to hold out her hand, and touched the wrist. His touch was icy cold, and shrivelled the tendons of her wrist. In the morning, when she woke up, she heard news of her brother's death. For the rest of her life she wore a black bandage around the shrivelled wrist. All of the ghost's other prophecies came to pass exactly as he had said.*

Aunt Dinah read me this story aloud. She then showed me the book, and let me verify for myself that it was not fiction. I read some of the other narratives in it, and they seemed to be well authenticated, with all kinds of sources quoted.

For a while, this convinced me – particularly when Aunt Dinah explained that Lord Tyrone's sister would have gone to hell if it had not been for her brother's warning. Human beings might be wrong, but surely a ghost would be in a position to know something more about the mysteries of life and death?

Aunt Dinah knew better than to try and press me too far; she told me to think about it, and to go back to her if I felt I wanted to know more. I thought about it all night and most of the next day. Then I decided that, even if Aunt Dinah was wrong, it could do no harm to look into it further. So I went to see her the same evening, and she was obviously delighted to see me. She made a specially large jar of rum and lemon for herself, gave me some cake and a glass of milk, and then began to instruct me. Halfway through the evening one of her friends joined us; she was also a spiritualist – a large, fat lady who always sat with her legs wide open, and rolled her own cigarettes. All their talk about life after death fascinated me. Aunt Dinah told me how the spirit of her father had given her a detailed description of what it is like to die – how he had found himself rising out of his body, so that he could look down on the people crying over him. It was all very moving, and Aunt Dinah almost had me in tears

* A version of the Lord Tyrone story can be found in *Lord Halifax's Ghost Book*. – H.G.

53

when she told me how her father had tried to comfort his wife – who was sitting by the body – by laying his hands on her head, until suddenly she looked calmer and gradually stopped crying. There followed a long description of heaven, which I found somewhat disappointing; it was apparently all pearl-grey, and the ground was like sponge-rubber, so that you couldn't hurt yourself if you fell down. Still, it was a most interesting evening, and a great deal more entertaining than I'd hoped – I had expected a kind of extended scripture lesson with obscure explanations about one-in-three and three-in-one. When I went home, Aunt Dinah's friend gave me a paper-covered edition of Swedenborg's *Heaven and Hell*, but I found this quite incomprehensible.

But the spell began to dissolve when I attended my first meeting. It was in a church, and it was very crowded. We sang hymns, then a skinny man with a London accent came and sat in a chair. He did not (as far as I could tell) go into a trance, but closed his eyes and sat in the attitude of Rodin's thinker. Then he said: 'There is a spirit called Jack. He wants to get in touch with someone called Mary. He is a middle-aged man with a stiff collar and a black tie.' Someone jumped up and said: 'That's my Jack.' A few messages followed: 'He says that you mustn't fret about him. You are heading into some financial difficulties, but if you take great care everything will be all right,' and other things of the same sort. It was not that I found this unconvincing; I didn't doubt that the medium was really in touch with someone called Jack. But my old distaste for human beings suddenly came over me; I found myself disliking all these silly people – and the spirits sounded as futile as the people in the church. Near my seat, close to the door of the church, there was a rack full of books and pamphlets, and one of them was called 'Are *you* descended from an ape?' On the cover was a picture of an ugly, simian face with piggish eyes. I looked at Aunt Dinah on one side of me, with her protruding lips slightly open, and at the man who, from his smell, was a fishmonger, and the answer seemed obvious.

I attended a few more meetings, and a Bible-reading in the home of the fat woman, but my enthusiasm had gone. I explained to Aunt Dinah that I was working hard for my exams – the eleven plus – and that I would be able to attend more meetings after they were over. But I took care to avoid Aunt Dinah after that. If the truth involved mixing with other human beings, I preferred to risk damnation.

2

There is a sentence in Uncle Sam's 'confession' that makes me realize how much alike we are: 'I have always been unusually sensitive to the idea of violence.' My feeling about violence has always been with me. I do not know why this should be so. Some people are born cheerful; they know about violence but it does not seem important; others can never escape the thought. I am one of these. If I think back on my childhood, all the most vivid memories involve violence or the fear of violence.

For example, I remember clearly a newspaper article that I read when I was very young. The journalist had been walking along a Glasgow street when he saw a gang of men beating up a youth. He tried to interfere, and was knocked unconscious. When he opened his eyes, he found a kindly-looking man bending over him, saying: 'Are you all right, son?' He said yes. The man said: 'Well, next time don't interfere in things that don't concern you,' and slashed both his cheeks with a razor.

This episode stayed in my mind for years, and every time I thought of it, I raised my hands to my cheeks to protect them.

I am not speaking simply of the fear of violence, but of a sense of the unending closeness of violence. For me, it was always present, as fatigue is always present to a sick man, or as stabs of gout might be present to an old man. There is no reason why this should have been so. Only one of my very early memories concerns violence. I remember, at the age of about five, being taken into a butcher's shop by my mother, and becoming suddenly convinced that the carcasses hanging from the ceiling were those of human beings with their head and limbs hacked off. I started to be sick in the shop and had to be rushed outside.

I had another uncle, my mother's brother Fred, who specialized in tales of violence; but as far as I can remember none of these impressed me very deeply, with one exception.

Uncle Fred was a huge man with the build of a professional weight-lifter (which he had been at one point in his career). He had spent most of his life in the army, on the North-West Frontier of India. When he came back, he married Aunt Amy, and then took to his bed, alleging a weak heart and feeble lungs. Because he disliked the toil of moving up and down stairs to the lavatory, he had his bed installed in the front room, where he could look out into the street. He had a small pension from the army, and Aunt Amy went out to work while Uncle Fred read library books at the rate of two a day, and occasionally took up his field glasses to look out of the window at the blank house-fronts opposite.

His conversation was difficult to follow; he spoke in a quick, elliptical way, punctuating the sentences with wheezy coughs. He liked to read travel books, and I think that perhaps some of his 'true stories' came out of them.

The story that impressed me concerned an old Indian who kept a snake in a box. It was a hooded cobra, and the box had a thick glass lid. Whenever there were new arrivals in the barracks he always made the same bet with them – to double their money if they could keep a hand on the glass for fifteen seconds. It seemed an easy bet; the glass was too thick to break. But as soon as the snake struck at the glass, no one could control the impulse to snatch the hand away. In this way, the old man made a great deal of money from the new arrivals. One day, a soldier with a wooden hand asked if he could be allowed to wear a glove while he laid his hand on the box. The old Hindu agreed; he was aware that a glove makes no difference – to the reflex of self-defence. The soldier laid a high stake; the old man had to go away to get enough money to double it. Everyone in the barracks gathered round, hoping to see the old man beaten at last. They were not disappointed; the soldier kept his gloved hand on the box while the cobra struck again and again. The old man suspected trickery and demanded to see the hand, but the crowd of British soldiers felt that he had been fairly beaten, and forced him to pay up. Two nights later, according to his own account, Uncle Fred was awakened by a faint noise, and watched the old man creeping from bed to bed, looking for the soldier with the wooden hand; he was naked, and shone in the moonlight from some kind of grease plastered all over his body. Probably he only meant to rob, although he carried a knife. Uncle Fred gave the alarm; the old man was collared and wrapped in blankets – the grease would otherwise have made him too slippery to hold. Outside the barracks was a deep well that had been sunk to an underground stream. The old man was gagged and tossed down this well.

The story horrified and fascinated me; I demanded all kinds of details: how deep was the well? how fast was the stream? (Too fast, Uncle Fred replied; they had given up using it because they had lost too many buckets.) Where did it come from and where did it go? Uncle Fred said he didn't know, and I found his lack of curiosity about these matters incredible. But for months after he told me this story, I woke up at night dreaming that I was falling down a deep well towards an underground stream that plunged to a lake in the centre of the earth.

I never ceased to be aware of this violence underlying the world. I once made a calculation of how many human beings had died in the past three thousand years, and worked out that their bodies would cover almost every inch of land on the earth. It seemed probable, then, that every handful of earth has at some time been mixed with decaying human flesh.

I realize that these speculations sound morbid, but I believe they may be more common among children than we realize.

Probably this fear of violence had something to do with my love of mathematics. The world of mathematics offered clarity and certainty. It was true that Archimedes had been killed by a stupid soldier, but in a sense he had triumphed. When a man became a mathematician, he ceased to be a victim and became a kind of god, and if he died he died as a god. Mathematics could make you feel solid inside, instead of guilty or helpless.

When I was very young, I showed a tendency to turn away from the idea of violence, to try to forget it. For example, my cousin and I used to attend the Saturday-afternoon matinee at a local cinema. The programme always included an episode of a serial. My favourite character, a man who called himself the Eagle, wore a black cloak and mask, and spent most of his time restoring law and order to the Wild West. The serial always ended with the Eagle in some position of apparently inescapable danger – hurtling over a cliff in a runaway stage-coach, trapped in a mine that was blown sky-high with dynamite, canoeing over a waterfall that was as high as Niagara. The following instalment, recapitulating the final minutes of its predecessor, would accomplish some clever sleight of hand and reveal that, contrary to all the evidence of the camera, the Eagle was never in the plunging coach or the collapsing pit-shaft. I never missed an instalment until one day the scene was a Mexican monastery that had been set on fire by bandits. For some reason, the Eagle went rushing back into the flames, climbing in through a high window. The camera showed pews and altar-hangings blazing convincingly; then the roof of the church collapsed. I sat through the rest of the programme feeling the same kind of sickness I had felt in the butcher's shop. On the way home, I refused to play cowboys and Indians with my cousin; the Eagle had become somehow unmentionable. The following Saturday I went to another cinema, and I never saw another instalment of the Eagle. I felt that he had betrayed me. He had left the world of romance and entered the world of violence.

This kind of nausea, this turning away from violence, disappeared as soon as I became absorbed in mathematics. When I was nine or ten I borrowed a book from the library called *Men of Mathematics*, the life stories of various mathematicians. I read it from cover to cover in one weekend, spending all the time in my bedroom. I can still remember that weekend clearly. It was midsummer; the lilac tree in our front garden was in bloom, and our neighbour mowed his lawn so that the cut-grass smell came into the bedroom. My father told me I should be in the garden because it was a shame to waste such weather, but I ignored him, and went on reading. I had always loved mathematics, but this book somehow altered my whole approach to it. It produced on me the kind of effect that the poetry of Keats and Shelley produces on some teenagers. It seemed to me that mathematicians were the elite of the world. Kings and Emperors treated them with respect. Most of them seemed to live to a great age. In a world of men who squabbled and intrigued, they stood apart. The article about Pascal infuriated me; I shared the author's contempt for Pascal's retreat into religion, and it came to me for the first time that all religion is a pernicious fake. (This was about a year before Aunt Dinah briefly convinced me otherwise.) I chortled aloud as I read the article about Gauss, particularly the parts about Napoleon – how Gauss had refused to beg the Emperor to remit the 2,000-franc fine and had accurately prophesied the downfall of his enemy. But the articles on Abel and Galois gave me a sense of luxurious melancholy. Both had died young, Abel of tuberculosis, Galois in a duel at twenty-one. I finished reading about Galois in the dusk, preferring not to switch on the light, then stared out of the window for a long time. The world outside no longer seemed real. I convinced myself that Galois, if he had lived, would have been a greater mathematician than Newton or Gauss; this intensified the tragedy.

From that time onward, I had the book out of the library almost permanently – until, some time later, I was able to buy a second-hand copy. Later still, I bought a paper-covered edition in two volumes and carried it around with me; probably I should have bought a dozen copies if I'd found them; it seemed to me one of the greatest books ever written. It supplied me with a basic attitude towards the world – that mathematicians are the only men who can ever be called free.

I have said that I disliked human beings. But that is a negative statement. It was Bell's *Men of Mathematics* that taught me to see its positive side: that what I really disliked about human beings was their capacity for self-delusion and their weakness. It was Uncle Sam's feeling that men are contented slaves who lack the spirit to rebel. Uncle Sam had tried to make his individual protest by separating himself from the rest of his species. But I was better off; I had before me a positive ideal of greatness: the detachment of the mathematician. No wonder

Newton said that God is a mathematician: he recognized that a man doing mathematics is very close to being a god.

I had a day-dream that stayed with me throughout my childhood and teens, and that still comes back to me. I imagined that the world had been invaded by a race of wise beings from another planet – beings whose civilization is far older than ours. They would land by space-ship one day, and interrupt the broadcasts of the world to explain that they had come to take over the leadership of the human race. They would not be visible; they would not interfere in most human affairs. Life would continue as before – but now controlled by the benevolent dictators from outer space. Crime would vanish; war would come to an end. The aliens would enter a city like Chicago; their intelligence system would locate every dangerous criminal, and all would be arrested and executed without trial. Crime would cease to be worth while, because the aliens would know about it as soon as it was committed. There would be no more popular leaders; politicians would be forced into their proper place – as anonymous public servants.

And finally, to educate the human race out of its stupidity and tendency to self-delusion, every man, woman, and child would be taught mathematics for several hours a day. There would be non-stop mathematical education, films about mathematics, articles in every newspaper every day, radio programmes about it; station bookstalls would sell books of mathematical puzzles instead of detective stories. All social distinctions would be abolished. The president or king of a country would automatically be its greatest mathematician. No man could be a knight or peer unless he was a superlative mathematician. No rich man would be allowed to keep his wealth unless he could prove that he was a better mathematician than every one of his employees. In this way, after a few generations, children would be born great mathematicians. And after a hundred years of this, the aliens would be able to leave our planet to take care of itself, in the hands of a race of men-gods, complete masters of their emotions, incapable of cruelty and self-delusion.

This dazzling Utopia occupied my mind all through my childhood. It seemed to me self-evident that human stupidity is due to involvement in personality; everyone is a petty egoist. Mathematics would teach men to forget themselves.

Incidentally, it was this idea of mine that turned me into a convinced atheist. I was certain that, if God existed, he would see at a glance that men could be made wiser and greater by simply giving them all a mathematical faculty. This would save all the trouble of preachers, missionaries, and churches, not to mention sending his only begotten son to try to reform the human race. I once expressed this point of view to an Anglican priest who was also a good mathematician. He agreed with my reasoning, but pointed out that anyone can develop the mathematical faculty; therefore God has already given us our means of salvation; all we have to do is to avail ourselves of it. 'He has led us to the trough,' said the priest, 'you can't expect him to eat and drink for us too.' I asked him why, if that was the case, Christ never pointed out the importance of mathematics, and the discussion came to an end.

At this point I should mention our neighbour Mr Sutton, because he plays an important part in the story later. He was an engineer who lived in the next street, and he was probably the only good mathematician in our district. I was at school with his son Gerald, a gentle, bespectacled lad who was not particularly brilliant. Like myself, Mr Sutton was interested in the theory of numbers. I had tea with Gerald one day and talked to his father; I produced my copy of Diophantus, and we sat over it for the rest of the evening. I began making a habit of seeing him two or three evenings a week and talking over problems that interested me.

Apart from his engineering, Mr Sutton had been self-taught. He had left school at fourteen and studied at night-school; consequently he had an enormous respect for education. He had taught himself German and French, and even to play the piano. He was not much liked by my father, who thought he was a know-all. Mr Sutton enjoyed standing in the garden on starry nights and explaining the names of all the constellations to me; if we walked in his garden on a sunny day, he would break off the talk about mathematics to tell me the botanical names of the flowers. He spoke a few words of a dozen languages, and liked to be considered a good linguist.

He had a few other harmless foibles. For example, he liked to tell us that his touch on the piano was so light that he could easily be a professional pianist; he would often listen to concerts on the radio and make scathing remarks about the pianist, implying that he could do far better himself. On one occasion, he decided to convince me of the lightness of his touch by touching me so lightly that I wouldn't even be aware of it. He told me to close my eyes, and then slowly raised his hand to my face. After a few seconds, I felt a clumsy pressure on my cheek. But I kept my eyes closed, and said: 'Go on, touch me.' Mr Sutton gave a shout of triumph: 'I touched you a minute ago.' 'I didn't feel you,' I said, and noted that Mr Sutton was in high spirits for the rest of the evening.

But I expected grown-ups to make fools of themselves, and felt no surprise or regret about it.

My father put an end to this friendship quite suddenly. Mr Sutton was a member of the town pistol-club, and took me there one evening, together with Gerald. I was not particularly interested in guns, but Gerald was always talking about them and explaining to me that it takes a great deal of courage to fire a pistol. Finally, I got so tired of his attitude of superior knowledge that I asked Mr Sutton to take me along to the club.

The shooting-range was in the basement of an office-building in the centre of the town – I was to get to know it very well later. The anteroom was full of posters and advertisements for guns. The gallery itself was a long, bare room like a skittle-alley. At our end of the room stood a long table, with several telescopes mounted on tripods; at the far end were a number of paper-targets suspended over a metal trough. The men stood sideways to fire with the pistol at arm's length, or rested the wrist in a wooden support. After each shot, they peered at the targets through the telescope.

I was startled by the tremendous noise made by the guns; it was louder than anything I had been led to anticipate from cowboy films. I found it even more unnerving when Mr Sutton allowed me to fire the gun. It seemed to explode in my hand when I pulled the trigger, and I felt my fingers peppered with small, hot fragments. After several tries, and a cup of tea in the café next door, my aim improved slightly, and I managed to hit the target once or twice.

Unfortunately, the terrific noise of the explosions made my ears ring, and for a few hours I was partly deaf. I didn't mind this in the least – it had been an exciting evening, and I had the satisfaction of knowing that Gerald was a worse shot than I was. But when I got back home, my father asked me where I'd been, and I didn't hear him. He repeated the question, and I explained that I was a little deaf from the explosions. He wanted to know why I hadn't asked his permission before going to a shooting-gallery, but I had to ask him to repeat the question. At this, he flew into a rage and declared that my ear-drums had probably been burst. My mother was called in, and she looked worried when she found that I couldn't hear her either. My father had a habit of envisaging unlikely accidents, and he shouted: 'Supposing he'd looked down the barrel and somebody had pulled the trigger?' I pointed out that you don't look down the barrel of a loaded gun, but it made no difference. As a child I had occasionally suffered from ear-aches, and my father was convinced that I had perforated ear-drums. He was in a state of indignation when he saw Mr Sutton walking through our gate. He immediately rushed out of the front door and began abusing him in the middle of the garden. I could not hear what they were saying, but at one point they almost came to blows. My mother sent me off to bed; from my window, I saw Mr Sutton striding off looking furious.

This kind of thing was typical of my father; he had sudden rages or fixed ideas, and nothing could be done about them. The next day, at school, Gerald Sutton avoided me, and, when I cornered him, told me that his father had ordered him not to speak to me. That night I waited round the end of the street until Mr Sutton came home from work on his bicycle. He looked embarrassed when he saw me. I said that I was sorry about the quarrel, but he interrupted me:

'No lad, I don't want you to say you're sorry. I want your father to come and apologize.'

He turned and walked off down the garden without saying another word.

I told my father about this – he had by now forgotten his rage, since it was obvious that the explosions of the guns had not made me permanently deaf. But he only shrugged and said: 'Silly bugger. You're better off without him.' So my visits to Mr Sutton ceased, although I eventually became friendly with Gerald again.

Several times as a child I was bullied by older boys. On one occasion, I was knocked unconscious. This happened one night when I was walking home from the park with a friend. We saw a gang of boys approaching on the other side of the road; they were around us before my friend realized that the leader was an old enemy of his. In the unpleasant, sneering way that these boys have when their instinct to bully meets no resistance, they began to ask us how we liked it now we were caught. Suddenly, one of them hit my friend in the stomach and made him double up, then kicked him in the face as he fell on to his knees. I saw a movement out of the corner of my eye and half turned my head, then I was hit under the jaw and collapsed. When I opened my eyes again, the boys had gone; my mouth was full of blood and bits of broken tooth, and blood flowed from a cut under my jaw. (I still have the scar.)

It was not serious; a patch of sticking-plaster stopped the bleeding, and the broken tooth gave no trouble, although later it had to be filled. The worst thing was the rage and impotence. I kept thinking: 'How *dare* he touch me?' and day-dreaming how pleasant it would be to torture them all to death. At this time I was keeping a kind of mathematical diary, and had been writing at length about Cantor and the infinite. I remember going up to my bedroom and staring at the notebook with disappointment and disgust. It seemed another kind of self-delusion. It was apparent to me that mathematics is not for human beings. If a man were a god, beyond the realm of accident, capable of striking down his enemies with a thunderbolt, then he could afford to be a mathematician. But for mere human beings to do mathematics seemed like fiddling while Rome burns. It is as if a pioneer in a wild country should decide to devote his days to landscape gardening instead of preparing for winter and fortifying the house against attacks.

For months after this happened I gave myself up to dreams of revenge. It happened that, some weeks later, I saw the boy who had been the leader of the gang leaving a cinema. I was walking fifty yards behind him. I had no intention of following him, but his way lay in the same direction as mine, and eventually I saw him turn into an entry. The house was in the slum district of our town, and was of an old-fashioned type with one backyard serving for several houses. In the centre of this yard there was a wooden structure – the communal lavatory. It was possible to cross the yard and leave it by any one of several entries; and because people walked in and out all the time no one paid any attention to me as I walked down the entry and across the yard. I saw the boy walk in through a back door. A woman who was standing in the entry spoke to him; she was hanging out clothes on a line that stretched the length of the entry.

I was on my way to see Aunt Bertha that night. All the time I was with her I kept wondering what use I could make of this piece of information. The idea of doing anything made me feel sick with excitement and self-doubt. This only produced a reaction of self-contempt and a feeling that I must do something about it. Late that night I returned home the same way and walked through the yard again, wondering if any idea would occur to me. The entry was still full of washing, and on touching one of the sheets I realized that it was now dry – it had been a hot day. I was seized with a temptation to set fire to the sheets; I had a box of matches in my pocket; there was a screwed-up ball of fish-and-chip wrapping in the entry. It would only take a moment to light the paper and drop it into the folds of one of the sheets, then walk away . . . Then suddenly I felt sick. The absurdity of it overwhelmed me, and I hurried out of the entry. What would be the good? There might be some point if I could meet the boy and challenge him to a fight. But this method seemed stupid and cowardly and – worse still – basically illogical. And yet on my way home I felt more strongly than ever that mathematics is only a turning-away from the basic problem. At least my reaction in the entry had been an honest attempt to face the problem, not a complete evasion.

At the beginning of the war I had a brief period of absolute certainty about the meaning of right and wrong. For some time before the war my father had been reading anti-Nazi books telling about Hitler's atrocities. My hatred of Hitler dated from the time when our science master told me that the Nazis had forced Einstein to leave Germany, and that Einstein would probably have died in a prison camp if he had stayed. This was Napoleon and Gauss all over again, but far worse.

Therefore, when war was announced, I danced with excitement. It was time England decided to do something about Hitler. I knew nothing about the economic motives of the war. I simply assumed that England, out of a sense of fair play, had decided that something really must be done about this bully. And I heard my father say that the war would be all over in six months – that all we had to do was to show that we couldn't be bullied, and Hitler would crawl back into his shell. Certainly, Hitler came to represent for me all the violence that made mathematics seem futile. He was a symbol of brute stupidity, like the youth who had hit me under the chin with a knuckleduster.

For the first time, there were simple lines of right and wrong across the world, and a simple hope for the future. All this crystallized in the series of broadcasts that J. B. Priestley made every Sunday evening in the summer of 1940. A few days ago I picked up a second-hand copy of these broadcasts. They brought back those early days of the war with great clarity, and I realize how perfectly Priestley expressed the feelings of everyone I knew. Nazism, Priestley explained, is 'an attitude of mind – the expression in political life of a very unpleasant temperament . . . the man who loves bluster and swagger-uniforms and bodyguards and fast cars, plotting in back rooms, shouting and bullying, taking it out of all the people who have made him feel inferior . . . That's why the gang spirit is so marked among these Nazis; and it explains, too, why there has always seemed something unhealthy, abnormal, perverted, crawlingly corrupt, about them and all their activities.' And he goes on to warn us that a country dominated by the Nazis will also find itself in the hands of its most unpleasant types – 'the very people who, for years, have been rotten with unsatisfied vanity, gnawing envy, and haunted by dreams of cruel power. Let the Nazis in, and you will find that the laziest loud-mouth in the workshop has suddenly been given power to kick you up and down the street . . .' And when he talks about Mr Churchill giving Mr Bevin a dig in the ribs in the House, he adds: 'When I saw that grin and that dig in the ribs, I said: "These are the men for us, but let them make haste, raise their voices and command the expectant people, who can, out of their kindness, humour and courage, yet defeat these cunning, ruthless, but crack-brained and small-hearted Nazis."'

I was ten when the war began – exactly the right age to enjoy it as simply as an adventure story. I think there was probably a lot of truth in the things Priestley said, even if they now appear over-simplified. They seemed to me then to be obviously and incontrovertibly true. Hitler represented stupidity and evil; there was nothing to be said for a man who would have executed Einstein. It did not strike me until ten years later that Hitler also believed in an absurdly simple form of right and wrong; that, like the rest of us, he was sick of the complexity and difficulty of our civilization, and dreamed of something simple and heroic – a pure Aryan race living with the strength and simplicity of the Norsemen. This kind of day-dream is like the fundamentalist religious revivals of our time – a return to the past, an attempt to crawl back into the womb of time. We combated it with another illusion.

Yet I think many of us were glad of the war. I know my father was. The thirties had been a hard time for him; he worked for a large firm of solicitors, and was always talking of starting in business on his own; but his only venture in that direction collapsed after a year, and he had to return to his previous job. Gradually, he became irritable and taciturn; just before the war he had a sudden wild outburst of rage against the cat, which was mewing for its supper; the cat was thrown out of the house with a few bruises, but my father got some deep scratches on his face, and almost lost his left eye. He was in hospital for a few weeks, and came back more moody than ever.

Then came the war, and he was revitalized. His weak heart kept him out of the army, but he became chief air-raid warden for our district. His work with his firm trebled, and so did his pay. He was up at six every morning and down at the local fire-watching post to take reports. In the evenings he arranged lectures or demonstrations of how to cope with incendiary bombs. He had to attend meetings of the town council and arrange for the distribution of family air-raid shelters and the building of public ones. I have never seen him so happy. He listened to every news bulletin on the radio, and followed up all the battles on a map. He also became convinced that Hitler had been responsible for the business slump of the thirties – making British businessmen afraid to invest in Europe – and that when Hitler was beaten there would be a new prosperity. When Quentin Reynolds, a war correspondent, did a famous propaganda broadcast against Hitler, referring to him as 'Mr Schickelgruber', my father somehow got hold of a copy of the script, and never tired of reciting pieces from it; he closed his lectures with it, and always got a loud ovation. He also made a habit of dropping into several pubs on his way home 'to check the black-out', and usually came home very cheerful and smelling of whisky. Mother didn't mind this – she preferred it to the gloom and irritation. They got on better than ever before, and the result was my sister Anne, who was born in 1942.

In those first two years of the war, I think we all thought of it as a crusade against the powers of darkness. The air-raids were a kind of game. (We only had about a dozen – the raiders were searching for engineering factories, and succeeded in destroying a few square miles of slums – including the house where I had almost become an arsonist.) Then, after two years, the inconveniences began to outweigh the excitement. A war lasting a year would have been a delightful change that would have been as welcome as a school holiday; five years of war exhausted everybody, so that even the excitement of victory seemed an anti-climax.

But for me, the war had been a different kind of holiday – a respite from my obsession with violence. For violence was conveniently symbolized in Nazism. And the end of the war, with its revelations of Auschwitz and Belsen, only seemed to confirm this.

There were other reasons why my horror of violence became less oppressive in the war years.

The most important of these was an idea I picked up from an article in some popular science magazine. It dealt with the progress of the Darwinian theory of natural selection. But one sentence struck me like a bullet, so that I re-read it a dozen times and watched its implications spread as quickly as a forest fire. I copied the sentence on to the title page of Caine's *Hollow Earth*; it is in front of me as I write. 'Among the millions of cavemen who then inhabited the earth, there were perhaps a hundred of the new species, homo sapiens; but natural selection saw to it that it was their type that continued, while their ape-like brothers died.' This is not a particularly striking idea; its impact on me came from the things I read into it. If this had happened once in the history of man, it might be happening again. Supposing that among the millions of ape-men now alive there are a few dozen 'new men', a super-species? Probably this idea had possessed me in a vague, instinctive way for years before I read the sentence in *Armchair Science*, but I had never grasped it clearly. Now it presented itself as a possibility that gave me a sense of liberation. I remember walking on my way to school on a summer afternoon – walking instead of travelling by bus, because I wanted to be able to think – and looking at the men and women in the streets, and thinking: 'You don't realize it, but you are a doomed species, played out.' It never occurred to me to doubt that I was one of the hundred 'new men'. What would these men be like? To begin with, they would feel that there is something vaguely wrong with the way other people live; generally accepted thoughts and ideas would seem to them untrue. They would find it hard to express most of their disagreements, just as a modern man would find it hard to express himself in the grunts of an ape. But without being sure of the reasons for their rejections, without having formed positive ideas of their own, they would nevertheless feel that there is something basically absurd about the lives and beliefs of their fellow human beings.

This theory gave me something I had always wanted: a conscious reason for retreating from human beings, for rejecting everything about them, for declining to make the effort of judging what is right and wrong in human history. *Everything* could be dismissed.

This tendency to world-rejection had always been strong in me, but it increased suddenly when I was about thirteen years old. This was through an accidental discovery that had an enormous influence on my development in my teens.

I came home from school one day with a slight headache, and took two aspirins from a bottle in the medicine cupboard. They left a curious after-taste in my mouth, and when my mother came home half an hour later I told her what I had done. She shrieked and ran to the telephone; I had taken some tablets that the doctor had prescribed for her stomach cramps, and she had been warned that it was dangerous to exceed the stated dose – one tablet per day. She had broken the bottle that morning, and transferred the tablets to an empty aspirin bottle.

The doctor's line was engaged. She told me to go and make myself sick by thrusting my fingers down my throat. I did, and this made me feel really ill; I staggered from the bathroom into my bed, feeling sorry for myself.

But when I stopped noticing the unpleasant acidy feeling in my mouth and throat I realized that I felt completely calm. My thoughts seemed as orderly as the planets in their courses. There was a silence inside me, as if all the machines in a factory had been switched off. My thoughts became surprisingly easy to control.

I had, of course, experienced this inner peace before, during illnesses; but an illness approaches slowly. This serenity had come suddenly out of an ordinary afternoon. I sat in bed, watching the dusk descend, and was amazed at the new economy of my inner being. And I reached a conclusion: that people produce far too much energy for their own good. When they sit still, this energy churns around inside them, producing a sense of discomfort. They are forced to get up and do something.

It also became clear to me that most of the world's history consists of acts committed under pressure of excess energy. I sat in bed, and contemplated this new accuracy of my thoughts; they seemed to move to their goal with a quiet grace, with no unnecessary writhing. I would now use a simile that would never have occurred to me then. It was like getting out of an old motor car, where the steering-wheel has to be twisted violently, and into a new car where the slightest movement of the steering-wheel will alter the car's direction.

One of the Eastern scriptures says that the moon cannot be reflected in disturbed waters, but that as soon as the waters are still they become a mirror. Certain Western mystics talk about a 'Sabbath of the soul'. But they should speak of a Sabbath of the body, for it is the body that has to be stilled. I realized that evening that the efficiency of my thinking is impaired by the turbulence of the mind and body; sickness, by exhausting the body, endows the mind with a new perceptiveness.

I began to make myself sick about once a week, usually at the weekend. Afterwards I would lie back in bed, my head on the pillow, aware of the tears on my eyelashes

75

and the trembling of my legs. Gradually this trembling would stop, and the peace would settle on me. It was the peace of exhaustion, and it made all the activity of the world seem vulgar. I would decide in advance what I wanted to think about; it might be a mathematical problem, or simply some idea out of a book that excited me. Under normal circumstances – without the exhaustion – my mind would have shown its usual tendency to change the subject, to run off at tangents, to follow a process of association of ideas until I ended by thinking about my dinner or the wart on the geography master's nose. It was like taking a large and badly trained dog for a walk on a lead; at one moment it would stop to sniff a lamp-post, at another suddenly try to rush after a cat. But with the body exhausted thoughts became well behaved. Newton's first law of motion applies also to the mind; a moving body will continue in a straight line until something alters its direction; a moving thought will also continue in a straight line if the body's stupid energies are kept in check. An even better simile comes from chemistry. Crystals will never form in a liquid if the liquid is shaken every few minutes; if it is allowed to stand still, crystals immediately begin to form. So in my mind, every thought quickly became covered with crystals. Every casual idea seemed to awaken echoes; every abstract thought turned into an intuition, cutting a path like a comet. I apologize for the mixture of similes; it is the only way I can express what happened. Here is one more: my 'convalescences' were like standing on a hilltop and seeing my daily life spread out below me, with all its relations clear.

In these moods I became a confirmed world-rejector. It is true that this development woud probably have occurred in any case, as a result of my interest in abstract ideas; but my habit of making myself sick hastened the process and also simplified it.

I realize, on re-reading the above, that it sounds absurd – the kind of thing that Gilbert satirized in *Patience*. And yet I believe that it is better to accept the idea of sickness consciously, and use it as an instrument to increase sensitivity, than to allow the subconscious mind to 'induce' sickness, as I believe it did with Pascal and Abel. Once the subconscious mind has been called in, the results tend to get out of hand and the process ends in a coffin. I agree that making yourself vomit is a primitive way of 'subduing the body', but I think it, on the whole, less harmful than De Quincey's laudanum or Poe's gin and water.

At the age of eleven I passed the scholarship examination, and went to the Alderman Collins School, which was noted for its teaching of science and mathematics. But although my science and mathematics always gained top marks, I took very little interest in most other subjects – history, geography, French, German and English. I was also bad at games. Consequently I was never in an 'A' form, and in fact spent my first two years at Alderman Collins in 'sub-C', a special class for dunces. I made no effort to improve until, at the end of the two years, I was told that I would probably have to leave and go to an 'intermediate' school instead. I then spent a term studying hard and, to my disgust, shot into an 'A' form, where the masters wanted to train me to take more scholarships. So I immediately stopped working, and over the next two years managed to drop quietly back into 'C'. All my reports stated: 'He has the ability, but is lazy.' But the truth was simpler. I disliked attention; I hated feeling that I had to 'live up' to someone's expectations. I took care even to conceal the exact nature of my mathematical studies and allowed the mathematics master to think that I made a hobby of 'puzzles', when in fact I was working steadily through G. H. Hardy's *Course of Pure Mathematics* and Knopp's *Theory of Functions*.

I now lived and breathed and ate mathematics. I had suddenly become aware that, even if I spent the next sixty years reading in and about it, I could never hope to cover even a quarter of the vast field of modern mathematics. And yet I believed that, with enough study, I could at least have a nodding acquaintance with every important branch of the subject. So I hopped indiscriminately from the theory of functions to non-Euclidean geometry to Hamilton's quaternions to Kummer's ideal numbers, and never lost the excitement of exploring.

All this made the world seem beautifully simple. There is no snobbery like the snobbery of the pure mathematician. Even science seems an inferior subject, because it is tied to experiment and observation. And history and geography and literature are so far below that they are pariahs. The world of the mathematician is all chromium and sunlight.

It is true that the fear of violence still hovered in the background, but usually it seemed as unreal as a childish nightmare. And two events that occurred in my first year at Alderman Collins increased this feeling.

The first was a visit to the theatre with my cousin Robert, when we saw a hypnotist. Robert's father, my Uncle Jeff, was sceptical about hypnotism; he had read popular books on psychology, and assured us that no one can be hypnotized to do something against his will. He believed that stage hypnotists were usually frauds. I asked why, in that case, weren't they denounced by the people they pretended to hypnotize? Because, Uncle Jeff said, people were too nervous, up there in the glare of the spotlights.

Robert and I argued about it on the bus going to the theatre; it was one of those unpleasant, jeering arguments that boys sometimes drift into, both trying to pierce the other's defences. So as we went into the theatre I determined that I would test Robert's assertion by offering myself as a subject for the hypnotist.

The latter called himself 'The Great Kaspar', and the posters showed a pair of compelling eyes staring out of a blue mist. He came on stage after a few feeble variety turns, and his appearance was disappointing. He looked small and apologetic, and his dress-suit had obviously been made for a bigger man; he spoke with a faint London accent, and his voice reminded me of our fishmonger.

He performed a few conjuring and card tricks, and then asked for volunteers to be hypnotized. Robert and I were sitting at the end of a row in the stalls, and I immediately stood up. Robert, not to be outdone, stood up too and preceded me down the aisle. I felt nervous, and was relieved to see that there were two girls ahead of us.

We halted at the bottom of a flight of steps leading on to the stage, and one of the girls went up, helped by Kaspar and encouraged by a clapping of hands.

The magician asked the girl her name, age and profession and whether she was married. She answered inaudibly and he had to repeat her answers. He then asked her to sit down, and went on talking to her in a soothing voice; but when he laid his hand on her forehead, she jumped nervously out of the chair, and the audience laughed.

The next ten minutes were farcical. The girl was obviously terrified and wanted nothing so much as to get back to her seat. Kaspar tried swinging a shiny glass object in front of her nose; to the delight of the audience, she sneezed and Kaspar dropped it. (I think he was probably suffering from a hangover.) Finally, he had to ask her to sit down on the other side of the stage.

I began to feel sorry for the magician. Robert was looking at me triumphantly. The second girl now showed no eagerness to go on stage, so I decided that I would go up and help the magician by pretending to be hypnotized. Robert may have guessed my intention; at all events, when I tried to go up the stairs he pushed me aside and climbed up himself.

Kaspar held out his hand and led him to the centre of the stage. There were a few cheers from the gods; evidently some boys from Alderman Collins had recognized him. The magician asked his name, and Robert replied in a firm voice. Kaspar looked at his thick legs and deep chest, and asked if he was good at games; Robert said modestly that he was. Someone in the gods yelled 'Up the Mortons' (Robert's house at school), and Robert looked up and grinned. He didn't seem in the least nervous.

The magician asked him to sit down; then he turned to the audience and began to talk to them about hypnotism, saying that there was a great deal of nonsense talked about it. This held their interest, and helped to restore the atmosphere after the failure with the girl. Finally Kaspar told Robert to relax, and to stare at the glass object at the end of the string. Then he began to swing it gently, talking in a soft voice that we could not catch. I wondered if he was asking Robert to co-operate with him and pretend to be hypnotized, but the appearances were against it. Robert looked drowsy. He closed his eyes. Kaspar went behind him and stroked his forehead. After a moment he lifted one of Robert's eyelids, and commanded him to stand up. Robert stood up slowly. Kaspar took his hand and pinched the back of it; Robert did not wince. Kaspar then told the audience that Robert was now hypnotized and would do whatever he wanted. He next took from his pocket a small glass bulb, which he dropped on the floor. There was a loud report, and everyone in the audience jumped. Robert remained perfectly still. This convinced me that he was really in a trance.

Kaspar now asked Robert some questions about school. Were there any subjects he particularly disliked? Robert said yes, chemistry. Why? asked Kaspar. 'Because I don't like old Bilge,' said Robert. There were cheers from the gallery. The chemistry master's name was Bluewater, and we called him Bilge. The magician persisted: 'Why not?' 'Because he grabs your arse and squeezes it,' said Robert woodenly. Part of the audience laughed; the others, realizing the scandalous implication of the remark, gasped. (It was true; old Bilge had a habit of asking small boys to stand in front of the class as he questioned them, and fondling their behinds with his enormous hand.)

Kaspar quickly changed the subject; he asked Robert what animals he liked, and Robert said ferrets. 'Good,' Kaspar said. 'Then I want you to imagine you are a ferret in its cage.' Robert immediately dropped on all fours, and the audience laughed. This convinced me more than anything else that he was not shamming; like his father, he couldn't bear to be laughed at. 'We're out rabbiting,' said Kaspar. He produced a rabbit out of a top hat (it was not alive) and showed it to Robert, who arched his back and hissed slightly. I shivered; it was almost as if I could see his short, brownish fur standing up. Then the magician tossed the rabbit across the stage and shouted: 'Get it.' With a bound, Robert was across the stage, and caught the bundle of limp fur in his teeth. 'Good boy,' Kaspar said. 'Bring it here,' and Robert trotted across the stage and dropped the rabbit at Kaspar's feet. The audience clapped.

Kaspar now looked happier; his voice had become more masterful. He announced: 'I think we'll try hypnotizing two subjects at the same time,' and his eye fell on me. Before I could retreat or feel nervous, he was walking across the stage and asking me to come up. I clambered up the steps and was led to the centre of the stage. This time there were no cheers from the gods; I was not as well known as my cousin Robert. There followed the usual questions; I mentioned that 'the ferret' was my cousin and that we went to the same school. At close quarters Kaspar looked much older than I had taken him for, and his breath smelt unpleasant. He had a yellowish complexion, lots of wrinkles and kindly eyes.

At once I became aware of the power he was exerting. It was something to do with standing on a stage, and realizing that several hundred people were expecting me to do what he told me. But he also established a feeling of intimacy between us, as if we were more than a match for the audience.

He asked me to sit down, and began to swing the coloured glass ball in front of me. I had a vague sense that I was already halfway to hypnotizing myself, for I was watching everything with extreme care and waiting for something to happen, and this tension relaxed every few seconds, producing the same kind of effect as being on the edge of sleep. The swinging light was soothing, and his face looked so kindly and I felt completely relaxed. I had expected him to say 'Look into my eyes', and then his eyes to swell and become masterful, like the poster outside the theatre, but he was actually as unfrightening as our family doctor. As he swung the glass ball, which reflected the light, he talked to me in a soft voice, and I became sleepy. He asked me if I kept ferrets like

82

my cousin; I said no. Then he asked me what I did as a hobby. This was his mistake. Still feeling dreamy, I said 'Mathematics'. This seemed to disconcert him; the pendulum wavered slightly. 'What kind of mathematics?' he asked. Immediately, my mind went back to the problem I had been studying all day, and that I was anxious to get back to when I got home: Kummer's attempt to prove Fermat's last theorem. Something like a bolt of lightning seemed to fall in my mind, and suddenly Kaspar was only a pathetic old man asking me silly questions. It all seemed a farce; I was sitting on a solid stage, in front of an audience, and not feeling in the least sleepy or like being hypnotized; on the contrary, my mind felt as cold and constant as a neon light. Kaspar must have seen this; he immediately changed his tactics, went behind the chair, and began running his hands from my forehead down to my neck, behind my ears. This only irritated me. Kaspar turned to the audience and said: 'Another difficult subject,' and beckoned the first girl to return from the far side of the stage; then he told me to go and sit in the chair she had vacated. Within a few minutes he had the girl in a trance. Watching Robert and myself had relaxed her tension, and she became an easy subject. He told her that she was a rabbit and that Robert was a ferret, and she cowered away, looking terrified, while Robert arched his back. He told them they were two acrobats, and made them both walk on their hands. Robert found this easy, but the girl had to be supported; her dress fell down around her head, and the men in the audience whistled their appreciation of her figure.

After ten minutes of this kind of thing, Kaspar slapped them both lightly on the cheek, and they shook their heads and looked startled; the band played a heavy chord, and the audience clapped. As Robert and the girl were escorted off the stage by Kaspar, a theatre employee standing below beckoned me down the flight of stairs close to my chair. As I reached the bottom step, he pressed something into my hand; it was two half-crowns. I went quietly back to my seat, and the next turn came on. I passed the girl and her friend in the aisle, and heard the hypnotized girl asking: 'What did I do?', and her friend replying: 'Show everything you've got.'

At first I felt numb and embarrassed about it – I had disappointed the audience; then I stole a look at Robert, who still seemed bewildered, and felt triumphant as it came to me that he had been hypnotized and I hadn't.

On the way home on the bus he was sulky and refused to talk about it; the bus was so crowded that we had to sit in separate seats, so I had no opportunity to press him. And when later I turned around to look for him he had disappeared. The next day, at school, he had already decided on his story: that he had been pretending to be hypnotized because he was unwilling to embarrass the magician. He became something of a school hero for his public remark about old Bilge (who never forgave him for it). He soon learned, from some of his admirers in the gods, exactly what he had done on the stage, and so was able to tell a most circumstantial story of how he had 'helped' the magician by faking a trance. It was not until fifteen years later that he finally admitted to me that his mind had become a complete blank after he went up on the stage.

Robert's story never troubled me; I knew it was untrue. I also saw the implications of the experience. Although Robert appeared to be belligerent and 'good leader material', he was actually easily influenced by suggestion. He enjoyed being popular and belonging to a crowd. (Later on, he made a career in the army; he is still a very heavy drinker.) Therefore he made a good hypnotic subject. I was more used to being alone; it takes a great deal of 'melting' before I feel happy in a crowd, so I had more resistance. Finally, the accident of thinking about Fermat's last theorem had suddenly switched off the emotional and physical warmth with which I was responding to Kaspar, and switched on the intellectual half of my being. But for the magician's remark about my hobby, I should probably have been as easy to hypnotize as Robert. However, I preferred to ignore this at the time.

Another incident took place in my first year at Alderman Collins that strengthened my conceit, and sowed the seed of an attitude that developed during my teens.

In our town there were a great number of gangs – of the kind that had attacked me. I experienced several such incidents before the age of ten, although it is not worth going into detail about the others. I suppose such gangs formed because the menfolk were in the forces and the police force was under-manned. Although we lived in a fairly respectable district of the town, there were two or three such gangs in our area. There was the Thames Street gang and the Moat Road gang and the Temple Road gang, and a rather younger gang of hooligans who specialized in robbing orchards and who called themselves the Frith Mob.

The lawless activities of most of these gangs were confined to playing football in the street and beating up boys from other areas who trespassed on their territory. There were ominous rumours from poorer districts of the town about rapes and woundings, but nothing of the sort happened in our area. But occasionally 'trouble' blew up; challenges were exchanged, brickbats and palings were collected, and an army of grim-faced urchins marched into enemy territory. The opposing army met them from behind barricades of dustbins and old chairs; for ten minutes, bricks and milk bottles flew through the air, and a few heads were broken. The police would arrive and find the street littered with broken glass and cabbage stumps, but no sign of the armies.

One day as I was crossing the Stoneyvale Park I saw a gang of roughs who were hanging round the gate by which I intended to leave. I did not like the look of them, but I was crossing a wide, open stretch of grass and could not change my direction without revealing my nervousness. Then, fifty yards away on my right, I saw a group of boys whom I knew vaguely; one of them delivered our newspapers. So I changed my direction and went towards them. Our newsboy was called Teddy Kirk; he was a tough-looking boy with red hair, but I had always found him friendly. I knew a few of the others by sight, and Teddy introduced me; they were members of the Temple Road gang, and they were holding a council of war. The boys by the gate were, in fact, members of the Thames Street gang, and they had just been warned that there would be an attack on Thames Street that evening. (This was not a matter of politeness; if the attackers turned up without warning the rival gang, they might find no one there, and the whole thing would be an anti-climax.)

Teddy Kirk now asked me if I would fight on their side that evening. The idea did not appeal to me, but I agreed so as not to be thought a coward. And in order to get away I said that I would go and reconnoitre enemy territory. Teddy immediately said he would go with me, and dropped hints to the others that I was known as a master of strategy, and could be expected to produce some brilliant plan of attack. I had been intending to go home and stay there, but this build-up made me feel that I would have to show some results. So Teddy and I walked to Thames Street, and I hid my nervousness. On the way there we met Fred Randle, the leader of the Temple Road gang, a scar-faced, crop-haired lad who

86

was about to leave school and work for a builder. He looked at me dubiously, and I could see what he was thinking. But since he had nothing to do he came along with us.

Thames Street was a broad road on the edge of the town, half a mile from the park. It was part of a council estate, and most of the houses had been built just before the war. Halfway along it, a cul-de-sac called Deep Dell ran off to the right. The cul-de-sac was narrower than Thames Street, and would therefore be easier to defend. Thames Street was also a kind of cul-de-sac, ending in a high wooden fence, with a spinney on the other side. This fence had lengths of barbed wire along the top, and carried a metal notice saying: 'DANGER, 10,000 volts.' There was an electricity-board kiosk in the middle of the spinney. There was also an absurd rumour that the council had set man-traps in the long grass; for this reason, the Thames Street gang kept clear of it.

Fred Randle had fought there before. He told us that the gang would set up their barricade halfway down Deep Dell. I walked up the street; it was obviously going to be difficult to attack and easy to defend. On the other hand, Thames Street would be easy to attack, and would, in fact, be indefensible if there was any way of getting across the spinney. I explained this to Teddy and Fred; Fred told me about the man-traps in the spinney. That was obviously a myth, so I asked them to give me a lift over the fence. Teddy came over with me, and I tore the seat out of my trousers on the barbed wire. Still, it was obvious that there were no man-traps in the spinney, and that it could easily be entered from a lane on the other side if certain strands of barbed wire were cut.

The main problem was how to get the gang to fight in Thames Street instead of in Deep Dell, and I finally hit on a plan that seemed worth trying. It depended on creating some kind of a disturbance in Deep Dell that would drive the gang to erect their barricades in Thames Street. I told Fred to divide his gang into two halves, and to send one of them through the spinney. When he asked me how I proposed to get the gang to fight in Thames Street, I winked, and Teddy told him to leave it to me. I warned him to take wire-cutters with him if he led the spinney contingent. Then I went home to change my clothes. At the end of Thames Street I stopped to talk to a woman who was weeding her front garden; she told me that the evening newspapers were delivered at about half past five, and that the boy came from a newsagent half a mile away.

Teddy came home with me; it was now about five o'clock, and the attack was due in an hour. We both drank some milk, and I took half a crown out of my money-box; I also borrowed my father's wire-cutters from the tool-shed in case Fred forgot to take some. We were too excited to eat, but chewed biscuits on our way back to Thames Street.

It was easy to locate the newsboy. I approached him as he was coming out of a front gate near Thames Street, and offered him half a crown if he would allow me to deliver his newspapers in Deep Dell. At first he was suspicious, but the sight of the money persuaded him. I wrote down a list of the houses I had to deliver to, and set off with the canvas bag, while Teddy waited around with the newsboy at the end of the street.

I felt terrified as I turned into Deep Dell. About forty boys were gathered at the far end. They were not building the barricade yet – probably in case the police were warned before the battle began – but dustbins, chairs and sheets of corrugated tin had been left discreetly in front gardens and under hedges. They appeared to be playing cricket peacefully enough. No one paid any attention to me as I delivered the newspapers, although a girl asked me what had happened to Frankie, and I replied that he was sick. I began to wonder if any of the gang would recognize me as the boy who walked over to the Temple Road gang in the park, and my stomach turned to water.

Near the top of the street were two front gardens with unusually high privet hedges. I had noticed these earlier, and was relying on them for cover. I went into the first front garden and delivered the newspaper, then looked round. Two boys – acting as fielders – were directly in my line of vision. I went out of the gate and into the next garden. One of the boys could still see me if he turned his head. Worse still, the house was not on my list for newspaper delivery. I stopped to tie my shoelace, to gain time. Then both fielders suddenly disappeared, chasing the ball. I acted quickly. Making sure that no one else could see me, I took a large round stone out of my pocket. The target was the front window of a house opposite. My aim was accurate; there was a shattering of glass, and I felt an awful panic, certain that someone would rush at me. Then I pulled myself together and walked out of the gate, whistling and assuming an air of innocence that would have branded me immediately as the culprit if anyone had noticed it. Fortunately everyone was staring at the house with the broken window and accusing one another of doing it. My stone had gone through the centre pane, leaving a hole about a foot in diameter. Then the front door opened, and a furious old man appeared and began to swear at them. I was feeling so sick with tension and alarm that I hardly noticed what was going on. I heard the man threatening to call the police. My chief problem was restraining a desire to hurry straight back to the waiting newsboy and hand him his bag, but I realized that this might spoil everything. I had twenty papers still to deliver, and I delivered them, carefully consulting my list. I was so frightened that I probably delivered them all to the wrong houses; anyhow, I rejoined the newsboy and Teddy a quarter of an hour later, and we had the satisfaction of seeing that the Thames Street gang was transporting its dustbins and corrugated tin to the far end of Thames Street. Teddy was so delighted that he kept jumping up and down and slapping me on the back.

The rest went as planned, and I stayed well in the background. (Teddy went off to make sure that everything was being done according to my instructions.) At six o'clock, a contingent of the Temple Road gang appeared, and the Thames Streeters constructed their barricade in a matter of seconds and met them with a barrage of missiles. From my position at the end of the street I saw Fred Randle's head appear over the fence behind the defenders, and snip the barbed wire. The Thames Streeters were too busy throwing things to notice that they were being attacked from the rear, and when they did notice it was too late; the Temple Roaders were on them with wooden palings, cabbage stalks and other weapons for fighting at close quarters. I was so excited by it all that I went a little too far along Thames Street, and was hit on the head by a half brick that split the skin. When Teddy Kirk came up to congratulate me he found me sitting on the ground clutching my head. The Thames Street gang had been completely routed, and the victorious Temple Roaders carried off one of their dustbins as a trophy.

I joined them for the victory celebration in an old air-raid shelter, and drank luke-warm lemonade out of a tin cup while Teddy explained my strategy to the rest of the gang. I enjoyed listening to their praises, but now felt a sense of anti-climax. I was invited to become a permanent member of the gang, and said that I would think about it.

Then I went home. I felt sufficiently proud of my exploit to write about it in detail in my journal (which I still have).

This episode exorcized the fear of 'rough boys'. To begin with, the Temple Roaders always treated me with cordial respect afterwards, and talking to them made me feel less nervous about boys with torn trousers. But I also felt that I had proved my superiority.

3

The most important episode of my early teens was my meeting with Jeremy Wolfe.

During most of my time at Alderman Collins, my old problem of belief held no interest for me. And yet I think that Uncle Nick had planted a virus in me; and, like malaria, it would return unexpectedly. It was always present somewhere in my mind, but only as a vague disquiet. For example, I once spent a morning helping Aunt Bertha and the vicar's wife prepare the refreshments-tent at a garden fête, and was fascinated by the conversation of some of the women who had been hired to help: 'I said to 'er – told 'er to 'er face – "You must think I'm a complete fool if you think I'll believe that kind of stuff".' 'So I said to her, I said . . .' There was a kind of naïve egoism about it all; the word 'I' was repeated ten times a minute; all the conversation was directed to showing how the speaker had won an argument and confused and confounded the person who had had the temerity to oppose her. I sat there for an hour, listening while we all drank tea, paying particular attention to a woman with a brick-red face and fat, powerful arms who seemed to command everybody's respect. When she told a story of how she defeated the attempt of some shopwoman to overcharge her, or of her next-door neighbour to tell her a 'bare-faced lie', the other women would murmur 'She ought to've known better than to try that on you'. After half an hour of this lady's stories I was convinced that everyone thought her infallible and in every way admirable. Then the fat woman went home to get her husband's lunch, and I was surprised by the comments that followed her departure. 'She must think we're crackers to believe that stuff', 'She's such a liar', 'I know what she *really* said to Mrs Battison', 'She hasn't paid her laundry-bill for two months'. They then proceeded to tell spiteful stories about the fat lady, and it now appeared that every one of them had beaten her in argument, proved decisively to her face that she was a liar, etc. This made me speculate on what would happen if they all left the room one by one – whether each one would be revealed as a liar and a 'show off'; what would happen when there was only one woman left in the room? Would she sit there, possessing 'truth' all to herself, secure in her knowledge that all her neighbours were self-deceivers; or would she be confronted with the possibility that she was also a liar, that even in her thoughts she was lying to herself?

The same kind of problem struck me one day when my father had spent an afternoon with a group of builder's labourers, and began to talk to my mother about the way that city workmen lie and try to impress one another. He also noticed this naïve boasting and self-praise: 'I told him I wasn't that kind of bloke at all,' etc. He then went on to contrast this with the taciturnity of the countryman, and mentioned an old man we both knew well, a quiet, pipe-smoking type with whom my father and Uncle Jeff sometimes went rabbiting or fishing. This old man was noted for his quiet but effective retorts, and my father told several stories in which some boaster from the city had lost an argument with him. But it seemed to me that this old man had only developed a more subtle system of inflating his ego, and that this was his only superiority to 'city boasters'. After pursuing this train of thought for a while, it seemed to me that the human race is only a collection of swollen egos, and that if human beings ever had the courage to contemplate themselves honestly there would be no alternative but suicide. Pontius Pilate had expressed a final judgement when he asked: 'What is truth?'

But then, Pilate had not been a mathematician, or he might have realized that it is possible for human beings to achieve a kind of knowledge untouched by the compulsion to ego-inflation. So I went back to my mathematics, and was glad to feel myself again in the company of sane men.

It was at about this time – shortly after the end of the war – that a cousin of my father returned from the United States and told us about a Negro 'Messiah' who had declared that he was God, and now had a vast following, as well as being a millionaire; wherever he walked, his followers prostrated themselves and kissed the ground. This story aroused in me the problems that had troubled me when Uncle Nick was committed, but only in a vague way, like pangs of toothache. I dismissed them and went back to the theory of functions.

Before I speak of Jeremy Wolfe, I must mention a curious episode that had repercussions later. When my sister Anne was six years old, I saved her from being sexually assaulted. Anne was a pretty but quiet child who looked like her mother. She was shy of strangers. There had been, at the end of the war, a number of sexual murders involving children, and in our district in 1948 there was some talk of a sex maniac who attacked children. 'Attacked' is perhaps too strong a word; he lured the children into quiet places with promises of toys or sweets, persuaded them into sexual games, and usually left them to find their way home in tears. So my parents spent a great deal of time warning Anne about talking to strange men.

One day, Anne went out to play in the street after tea,

and could not be found an hour later. We looked through the surrounding streets, but no one had seen her. My father went off in the car looking for her, and I decided to search in the park. Some boys there told me that they had seen a small girl in a blue dress watching a cricket match, and someone else said that she had been seen walking off with a man who was pushing a bicycle. The chances were against this child being my sister, but I walked off in the direction in which they had been seen walking. This brought me to the back of the spinney through which the Temple Road gang had launched their attack. I called Anne's name, and to my surprise, her voice called back. I found a hole in the hedge, and as I scrambled through she came running towards me. I asked her what she had been doing, and she said she had been talking to a 'nice man'. I walked into the spinney, and was in time to see a youth clambering over the fence that led into Thames Street. He grinned and waved at me, said: 'Can't stop', and dropped on the other side. I recognized him as a youth whom I had seen around in the park; I thought he was a member of one of the gangs. Anne and I walked home; she was not in the least excited about her exploit. She had walked into the park with two girl friends, looking for butterflies, had watched a cricket match, and had then got into conversation with the 'nice man', who told her that he knew where she could catch butterflies. He took her into the spinney, telling her stories as they walked along; when they got into the spinney, he told her that she would have to take off her dress if she wanted to keep it clean, because the butter-flies lived in a treacle barrel. She was mildly objecting to this when I appeared.

I warned her about talking to strange men, but she insisted that this one was 'nice'; I agreed that this was probably so, but made her promise that, in future, she would never again accept an invitation to look for butter-flies. She agreed readily enough, and I felt pleased with myself; I did not want to frighten her. But my parents immediately undid my good work; my mother had hysterics and clutched Anne in her arms, screaming: 'My baby', and my father spanked her and told her that the 'nice man' was a bogy who would have killed her. Then Anne had hysterics too, and for a long time afterwards was nervous, mistrustful and shy. My father reported the matter to the police, who questioned me about the appearance of the 'nice man', and Anne was taken to the park to try to pick him out. But nothing came of all this except that Anne caught my parents' neurosis about murderers and sometimes woke up in the night screaming.

In September 1948, I found a book in Aunt Dinah's living-room; it was called *Old Truths With New Names* by Jeremy Wolfe. The title interested me, and I started to read. On page one the author remarked that Euclid's fifth postulate could be reversed and combined with the others to make a consistent non-Euclidean geometry. (The fifth postulate, of course, states that if you put a dot near a straight line, only *one* straight line can be drawn through this dot parallel to the other line.) He went on to remark that any one of the 'obvious truths' about the universe can be turned upside down, and a consistent philosophy constructed on the result. For example, the thugs of India accepted all the ten commandments except 'Thou shalt not kill', which they changed to 'Thou shalt kill as much as possible', and the result was a consistent and reasonable kind of religion.

Now this remark astounded me; it expressed something I had felt since Uncle Nick taught me that the earth is hollow, but had never been able to express with clarity. I sat down and began to read the book. It was not easy to follow, but the style had a hard, dogmatic quality that reminded me of a mathematical textbook. I asked Aunt Dinah where the book came from; she said that the mother of the author had lent it her. This excited me; I asked if I could borrow it, but she refused, saying that she had to return it that day. I asked her what she knew about the author, but she was vague. She had only met the mother once at a spiritualist meeting. I noted that the book was published by a local bookseller. I went to the central library and enquired about it. The librarian asked me if I knew the author, and I said I didn't. He produced a copy of the book, and told me that the author had been in personally to present it to the library. It had been on the shelves for several months, but so far no one had taken it out. So I was its first borrower.

The librarian was not able to tell me much about the author except that he was a young man who lived alone and sometimes played the organ in the cathedral.

I went home and read the book straight through. It was well written, and since I had read no philosophy it struck me as completely original. The author contended that, although we must reject orthodox religion as old-fashioned, nevertheless most religions are based upon certain truths that can be expressed in scientific terms. The most important of these is that human beings are evolving by devotion to the mind and things of the mind. A great deal of the book was occupied with attacks on the modern world, on advertising, journalism, the cinema, the theatre, democracy, fascism and communism, and on modern religious revivals. The author demolished these so briefly and devastatingly that it was obvious to me that he was in possession of some profound truth. I was particularly struck by a paragraph on the final page of the book:

'In an age that has no belief in the "spiritual", we might well start from this self-evident truth: *Life is subsidized.* What do I mean by this? During the war, the government gave farmers financial subsidies to produce certain kinds of crops; the farmers' losses were therefore turned into profits. Human life is also subsidized by the power behind evolution. Common sense tells us that self-interest is the only sensible motive; but the life-force prefers to subsidize disinterestedness and idealism. But apart from this, life gives sudden generous allowances of intensity and vitality to people who seem in no way to deserve it – wasters, drifters and sensualists. I suspect that the history of every idealist is a story of sudden "subsidies" of vitality and joy that deflected the energies from self-interest into generosity of spirit.'

This struck a chord; I recognized it immediately as my own intellectual history: moments of intensity in which I abandoned caution and embraced the absolute with as much joy as if it were the girl of my romantic day-dreams. Jeremy Wolfe's book was a mirror in which I saw my face; and a highly flattering mirror at that.

The next morning, I called on the bookshop that had published *Old Truths With New Names* and talked to a little, bent Jewish man called Kant whose identity was concealed by the word 'Thornhill Press'. He loved literature, and had apparently published a dozen or so volumes by local writers. He lost from twenty to a hundred pounds on every volume published, unless the author could be persuaded to bear the loss. But he still believed that several of his authors were undiscovered geniuses, and that one day his name would be famous as their first publisher.

Mr Kant (his Christian name was, strangely enough, Immanuel) told me a little about Jeremy Wolfe. He admitted that he did not like his work, but had agreed to publish the book when the author offered to pay for it. Wolfe, he said, was a lonely and gloomy young man who lived alone in a cottage near Cranthorpe, a village five miles out of town. He was a good pianist who occasionally helped out the local drama group. But he was difficult to get along with, and had twice refused to come to Mr Kant's small literary gatherings. Last time he came into the shop, he had criticized Mr Kant for offering for sale various books on sex, and had left in a self-righteous mood.

Mr Kant gave me the author's address, and I immediately went to the local reading-room and wrote a letter to Jeremy Wolfe, explaining that I was an admirer of his work, mentioning my age, and asking if I could meet him. A reply came two days later, offering to meet me – of all places – in our local park. I kept the appointment, and waited, as he suggested, outside the pavilion, carrying the copy of *Old Truths With New Names*.

He was very late – more than an hour. I was about to go home when a tall young man approached me and asked me if my name was Hugh Greene; the question was superfluous since I was carrying the book.

At first I was disappointed. He was tall and thin, about twenty-three years old, with a very slight moustache, a weak mouth and receding chin. He was beautifully dressed in a light brown suit, and pointed, highly polished shoes. His voice was weak, and had a suggestion of a bleat; he also had a habit of trailing off sentences as if too tired to finish them.

He apologized for being late, and then said immediately that he would have to go home again in half an hour. For the past two days I had been building daydreams of an intellectual giant with whom I would talk for hours and exchange great ideas; this casual young man with his faint voice was an anti-climax.

However, we went into the pavilion and bought tea. For the first quarter of an hour we both felt awkward. He kept glancing at his watch, and when he finished his tea made unmistakable preparations for going back home. I decided that something had to be said to start a conversation, and mentioned his reference to Euclid in the first paragraph of his book. In a slightly patronizing way he started to explain non-Euclidean geometry to me; I listened silently until he remarked that Riemann had invented it. I corrected him, telling him that Lobatchewsky should be given the credit. He looked startled, and I talked about the achievement of Lobatchewsky, then, seeing that I held his interest, gave him a brief sketch of the history of non-Euclidean geometry. I was delighted to see the astonishment on his face. He mentioned that he had been trying to read Einstein's book on relativity but had been forced to give up after two chapters. For the past few weeks I had been studying Milne's *Space, Time and Gravitation*, so the special theory of relativity was child's play to me, and I clarified the theories of Lorentz and Poincaré for him.

He was a good audience. Like most writers he was a poor mathematician, and seemed to feel there was a kind of black magic involved in the subject – not in the figures themselves, but in the ability to be interested in anything so basically repellent. He tried to get me to explain how my interest in figures had developed, and took my inability to explain for another proof that the matter verged on mysticism. Half an hour later he asked me if I would like to go back to his cottage for supper. I accepted delightedly, but asked him about his 'appointment'; he immediately admitted that this had been an excuse in case he found me tiresome. He had suggested meeting in the park because it would be easy to leave me there, while if he invited me to his cottage or his mother's house it might be more difficult to get rid of me if I proved tiresome.

This frankness naturally turned us into close friends, and we talked with complete freedom on the bus that took us out to Cranthorpe. This was the first time I made a journey that I was to make hundreds of times afterwards. I soon began to wonder why I had been disappointed by his appearance; when he was excited his face coloured, his eyes brightened, and there was no longer any suggestion of weakness about his appearance – on the contrary, there was a gleam of fanaticism that reminded me of a picture of Torquemada in our school history-book.

At about half past eight the bus arrived in Cranthorpe. It was a warm autumn evening, and the sunlight on the old cottages and the war memorial was golden. Jeremy's cottage was half a mile outside the village, along an unfrequented road; this road rises steeply on the far side of the village square, past the church, and then turns a hairpin-bend above the village. From this road the whole village could be seen – a picture-postcard village with white cottages, thatched roofs and flower gardens. Then the road turns another bend, past a wood – and a hundred yards further stands Jeremy's cottage, also thatched, and with a small, neat garden.

He pushed open the door – which was always left unlatched – and I found myself in his living-room.

The cottage was very small, with only one room up and down, and a kitchen with room for only one person. There was a fawn pile-carpet on the floor, and the furniture was new and expensive. There was an upright piano, and also a Hammond organ; these two, together with the armchairs and two antique occasional tables, took up most of the available room. There were bookshelves around the walls, as well as on the stairs; I looked through these while Jeremy made coffee, and was impressed at the range of his interests – from Elizabethan playwrights to modern philosophy. There were only a few volumes on science or mathematics, and these were popular expositions.

We spent the next three hours talking and drinking coffee, then I had to hurry off to catch the last bus. I missed it by a few minutes, and had a five-mile walk back home. I didn't mind this; it was a cold, starry night, and the air sometimes had a sweet smell – as if, I thought, it blew from an ice-cream factory. Jeremy had told me something about himself. He was an only child, and his father was dead. His mother was well provided for, and had bought him this cottage (for twenty-five pounds) where he could work at composing. (She lived in a block of flats in town, and the other tenants objected to Jeremy's habit of playing the piano at three in the morning.) Here he lived very cheaply – she allowed him only two pounds a week – and wrote books and some music. At the end of the war he had been in the navy for a short time, but had been discharged as 'nervously unsuitable' after a few months.

A number of things about him puzzled me. At the age of fifteen I was aware of the presence of vital urges that distracted me from my total absorption in mathematical truth. Boys of my own age at school talked endlessly about sex, and some of this fever communicated itself to me. But my own attitude to sex was casual; I never deliberately indulged in sexual fantasies, but neither did I try too hard to escape them. I was continually aware of its importance, but still gave most of my mental energy to mathematics. Jeremy had not mentioned sex in our first evening's conversation, and I got the feeling that he fought shy of the subject. Was he afraid of it? Or simply a puritan? Or did he have a mistress? And did he have no friends? And if his culture was as wide and profound as it seemed to me, how could he take any pleasure in talking with me, eight years his junior?

Slowly, over the next few months, I found out the answer to these questions. I discovered that he liked talking to me because he enjoyed playing the pedagogue. He was lonely, he was bored, and he thought of himself as a world-betterer. But he was also lazy, shy and subject to sudden attacks of nervous apathy. He found me intelligent, receptive, and totally uninformed about music, literature and philosophy. I was an ideal audience. And Jeremy Wolfe taught me more in a year than I had learned in ten years of schooling.

His character was one of the most curious and complex that I have ever met. I have never discovered strength and weakness mixed so strangely – and so completely bound up with one another. His writing was forceful and witty. (His models had been Bernard Shaw and Bertrand Russell.) A reader of his books might have expected their author to be a strong personality, a good talker, a man who was made to dominate any gathering in which he found himself. Jeremy was none of these things. His temperament was affected by the weather; a rainy day left him depressed and exhausted. He was never punctual; he admitted to me that as the time for some appointment came closer, he began to feel it as a limitation of his freedom, and finally as a constant irritation that drained him of energy, so that he had to lie down on the bed and watch his motive power seeping away like blood from an open artery. Finally, half an hour after he was due for the appointment, he would drag himself to his feet like someone rising from the dead and force himself to leave the house. Alternatively, he might decide to phone and pretend to be ill; but this made it no easier, for he would then begin to postpone the act of phoning

103

until it became an obstacle that demanded all his will-power; he would sit in a chair, or lie on the bed, watching the clock, and deciding when would be the last possible moment to telephone; having decided, he would stare at the second hand of the clock like a condemned man watching for the dawn that would bring the executioner. Finally, the telephone would seem to be too heavy for his wrist, and every turn of the dial require an act of will to frustrate the urge to drop the receiver back into its cradle. And having made his excuses, he would fall back on the bed, shivering with distaste and thinking how much more convenient it would have been if the person he was supposed to meet had dropped dead earlier in the day.

The second time I met him I discovered the way that he set his intellect to work to justify these peculiarities of disposition. It was the next evening. It had rained all day, and was still drizzling as I walked up the hill out of Cranthorpe square. I found Jeremy drooping in an arm-chair, looking like a fungoid growth or some limp and glutinous object that had found its way through a hole in the roof. I asked him if he felt ill; he said no, merely tired. I looked around the room, expecting to see piles of manuscript or music paper; none were visible. I asked him what he'd been doing.

'Nothing. Just wrestling with my temperament.'

I grinned and asked: 'Why, what's wrong with it?'

This prompted a torrent of confession and explanation. He said that he sometimes felt as if his body was like a team of untamed horses. Most men, he said, can be exhausted by a hard day's work, but he was far less fortunate, because even the preliminary of work – concentrating his forces – often took more energy than he had available. He spent the whole day wrestling obscurely with a kind of grey octopus of feelings. I asked gently – trying hard not to seem critical – whether this might not be the outcome of having nothing to do. Immediately he became vehement in repudiating my mistake. He agreed that this might be true of most men, who had nothing to do but work for a weekly wage-packet, because they possess energy without real purpose. But his energies were all turned into the work of creation; he was working, in the deepest possible sense, 'for himself'. And as soon as a man began to work for himself – that is, out of some impulse connected with a basic need – then he began to tap a source of energy beyond the understanding of any wage-slave. There are, he explained, many different kinds of energy, just as, in the industrial world, there are many kinds of fuel, ranging from coal to atomic energy, from diesel oil to high-octane petrol. When we normally speak of 'an energetic man', we mean a man who makes a lot of commotion as he expends his energy; but such a man is always driven on the coarsest fuel, mere coal or diesel oil. The true artist is driven by something more like atomic energy. Atomic energy is a 'smokeless' fuel; its use involves no fuss or commotion. On the other hand, a cyclotron is a far more complicated machine than a steam engine; it is more difficult to start; when it goes wrong, it is infinitely more difficult to repair. An old train, belching out greasy clouds, will keep on running until its joints fall apart; but the slightest speck of rust can affect the cyclotron.

Moreover, Jeremy said, his simile of the cyclotron was more exact than I might suppose. For creative energy is also a 'chain reaction'; when he found himself working well, he also found that he was not expending energy but creating it. For a long time there would be an increase in clarity and strength until all the mind and body seemed involved in the process; and when exhaustion came, it was a healthy exhaustion, not like the nervous prostration that he felt after a 'bad day' like today.

105

I had got Jeremy on to his favourite subject – the 'higher energies', which are actually far stronger than the animal energies of the body, even though they may seem weaker when in direct competition.

So Jeremy need feel no self-contempt about his inability to lift the telephone or cancel an appointment; it was all part of an 'unseen warfare', an interior struggle that would have killed any healthy navvy or farm-hand. It was inevitable that he should vacillate between periods of creative fever and nervous exhaustion. For the evolutionary force has not yet perfected its human cyclotrons, and the artist could only wait patiently through periods of 'mechanical breakdown' – always due, of course, to 'technical faults at present beyond his control'.

I remember sitting there, impressed by this terrific flow of self-explanation, and by the extent to which he could use his intellect to define the complexities of his own being. And my admiration stimulated him to more definitions, until he suddenly said: 'Now, you see, I could settle down and begin a new book right away if I was alone. The cyclotron's working again.' I asked him if he would like me to go home. He dismissed the idea (perhaps he didn't want to be forced to accept his own challenge) and made some coffee.

Now a curious thing occurred. The fire was low, and he asked me if I would mind getting in more coal, since my shoes were thicker than his and therefore more waterproof. The coal was kept in a lean-to shed at the bottom of the back garden, on the other side of the lawn. I took the scuttle and a shovel, and walked across the wet lawn; it was dusty and the rain had stopped. Behind the coal-shed flowed a stream, and I pushed my way through some stinging-nettles to peer down at it. (I have always loved the sound of running water.) It was so pleasant that I stood there for a few minutes, enjoying the clean air

106

and the smell that came from the orchard on the other side of the stream. Then I turned back to the shed, and began to fill the scuttle with coal. As I did so, I had a feeling of someone standing behind me, and I thought for a moment that Jeremy had walked down to join me. I went on shovelling without turning round, and soon realized that although there *was* no one directly behind me there was someone looking at me from the cottage. I cannot explain why I felt sure of this, but it seemed an extension of the feeling that there was someone behind me. When I turned round, holding the full scuttle, I was aware that someone was looking at me from the upstairs window of the cottage, and I thought I could see a face through the dusk.

This struck me as interesting; such sensations are not very common with me; I thought that perhaps my talk with Jeremy had established a contact between us that made me feel that he was looking out of the window, wondering what had happened to me.

I went back into the cottage, and found Jeremy poking the fire. He asked me if I was hungry, and I forgot about my 'telepathic sensation' as we made up the fire, poured the coffee, and then made cheese sandwiches. For the next two hours we talked of various things, and he ended by playing me some of Bach's Well Tempered Clavier on the piano. I listened for nearly half an hour; then he broke off for a moment to observe that he often thought that music helped to 'prime' the cyclotron and make it run more easily. It elevated the mind, made it aware of subtler vibrations; and when two minds were moved by the same music, it made them aware of one another's vibrations.

I interrupted him to say: 'I know. But I think that good conversation has the same effect. For example, while I was getting the coal I was aware that you were watching me from the house – and not only that, but that you were watching me from the bedroom window.'

He went pale and stared hard at me. Then he said: 'Why do you say that?' I explained. He listened with a strange look – not frightened, but as if he had heard some bad news – then said: 'I wasn't upstairs. I was in here all the time.'

We sat silent for a moment, absorbing this. Then I said: 'I suppose I could have been mistaken.'

'No. You weren't mistaken. I have experienced it too. There is someone in the upstairs room.'

I can still remember the way my hair stirred as he said this.

'How do you mean – someone? You don't believe in ghosts, do you?'

'A ghost, a presence – I don't think it matters what you call it.'

'Up there *now*?'

He stood up. 'Let's go and see.'

The room, of course, was empty. It was a pleasant room, with a thick carpet, many bookshelves and a warm, comfortable appearance. It looked so 'normal' and pleasant that my nervousness evaporated, and I became convinced that we were talking nonsense. And yet when I thought of shovelling the coal at the bottom of the garden, I could not doubt that someone had been watching me. We went downstairs again. I asked him why he thought there was someone in the bedroom.

'Not just in the bedroom. There's a presence in the cottage – sometimes down here, sometimes in the garden.'

'Do you mean he can see us and we can't see him?'

'I doubt whether he can see us either.'

He told me that he had also experienced this sensation

of being watched – sometimes from the garden, some-times from the house.

'Doesn't it make you nervous?' I asked.

'I suppose so. At least, I don't like it. But I don't think there's any harm in it, any more than in a smell.'

'But how do you explain it?'

From his explanations I could see that he had thought about it for a long time. To begin with, he was not willing to call the 'someone' a ghost, but preferred to speak of 'a presence'. I said that if the 'presence' was conscious of us, then it could be called a ghost. Jeremy said he doubted whether it was conscious of us in the sense I meant – that is, the sense in which we were conscious of one another. Consciousness, after all, depends on a 'reference system', on the brain and the memory. Could a ghost be said to have a memory, since it has no brain?

'Supposing,' Jeremy said, 'you are sitting in that chair, and you think of something pleasant. Then a noise outside breaks your train of thought. You try to remember what you were thinking about, but it has gone. As you try to jog your memory, you have a sense of groping in a void, of being helpless. So you deliberately look around the room, and try to remember how the train of thought started. Your eyes rest on a certain book, and you remember looking at it ten minutes before and thinking about it. Starting from there, you reconstruct your chain of thought until you finally arrive at what you are trying to remember. It is like climbing a stair by means of a handrail, pulling yourself up. That handrail is *the external world*. And part of the external world is your material body. That is the anchor of consciousness. A ghost could have no memory in this sense.'

'But it might have some other kind.'

'I doubt it. Recall how you feel on those days when you find it hard to concentrate. Your mind jumps like a grasshopper. Everything distracts you. Well, imagine that state of mind magnified ten thousand times, and you probably have an idea of the state of mind of a ghost. Almost no memory – nothing to hold it together but a few obsessions. It would be like being very, very drunk.'

I asked him how he would define a ghost.

'As a kind of stagnant state of mind, a little floating island of unattached consciousness. It is the body that stops us from stagnating. With its hunger and thirst and other needs, it drives us forward. Since a ghost has no body, it could have very little that we associate with consciousness – no power of reasoning, no attention, no memory. It is, after all, about as real as a smell.'

But he had no theory to account for the existence of ghosts – or rather, presences. I asked how they fitted into his scheme of evolution. He said: 'Your guess is as good as mine.' Before I left that night, he lent me three books. They were Tyrrell's *Apparitions*, Sacheverell Sitwell's *Poltergeists*, and Dunne's *Experiment with Time*. I started reading Dunne on the bus going back home, and was fascinated by it. It seemed that I was back in the world of Uncle Nick and his theories, but that all this was better authenticated. Admittedly, I had some doubts about my own experience of being 'watched'; it might, after all, have been an illusion, a subconscious observation of some movement behind me that made me think that someone was there. Having a scientific turn of mind, I tried the experiment of staring at someone who was not aware of my presence, and seeing if my 'stare' could be felt; but a dozen repetition of this experiment gave no definite result. A few weeks later, however, I was presented with some more definite evidence. Jeremy had been speaking to me about the music of Beethoven. He explained that he felt that Beethoven's music was an exhaustive diary of his spiritual progress, and that the later works express spiritual states that are almost beyond human comprehension. He played me passages of the early sonatas, and ended by playing me the final movement of opus 109. This moved me deeply in a way that I could not understand. It almost hurt. Something was happening inside me analogous to the breaking of the ice on a river in spring, and the first sensation was painful. Nevertheless, I was fascinated. I said later to Jeremy:

'Now I know how a chrysalis must feel as it changes into a butterfly.'

As he finished, I stood up and went into the kitchen for a drink. It was a Saturday afternoon, and the dusk was falling. At the bottom of the garden Jeremy had raked the fallen leaves into a pile, and set fire to them. They were smouldering now. As I stared, I noticed a man on the far side of the leaves; he was holding a gardening tool that might have been a rake or a fork or a broom. I supposed that Jeremy had persuaded one of the local farm-workers to do a few hours' work in his garden. I glanced down at the tap, filling my glass, then looked up again; the man was not there. This did not surprise me either; he might have gone behind the coal-shed. Then a vague suspicion came into my mind, and I called:

'Jeremy. Who's the man in your garden?'

'Man?' he said, hurrying out. 'Where?'

'He *was* behind the bonfire,' I said. Jeremy opened the door, and I walked down the garden with him. I knew already that we would find nothing, and that I had seen the 'presence'. There was no one near, and nowhere a man could have hidden in the few moments since I had see him.

'It looks as if that's your ghost,' I said, as we walked towards the cottage.

'What did he look like?'

I said I didn't know. He just looked like a man raking leaves into a fire.

That evening we went down to the local pub, and both drank ginger-beer shandy. (I was not old enough to be allowed in, but the village had no policeman, so no one bothered.) The landlord knew Jeremy only by sight, and was surprised to see him there. Jeremy had warned me not to talk about 'ghosts'; he didn't want to become the talk of the village. However, he asked the landlord casually who had lived in the cottage before his mother bought it, and the landlord said: 'Old Mrs Clark, the postmistress.' 'And before that?' Jeremy said. The landlord looked at him hard, and asked: 'Have you been seeing ghosts?' Jeremy promptly replied: 'No, but I've heard stories about them.' The landlord became friendly, and admitted that the cottage had a reputation for being haunted, and that this was probably why Jeremy's mother had bought it so cheaply. He had no idea who the ghost was supposed to be. An old man who came in before we left was a little more helpful. He said: 'People do say it be old Tom Davis, who worked for Mr Braithwaite, the great-grandfather of the Braithwaite who owns Kidbrook Farm now.' But he also could tell us very little, except that Tom Davis had been the cow-man, and a good gardener, and had died of 'a swelling on his neck'.

I should add that this ghost story has no conclusion. I should like to be able to say that we discovered some mysterious bones in the cellar, and an ancient manuscript hidden in the chimney, but nothing of the sort happened. I never saw the ghost again, and never again felt that I was being 'watched'. Jeremy once thought he saw it on a winter's night, as a dim figure in the house, but admits that he might have been mistaken. I do not know anything about Tom Davis, or even whether he was the ghost. Jeremy had one theory that seemed to me fairly plausible, and in keeping with his other theory about ghosts. If Tom Davis died with a boil on his neck – or a swelling – then he almost certainly died of blood poisoning, and probably in a fever. The fever might well have lasted for days. In a state of fever, the mind 'wanders' and reality becomes a kind of dream where thoughts and 'actuality' become tangled. If a man died in such a state of confusion, the effect might be similar to that of falling asleep in confusion or excitement – a fitful slumber, disturbed by dreams. The ghost of Tom Davis might simply *not know it was dead*.

Yet it seems to me that I saw the 'presence' in the garden because I was in a disturbed state after listening to the Beethoven, and some new faculty in me had been awakened. This, of course, raises a curious speculation: if I could see a ghost when my mind had been 'sensitized' by Beethoven's music, would Beethoven himself have been able to see the ghost all the time, since presumably his mind was 'sensitive' all the time? Jeremy was inclined to doubt this, pointing out that even great creators only achieve these moments of insight occasionally; for most of their lives, their senses are probably as obtuse as those of the rest of us.

The 'ghost business' interested us less than you might suppose. As far as I was concerned, it was only a symbol of Jeremy's alien world. For a few months I thought and talked of nothing but Jeremy; my parents got tired of hearing his name. I suppose that Jeremy seemed to me to belong to a different order of reality from my own world. There is something insidiously stupid about the world of a provincial town – the kind of stupidity represented by my father's quarrel with Mr Sutton. It is like the world inside one of those glass balls that you turn upside down to cause a snowstorm, and its state of mind is as savourless as a greenhouse rose. Probably my interest in mathematics made me more aware of it than I might have been otherwise, for mathematics belongs to the greater world and ultimately to the universe, while the people in our town seemed to believe that the universe is as stagnant and predictable as their own backwater. There were times when its mental atmosphere seemed to become so stuffy that even mathematics had no power to stop me from feeling suffocated. Jeremy showed me that there are more windows than I had ever suspected, and it took me some time to discover that his world also had curious limitations.

The 'ghost business' happened at the beginning of my acquaintance with Jeremy, and it is associated in my mind with chilly autumn evenings and the smell of churches. This was because Jeremy was fascinated by churches. He was not a Christian, but for him they represented 'the past', and he loved the past as I love mathematics. Sometimes he played the organ in the cathedral, and I sat with him in the organ loft, staring through the stained glass at the bare shapes of trees until the dusk left us in semi-darkness. Jeremy's favourite piano piece was Debussy's 'Submerged Cathedral', and I believe he wished our own cathedral to be submerged so that he could feel himself completely isolated from the world. When we went out into the street, I was always glad of the noise of traffic and the lights; Jeremy hated it, and shrank as if he was cold. (We often were; the cathedral was icy.)

It was on one of our visits to the cathedral that I discovered the 'other side' of Jeremy's nature. The first evening we went together, it was to hear a performance of the St John Passion given by the local choral society. It was very long; I was very cold. I was impressed and moved, but long before the end I was more aware of the hardness of the seat and the draught down my neck than of the music. As soon as we left, I suggested that we should go into a milk-bar I knew. He looked at me in a pained way and said: 'Do you mean to say that, after hearing that music, you could go into a milk-bar?' As he said this, we drew level with the place; it looked warm and comfortable and very crowded. I looked at him in amazement and said: 'Why not?' Finally, he agreed that I should buy two hot dogs at the stall opposite the Palais de Danse, while he stood twenty yards away. A few bus-drivers and cab-men were there, and an old man and an old woman were eating hot dogs and dancing a little jig and singing 'Don't have any more, Mrs Moore'. When I returned to Jeremy with the hot dogs, he said: 'Well, what did you think of that?'

'Of what?'

'That old man and woman behaving like that?'

'I expect they've just come out of the pub.'

'I know.'

We ate the hot dogs and walked on. The streets were full of people, for it was closing-time in the pubs. Jeremy said:

'This is why I live in the country.'

I was still puzzled. Now I had my hot dog I felt happy and comfortable enough, and I found the sight of happy people quite cheering.

'What's wrong?' I asked.

'Stand still and look,' he said.

We were standing opposite a row of hoardings and a new, modern-looking garage. Trams came rumbling by. (Trams ran in our town until 1950.) It was a Friday night, and I felt cheerful about not having to go to school the next morning.

'Look,' Jeremy said indignantly. 'Tinsel and cheapness.' He gestured at the overhead lights. 'Imagine what this road looked like two hundred and fifty years ago, when Bach wrote the St John Passion. Try to imagine it, and then look at it now. Look at that.' He pointed to the hoardings. They seemed all right to me. One of them advertised a new Hollywood spectacular, and the rest were the usual advertisements for cigarettes, Guinness, Horlicks and so on. During the war, of course, there had been none of this because of the paper shortage, so I found it exciting. But I listened respectfully while Jeremy denounced the cheapness and nastiness of the modern world. To some extent I sympathized, for I also lived in two worlds, and rejected one of them because it was complacently ignorant. But I could not see what advertisements and public houses had to do with it. In Bach's time, people still spent their evenings in pubs (or taverns); the streets were narrower and dirtier than ours, but otherwise probably much the same.

'And that old couple,' Jeremy said. 'You'd think they'd have something better to think about at their age than dancing in the street. Doesn't it make you despair when you look at human beings? Nasty, vulgar, stupid . . .'

We caught a bus back to Cranthorpe (I was staying the night), and he sat hunched up, staring out of the window. The bus was crowded, and we were forced to sit in different seats. I sat looking at him, and wondering if there was something wrong with me for not hating these people as he obviously did.

That night he talked for several hours and we emptied a huge pot of coffee. He told me about his parents and his childhood. I found it interesting enough at the time, but have now forgotten almost everything he said. It was the kind of story I might have expected – an over-sensitive child who hated his father because his father thought him a coward and a weakling. He admitted that he felt little regret when his father was killed in the war. His mother pampered him and found a doctor who signed a certificate excusing him from games and gymnastics at school. In the last few months of the war, Jeremy had been in the navy; naturally, he hated it. One day, during his training period, they heard the sound of a flying-bomb overhead; suddenly the engine stopped. The sergeant in charge of the class ordered everybody to take cover under the desks. 'My mind went blank,' Jeremy said. 'Half an hour later I seemed to regain consciousness, and found myself crouching on all fours under the table, and clinging to one of its legs, while the sergeant kept saying: "It's all over now; you can come out".'

Jeremy told this story seriously to explain why he found the navy unbearable. The idea of Jeremy, on all fours, refusing to come out while the whole class tried to convince him that the danger was past, struck me as so funny that I wanted to laugh, but I was afraid of offending him. Yet the harder I tried not to laugh the funnier it seemed, until finally I had to give way. He looked puzzled while I flung myself back in the chair and shrieked hysterically. When I stopped he asked patiently: 'What's funny?' 'I'm sorry,' I said, 'but the thought of you under the table . . .' He didn't seem offended, only a little hurt. 'But that's my point. All these boys were thinking: "He's a coward," but they didn't realize that they were really congratulating themselves for being stupid.'

Jeremy never expressed his basic ideas to me as clearly as on that night. I asked questions, and he answered frankly. I asked, for example, about his attitude to women.

'I don't dislike women, although I imagine I'd find it difficult to find a woman I could live with. Women rather frighten me. That's another problem of living as I do. Women like to be bossed and bullied. You'll often meet an intellectual woman married to a stupid man, because

117

all women want to be dominated physically. They don't mind being dominated mentally, provided they can be dominated physically as well. Now I could never dominate anybody physically . . .'

I suggested that there are probably many women who would prefer a brilliant man, but he wouldn't have this. From a cupboard he produced the manuscript of a play he had written the year before, and I read some of it while he made the coffee. It showed me a new side to his character – a sense of satiric humour, seldom visible in his conversation. It was about the prince of some Ruritanian country whose only interest in life is in his performing fleas. He cannot be persuaded to hunt, or go to war, or even open a public library. His family think him a poor fish, but his mother decides that he may make a tolerable king if he is married to a queen who has her head screwed on the right way. So they tell him that he is to be married to a princess from a neighbouring country. He detests the idea. So does the princess, who happens to be a shy, quiet girl. But as soon as they meet, they fall in love, being perfectly suited to one another.

I was enjoying the play when Jeremy brought in the coffee. I asked him how it finished.

'Oh, he loses her to his cousin – a typical army type. You see, although she's very attracted by him at first, she's like all women – she wants to be dominated physically. And he's much more interested in his fleas than in the princess.'

The fleas, he explained, were a symbol of the life of the mind – a comic symbol, admittedly, but Jeremy was capable of laughing at himself. How can the flea-loving prince hope to keep the affection of an attractive girl?

The 'typical army type' cousin, it appeared, was based on Jeremy's cousin, who was intelligent and yet a stranger to the 'life of the mind'; he spent most of his time in pubs, was fascinated by guns and was a good shot, seduced girls at the rate of one a week, and enjoyed a brawl now and then. 'I once spent a day with him,' Jeremy said. 'His idea of fun was to go from pub to pub, having the most pointless conversations with all sorts of people. We ended up at some party . . .' He brooded on this for a while, then said: 'You see, I live in a world he just wouldn't understand. I'm happy to spend an evening listening to Delius. He hates Delius. I played him Brigg Fair, and he said he thought that Delius sounded a weakling . . .' (After Debussy, Delius was Jeremy's favourite composer.)

He produced me a letter that his cousin had written after their day together, and it made it clear that the day had finished with something like a quarrel. From the sound of it, Jeremy had held his own. Part of their quarrel had been about sex; the cousin had jeered and called Jeremy a 'half man'. Jeremy retorted that in that case all the saints had been half men, beginning with St Paul. But in fact they were not half men, but the highest type of man. All the 'higher men' are naturally ascetics, all the saints, philosophers, even the poets . . .

It was this last assertion that had led the cousin to defend himself in a letter, and it was obvious that Jeremy had got 'under his skin'. Saints and philosophers, perhaps, he admitted, but certainly not the poets. How about Burns? How about Shakespeare? And he then went on to quote Whitman and Blake on the holiness of the sexual impulse; there was a whole page of some poem of Blake's glorifying sex.

I asked Jeremy what he had replied to this. 'Blake ought to have been ashamed of himself,' he said.

And yet when I finally went off to bed I was not sure whether I agreed with Jeremy or with his cousin. Before he turned off the light, he handed me a small book by

Lagerkvist called *The Dwarf*, and told me that it summarized his own attitude to life. He said that the sentence he admired particularly was the dwarf's remark: 'I delight in nothing.' This meant, Jeremy said, that he delights in nothing 'of this world'.

I read through the book before I went to sleep – it is not long – but when I finished, I was more puzzled than before. In its first dozen pages I could see why Jeremy admired it – for its feeling of world-rejection, its disgust with sensuality and the 'human world'. But it is obvious that Jeremy was reading into it something that the author never intended. The dwarf is malign and treacherous; he loves war and murder, and instinctively detests Leonardo, the life-worshipper.

When I challenged Jeremy about this, he only said: 'Perhaps Lagerkvist didn't dare to say what was in his mind,' then, to put an end to the discussion: 'It's not a very good book anyway.'

So Jeremy had evolved a philosophy in which loneliness and misunderstanding were the price he paid for his refusal to flatter the world. He had published three books at his own expense, but even the literary circle in our town ignored them. He presented copies to several libraries, and periodically checked up to see whether they went out. The results were disappointing. Again, he assumed that this was because his fearless criticism was unpalatable, even to the kind of intellectual who could enjoy *The Waste Land*. A writer can attack modern society and become rich and popular; but if he attacks *people* and tells them that they ought to be living a higher life he can expect derision and fear. 'Perhaps it's as well I'm not read,' he said once, 'otherwise they'd find an excuse to kill me, as they killed Socrates and Jesus.'

* * *

One day when I was travelling out to Cranthorpe I found a romantic woman's magazine on the back seat of the bus; it was called 'Thrilling Confessions' or something of the sort. I opened it, having nothing else to read, and found it so amusing that I began to read it from cover to cover. The stories had titles like: 'My husband fell in love with his step-daughter', 'I led my sister into sin', 'Should a girl forgive?'. There were posed photographs showing worried-looking girls spying on their unfaithful lovers; all the girls were pretty, and all the men wore tweed jackets and smoked a pipe. What amused me were the underlying assumptions of value, the things that the writers and readers felt to be important. 'Jack is handsome and dashing, but a flirt; Ned has a club foot and stutters, but I am sure he loves me sincerely. Which shall I marry?'

I finished reading it as I walked to the cottage. When I saw Jeremy I said jokingly: 'I've brought you a present.' He looked pleased, then incredulous when he saw what I was holding out. He glanced inside it, grimaced with disgust, and then dropped it into the kitchen boiler, holding it gingerly by its corner. I was disappointed; I had meant to take it home to my mother, and I told him so.

'Then you shouldn't have said it was a present.'

'I found it on the bus. It was just a joke . . .'

'I don't find that kind of trash funny. I find it agonizing.'

I tried to explain what I meant, but it was useless.

'I agree that it's interesting from a certain point of view. It would also be interesting if the village idiot came and relieved his bowels in the middle of this carpet – from the viewpoint of a psychiatrist. But I can't be expected to enjoy it.'

I suppose I was irritated by the way he had promptly

destroyed it – as if I had committed an act of bad taste bringing it into the house. This made me say angrily:

'But what's the good of turning away from it? That's just escapism.'

It was a pointless kind of argument, because I was overstating my case and he was angry and defensive. I argued that if you read this kind of thing with emotional detachment you could learn a great deal from it; he declared that the only thing you could learn from it was that modern life is unbelievably nasty. Inevitably, we began to drag the saints and 'higher men' into the argument. I said that any saint would find 'Thrilling Confessions' interesting because of the light it throws on human nature. Jeremy said sweepingly that half an hour of 'Thrilling Confessions' would give a saint moral indigestion. He then suggested that we drop the discussion and talk about something else. Naturally, this was almost impossible. I felt snubbed and provoked, and inclined to criticize everything he said. After an hour of wrangling and snapping at one another I went home. The next day, he wrote me a long letter, repeating all his points, and warning me that it is too easy to slip from detachment into corruption, that you cannot play with tar without dirtying your hands. The letter was evidently written while he was still in a state of indignation about my use of the word 'escapism'. 'Strike that word from your vocabulary,' he wrote. 'It was invented by clods and swine to sneer at their betters . . . Next time you walk through the town on a Sunday afternoon, take a look at these members of the great proletariat, these honest workmen. Watch them streaming out of a football match or into a cinema showing the latest and silliest Hollywood epic, and then ask yourself who is the escapist . . . And what is it that I am supposed to be escaping? Reality? What do these fools know of reality? No doubt they

122

congratulate themselves because their work brings them into daily contact with stupidity and futility. But place one of them in my position for a week, and see what happens. Within a few hours he would be looking around for his morning paper; within two days he would be inviting his friends in to play poker; within a week he would be on the way to a nervous breakdown. You at least should know better than to throw these heresies in my face. Force one of these "honest workmen" to spend a week listening to Bach or learning the higher mathematics, and he will beg you to allow him to go back to his workmates and the morning paper and his nightly pint and the rest of his favourite tediums . . .'

It only dawned on me slowly that, in spite of his admiration for Shaw and Bergson, Jeremy was an old-fashioned Calvinist of terrifying consistency. He had two favourite quotations. One was the dwarf's 'I delight in nothing'. The other (whose source I have forgotten): 'God demands from us a terrible purity of intention.' But Jeremy's purity was the kind that throws the baby out with the bath water.

It was through Jeremy that I decided against going to Cambridge. I have been writing as if we spent most of our time quarrelling, but this is untrue. Jeremy introduced me to literature and philosophy; he also introduced me to myself. Before I met him I was unaware that I kept my life in two separate compartments; I thought of mathematics as an oasis of order in a universe of chaos. I had always been afraid of the chaos; I lived in my ivory tower as if I was in a state of siege. After six months of knowing Jeremy, all that was changed. Ever since I had read the article on Pascal in *Men of Mathematics* I had thought of religion as a product of ignorance and superstition, another proof of man's capacity for self-deception. The first time I expressed this view to Jeremy was also the last. He gave me a lecture that lasted for two hours; he pointed out that religion is at least an attempt to see the world whole, while science deliberately ignores three-quarters of human experience.

'How would you explain the colour red in terms of mathematics?'

'As a wave-length,' I said.

'But how do you explain the difference between red and green? Wave-lengths won't explain it, will they? They just *look* different.'

This kind of argument battered down the door of my tower; but after a few weeks I needed no further convincing; the change in me was as complete as the difference between winter and spring. Things seemed to be happening inside me that made mathematics repellent. At first I was glad of the excuse to treat the outside world as being as real and valid as the world of mathematics; after a short time I needed no excuse; the new feeling of warmth was enough. Again – to change the simile – I felt like an Eskimo suddenly transported to Tahiti. After six months I barely recognized myself, my internal landscape had altered so completely. Where before there had only been Newton and Gauss and Einstein, there was now the music of Delius, the dialogues of Plato, the novels of Tolstoy.

It was at this point that our headmaster told me I had to make my decision about a career – whether I wanted to stay on at school for another year and try for a Cambridge scholarship. The idea was unwelcome. I had hardly looked at a book on mathematics for six months. Admittedly, my standard was probably high enough to pass the Cambridge entrance examination without further study, but that was not what bothered me. It was like receiving an ultimatum that I had to leave Tahiti and go back to the North Pole. If the problem had been left for another year I might have felt differently. But Jeremy's world was new to me; it had possessed me; I didn't want to lose it so quickly. I no more wanted to become a professor of mathematics or an industrial scientist than I wanted to live in Siberia. So I thought about it for a week, discussed it with Jeremy, and then told the headmaster that I wanted to be allowed to work at mathematics on my own, not study it at a university. He pointed out that a university would give me more time to study on my own. He wanted me to get a scholarship – for the honour of the school – and might have persuaded me if it had not been for the attitude of my parents. But my father was ill again – this time with duodenal ulcers – and the idea of supporting me at university depressed him. He and I had been out of touch for years; he often accused me of treating the house as a hotel. If I went to work, I would at least be supporting myself. So he wrote the headmaster a letter saying that he agreed with my decision not to try for a Cambridge scholarship, and the matter ended. The headmaster pointedly ignored me for the rest of the term, and looked away if he happened to pass me in the school corridors.

PART TWO

The Inner Dark

4

I left school when I was sixteen years and two months old. My father asked me what kind of work I wanted to do; I thought about this for a few days, and decided that I didn't want to do any. But I could not expect him to sympathize with this feeling, and I knew that he thought of making me office boy at Cheesman, Greene and Hake, his own firm, which I wanted to avoid at all costs; it was enough to have to live with my father without working under him. So I said that I thought I might enjoy some job involving 'figures'; and in September 1949 I found myself working as a clerk in the offices of the local electricity board. The less I say about this, the better. For the first time in my life I found myself acutely bored. Probably the people in our office were averagely intelligent, but they seemed to me indecently, unbelievably stupid. Mixing with them reminded me of eating cabbage soup. From the age of four, I had been used to living with ideas; even if I found my home- and school-life dull, they were seen against a continually changing landscape of ideas. Most children have to learn to swallow and digest huge quantities of boredom – in churches and schools and the homes of relatives; I had been lucky, but I didn't know this. So my first reaction to the people in our office was furious incredulity. It was like being dropped into a world in slow motion. There was Marion, a beefy but very pretty married woman, who thought of nothing but clothes; Miss Roberts, a white-haired, sweet-looking old lady with a malicious tongue, whose only interest in life was the Royal Family. (She had their photographs stuck all over the wall next to her desk, and could tell you exactly who was the second cousin of the Duke of Richmond, or what was the relationship of the present Prince of Wales to George the Fourth.) There was a freckled girl on the telephone switchboard with a whining voice; she had no boy-friend, but talked of nothing but boys. There were two or three typists, all ugly and unmarried, and two married men who were so nondescript that I can no longer remember their names or faces. The head of the department was a skinny, embittered man named Coles, who had a yellow complexion and teeth like a ferret; his uncertain temper provided one of the constant topics of discussion in the office. The pleasantest man in the office was a big ex-paratrooper named John Duncan. He was six feet tall, had the red face of a farmer, and seemed to like everybody and everything. He was in charge of accounts, and enjoyed adding up columns of figures, so we got along excellently. He was amazed at my speed in adding up, and often brought his columns of figures to me if there was a mistake that he could not find.

When I had been in the office two or three days I established a reputation by an absurd accident. No one knew about my interest in mathematics. One day a man called Cayley came in to pay his electricity bill; but he had forgotten to bring the bill with him, and John Duncan asked his typist to look up the duplicate in the files. I happened to be standing at the counter, and told the typist that she needn't bother to look it up – that the bill was for seventeen pounds, two shillings and ninepence. The customer immediately said: 'Yes, that's right, I remember.' The typist found the carbon, and it proved to be correct. John Duncan was amazed, and asked me how I did it; I said carelessly: 'Oh, memory. I happened to see the bill when we sent it out.' But later, when the customer had gone, I explained more fully. The customer's name, Cayley, had struck me because it is the name of the great English mathematician; the figures, £17 2s. 9d., had stuck in my mind because 1729 happens to be the smallest number expressible as the sum of two cubes in two different ways – an observation I owe to Ramanujan.

John Duncan told the story all over the office – in fact, all over the building (which also contains the gas board and housing department). Mr Coles asked me into his office, and succeeded in making his lemon-yellow face look amiable for half an hour while he questioned me about my interest in mathematics. On my way home that evening I regretted my piece of show-off, since it had lost me my total anonymity in the office. But Coles soon let me alone – he was too bad-tempered to be amiable for more than a few hours together – and John Duncan proved to be a useful ally; when I got too bored he would find excuses for sending me out to carry instructions to the foremen of street-gangs in distant parts of the town.

After a fortnight in this office I began to realize my mistake in rejecting the idea of Cambridge. I began to drop hints to my parents about changing my mind, and went to see my old headmaster to find out what could be done about it. He could not resist a smile of satisfaction, and said that he'd told me so. He advised me to speak to my father about it. But I guessed that he would probably be helpful when he had given me time to feel even sorrier about leaving school, so I decided to concentrate on my father. He pretended not to notice my hints, but I knew that a few weeks of gentle persistence would alter that. After a fortnight I began to feel distinctly hopeful. Then a number of things happened that made me forget about my eagerness to escape the electricity board.

* * *

One Saturday afternoon I went out to Cranthorpe to see Jeremy, and found myself sitting on the back seat of the bus with a pretty red-headed girl and a well-dressed military-looking man of about Jeremy's age. We were squeezed into the seat by a farmer and his wife, so I could not help being aware of the warmth of the girl's thigh as we sat pressed together. Since I had decided to try for a Cambridge scholarship, I was brushing up my theory of functions and skimming through Hardy's *Course in Pure Mathematics*. I was aware that this might seem to be show-off to my neighbours, who could obviously see what I was reading, but I had nothing else with me except a score of Haydn's Seasons, which was equally unsuitable. The farmer and his wife got off a mile before Cranthorpe, and I was sorry to lose the warmth of the girl's body as we made ourselves more room on the seat. But just before the bus stopped in Cranthorpe square the man leaned forward and said to me: 'Excuse me, but are you Hugh Greene?' I was flattered that he knew my name, but the explanation was simple enough; he was Jeremy's cousin Monty, and had heard about me from Jeremy's mother. He introduced me to the girl Patricia, and I was glad of an opportunity to look at her face, since I already felt so well acquainted with her body; she had a few freckles, a wide, attractive mouth, and the kind of smile that a girl develops when she has been used to a lifetime of admiration. She immediately turned my head by treating me as an adult. Monty flattered me in the same way – although I have no doubt this was unconscious. Jeremy's mother had talked so much about me that he was curious to get to know me.

He told me that Patricia was interested in ghost stories, and they had heard about Jeremy's ghost. I was able to tell them about this as we walked up to the cottage. It also transpired that Patricia had read one of Jeremy's books and was curious to meet him; this made Monty impatient, and part of his intention in bringing her along was to show her what a poor fish Jeremy was.

It was a windy, chilly October afternoon, and Patricia pulled up a blue hood over her head; I can still remember my excitement, glancing sideways at her face, made pink by the wind and alluring by the half-concealment of the hood. I found myself envying Monty; yet I also felt a kind of part-ownership of her, since she seemed to turn the same kind of feminine admiration on both of us.

I was not sure how I felt about Monty. He had a square, strong sort of face with a big chin and a slightly broken nose (acquired in amateur boxing). He talked with a clipped, upper-class accent that he made more clipped and upper-class to emphasize that he was a military type. He wore an officer's greatcoat, and somehow contrived to look as if he had been born in the army. I found his appearance easy enough to reconcile with what Jeremy had told me about him, but not with the letter I had read. How did a type like this come to be quoting Blake and Whitman?

In retrospect, I think that Monty acted the officer with me exactly as I acted the mathematical prodigy with him. To some extent, he acted it with everyone – but he exaggerated it with people he wanted to impress. But he was too intelligent for the role in which he had cast himself. He had constructed a personality that he thought ideal for impressing everyone he thought worth impressing. As an 'officer and gentleman' he had the slightly insolent, Byronic touch; he also cultivated an ironic glance that was supposed to indicate that anyone who took him for a mere officer would be a fool. He was undeniably intelligent; he spoke German and French perfectly, and was as fond of music as Jeremy, although he knew less about it. But fundamentally he was too moody and sensitive to be the simple officer type; like Jeremy, he was a prey to moods.

I guessed nothing of this on that first afternoon we talked together. His brisk, hard, slightly nasal voice gave me the impression of a man who knows exactly what he wants and what he thinks. His face wore an habitual expression of mild contempt, and I was puzzled that I seemed to be excepted from it. I discovered what I think was the solution only about six years later. Monty had a number of German books on his shelves, and he told me several times that he thought Musil's *Mann Ohne Eigenschaften* to be one of the greatest modern novels. I had no chance to check on his opinion until a translation began to appear in England in the nineteen-fifties. As soon as I started reading it, I realized that Musil's hero Ulrich was probably the man on whom Monty modelled himself: ex-army officer, but too intelligent for the army, irresistible to women, a superb athlete. But Ulrich is also a fine mathematician. Monty, as I soon realized, had no more capacity for figures than Jeremy had. It was the one quality in which he fell short of his model. Hence his readiness to admire a mathematician.

As we drew near the cottage, Monty suddenly asked me:

'What do you think of Jeremy?'

I floundered for a moment, then said:

'That would take about two hours to answer.'

'All right,' Monty said. 'Come and have a drink with me this evening. We'll talk about it.'

I was too flattered to refuse, although I had intended to spend the evening with Jeremy. I asked:

'But shan't I be in the way . . .?'

'No. Pat's got to go to a family party.'

So before we arrived at Jeremy's door it was arranged that I should leave with Monty and Patricia, claiming that

I also had to attend a family party. I knew Jeremy would be offended if he thought I was going to spend the evening with his cousin.

Jeremy looked disconcerted to see us. His manner was offhand and rather cold, but I knew that this concealed his shyness with Patricia. I could also see that she was favourably impressed by Jeremy – by the immaculate clothes, the delicate profile, the rather thin blond moustache. We drank tea, then all went out for a walk before it grew dark. Children were gathering chestnuts in the woods, and others were playing with kites in the meadow on the edge of the wood. Some of the best chestnuts were on the highest branches, and they were throwing sticks to try to knock them down. Monty saw an opportunity to display his athleticism; the lower part of the trunk was too smooth to climb, but he asked me to bend down so that he could stand on my shoulders. Then he leapt on to a low branch, and swarmed up to the top. The boys cheered as he broke off the branch and threw it down. Jeremy stared at him gloomily, then said to Patricia: 'I could never climb trees – I get dizzy at the heights.' This comment struck me as a piece of masochism, since she had probably not even thought about whether Jeremy could climb as well as Monty. Monty dropped down and slipped into his overcoat, and we walked on. Somehow, the conversation turned on the question of athleticism, and Jeremy remarked: 'There'd be no point in my having a physique like yours. I hate doing most of the things that athletes do – like skiing and climbing mountains and things. And I don't like games and I don't like swimming.'

Monty said, rather cuttingly: 'You talk as if physical courage had anything to do with physique. Your favourite poet Shelley was all skin and bones, but even Byron admired his physical courage.'

'So he might,' Jeremy said. 'They were both fools. And

135

they both came to a violent end because they were stupid enough to want to prove their physical courage.'

I felt uncomfortable because I felt that Jeremy was including me with himself in this generalization, whereas the whole argument touched on the matters in which I most disagreed with him. So I walked on behind, kicking up the dead leaves, and admiring Patricia's slim legs.

We stopped on the outskirts of the wood above the village, looked at the view for a few minutes, and then turned to walk back. At that moment, a boy came running up to us.

'Mister, can you help us get a kite down? It's stuck in a tree.'

Jeremy made no secret of his irritation, and I understood how he felt. Monty had proved he could climb trees and neither Jeremy nor I particularly wanted to stand by while he gave us another display. However, we followed the boy back into the wood. When we saw the tree we felt more cheerful; it was a very tall elm, and there were thorn bushes round its base that made it almost unapproachable. Two more trees grew near by whose branches touched it, but the branches looked very thin. The owner of the kite had already climbed one of these smaller trees and was trying to reach the kite by throwing a stave cut from a hedge. It was already dusk, so it was not easy to see how the kite could be approached. However, Monty saw that he was expected to climb, so he threw off his overcoat and jacket, and climbed. He managed to get a great deal higher up the smaller tree than the kite's owner had climbed, and could touch the kite with the stave; but the string was tangled in the branches, and he could not dislodge it. I watched this for a moment; then, when no one was looking, dropped my own coat and climbed up the other tree. I soon saw that I could get from here on to the elm if I was willing to jump across a space of about

136

six feet; it was not as dangerous as it looked from below, because the branch from which I would jump was several feet above the branch on which I would land. My light weight was in my favour; I got into a good position, steadied myself on an overhead branch and jumped. I managed to scramble on to the other branch without difficulty. From there on, it was easy; I climbed the tree, which was as uncomplicated as a ladder, untangled the string, and let the kite float across to Monty, who caught it and took it down. Then I went down myself, descending the lower part of the trunk as if it had been a drainpipe; this made my hands dirty, and took the skin off my ankles, but was not difficult or dangerous. I remember, as I came down the tree, feeling again exactly as I had done six years before when I helped the Temple Roaders to win their street battle. I concealed my complacency when I got down by pretending to examine my hands and then putting on my coat. Monty slapped me on the back and said: 'Good man.' I caught Jeremy's eye and his look of reproach, but I turned away and refused to think about its implications. I had not taken sides against him, only helped to get a kite out of a tree as anyone else might have done. Nothing more was said about it on the way home, but when we got back into the cottage Monty and I stood together at the sink washing our hands, and again I caught Jeremy looking reproachfully at me.

I made my excuse about the family party before Monty talked about leaving, and was on my way out of the house before Monty said: 'Hold on a moment. We've got to be on our way too.' By the time Patricia was ready, I knew I had missed the six o'clock bus. Monty then suggested that Jeremy should walk down to the village with us and have a drink at the pub before we caught the next bus. Jeremy refused – rather sullenly, I thought – but then mustered enough good temper to give Patricia a copy of one of his books – a rather esoteric satire on Kierkegaard – and to sign it 'with warm regards'.

'I think he's rather sweet,' Patricia said, when we were outside.

'I couldn't get him into an argument,' Monty said. 'Wait until you hear the way he argues.'

In the village, Monty proposed that we should go into the pub; Patricia protested that she was not yet allowed in pubs, being only seventeen. (This startled me; I thought she was Monty's age – twenty-four.) So Monty went inside and brought drinks out to us on a tray – sherry for Patricia and whiskies for the two of us. We sat on the bench, feeling very cold and envying the warmth and light inside. I then timidly proposed that I should pay for a round of drinks, if Monty would fetch them. He said: 'All right, it'll keep out the cold,' and went in. By the time we had finished these I was warm and happy, although I felt signs of an approaching cold. We had to run for the bus. Once again, I sat on the back seat next to Patricia; once again, other passengers were obliging enough to crowd us into a corner.

Back in town, we delivered Patricia to the door of her aunt's house, and she agreed to find her own way back to Monty's room as soon as she could escape. We immediately went into the pub opposite. I was afraid I looked too young but Monty told me to go and sit in a corner, and he returned with two glasses of hot grog.

By this time I knew I was well on the way to being drunk; but the sensation was so novel and so pleasant that I was not worried. I can no longer remember the exact course of the conversation over the next three hours. We began by talking about Jeremy, and I told the story about the woman's magazine I had found on the bus. Monty seemed delighted by my analysis. 'That's right,' he said. 'He's a Calvinist without the Christianity. Given the powers, he'd have me burned at the stake.'

I said I thought this was unfair to Jeremy.

'And why not?' Monty said, finishing his hot rum. 'That's what we need. A bit of violence.'

'I hate violence,' I said.

He looked surprised.

'Why? You don't strike me as that type.'

'What type?'

'Thin-blooded, like Jeremy. Don't think I don't know why you went up that tree this afternoon.'

I blushed. I thought he was about to say that I wanted to impress Patricia. But that was not what he meant.

'I could see you writhing as Jeremy talked about the great man always being a coward. [This was untrue; I was walking behind them; and anyhow, Jeremy hadn't phrased it that way.] You wanted to show you were on my side, didn't you?'

'Perhaps,' I said, too weak to stand up for Jeremy.

'That's right,' he said, slapping me on the shoulder. 'Don't commit yourself. Let's go back to my place. I've got a bottle of rum there.'

Monty had a flat within five minutes of the centre of town. He lit a fire, made a saucepan of grog, and produced cheese and biscuits. I was impressed by his bookshelves, but he pulled me away before I could examine them too closely.

'Never mind them. Think about life instead.' He was fairly drunk by this time; so was I. There was no point in arguing with him. I sat down and let him talk. He told me about his army experiences, and said that he was sorry to be out of the army. He had been in the tank corps, and had served some time as a military policeman. He talked about guns, and showed me three revolvers – all illegal, since he had no permits. He also showed me an interesting collection of pornographic books, some in French and German, and an edition of Burns with woodcuts that would have made the poet blush. I said jokingly:

'Talking of sex, what time is Patricia due here?' I immediately felt I had gone too far, but he only laughed.

'Any minute now. She won't hurry. Her aunt's supposed to be her alibi for the night, so she'll stay as late as she can in case her parents ring up.' He looked at his watch. 'How about slipping out for a final drink before the pubs close?' It was about a quarter to ten.

There was a pub within five minutes of his flat. It was so crowded that it was almost impossible to push our way to the bar. I found a corner near the fire, and waited for Monty to return with the drinks. Two girls with bright orange lipstick were standing close to me, and one of them looked at me curiously, then said: 'You're a bit young for this place, aren't you?'

The other girl peered at me, and said thickly:

'Is it a boy or a girl?'

A black-haired youth who was standing next to her told her to shut up. At this moment, Monty returned with the drinks. The girl who had spoken to me made eyes at him and said:

'If you're his father you ought to know better.'

It was a feeble joke, but not intended offensively. To my surprise, the black-haired youth grabbed her arm, shook her, and snarled: 'Are you going to shut up?' I now noticed that a second youth was sitting in a basket-chair in a lounging attitude, and was staring me up and down with a sneering expression that he had probably picked up from a gangster film. Monty noticed this as he handed me the drink, and stared back at him. The youth dropped his eyes, but his friend noticed it, and said to Monty: 'You looking for trouble, are you?

140

It was an absurd business – a typical Monty situation. (For some reason, this kind of thing always seemed to be happening to Monty.) It had all the elements: two girls to be impressed, and two aggressive teenagers. Monty drained his glass very calmly, and then said:

'Like to step outside?'

'No, they wouldn't,' the drunk girl snapped.

'What, your friend too?' the black-haired youth said, grinning contemptuously at me. This didn't offend me; he reminded me of Teddy Kirk, so I rather liked the look of him. Besides, I guessed that he wanted to avoid a fight.

'He can hold my coat,' Monty said.

The lounging youth suddenly stood up, and said: 'Oh, come on.' I think he probably meant that they should leave the pub, but Monty took it as an acceptance of his challenge, so as both youths started for the door he went ahead of them. The girl who had first spoken to me now said:

'Can't you stop your friend? They've got flick knives.'

I had drunk too much to feel worried. So I said:

'So has he.'

There was a piece of waste ground behind the pub, and Monty marched around on to this. I think the business of the knives was bluff, because as soon as we got behind the pub one of the boys leapt forward and tried to get his arm around Monty's neck. I shouted a warning, but there was no need; Monty leaned forward, and the boy shot over his head and landed on his back. The other one ran in, his head down, and was met by Monty's knee.

It was obvious that neither of them was a match for him; he went into it like a machine, kicking and punching as if he was following an instruction book. The black-haired one got in a good blow at Monty's cheek, and

Monty snarled: 'It's like that, is it?' and went in ferociously; a moment later, the boy was on the ground. Monty turned to me, panting, and said:

'Come on, let's go.' He said to the girls as we went: 'You want to teach them how to fight.'

His cheek was cut – he explained that the boy had been fighting with pennies clutched between his fingers – but his expression of self-satisfaction was almost grotesque. And I could see that he was delighted to find Patricia waiting for us when we went into his flat. She said:

'Oh, you haven't been fighting again!'

'Couple of yobs,' Monty said, and went into the kitchen to clean himself up.

I said it was time for me to go, but he insisted that I should stay and have another drink. He then recounted the whole affair in detail to Patricia; I was pleased to note that she looked a little impatient. It was nearly midnight when I left. Halfway home, I stopped and vomited in someone's front garden.

The next morning I was tempted to go and see Jeremy; I wanted to discuss his cousin. But it was a rainy day, and my head ached, so I lay in bed and stared at the ceiling. Anyway, it would have been pointless; I could no more discuss Monty with Jeremy than I could discuss Jeremy with Monty. Neither was capable of being fair to the other. I could now understand why Jeremy had been so revolted by Monty. The cult of athleticism and violence was a dead end. (Some time later, I discovered that Monty was an admirer of Hemingway, and had cast himself in the role of the Hemingway hero – sensitive and intelligent, but hard-fisted and a great lover. He exalted the love of fresh air and cold water into a kind of mysticism.) But it was equally obvious that Jeremy's cult of anti-violence was also a dead end. Jeremy stood for

How could I communicate? What did it matter whether I communicated or not?

After half an hour of this, I was about to go when she stood up. 'I'm going to take a drink up to your uncle. I'll tell him you're here.'

I had not seen Uncle Sam for two or three years. I pretended that this was because I respected his privacy, but the true reason was that the smell of his room revolted me. I have already quoted Uncle Sam's last 'testament' to me; this makes it appear that his reasons were wholly 'idealistic'. This is only partly true. There was also in him a strange emotional bias towards degradation. I cannot understand this, although Jeremy once suggested that Uncle Sam might be suffering from some physical disease – he hinted at syphilis – that gave him a feeling that there was no point in making an effort. On the evidence of his last letter to me, I doubt this.

When Aunt Bertha came down and told me that Uncle Sam would like to see me I thought of making an excuse; but I felt too tired to make it sound convincing. So I followed her upstairs, and noted that nothing had changed since the first time I had done this eight years before.

I noticed at once that the room, which was lighted by a very small, dim bulb, painted blue, had been recently tidied. It still smelt stale, but not offensive. Uncle Sam looked exactly the same; if anything, perhaps younger. Aunt Bertha left me alone. I sat down in the only chair. When he spoke, his voice sounded exactly the same as the last time I had seen him.

'Well, boy, how is life treating you?'

'Very well, thank you,' I said automatically.

'I don't believe that. No one was ever happy at sixteen. You're sixteen, aren't you?'

I had forgotten about this habit of firing blunt questions. But it was exactly what I needed. I said:

'I don't suppose anyone's ever happy.'

'Oh yes. Most people are. More or less. And they'll make you feel guilty for feeling unhappy. They say you'll grow out of it. So you will. But that doesn't mean they're right and you're wrong. In fact, you probably see the world more clearly in your teens than at any other time in your life.'

This cheered me. Uncle Sam went on talking, in his low, throaty voice, and I suddenly realized that the feeling of oppression had gone. Somehow the *way* he approached problems gave me more hope for human life. Besides, he stimulated me with a kind of question that made me think in an unaccustomed way. He made me realize that half the confusion of philosophers is not a failure to find the right answers, but a failure to ask the right questions.

He said something about the way that young people are easily embarrassed, and how older people have somehow learned the trick of turning away from embarrassment. He said: 'But do you think they're better off because of it? No; their solution is wrong. I'll give you something to think about. You're in a public place, and you see someone you think you recognize. He is walking away from you, so you hurry to catch him up. And as you draw level, you put your hand on his shoulder, and call: "Bill". He turns round, and you realize it's a stranger. Immediately you blush. You feel embarrassed. You feel you've made a fool of yourself in front of all these people. Why?'

I thought about this, then said: 'I suppose because you've made a mistake.'

'Yes, but not an embarrassing mistake. If you called "Bill" and it turned out to be a woman dressed mannishly, you'd have a reason to feel awkward because you might

146

have hurt her feelings. But otherwise, it's a perfectly natural mistake; anyone can understand it. So why feel ashamed?'

'Because we don't like to make mistakes.'

'That would answer my question if you were trying to pose as omniscient and infallible, and you were upset at giving yourself away. Is that the reason we feel embarrassed – that we want people to think us infallible?'

I give this as an example of the kind of question that Uncle Sam would ask me. I have still not solved it.

After some more discussion of this kind, Uncle Sam asked me whether I had any friends, and I told him about Jeremy. He encouraged me to go on talking. I suppose he must have developed an appetite for conversation, lying there on his own. I finished by describing Jeremy in some detail, and then going on to talk of his cousin Monty. Whenever I tried to break off, he asked me more questions. He ended by saying: 'You'd make a good novelist. You've got an excellent eye for the right detail.'

Aunt Bertha interrupted us with a pot of tea. I immediately offered to go, but Uncle Sam said he'd prefer me to wait. I could see Aunt Bertha was delighted that he was taking an interest in seeing one of the family. And I ended by staying until after ten o'clock, then eating supper with Aunt Bertha before I left. And the last part of his conversation interested me so much that I made notes on it when I got home. We were still talking about Monty, and then about militarism in general. I said that I could sympathize with Monty to some extent because I could remember how delighted I felt when the war started. What Uncle Sam then said strikes me as in some ways more important than anything he put into his testament to me.

'You're confusing yourself because you think that these friends of yours are choosing to be pacifists or militarists of their own free will. You don't understand that man has almost no free will.'

I said that I had been thinking about the subject only that afternoon.

'Good. But you still don't quite see what I mean. You've got to get a clear picture of what human beings are like. For example, you've seen pictures of knights in armour. Now imagine a man dressed in an armour made of slabs of concrete six inches thick and tied on with wire. Imagine what it would be like – to drag yourself around under that kind of burden. Now if some alien being from another planet asked me what it was like to be human, I'd describe that man wearing his concrete slabs, and I'd say: "That's one of the first things you have to learn about being human." We carry around an incredibly heavy load, and we're so used to it that we don't even notice it. Now another thing. If I held out my arm and you jabbed a pin in it, you'd expect to see me wince. Supposing you saw a man who could stick pins half an inch deep into any part of his body without feeling it – what would you think?'

'I'd think he had some disease that had deadened his nerves.'

'Quite. Well, that's another thing you have to realize about human beings. As well as being weighted down under half a ton of concrete, they're almost incapable of feeling. We're so busy living that we hardly notice how little we feel. Now supposing you heard that I'd died in the night. What would you feel?'

'I'd feel sorry, of course . . .'

'Don't talk nonsense. Of course you wouldn't. You hardly know me. But why did you just *say* you'd feel sorry? Because you're ashamed to admit that you don't care a damn. We know we *ought* to feel more, and we're always pretending we feel a lot more than we do; but the

148

flat truth is that we're all like a man without nerves – jab him where you like and he won't wince. How do you suppose Bertha would feel if I died tonight? She'd be sorry, I know that. She's got used to me, even if I am a damned nuisance. She'd wear black and cry at the funeral. But she'd do it because she'd know she *ought* to be miserable, not because she really felt it.'

He sat in silence for a while. I did not speak, because what he said gave me the same kind of sensation as thinking about infinity. He went on finally:

'I remember when I was your age – a bit older – I had a friend, Nigel. We used to walk about talking all night. We told each other everything. There was nothing we didn't discuss. Well, he died of pneumonia. When they told me I went and locked myself in my room, and wouldn't come out for two days. Everybody said: "Naturally, he's heartbroken about his friend's death". But that wasn't true. Shall I tell you why I stayed in my room? I was furious with myself for not feeling more. It was like jabbing a needle into myself and not feeling it. I kept saying: "Nigel's dead", hoping that it would suddenly burst on me with tremendous pain. Because I *know* I was fond of him. Not only that – it had deeper significances. We'd discussed life and death and infinity. Yet here I was, like a constipated man – nothing happening inside me.

'And that, you see, Hugh, is what's wrong with all human beings. You ask me why men are cruel. There's your reason. The less they feel, the more they need to whip themselves with strong sensations. That's why we go to war, when any rational man can prove that war is illogical. All the nerves are dead. Boredom accumulates inside us. The skin's made of concrete. The scientists tell us that man's the most sensitive organism that nature has yet produced. They compare us to the dinosaurs with their tremendous bodies and tiny brains. But they don't realize that we're still dinosaurs. There's still a tremendous burden of dull, dead flesh with only a tiny bit of spirit to animate it. Have you ever tried to light a bonfire made of wet rubbish? Well, that's what God's trying to do with human beings. We're all wet rubbish, and a tiny little spark trying to set it ablaze. We never stand a chance.'

I asked him: 'Is that why you live in here?'

'Partly. I'll tell you the whole story one of these days.'

We talked for a long time that evening; what is more, we talked as two intelligent human beings, not as uncle and nephew. I have no more notes of what he said, but I remember one more thing – something like this:

'The tragic thing about human beings is that they need pain and hardship. Otherwise they'd die of boredom. Notice how easily you forget the pleasant things that happen to you. You want to buy a certain book; you save for months perhaps, dreaming about it. Then you get it, and within a couple of days you no longer care whether you have it or not. That's typically human. That's because man's half dead. You don't expect a dead man to appreciate a good meal; you can't expect a half-dead man to appreciate being alive. Make life unpleasant for him and he'll appreciate it when you stop – for ten minutes. Threaten him with death, and he'll be grateful for life – for ten minutes. But give him pleasure, and he's bored with it in ten minutes. This is the strangest thing about human nature – our capacity for pain is infinitely bigger than our capacity for pleasure. Where pleasure's concerned, we're all like rich men who over – eat a little of it gives us indigestion. No man is a judge of what's good, but every man knows what's bad. Never believe a man who tells you he knows what he wants out of life. The only thing we know is what we don't want. The only time a man knows what he wants is when he's suffering. Then he knows he wants it to stop. Apart from that, we're all blind and deaf.'

At ten o'clock I decided I had to go home. Uncle Sam told me to come again, and as often as I liked. When I got downstairs Aunt Bertha asked me to stay and eat some cold beef; looking at her, I no longer had that feeling of non-communication – or rather I had it, but could now understand it. Her only thought was obviously that Uncle Sam had enjoyed talking to me. While we ate supper – washing it down with brown ale – she talked candidly about Uncle Sam. She was certain that he had retired into his room because he was a genius, and the world had failed to appreciate him; it was a gesture of disdain. But if he was ready to talk to me, it might be a sign that he was ready to come out again . . . I took care not to contradict her, promised to come again, and refused the five shillings that she tried to press on me.

It was a clear, cold night. I walked back over the park. I was feeling something analogous to what I'd felt when I first read about Abel and Galois, the same sense of tragedy. But what I now felt was that all mankind is involved in a tragedy. Man is like a dray-horse, which never has a chance from the moment it's born; only long days of hard work, a bag of oats at night, and the knacker's yard after ten years. But somehow it seemed better to face this squarely. Now I thought of Jeremy and Monty, both tangled in the same net, believing that they'd found a way out. I thought of my own bewilderment earlier in the day, and it vanished when I remembered what Uncle Sam had said. A man covered with heavy concrete slabs . . . a man whose nerves are all dead so that he feels nothing . . .

These thoughts gave me a curious feeling of freedom, of *recklessness*. It was the kind of recklessness that a peasant might feel on suddenly realizing that he has nothing to lose by revolt, because the lord of the manor intends to have him shot in a few days anyway. I felt that, in knowing the worst, I was freer than Jeremy or Monty. There was no point in feeling envious with a man like Monty, or shy with a girl like Patricia. Because no human being has anything to lose or to gain.

At the office the next morning, this feeling of freedom persisted. These people usually aroused in me a kind of incredulity; I sometimes even suspected that they were deliberately behaving like half-wits to make fun of me. (If a playwright or novelist had created an accurate picture of our office in one of his works, people would have accused him of exaggerating its stupidity, and claimed that the characters were 'types' and not human beings.) My talk with Uncle Sam altered my way of seeing them; they fitted his description exactly: creatures made dull and trivial by long imprisonment. Strangely enough, they no longer irritated me. But at mid-morning, when John Duncan sent me to the post-office, I found myself repeating as I walked through the town: 'What can be done about it?' It was not that I seriously thought anything could be done; only that repeating it gave me a new kind of detachment. On my way back to the office – it was after midday – I saw Patricia on the other side of the road. She caught a bus before I could attract her attention. This disturbed the detachment; I was aware how much she attracted me. It struck me then that, even if human beings are spiritual dinosaurs, the one positive and unfailing instinct in them is sex. But as I ate my sandwiches, and tried to read Russell on the foundations of geometry, I felt my insight slipping away, and the resentment and boredom returning.

Monday was 'overtime day'; during the busy season, everyone stayed on in the office until seven. This was compulsory, and I resented it since I had nothing to do. At six I was usually sent out to buy tea from the café opposite, and we had a ten-minute break.

On this Monday evening, John Duncan asked me to get him some cork-tipped cigarettes. The café had run out of stock; so I left the tea jug there, and walked to the tobacco kiosk near the Palais de Danse. It was already dark, and there was a thin rain. I had come out without my overcoat, so I turned up my collar and ran with bent head. Outside the Palais I cannoned into someone, and recoiled. A sullen-looking youth said: 'Look where you're goin', you bleedin' fool.' I apologized, and took my place in the short queue outside the tobacco kiosk. I glanced furtively at the youth who was leaning against the glass photograph-frame outside the dance hall. As I did so he moved his head, as if giving a signal. I looked round, and saw about five other boys, all dressed in leather jackets, standing in a group a few yards away. For an unpleasant moment I thought the signal was meant to draw attention to me; then a youth and a girl joined the queue behind me, and I saw that it was these they were watching. I looked away, anxious not to seem curious. The youth left the photograph-frame and said: 'Hello Johnny.' By this time it was my turn at the counter; as I moved forward I noticed out of the corner of my eye that the group of leather-coated boys had moved in. Then, very quickly, the first youth hit 'Johnny' in the stomach, and the others closed in. The tobacconist woman, seeing what was happening, shouted: 'Here, stop that or I'll call the police.' They ignored her. The boy was down on the pavement, and two of them were kicking him. The girl had backed away, and looked as if she wanted to scream, but she made no sound. It was all over in a few seconds. The boys simply walked away. 'Johnny', a youth in a white-belted raincoat, lay on the pavement, his face bloody. I noticed that the ringleader of the gang was lighting a cigarette as they strolled away. The girl and I both moved to the side of the boy on the ground. He sat up, and I saw his eyelid was cut. He said: 'The lousy sods' and then gasped and clutched his ribs. He said: 'I think they've broken a rib.' This did not convince me; I felt he was acting; but there could be no doubt that he was hurt. People now stopped to look at him, and the commissionaire came out of the entrance to the dance hall. He stood staring, while the woman in the kiosk was saying: 'They ought to give 'em the cat. That'd teach 'em.' A policeman came up, and asked the boy: 'Who were they?' and he said, gasping: 'I don't know.' I picked up my cigarettes and change, and walked away.

The episode had shocked me as completely as if I had been the one to be attacked; it brought back similar episodes from my own childhood with such clarity that I could feel the blows. It revived a familiar taste of fear. When I was halfway back to the office I regretted not staying to talk to 'Johnny'; the memory of violence was too sharp and clear, and learning the details might have helped to blur it. I also found myself thinking about Monty's fight on Saturday night, and suddenly understanding his aggressiveness. It seemed to me that my own dislike of fighting was an ostrich's attitude. These things were happening all the time, and Monty was responding to the challenge instead of pretending it did not exist. If everybody was as courageously aggressive as Monty, these thugs would not dare to carry their violence into the streets.

Back in the office with a jug of luke-warm tea, I explained what had happened. Everybody was interested – any subject of gossip was welcome. Miss Roberts said that it was a disgrace to England, and that we ought to use troops to keep order if the police failed. Then John

Duncan came in, and in a lull in the conversation said mildly that he had had some experience of the 'leather-jacket crowd'. They were, he said, always to be found outside the Palais on dance nights. Sometimes they had fights with rival gangs. But one of their favourite diversions was to bait passers-by – particularly men out with women. John then described how he had been walking past the Palais with his wife on a Saturday night. When they saw him coming, the gang spread out across the pavement, completely blocking it, meanwhile shoving and jostling one another as if they were preoccupied with the horseplay.

'What did you do?' I asked.

'Got out of their way.'

'How do you mean?'

'Walked in the roadway!'

Miss Roberts said:

'But surely a man of your size . . .'

'What's the point?' John said. 'They don't really want a fight. They just want to show off. Anyway, most of them carry coshes or razors.'

'Why didn't you report them to the police?' I asked. John's good nature sometimes irritated me.

'That wouldn't make any difference. The police know about it. But they haven't got enough policemen for all the gangs of Teddy-boys in the town.'

This struck me as shocking. I could understand that John might not like to start a fight when he had his wife with him. But it seemed intolerable that these boys should be allowed to practise this kind of insolence in the streets, and that the police should ignore them.

I thought about it as I left the office that night. As the bus passed the Palais I saw that there were still a few youths hanging about outside.

The whole episode made me vengeful. I imagined how

155

pleasant it would be if a few public-spirited citizens decided to carry guns, and took every opportunity of shooting down these thugs. But this kind of day-dreaming is like imagining a cool drink when you are thirsty; it only seems to make things worse. As I got off the bus, I had to walk past a gang of boys who were playing football on a car-park. They were younger than the leather-jacketed boys in front of the Palais, but it struck me that they would be just like them in a few years' time. It suddenly seemed to me that the whole town was full of this potential violence, lying just below the surface. I wondered why I had never noticed it before.

When I got home I found a phone message from Jeremy, asking me to go over the next evening. I had no wish to see Jeremy. He was another ostrich, playing his records of Delius and reading Plato.

Everything seemed to remind me of the violence. I picked up the newspaper; it carried a story about an old woman in a shop being beaten to death by two burglars. The radio brought news of further bomb-tests. My mother told me that my cousin George had been badly hurt in a motorcycle accident.

I went up to my room and lay on the bed. The more I thought of it, the more it was obvious that human beings are hopeless cowards. These boys in leather jackets were bullies because they were also cowards; they were aggressive to soothe their fear of aggression. The police were too cowardly to do anything to stop it. On Saturday night I had been irritated by Monty's aggressiveness because I felt he was trying to prove something to himself. But as I thought about my 'ideal public-spirited citizen', the man who would be prepared to take action against the thugs, I began to feel less critical of Monty.

My train of thought suddenly became clear. I felt irritated with myself for lying there day-dreaming about retaliating against these thugs. Such day-dreams were a coward's revenge. But was it possible to do anything practical?

I had been imagining that I was 'Johnny', standing in the queue outside the tobacco kiosk with a girl, and suddenly surrounded by half a dozen young thugs. But before they could hit me, I pulled a revolver out of my pocket and . . .

I stood up and went to the window. Suddenly, the day-dream was no longer an imaginative compensation. Monty had revolvers, and he hated these thugs as much as I did. The picture was now clear in my mind. Monty and Patricia and I were walking along the pavement towards the Palais de Danse. The Teddy-boys spread out across the pavement to drive us into the road. But instead of giving way, like John Duncan, we walked straight into them, and as they closed in . . .

I went downstairs and pulled on my raincoat. My mother said: 'You're not going out at this time?' It was after ten o'clock. 'I shan't be long,' I said. I wanted to talk to Monty about it.

Before I was halfway there, the absurdity of it struck me. Monty had told me that he had no permits for the guns, and that in England it is illegal to own a gun without a permit. Then what right had we to be carrying guns? We would immediately be arrested.

My enthusiasm collapsed and I got off the bus. Then I began to walk back slowly in the direction of home.

As I passed the working-men's club, I saw Mr Sutton outside, talking to a man and woman. I said goodnight (over the past year, we had got into the habit of saying hello to one another when we met in the street). He signalled me to wait for a moment, then walked along with me. He asked me what work I was doing, and about my father, and whether I intended to go to a university.

157

When I had answered his questions, I asked him about the revolver-club. He told me he was still a member, and that the club was expanding.

As I left him, I asked suddenly, on impulse:

'Do you think they'd let me join if I had a revolver?'

'Well yes, of course. Have you got a pistol?'

'No. But I know somebody with one to sell.'

He immediately began asking me about its make, age, and so on. I said I wasn't sure. He ended by making me promise to show him the gun before I paid hard cash for it. Then we said goodnight.

5

The day after I had talked to Mr Sutton, I still treated it as a kind of game, a day-dream. I cannot explain this easily. I was determined to go through with it, and yet I was not serious about it. When I went into the office next morning I had already formulated my plan. It is against the law in England to carry a revolver, or even to own a revolver unless you are a member of a pistol-club. But even a member of a pistol-club is not allowed to carry a gun, unless he is travelling to or from the club: it is, in any case, against the law to carry a loaded pistol. One member of our club had left a round in his pistol when he'd finished practising, and by some accident the gun went off as he was putting it away in the anteroom. No one was hurt (there was only one other person in the room, and the gun was pointing at the floor), but the member was instantly expelled. He would have been expelled from any club in England for the same carelessness.

Basically, my plan was simple. As a member of the pistol-club, I would be allowed to carry the gun on my way to shooting-practice. This, I knew, was on Wednesdays and Fridays. There was a dance at the Palais on Mondays, Fridays and Saturdays, and sometimes on Wednesdays too. I would be on my way to the club one evening; I would dismount at the bus-stop before the Palais. If it was after eight o'clock there would probably be the usual crowd of Teddy-boys outside. If they were blocking most of the pavement I would push my way through them.

On the other hand, it might prove to be impossible. I was not yet seventeen; I might not be allowed to own a gun. I thought of making Monty an offer for one of his pistols; he might not want to sell. But even if he agreed to sell, he had no firearms certificate for the guns; I would not be allowed to use an illegal pistol at a club.

So it remained a kind of day-dream; and I believe this was my main reason for not talking to Monty about my plan. He might dissuade me; on the other hand, he might agree with me, and then there could be no backing out. While the plan was in my head, I could pursue it or forget it as I felt inclined.

I find it most difficult to explain why I wanted to do this. The sight of the brutality outside the Palais had come as a sort of challenge. During my childhood I had been balanced between two worlds, violence and mathematics, and I was never certain of either. But at the time of my meeting Jeremy I'd changed so completely that I could no longer remember how I'd felt two years before; I was far more certain of myself and of my choice. Jeremy had only confirmed me in that feeling of certainty. The meeting with Monty and Patricia seemed another milestone; then the talk with Uncle Sam left me with a feeling of understanding something for the first time. And at this point, the scene outside the Palais threatened to throw me back eight years, to the time I had been beaten up outside the park. It was as though an unseen fate was saying 'All right, let's see if you've really changed . . .'. My first impulse had been to turn away, to accept my own defeat, as I had eight years ago. Then something in me made that impossible.

One of the reasons, I know, was Patricia. At midday on the Tuesday John Duncan sent me out to the post-office again. This time I went ten minutes earlier. When I came out of the post-office I waited on the corner, a hundred yards above the spot where I had seen her the day before. As she came past I waved to her, and she stopped to talk. She told me that she came that way every day, since she was a typist in the office of the Inspector of Taxes. She was in a hurry to catch her bus, being on her way home for lunch. I asked her what time she came out in the evening; she said five o'clock. I suggested meeting her for a coffee before she went home that evening. I think I was surprised when she agreed. Then I went back to the office, wondering whether I was delighted or embarrassed. I told myself that I was a fool to treat this as anything out of the ordinary. I was a friend of Monty's; Patricia and I worked within a few hundred yards of one another; we had obviously taken a mild, friendly liking to one another on Saturday night; why should we not meet and talk? – I had to reason with myself like this to soothe my nervousness. But I prepared myself in advance for defeat. The thought that she was Monty's mistress, which had aroused obscure longing and jealousy two days before, now helped to increase my confidence for this meeting; I told myself that it could lead to nothing. Then I thought about my 'revolver plan' – I called it this mentally – and no longer felt unsure of myself. Perhaps I might even persuade Patricia to come to the pistol-club with me. John Duncan had said that the Palais hooligans paid more attention to youths who had girls with them.

I can still remember my feelings that afternoon. The office usually depressed me, because it made me aware of myself as a machine; its dullness affected me as a kind of hypnosis. No matter how far I tried to control my reactions, the sight of the girl at the telephone switchboard, the sound of Miss Roberts's voice, the taste of the mid-afternoon tea, sterilized my capacity to feel and think; it seemed as automatic as switching on a light.

Boredom would affect me like an anaesthetic. This afternoon was different; the same stimuli no longer produced the same responses; or rather, the responses could be controlled. It came to me that most people allow themselves to be paralysed by boredom and the repetition of experience because their sense of urgency is never touched. A man having a nightmare can make great efforts to awake, but basically he realizes it is a dream, and the sleep-net is almost unbreakable; and yet the slightest sound in the room will waken him; the unbreakable mesh falls apart as if it was rotten.

As I stood waiting on the corner of the street at a quarter to five, Gerald Sutton came by. He was working in the newspaper-office. He told me that his father had mentioned my interest in the pistol-club at lunch-time and asked me to go and have a cup of tea with him; I had to explain that I was waiting for someone, but promised to see him later in the evening. Gerald was a member, although he was six months younger than I. It was easy for him, since his father was treasurer of the club. He asked me about the pistol I meant to buy. I told him that an ex-army friend had one for sale. He pulled a face.

'Are you sure it's legal?'

'Probably not,' I said.

'But in that case it's no use. You've got to send the bill of sale to the police when you fill in your application for a firearms certificate.'

This was an unforeseen complication.

'Is there no way out of that?' I asked. I think I already felt a certain relief that the whole thing was turning out impractical.

'There's no way of using an illegal gun in our club. You see, the mayor and the chief constable are members. But

162

why get an illegal gun anyway? What's to stop you buying one in the normal way?'

'The price, mainly.'

'How much do you want to pay?'

I had not thought about it, but I said 'About five pounds'.

'Mmm. That's not much. But I might be able to help you. I think I might know somebody . . .'

As he was going, I asked:

'How long would it take to get a certificate?'

'Oh, it could take anything up to two months. But that's the advantage of having the chief of police in the club. We could probably do it in two days if you want to shoot this week.'

I saw that fate was making it difficult to back out. I thanked him and promised to come later in the evening.

When Patricia said: 'I'm sorry I'm late,' I was almost surprised to see her, although it was now five-fifteen. I suggested we should go into a nearby café, but she said she knew a far nicer place – a sort of youth-club. As we walked along, she said: 'The only trouble with it is that Monty sometimes meets me there.'

'Suppose he's there now?'

'He won't be. He rang me just before I left the office, and I said I had to go straight home.'

'Why?' I was startled and flattered.

'He doesn't have to know all my business.'

The club was known as the 'O.A.C.' – this stood for 'Open Air Club'; it had a café downstairs and two or three rooms upstairs with games and comfortable but somewhat tattered armchairs. It was designed to keep teenagers out of the pubs. At half past five it was almost empty. We bought tea and sandwiches and went upstairs. A couple were playing table tennis, but we found the magazine-room empty. Having nothing else to talk about,

I pressed her about why she hadn't told Monty she was meeting me. It was only supposed to be a conversational gambit, but it had the effect of launching her into explanations. She said she was sick of Monty's assumption that he could treat her as casually as he liked, and yet expect her to rush to see him every time it occurred to him to phone her.

'Is he in love with you?' I asked. It was a silly kind of question, and I asked it simply because I could see she wanted to talk about Monty. She shrugged:

'He's not in love with anybody but himself.'

I wanted to ask if she was in love with him, but didn't have the courage. Instead, I asked:

'Why are you in such a bad mood with him?'

'Oh, because he's a . . .' She groped for a word: 'A . . . liar.'

Finally, she told me about it. Late on Saturday evening – after I had gone – a girl had walked into the room. Evidently she had let herself in with a front-door key. She had stared at Patricia, then at Monty, and Monty had smiled and said 'Hello Dorothy'. Then the girl turned and walked out. (I wanted to ask what Monty and Patricia were doing as she came in, but decided against it.) Monty was obviously ruffled. He told her a few lies about the girl, pretending that she had borrowed the flat once when he was away; when Patricia asked why, in that case, she had walked out without speaking, he looked awkward and admitted that there had been something between them. Finally – although it was now very late – Patricia decided to go home. Monty made no attempt to dissuade her.

She looked embarrassed as she said this. She knew that I knew she had been Monty's mistress; but it was not something I was supposed to take for granted. To cover up her confusion, I started to talk about Jeremy and

Monty. She was very curious about Jeremy. She was a member of a literary group, and had heard of Jeremy's work. She obviously felt that appearing in print endowed a writer with a kind of mystical distinction. This aroused a kind of jealousy in me, so that my analysis of Jeremy's character and ideas was less charitable than it might have been otherwise.

While we were talking, a man came in with an armful of cardboard boxes, saw us and said: 'Oh sorry. I didn't know there was anyone in here,' and backed out. Patricia went to the door and called: 'It's all right. You can come in,' but he had gone. As she came back, past my armchair, I caught her hand, and said: 'Patricia.'

She said: 'What?' standing still and not attempting to disengage her hand, which felt limp and damp.

'I wish you weren't so enthusiastic about the Wolfe family.'

'I'm not!'

'Good,' I said, and let go of her hand.

That was all that happened between us that evening but I thought about it repeatedly for the rest of the night. Shortly after this, she said she had to go home. I saw her to the bus-stop. As she left I asked her if she always went home for lunch; she said that she would be staying in town the next day to do some shopping. The bus pulled out before I could say any more. And yet I walked off feeling strangely pleased with myself. I decided to call in and see Monty before I went home; his flat was only a few minutes away. On my way there I stopped at a pub, and ordered a whisky. This was not because I felt I needed a drink, but out of bravado. I wanted to prove that I belonged to the adult world. Then I thought about the shooting-club, and my heart sank like lead. And yet I was curiously happy and optimistic. The lights of the town seemed brighter than usual. I felt that, basically, fate meant well by me. Besides, I could drop the shooting idea; I was not forced to go through with it.

Monty answered the door, and said: 'Oh, it's you. I was expecting a girl.'

'Patricia?' I said disingenuously.

'Don't talk to me about that!'

He offered me a glass of beer. We opened a pint bottle of ale, and sat in front of the fire.

'What about Patricia?' I asked.

He told me the story I had already heard, except that his version was franker. Patricia had been undressed and in bed when the other girl came in. (Monty's bed – a divan type – was in the living-room.) The other girl was supposed to be Monty's fiancée, and she was taking a domestic science course in Bath; he had no idea that she was in town. The result had been awkward; he had a suspicion that he had lost both girls.

'I rang Pat this afternoon, but she said she had to go straight home.'

He started to laugh.

'It's just about the awkwardest thing that ever happened to me. Except the occasion when I was in bed with a girl called Gretchen, and I said: "I love you, Mary." Luckily she didn't seem to notice, or pretended she didn't.'

'Can't you find some convincing explanation for your fiancée?'

'She wouldn't believe me. Anyway, I don't care. Actually, I'm more sorry about losing Pat. She was a delicious little thing.'

I said without enthusiasm: 'I expect you can get her to come back.'

'I don't know. It'd be different if she just suspected me of infidelity – or even if she knew for sure. But if there's

166

one thing a girl won't forgive, it's being made to look a fool in front of another woman.'

'Did she look a fool?' I asked, tormenting myself with a picture of Patricia sitting up in bed, trying to conceal her naked breasts with the sheet.

'Oh no, I suppose not. But she must have realized that Dorothy had some right to come barging in like that. So she probably felt as though she'd been caught in an act of burglary.'

'And how about Dorothy – was she trying to catch you out?'

'No, that's the silly part. She'd got a telegram saying her mother was ill. Her train didn't get in until two in the morning, so she thought she'd stay the night at my place.'

There was a ring at the door bell. I asked:

'Is that Dorothy?'

'No. She won't speak to me. It's a girl called Betsy. She's the boss's secretary.' (Monty held a good position in a firm of wool merchants.)

I went to the door with him. The girl who came in was a plump brunette with a round, gentle face. I was introduced to her, and we shook hands. Then I went. I had not talked to Monty about either of the subjects I wanted to bring up – the pistol-club, and the incident outside the Palais. Probably this was as well. As we had sat there talking in the firelight (Monty had switched off the light in preparation for Betsy), I had felt an urge to return confidence with confidence, and to tell him of my plan.

When I went up to my room, I lit the gas-fire and read Vinogradoff on number theory. I no longer felt any revulsion from mathematics – on the contrary, some of my early delight in it had returned. But every few minutes I put down the book and thought about Patricia or Monty. The thought of Monty was particularly pleasant.

His room had been laid out for a seduction – with a bottle of red wine near the fire, and a decanter of whisky on the sideboard; the kitchen and living-room spotlessly tidy (a characteristic Monty shared with his cousin) and a cover arranged over the bed so that it looked like a couch. Somehow, that room with the firelight on it symbolized a way of life that I had not even suspected. When I thought of Jeremy and his talk about 'higher men' I wanted to laugh out loud. The life of the spirit was all very well – and Bach and Delius and Schopenhauer had been an incomparable enrichment to the world – but it was never supposed to be kept separate from the life of the body. Music and philosophy were like wine – they were intended to enhance the pleasure of being alive, not to replace it. What surprised me most was that I had starved my humanity for as long as I could remember, feeding it on a diet of ideas and mathematics – and yet I had not starved it to death, for here it was, as healthy as ever, revelling in the thought of Patricia's damp hand. The truth suddenly seemed very simple; life was *supposed* to be many-sided, and the happiest human being is he who succeeds in perceiving as many sides as possible. I had spent my whole life living with an error – that life is supposed to be dominated by one truth; and it had worried me that life has an aspect of violence as well as of order and reason. But the truth is that life has hundreds of aspects, and every philosophy represents only one of them.

And it was at that moment that I had my great idea; I still believe it is the most important idea that has ever come to me. If I thought about it for the next fifty years, I should not become aware of all its implications.

It was this. We take it for granted that a man can adjust his intellectual viewpoint as easily as he can adjust the

168

range on a telescope. One day he can agree with Schopenhauer that the world is a death-trap and that the most sensible thing would be suicide, and the next day agree with Dr Pangloss that everything is for the best in this best of all possible worlds. He can take any one of a thousand points of view about life, from optimism to total pessimism. He can take up a dozen books in succession, from *The Fifth Form at St Dominic's* to *The Brothers Karamazov*, and see the world through the eyes of each author. We all take these intellectual quick-change acts for granted.

Why, in that case, does man accept his emotional states as somehow unchangeable? A man gets up early in the morning in a state of nervous tension, and feels depressed at the prospect of having to live through another day. Then he goes outside; it is a spring morning and the sun comes out; immediately he feels cheerful. His emotional climate has altered in a few seconds, yet he accepts this as a kind of *natural accident*, like the sun coming out – something beyond his control.

Admittedly, man knows a little about altering his emotions. If he likes music, then he will play a Tchaikovsky symphony when he feels a need for romantic emotion, Chopin when he feels melancholy, Wagner when he wants heroics, and so on. But he is still submitting himself to new *experiences* to change his emotions; he never asks himself why he should not have as much control over his emotions as over his ideas.

When I read what I have just written, I see that I have still not conveyed my central idea. Because I am not talking about mere emotional changes – from sadness to happiness, for example. We do not spend most of our lives in states of gloom or optimism or pity or excitement; we spend them in a state of emotional constipation – *feeling nothing*, or very little indeed. That is why the people in our office lived in such a state of dullness. They accepted this; they waited patiently for destiny to present them with some state of happiness or excitement. It never struck them that this state of emotional constipation was thoroughly unnatural – as unnatural as physical constipation.

It seemed to me that a person should be able to wake up and say: 'Now, how shall I feel this morning? Shall I wear my Tchaikovsky mood? Or my Bach mood? Or perhaps my Beethoven mood?' Obviously, certain moods would be unsuitable for a morning spent adding up figures, or doing the spring cleaning, or attending a parents' meeting at the school, just as a fur coat would be the wrong garment for a summer's day. If I woke up on a cold morning and found myself wearing a swimsuit, I would not feel bound to go to work in it. And yet we feel bound to accept the mood in which we wake up in the morning – or the complete lack of mood, which is more usual.

These ideas came to me as I sat in front of the fire, reading Vinogradoff; I still have the copy of Vinogradoff with the clean pages at the end (intended for calculations) covered with my handwriting. When I had written these ideas down, I remembered that I had promised to see Gerald Sutton, so I walked over. It was a clear cold night, and I looked at the sky and thought: 'Man is static because he has no reason to be anything else. No one teaches him any differently. Zoologists tell us that an animal takes three times as long to learn how to behave if it has no mother. Well, man has no mother and father; he is completely alone. One god, one god-like human being, would change the course of history by showing men how to behave . . .'

These thoughts were more intoxicating than an evening with Patricia or drinking Monty's hot rum.

Gerald had gone out for a while. Mr Sutton asked me in – it was the first time for eight years that I had been into the house – and offered me tea. To my surprise, he avoided the subject of the pistol-club, and asked me about my family. Twenty minutes later Gerald came in. He handed me a pistol – a Biretta .22 – and said: 'Tell me what you think of that.'

I tried it, and peered along the sights. 'It's a nice gun,' I said.

'If you want it, you can have it for seven pounds ten.'

Mr Sutton looked surprised. 'Seven pounds ten's very cheap. How did you get him down to that?'

The Biretta, it appeared, belonged to a friend of Gerald who had sudden and intense enthusiasms. But like Toad of Toad Hall he was as changeable as the weather. His latest enthusiasm was for long-playing records, which had been on the market for only a few months. As he had not been to the pistol-club for quite a time Gerald rightly guessed that the pistol would be for sale.

Mr Sutton said: 'I'll have it myself if you don't want it.'

It was obviously impossible to refuse. I thanked Gerald and said that I would get the money out of my post-office account the next day.

'Don't worry about that. You can say the gun's yours already. I've brought you the forms to fill in. You'll need your father's signature too as you're under seventeen.'

I felt embarrassed by all this helpfulness, so I covered my embarrassment by carefully filling in forms.

'Do you want to come to the club tomorrow?' Gerald asked.

'Can I do that before I get a firearms certificate?'

'Do you want to come?' he repeated. I had no alternative than to say yes.

171

'All right. Drop the form in here on your way to work tomorrow, and I'll see what I can do.'

I went away feeling awkward and guilty. Gerald and I had always been friendly at school, but in recent years we had seen little of one another. Apart from the pistol-club, his chief interest was now a cycling-club, and he spent his weekends pedalling around the countryside on a racing-model with no mudguards and special tubular tyres. I could see that he felt delighted to have me in the club, although I think he was a little puzzled by my sudden conversion. At all events, he hoped that it would be permanent. I felt so guilty about this that I began to wonder how I could back out. There was still one possibility – that my father might refuse to sign the form – which, in effect, made him true owner of the gun, and gave me permission to borrow it.

Always capable of the unexpected, my father signed it without even bothering to read it, merely muttering: 'I hope you know what you're doing.'

The following morning I handed it to Gerald. At mid-afternoon, he rang me to say that he had 'fixed things', and that I could come and practise at the club that evening.

I attended my meeting, together with Gerald and his father, and was introduced to most of the members. They were a mixed crowd; Gerald and I were the youngest; but there were two or three other members of Gerald's cycling-club, raw-boned young men who talked in technicalities and gave a curious impression of innocence. The best shot in the club was its secretary, Bob Salomons, a narrow-chested man with a sad-looking face and an unexpected snorting laugh. The mayor, Ewen Waite, was not there on my first evening; he was the president of the club, and Chief Superintendent Gibbs – known as Scottie

– was treasurer. Gerald had 'arranged' my firearms certificate with him. He had the build of an old-fashioned sergeant-major, with a bristly moustache and a stiff manner; Gerald assured me that under this surface he was the friendliest and nicest man in the club.

I practised for only about a quarter of an hour, then watched the others shoot. I had forgotten how deafening a pistol can be. As before, I found it difficult not to jerk the trigger instead of squeezing it; this, of course, has the effect of spoiling the aim of the pistol. Mr Sutton demonstrated this to me by pretending to re-load my gun, and handing it to me with one chamber empty; the hammer clicked on an empty chamber, but I was able to see that I allowed the barrel to jump slightly in preparation for the explosion. I was glad to stop practising, because I found my aim getting worse as I failed to control this tendency. After the shooting we all went into the pub next door, where Gerald and I drank shandy – nothing else was possible under the eye of the chief constable. But on the way home, I persuaded Gerald to walk with me to the hot-dog stall opposite the Palais. I pointed out to him the crowd of youths hanging around the entrance. He seemed to think they were harmless enough until I told him what I had seen two days before. Then he patted his brief-case and said: 'I'd like to see them try anything while I'm carrying this.' 'But it's not loaded.' 'I know. But they don't, do they?' We stood watching them for a while as we ate our hot dogs; I wanted to see whether they blocked the pavement, as John Duncan had described: but as Gerald said, they looked harmless enough. On the way home that night I again made up my mind to drop the whole thing.

I had seen Patricia at midday; she was obviously expecting me. We ate sandwiches at the Woolworth's snack-counter, and I wondered whether to tell her that I had seen Monty. When I told her about the pistol-club, she said:

'Don't tell me *you're* fascinated by guns, like Monty!'

I found it difficult to produce convincing excuses. Some months before, Jeremy had lent me a book called *Zen in the Art of Archery*. I converted its argument to pistol-shooting; but Patricia was unconvinced.

She had been reading the book Jeremy had given her, and said she would like to talk to him again. This raised a problem; I knew Jeremy would resent it if Patricia came with me. I told her I would think about it. That afternoon I rang Jeremy from the office. I told him that Patricia had got in touch with me, and that she wanted to talk to him about his book; I added that she had quarrelled with Monty. Jeremy sounded puzzled and suspicious.

'*Why* does she want to talk to me? Tell her to write me a letter.'

I tried flattery, told him that she admired his intellect and probably wanted to boast about her acquaintance with him to her friends. Jeremy muttered for a moment, then said, with the sudden frankness that was one of his most likeable characteristics:

'Look here, Hugh, women make me nervous. I just wouldn't know what to say to her. It's not that I don't want her to come . . .'

'Suppose I came over too? Then we could both talk to her.'

'That's an idea,' he said, brightening.

'I'll suggest it to her,' I said, then added: 'I'll have to ring off. The boss's coming.' This was untrue, but I didn't want to give him an opportunity to change his mind. That evening I met Patricia out of work, and told her that I could take her out to Cranthorpe the following evening.

It was not a success, from Jeremy's point of view. Patricia and I could not decide whether to arrive together;

finally, we agreed that there would be no point in travelling separately. On the bus, I told her in detail about Tom Davis's ghost; she immediately became nervous and wanted to turn back. I dissuaded her by pointing out that she was hardly likely to see the ghost. She talked about it all the way up to the cottage. She also took my hand as we passed by the woods and she thought she heard a strange noise; but she made no attempt to withdraw it when we had passed the woods. I always carried a pocket-torch for this walk, for the road was unlighted, and the ditch had a stream in the bottom; unfortunately, the bulb had burnt out, so we had to walk cautiously in the middle of the road. Jeremy sometimes hung a storm-lantern outside the cottage when he expected me, but this evening – perhaps because Patricia was unwelcome – he had not done so. When we arrived at the cottage I groped along the hedge, searching for the gate; somehow, we went past it, and I turned back, and stumbled against Patricia. As we stood there, keeping one another upright, I felt that she expected me to kiss her. So I put my arms around her, and pressed my lips against her cold face. She moved slightly, so I found her lips; they were warm, and I felt as if I were falling down a well. What surprised me most was that she had moved her face to allow me to kiss her. I wished we were not outside Jeremy's cottage; I wished we were somewhere where I could keep on kissing her all night. Then the cottage door opened; light came out, and Jeremy called: 'Is that you?' We broke apart guiltily, and went in through the gate. I was sure Jeremy had not seen us; but if he had heard us approaching the cottage he must have wondered what was keeping us outside. I muttered some explanation about my torch being broken. Luckily, Jeremy was also feeling awkward in the presence of a female guest, and hardly looked at us.

Patricia went upstairs to leave her coat on the bed, then went into the bathroom; Jeremy was filling the kettle in the kitchen. I quickly looked in the mirror to see if I had lipstick on me; no. What had just happened was incredible to me; ten minutes before, as we got off the bus, I would have thought it impossible. But I also felt as if I had betrayed Jeremy, and was now in his cottage under false pretences. Then, to anticipate disappointment, I told myself that it meant nothing, and that it would be fantastic if an attractive girl could find any interest in a sixteen-year-old mathematician after being involved with Monty. Perhaps she wanted to use me to make Monty jealous, and relied on Jeremy telling Monty about our visit.

Jeremy came in looking worried, and asked in a low voice:

'Do you think she's really read my book?'

His question was answered a moment later when Patricia came downstairs, carrying *Old Truths With New Names*. She looked absurdly beautiful in a grey woollen dress, and with her hair tied in a pony tail with a green ribbon. I suddenly felt as if I was steering a small boat down a very fast stream, and could hear the roar of a waterfall in the distance. I was ashamed of having spent my life reading books, and ashamed of being here with Jeremy, who was a symbol of the sedentary life. What surprised me was that Patricia seemed so much at home here. She sat at the table and opened the book, and I noticed that it was heavily marked in pencil. Jeremy also noticed this as he set down the coffee pot, and I saw him redden with pleasure.

While we were drinking the coffee Jeremy suddenly looked at his watch, and asked us if we would mind listening to the radio for half an hour. The Delius violin concerto was being performed on the Third. He turned

176

off the light and we sat in the firelight. The Delius concerto always makes me think of that Yeats poem about the fairies luring away a child; it is beautiful but life-denying. I enjoy the work – particularly if I am tired and need soothing – but on this evening my feelings revolted against it. I sat watching Patricia, who was now sitting opposite me, and kept thinking of her sitting up in bed, trying to draw the sheets over her breasts. I felt impatient of Jeremy and his hermit existence. Then the thought of the pistol cleared away my annoyance like a wind blowing into fog. I thought: I must get away from this town. I remembered the episode of the Thames Street battle with pride; it was one of the few episodes from my past that proved that I was made of different stuff from Jeremy. It proved that I was somehow at home in the world of action. And I thought nostalgically about Gauguin – whose biography I had just read – and wondered if I could raise enough money to go and live in Paris or Berlin for a year.

The concerto came to an end, and Patricia, to my surprise, said: 'That was beautiful.' I could not resist saying:

'But I don't know what the higher men will think of Delius. I imagine they'll burn everything he ever wrote.'

Patricia asked: 'Why?'

'There's a hothouse feeling about it. It's not healthy music – it's the music of a sick man dreaming of health.'

Jeremy looked startled; he interpreted this as an attack on his liking for Delius. It was not; I was only trying to express my response to the music. He shrugged and said:

'It's unearthly, but so is Beethoven's *Heilige Dankse-gang* from opus 132. All great music is unearthly.'

'I think I agree,' Patricia said.

Jeremy picked up his book from the table, turned to the section on music, and read it aloud. It stated that the appetite for music is the highest man possesses. I agreed with some of it, but again I had the feeling that Jeremy was trying to keep the flesh and its appetites in some lower compartment, as if they were a disgrace to human nature. I had always felt vaguely uncomfortable about this; but with Patricia sitting opposite me it seemed nonsense.

The result was that I criticized what he said more radically than ever before. According to Jeremy, man evolves by cultivating the 'higher part' of his nature, and if he does this honestly he leaves the world and its false values behind – and develops a set of values that worldly people call anti-life – which indeed for worldly people *are* anti-life. Nevertheless, they are the only way in which we can evolve. For example, Jeremy said, most people prefer Tolstoy's *War and Peace* to the works of his Christian period, and yet to any higher man a book like *The Kingdom of God* or *Resurrection* is worth ten times as much as *War and Peace*. In fact, when all mankind has evolved a stage further, we shall burn *War and Peace* as an unbearable frivolity – except for certain passages about God and religion.

When Jeremy became excited he talked with the fervour of a prophet. If he had been less shy he would have been a fine orator. He referred to the sex in *War and Peace* and *Anna Karenina*, and pointed out that Tolstoy had later been ashamed of it as a pandering to our everlasting, trivial interest in adultery and fornication. As he said this, his eyes wandered casually over Patricia's pointed breasts standing out under the tight grey wool, and he looked like Calvin sentencing Servetus to be burnt. I suspected that he thought of himself as a St Anthony defying all the devils of concupiscence. But Patricia looked impressed, and almost ashamed of the curves under her dress. I understood how Savonarola had persuaded the women of Florence to wear loose, sack-like dresses. Finally, Patricia said wistfully:

'But you have to be a man to live that kind of life. A woman is too tied down. She has to bring up children . . .'

'Quite,' Jeremy said. 'And because they're tied down, they've chosen to tie the men down too. They've poisoned our culture with a kind of feminism. A woman secretly knows that she owes her beauty to the evolutionary force, which wants her to bear children. After a few years she loses it and has to get used to being a household drudge. And by that time a man should have outgrown the allure of sex; when his wife loses her beauty he should already be thinking about other things – music, religion, mathematics. But women hate this idea, so they've filled our culture with a kind of feverish eroticism that affects men like a virus. They can't throw it off. It takes a man of Tolstoy's stature to denounce all the rubbish about sex and declare that religion is more important. His early works are full of feminism.'

I was somehow aware that this tirade was really directed at Patricia – and perhaps at Monty. Its tone of implied self-congratulation annoyed me. I found myself wondering how Uncle Sam would react to it, and this made me understand my reason for rejecting it. Because basically men are no more free than women, and the 'higher men' no wiser than the lower men.

I tried to explain Uncle Sam's point of view to Jeremy – his picture of men weighed down under concrete armour, and their lives spent in a constant state of emotional constipation. Then – gropingly and very badly – I tried to explain my own idea about the human slavery to moods. But as I talked the ideas became clearer.

I argued that all human acts of will are directed towards freedom. Why does a schoolboy want a bicycle? Because

179

he thinks that it will increase his freedom. Why does he want a stamp collection? Because it stimulates the imagination, makes him aware of 'far-away places'. Whatever human beings want they want because they think it will increase their freedom.

But what actually happens is that a schoolboy spends years saving up for a bicycle and dreaming about it; but when he gets it he takes it for granted within a month. There seems to be a mechanism in our nature that prevents us from feeling 'free' for more than a few minutes at a time. We get used to everything. It might be compared to the way that a clever government could cheat the workers. The workers demand higher wages; the government orders that they are to have higher wages. But it also announces that the price of food is to be raised – so the workers are back where they started. So men strive for freedom; they achieve what they want; then they get bored with it, so they have to find something else to strive for. This might be called 'the law of the conservation of freedom': human freedom seems to be a fixed quantity; it cannot be increased or decreased.

I did not believe all this myself; but it expressed something that Jeremy preferred not to recognize. He talked as if evolution was a perfectly simple affair, a climb up a ladder, away from the body and emotions, towards pure intellect and religion, away from Patricia towards late Tolstoy.

I turned the attack full on Jeremy.

'For example, you are in a position that many would consider enviable. You live in a pleasant cottage, with plenty of books and records. You told me that you used to dream about having a place of your own when you were in the navy. When your mother bought this cottage, you couldn't sleep for excitement. And yet now you take it for granted. Can you claim to be happy here? Don't you spend whole days in a state of boredom and nervous irritation, not knowing what to do with yourself?'

'I really don't see what you're getting at,' Jeremy said.

'Only that human beings are the victims of a continual confidence trick. The problem is far more complicated than you seem to realize. Your idea of evolution doesn't solve anything. It doesn't even touch the basic problem of why men are slaves. You only confuse the issue by claiming that we are slaves of the flesh and the devil, and that when we renounce these, we shan't be slaves any longer. Well, you claim to have renounced them. Are you any less a slave than the rest of us?'

Jeremy said that he didn't claim to be perfect; but I felt that he was trying to evade my objections.

Like all arguments of this sort, this one went on for too long, and the thread got lost. At half past nine I said that I wanted to get home early to do some studying. I had a sense of emptiness, of an argument that had been a waste of time and got nowhere. Patricia went upstairs again; Jeremy switched on the gramophone, put on a record of Schweitzer playing Bach, and leaned back in his chair with his eyes closed, as if cutting himself off from the rest of the world – and from me. When Patricia came back downstairs with her coat on, I said quickly:

'Don't bother to get up. I'll phone you tomorrow.'

Patricia thanked him for a pleasant evening. He said: 'I'm glad you enjoyed it,' and I suspected a tone of sarcasm. We went out into the darkness, followed by the thunder of the Bach Passacaglia. I had forgotten about the torch – I had meant to ask Jeremy for the loan of one, but I didn't want to return now. So we stumbled on through the darkness. When we came to the top of the hill, within sight of the lights of Cranthorpe, I kissed her again, but our faces were icy, and the wind blew around us. Then we walked down the hill, and I told her that I

181

wanted to go away for a year – to some other city. We saw the bus arriving in the square, and ran for it; she shouted something to me as we ran. We arrived just as the driver started the engine, and went down to the front seat. I asked her what she had said.

'I said I'd like to come with you.'

'Could you?'

She said: 'No. My parents wouldn't allow it.'

We arrived back after ten, and I walked her home. When we got to her front gate, she said:

'You can come in if you like. There's no one here.'

Her parents were out playing bridge, and would not return for another hour.

'Suppose they came back suddenly and found me here?'

'They wouldn't mind. But I'd rather they didn't find you. They're terribly nosy.'

Her home looked very much like mine – it even had the same kind of carpet on the floor. She asked me if I would like tea, or some sherry. I asked for sherry – I didn't want to waste valuable minutes making tea. Then it turned out that the sherry decanter was empty, but she found some cooking sherry. I couldn't tell the difference anyway; we never kept any kind of drink at home except at Christmas. She said:

'Let's take it into the front room. Then if we hear them coming in the back way, you can slip out of the front door.'

We lit the gas-fire and sat on the settee. I drank my sherry in one draught; I knew why we were there, and didn't want to waste time. She did the same, then kicked off her shoes and stretched out. I reached up and switched off the standard lamp. Our faces and hands were still cold, but it made no difference. I felt the length of her

182

warm body pressed against me, and wanted to laugh when I thought about Jeremy's 'higher men'.

Patricia was a great deal more experienced than I was (in fact I was totally inexperienced, never having kissed any female except relatives, and small girls at Christmas parties; I learned later that Patricia had had lovers since she was fifteen). She was a warm-blooded girl, of quick responses. I had always felt slightly ashamed of my sexual responses to the opposite sex, and thought that they should be concealed at all costs. It amazed me to feel that Patricia not only understood them but shared them. Kissing her was like falling: I was no longer aware of the room or the settee or the fire on my back; only of her body. I wanted nothing more than to lie there, feeling her warmth; at this stage, I was unaware that she was puzzled by my lack of responsiveness. And yet the pressure of two bodies will dissolve almost any inhibitions, and mine had almost vanished when we heard her parents outside. Within fifteen seconds I was out in the cold, pulling on my overcoat. I turned up my collar, buried my hands deep in the pockets, and walked back home through the fine drizzle that was now falling.

Back at home, I lay in bed and thought back over the events of the past hour, and the erotic excitement expanded, having no shyness to restrain it. It was intolerable to be lying in bed without Patricia. I remembered that only five hours earlier she was still, relatively speaking, a stranger. Then I realized that I was having to *tell myself* this, and yet did not feel it. The full truth of Uncle Sam's remarks came to me. I lacked feeling, consciousness; something important had happened to me, yet it seemed almost as unreal as if I had imagined it. Five hours before Patricia had been a stranger; an hour before, I had been lying beside her, very aware of the shape of her thighs and that her dress had climbed above the top of her stocking and that I could see the white flesh. With this thought, the tension dissolved, my body was convulsed; the stupidity flowed back and my consciousness became unlimited; my body no longer felt as if it was made of bakelite. I pressed against her, kissed her invisible face between my own and the pillow. Then the excitement subsided, and I felt ashamed – not of having allowed imagination to go beyond what had actually happened, but of the singleness of the need that had driven me. With the sheets giving back my warmth, I wondered whether Patricia was worth this surrender of identity.

I fell asleep almost immediately, without having decided.

The problem that preoccupied me the next morning was where I could see Patricia alone. I envied Monty his flat. There was nowhere for us to go. My parents went to bed early – sometimes as early as half past nine – but my sister Anne was quite capable of coming down to make herself a cup of cocoa when she ought to be asleep.

I thought about this when I had finished my filing in the office. Marion stood by my desk as she talked to Miss Roberts, and I found myself idly observing the way her suspenders showed through her dress as she leaned against the table. Suddenly it came to me that sex is a kind of insanity. It was too late to escape; it had caught me; but at least I could observe what was happening. What I now observed was a revelation. This world of sex had nothing – absolutely nothing – in common with the world of mathematics. And I could now see it in the office, as if I had been given the power to see the invisible. Everyone was caught in this current. I looked at Marion's green dress and the shapes of the suspenders, and I felt a dizziness, as if the dress and her underclothes had dissolved and there was a whirlpool in the region of her thighs. Then there was Susan on the telephone switchboard; with her flat, northern voice and freckled face she had never struck me as remotely attractive: now I was aware that the same power was emanating from her as she sat opposite me. I had been looking for truth in mathematics, but I had made the same mistake as Newton – I had overlooked an invisible force. Marion's thighs were only a small vortex in a larger vortex that dragged us all along; perhaps the earth swept round the sun in the same whirlpool. But where did it get you? People in whirlpools disappear.

A great change had come over me since the previous night. Twenty-four hours before Patricia had been an alluring idea, something exciting but undefinable like a perfume. Now all the glamour had disappeared, but she had caught me in a stronger grip; I was aware of a poison in my veins; I kept wanting to ask, absurdly: 'But what about mathematics?' Then an image fell into my brain, with no train of thought to prepare it. It was the image of a youth slouching away down Thames Street, and looking at me over his shoulder – the youth who had lured my sister into the spinney. I do not know why I thought of him. But the thought made me aware of all the implications of this current into which I had fallen. Mathematics is a cold flow; it leads into seas of abstraction. Sex is a self-enclosed current, leading nowhere but to procreation. And because it flows in a circle, it cannot be said to progress. But in that case, I was spinning in the same whirlpool as the youth who wanted to assault my sister; he was simply closer to the centre.

For some reason, I decided I wanted to talk to Monty; I rang him at his office, and asked him if I could see him later. He asked me to meet him out of work, but I explained that I had to go to the pistol-club. He told me to come round afterwards.

At twelve o'clock I met Patricia. And it was during the next hour that I observed the curious way that chance sometimes produces the appearance of logic, just as potatoes may appear to imitate the shapes of animals. Patricia and I had bought sandwiches and walked down to the cattle-market – Friday being a market day. She wanted to see the bicycles that were auctioned. Suddenly she looked startled and her hand tightened in mine. She said: 'That man who's just gone in there,' pointing to a shed, 'he's a burglar.' I asked her to explain. She said that, about six months before, she had gone to see an aunt who lived in Stoneyvale – the expensive end of town. As she walked into her aunt's front garden, a man hurried out past her; she assumed, from his clothes, that he was a bricklayer or labourer. She noticed him particularly because she thought he looked guilty, and mentioned him to her aunt. There had been a number of burglaries in the district recently. That night, the house next door was broken into, and an old man who went to investigate the noise was knocked out with a brass candlestick. Patricia was sure that the man she had seen was one of the gang.

We stood staring at the shed, when Patricia said: 'There he is.' The man who came out was the youth who had lured Anne into the spinney. He turned away from us and disappeared into a crowd. When I told her about my own encounter with him Patricia said: 'What ought we to do? Go and tell a policeman?' We discussed it for a few minutes, and agreed that it would probably be pointless. I decided that I would speak to Scottie Gibbs – the chief constable – that evening.

On the way back to the office I mentioned to Patricia that my parents often went to bed early, and that we might go back to my home some evening – after ten o'clock. She said casually 'All right', but I sensed that the casualness was deceptive; she knew what I was thinking.

That evening, before I left for the club, I carefully loaded my pistol, and made sure the safety catch was on. I had already made an excuse to Gerald for not travelling to the club with him; I said that I might be staying in town after work. At half past seven I got off the bus outside the Palais de Danse. A few youths were standing around, but close to the door, and talking. I stopped and pretended to look in the glass case, showing photographs of a jiving competition. No one paid any attention to me. I walked on to the club, feeling pleased with myself; at least I was keeping my promise.

The first person I saw as I got into the club was Scottie Gibbs. I was about to take the Biretta out of my brief-case when he said:

'Oh, Hugh, I'm glad you're here. Could I have a look at your gun? I need the number for this permit.'

This was awkward; luckily, I had my back to him, holding the case. I said:

'Just a moment. Let me finish loading it.'

'No need for that. I only want the number.'

I pretended to fumble for a few minutes longer, afraid that he would come and look over my shoulder and see that the gun was already loaded. Luckily, he stayed where he was. I turned round, pretending to slip on the safety catch, and handed it to him. He said casually:

'You shouldn't load until you're ready to fire, you know.'

'I know. I'm ready to fire now.'

'You can't. Mr Thomas is doing his match out there.'

To conceal my embarrassment – I looked as if I had been caught in the act of breaking and entering – I started to tell him about the man at the cattle-market – Patricia's

187

burglar and Anne's 'nice man'. He listened carefully, then said:

'I don't know there's much we can do. But you might come into the station when you have a moment and look through our rogues' gallery.'

At that moment a man came out of the other room, and said: 'All right, I've finished now.' I was glad of the opportunity to go and shoot. After a few rounds, I realized why this sport takes such a hold on such different types of people. Why is it that holding a gun seems one of the natural situations of man's life, like eating or sex? It is as if there is a natural affinity between weapons and man's deepest nature. It came to me now, as I sighted the barrel, taking care to prevent it from wavering and to allow my finger to squeeze the trigger without an act of volition, that in such a moment the whole inner being concentrates, and illusions are thrown off as when a dog shakes itself. No poet or artist ever needed the inner grace of inspiration more completely than a good marksman. Then the explosion requires an inner hardening. Ten minutes of good shooting can produce a feeling of health as complete as a moorland walk in a high wind.

'You're improving,' Scottie Gibbs said. 'Keep improving and you'll be a first-class shot.'

I found the compliment meaningless; its truth was self-evident to me.

At half past nine, Ewen Waite, the mayor, turned up with a plump young man who was introduced as Nigel Lever. I had not seen the mayor before; he was a big man, but had a curiously sad face, with eyes that reminded me of a bloodhound's. I was struck by his good manners; he shook my hand as gravely as if I had been an alderman and asked me my opinion of the club and why I had decided to join. I told him I had been along when I was eight years old. He looked surprised, then said:

'Ah, during the war, of course. The rules are a bit tighter now.'

My first impression of Nigel Lever was a bad one; he had a pink, plump face and an old Etonian voice (the kind of voice that seems perfectly adapted to saying 'ode bo-ooy' in a drawling bleat), and his brown eyes struck me as having something wrong with them. They were not exactly shifty, but their glance seemed slightly askew. He turned out to be an excellent shot – better than anyone in the club except Bob Salomons and a youth called Ernie Timson – and when he had finished shooting he talked to me about big-game hunting in Africa. He had some kind of a job in Tanganyika, and often acted as white hunter to parties of American tourists.

As Gerald and I were cleaning our guns, I asked Gerald what he thought of Nigel Lever.

'I don't like him. There's something morbid about him.'

The adjective struck me as curious. I asked him to explain it.

'I mean that some people like shooting because it's a good sport, and others have a sort of morbid interest in guns. They're kind of childish. They'd really like to shoot people.'

Gerald had never struck me as very bright, but his penetration startled me.

Nigel Lever came in a moment later, slapped me on the shoulder and said:

'You boys coming next door for a drink?'

I explained that I had somewhere to go. He said, grinning: 'Girl?'

'Oh no. A friend – Monty Wolfe.'

189

'Monty! You don't say! That old sod's still in circulation, is he?'

And he immediately declared that he would change his mind about the pub, and come with me to see Monty.

'I don't want to butt in, you know, but I'd just like to say hello briefly. Where's he live? I'll give you a lift in my car.'

This was welcome; it was raining heavily. Gerald watched us go wistfully, making me feel guilty at deserting him again.

'What fun,' Nigel Lever said, as we drove through the rain. 'Coming across old Monty on my first day home.' He was treating me with less condescension now he thought of me as a friend of Monty.

'Is this your car?' I asked. It was a two-seater with a canvas hood.

'Yes. My father bought it for me. I always buy a car when I come home on leave, then sell it again when I leave. It's worth it to me. I get used to long distances in Africa, and like to pop around the countryside. Last time I was home I drove to Cornwall for a one-night party.'

Monty answered the door, and I thought he looked unwelcoming when he saw Nigel Lever. Nigel said quickly:

'I don't want to butt in. But I couldn't resist saying hello when Hugh here said he was on his way to see you.'

Monty invited us in. He said:

'I'm afraid I can only offer you beer. I finished the spirits last night.'

'That's OK. I've got some Scotch in the car. Lend me that umbrella.'

Monty cheered up immediately. Nigel returned with the bottle; he pulled out the cork and tossed it into the fire, saying:

'That's the way we do it in Tanganyika.'

190

I said I would prefer beer; they ignored me, and handed me a large whisky. The phone rang. Monty said:

'Damn. I suppose that's Jeremy again.'

He went out and talked for a few minutes, then returned:

'No, it was Betsy. She says she can't come tonight.'

'Did you say Jeremy *again*?'

He looked at me ironically.

'Oh yes, he rang me earlier this evening – on family business. But he mentioned he'd seen you . . . and Patricia.'

'Who's that?' Nigel asked.

'An attractive redhead – stimulating and easy to stimulate.'

'She wanted to talk to Jeremy,' I said, irritated to feel that I was showing my embarrassment.

'That's all right, I don't mind. I'm not selfish. Hope you're enjoying her as much as I did.'

'She's a pleasant girl,' I said, trying to be non-committal.

'I don't know how you feel,' Monty said to Nigel, 'but no matter how pretty a girl is, I prefer her to put up a certain resistance. You know, she ought to pretend she doesn't like it, even if . . . oh well, I hadn't better say any more in case I upset Hugh.'

'Don't bother about me,' I said. 'We're just friends.'

Monty and Nigel both laughed noisily, and Nigel slapped me on the back. I realized that they thought I was making the usual masculine disclaimers; I also realized that Monty was not irritated about Patricia. Nigel poured more drinks – this half-emptied the bottle – and Monty brought out a scratch meal of cheese and biscuits. Within ten minutes they were completely absorbed in exchanging stories about the army, big-game hunting and women. I made no contribution; besides, I was fascinated

191

to watch the picture they built up between them. Monty's family, from remarks dropped by Jeremy, were of about the same social status as my own. I knew nothing whatever about Nigel's background. But their talk, the drift of their stories, indicated that their common territory was the world of the aristocracy. There were a lot of officers' mess stories, all involving people with titles. Monty's voice seemed to become slightly more nasal, more drawlingly upper-class, as he told his stories, and he kept producing a kind of barking laugh that I had never noticed before. Both made a lot of jokes about the stupidity of the army, and Monty produced a remark that I had already heard twice:

'Then there was the story about the lieutenant who was so stupid that even his brother officers noticed it . . .'

This got them into stories about cavalry officers and bestiality, and from there into stories of seductions. Nigel looked around the room, and said:

'I should imagine this is a pretty ideal place for seduction.'

'Pretty good,' Monty said. 'I'd like to write a book one of these days about its techniques.' I could see that he was glad that the talk had turned to this subject; I had noticed signs of slight impatience when Nigel's stories of big-game hunting threatened to go on too long. Monty took a long drink of whisky, then said with an enthusiasm that was obviously real: 'You know, I can't understand why all men don't go in for seducing virgins. It's the best sport I know.'

'Let's face it, old boy, all men don't have your advantages . . .' From the way Nigel smiled I could see that he was adding mentally 'or mine'.

'Bosh,' Monty said. 'The real trouble is that they're all such damn wets. They're too shy. They don't know the secret – that almost nothing counts but self-confidence.

A man could look like the hunchback of Notre Dame and still be a Casanova if he had the right kind of belief in himself. I said the *right* kind. I don't mean a pimply, smirking swagger. I'll give you an example . . .'

He told a story in which he had managed to sleep with a girl immediately after her engagement-party to one of his brother officers. He then turned suddenly to me and said:

'How about you. Have you had Patricia yet?'

'No.'

'Why not?'

'The question hasn't arisen,' I said untruthfully, 'I hardly know her.'

'Balls. Do you mean to say you wouldn't have her like a shot if she got into your bed?'

'I suppose so . . .'

'Who is this girl?' Nigel said.

'I'll tell you about Patricia,' Monty said, 'since Hugh isn't as involved with her as I thought he was.' He grinned with cheerful malice. 'That girl has everything to make her the wife of a millionaire – except one thing.'

'What's that?'

'She likes sex too much. She's a desirable dish. If she acted demure, she could drive anybody crazy. But after about three kisses, she groans and starts to undo her suspenders.' He winked at me. 'You try it.'

'That's awful,' Nigel said. 'Terribly off-putting.'

'Ah, but what a subject,' Monty said, sighing. 'I could talk about it for ever.' Nigel looked dubious, but Monty kept on, perhaps to get his own back for all the African stories. 'The world's full of lovely women – millions of 'em. And for some reason, they're one of the few delights that never pall. Of all other things you can get tired – books, plays, even shooting. But every woman is a new mystery. And that's the astounding thing. How does it work? You look at a pretty woman, and feel an insatiable curiosity to know what she'll be like in bed. And yet close your eyes and use a little imagination, and you know exactly what she'll be like in bed. I've often noticed that if I wake up a little drunk, and find myself in bed with a girl, I can make love to her without having the slightest idea who she is – whether I've slept with her a hundred times, or just got into bed for the first time.'

'So it's an illusion?' I said, fascinated by all this.

'No, and that's the odd thing. Because every time it happens, you feel you've got closer to the mystery.'

I noticed on Monty's face an expression that reminded me of Jeremy – a kind of excitement. He said:

'I used to have a Sunday-school teacher who was always talking about some female saint – I think it was St Theresa – and she said this saint wanted to talk about nothing but God. Nothing else gave her any pleasure. But I tell you, *I* think no one has ever done justice to sex . . . no one but Casanova, anyway, and he's not all that good. I could talk about it from now until this time next year. The tremendous fascination of women. You know Sherlock Holmes is supposed to have written a monograph on a hundred different kinds of tobacco ash? Well I could write a monograph on the hundred different kinds of women . . .'

'Why don't you?' I said. 'You'd make a lot of money.'

'I shall, one day. But we're not allowed to write frankly enough.'

'That's modern prudishness,' Nigel said. 'Shakespeare said exactly what he wanted to.'

'No he didn't. What's more, he couldn't in a play. But even if he'd written novels, he couldn't have told the whole truth. Anybody can write about a young couple being attracted to one another, the blushes and sighs and the rest of it. It's all right up to the first kiss – we've got plenty of literature that goes that far. But no one ever writes about the next stage. The next thing that happens is that Romeo and Juliet are in bed together. But there can be about a hundred stages between the first kiss and sleeping together – particularly if the girl is frightened. And all the paradoxes of the female mind! It's all right for the man to slip his hand into the top of her skirt as he kisses her and to caress her behind, but she'd be horrified if he tried to get his hand up from the bottom of her skirt.'

Monty poured himself another drink, and said:

'I'd better get plastered or I'll go out and rape somebody tonight.'

At this point, Nigel took up the theme:

'You can't wonder that people talk about the sex war. It *is* a war, isn't it? Women are like female spiders and scorpions who eat their husbands. They'd all like to destroy the man they've been to bed with.'

Monty said, laughing: 'I can see you've been bitten.'

'Not exactly, although I can understand why men get so aggressive about women. For example, these snipers. They say that the number is increasing all the time in America. I expect it'd increase over here if everybody could buy a gun.'

I asked him to explain about snipers, and I noticed that he talked with relish – the same relish that Monty had shown when talking about the mechanics of seduction. He told us about a young man in Johannesburg who had felt a compulsion to shoot at pretty girls when he saw them out walking with their lovers. He had killed six girls and wounded several more when he was caught. He also talked about *piqueurs* – men who would drive a sharp knife or a needle through a woman's clothes in a crowd, then hurry away.

'But can you wonder?' Nigel said. 'It couldn't happen

195

in the East, because women are looked on as cattle. They're expected to give a man pleasure when he asks for it – that's their main function. In the West we treat them as equals. You talk about seduction, but if you lived in India you wouldn't have to seduce – you'd have all the women you wanted for the asking. As soon as we give a woman the right to refuse a man pleasure, we place her in the position of an enemy. The healthy males resent it, and they turn into sadists to get their own back. And the result is a rise in sex crime and sadism.'

Monty asked, grinning oddly:

'What would you do then? Pass a law that all women should be whipped once a week until they've learned their place?'

Nigel saw he was being baited, but took it easily.

'Why not? Wouldn't you enjoy beating a girl once a week? I know I would.'

'Why?' Monty said.

'Oh come, don't be a hypocrite. Do you mean to tell me that if a pretty girl came into this room, and said: Beat me, you'd refuse?'

'Perhaps not,' Monty said. He glanced at me as he said it, and I caught the expression of irony.

'Of course you wouldn't,' Nigel said. 'Nobody would.'

We had been talking in the dark for a while, with the fire sinking low, and the whisky bottle almost empty. A light came on in the house next door, throwing the shadow of our window-frame on the opposite wall. Monty jumped up and looked out of the window. He said:

'Ah, this is what I've been waiting for.'

We also stood up and looked. A woman was moving around in the room next door. After a moment, the light went out. Monty said: 'Quick, upstairs.'

We followed him upstairs in the dark.

'She's my private strip-tease show,' Monty said. 'She always undresses with open curtains.'

A bedroom light had now come on, and we watched by the window in the icy cold. I had banged my shin on the way into the room, and was standing on one leg and nursing it. The woman next door proceeded to get undressed in full view of the window. Nigel said suddenly:

'God, I wish I'd got my pistol here.'

We ignored him. The woman – who looked in her middle thirties – finished undressing, pulled on a nightgown, then came and closed the curtains. Monty said, sighing:

'Show's over.'

He switched on the bedroom light. I asked:

'Won't she guess we've been watching her if she sees the light?'

'It doesn't matter. She knows damn well I always watch her.'

We went downstairs again. I was glad to be back in a warm room; we had been upstairs for about a quarter of an hour, and the cold had gone to my bones. Nigel asked:

'Why don't you get to know her? She probably wants to go to bed.'

'Why should I?' Monty said. 'If I go to bed with her, I get to know her, and I wouldn't enjoy watching her get undressed. I get more fun this way.'

His room was getting cold, and I knew I should go; but we sat there because it is difficult to go without any particular reason for leaving. I asked Nigel:

'Why did you say you wanted your gun?'

He went red, and said:

'No reason in particular. She just made a good target.'

Again I caught Monty's ironic look.

Finally, Nigel drove me home. He asked me questions

about my interest in mathematics, as if to make up for excluding me from the conversation for most of the evening. I also suspected that he wanted to make me feel that he had normal, human interests as well as a secret longing to shoot girls.

I thought about Patricia before I fell asleep, but the thought no longer brought pleasant anticipation. I felt as if I was sliding down a hillside towards a lake of dirty evil-smelling water.

6

The following morning – a Saturday – I met Patricia in town, and we went to the police-station to look at photographs. Scottie Gibbs was not there when we arrived; I told my story to the sergeant in charge, and he produced two leather-bound volumes. Patricia and I sat on a bench and looked through them. Every 'offender' was shown in full-face and profile. No details or names were given; each picture had a number underneath.

We had looked through the first volume – and both of us had seen several men we thought we recognized, but not the one we were looking for – when Scottie came in. The sergeant said:

'This young man says he knows you.' His tone suggested that he thought this unlikely. But Gibbs said affably:

'Hello, Hugh. This is the young lady, is it? Come into my office.'

He looked through papers while we turned over the pages of the second volume. Patricia and I saw the picture simultaneously, and both exclaimed. We showed it to Scottie Gibbs. He said into the talking-box: 'Bring in the file of eighty-three.' While we waited, I stared at the picture. The youth looked about nineteen. He had a strong, square-looking face, with overhanging brows and dark hair. But he was looking at the camera blankly, emptily – not glaring defiance, like some of the other photographs. His eyes had an abstracted look.

The sergeant brought in a folder and went out again.

Gibbs looked through it for a few minutes, ignoring us. Then he said to Patricia:

'It looks as if you could be right. He's done a stretch in a reform school for breaking into a warehouse.'

'But what about the sex crime business?' I asked.

'You're sure this is the man?'

'Yes.'

'How long ago was it you saw him?'

'Nearly two years, I know . . .'

'And he was walking away from you, with his back to you?'

'Yes. But I'd seen him several times in the park. I already knew him by sight.'

'Hmm. That's interesting.'

He looked through the file again, then said, almost to himself:

'There's a psychiatrist's report. Says he's co-operative and easily influenced, but liable to fits of rage. No mention of any sexual abnormality . . .'

I began to feel defensive, as if he was accusing me of trying to mislead him.

'But what about those cases two years ago? There was a piece in the newspaper warning parents about it.'

'But we caught a man, you know.'

'Did you?'

'He was an idiot. He's in the asylum now.'

'Perhaps I was mistaken,' I said.

'How do you mean, mistaken?' He jumped on this immediately.

'Perhaps he really *wanted* to show my sister where she could find butterflies.'

'Perhaps. Anyway, it's worth knowing.' He wrote something on a sheet of paper, and inserted it into the file.

Patricia and I left. We went into the café at the bus

200

station and had tea. I wanted to tell her about the previous evening, which was in the forefront of my mind, but I felt that she would fail to understand. Besides, I didn't want to remind her of Monty, in case she thought of the previous Saturday and regretted what had happened since.

Looking through the photographs had depressed me. None of the faces had looked particularly criminal, but all looked as if they had been reduced to objects by the camera. Patricia seemed cheerful; she talked about a boy she had once known – and whose photograph she had seen at the police-station – who hated his parents. I was surprised that she could talk as if these faces in the police-album were somehow of the natural order of things. For me, they were a world of stupidity, boredom, emptiness, a kind of denial of all culture. As I sat listening to her, several youths came into the café and stood at the counter. As they stood waiting for tea, they stared at a cigarette advertisement behind the counter. I had stared at it too. It showed a very pretty girl lying on a bed in her bra and panties, smoking a cigarette and talking into a telephone – probably to her lover. I had stared at it because the picture seemed to catch a whole way of life, as if it was an illustration to a novel: the warm and intimate look of the room, the suggestion of money – as if the man on the other end of the line was wearing a top hat and carrying a gold cane – and then all the life of sex. It was what I had sensed the other day in the office – the invisible vortex – but here it was unveiled, obvious. And it was behind the counter in a bus-station café, where men would stare at it on their way to work, or waiting for a bus to take them home in the evening. It was like advertising an expensive restaurant in a poor-house. I had no doubt of the feelings of the youths who were looking at it. There would be no nostalgia, no dreamy imagining: only a hard desire to force her backward and possess her – one after the other if necessary. It struck me that keeping a picture like this in a station café was like keeping a burning torch in a powder magazine.

But Patricia talked on happily; it was strange to me that her world seemed to contain no conflict and no ambiguity.

She told me that she wanted to wash her hair during the afternoon, and had to go home soon. This solved a problem that had been bothering me – where we could go on a rainy winter afternoon.

I took her home, intending to leave her at her gate. But as we turned into her street, she said: 'Hello, the car's gone. That means daddy's out.'

We stopped at her gate, and she said:

'Come and meet my mother. She knows all about you.'

I protested, but she insisted. When there was no reply to her ring at the front-door bell, she said: 'They can't both be out . . . it's very odd.' We went round through the back gate. Stuck on the back door with a pin was a note: 'Call me at Aunty Meg's. Mummy.' 'They *are* out,' Patricia said.

'Come on in.' I was glad that I had resisted the impulse to leave her at the front gate.

The lunch table was still set; the plates had not even been taken into the kitchen. Patricia told me to wait in the front room and light the fire. I sat there, on the settee on which I had embraced her a few nights before, and listened to her voice coming faintly through the closed door. It was a short conversation. Then she came in and said:

'Oh lord. It's mad. My Uncle James has committed suicide.'

'How?'

'I don't know. Mummy couldn't tell me anything over

the phone. She didn't even say he'd killed himself, but it was obviously what she meant.'

'Why should he do that?'

'Oh, I don't know. Debts, I suppose. He's always in debt.'

'Tell me about it.'

'I think I'd better clean up first. Come and help me wash up.'

We cleared the table and re-set it for tea, and washed up the dishes. I asked her if she had mentioned my presence to her mother.

'Of course not. I didn't think.'

'When will they be back?'

'I don't know. She says she'll ring me.'

'What shall I do?'

'You can help me wash my hair.'

This was unexpectedly pleasant; I felt grateful to the deceased Uncle James. As we washed up she told me something about him. He was not Aunt Meg's husband, but her brother-in-law; but since her husband was dead, he lived in her house. I gathered that Uncle James was a black sheep; he had even made advances to Patricia as they drove back from the funeral of Aunt Meg's husband. He had been bankrupt twice; he sometimes worked as a commercial traveller; and he had a taste for tall women.

'But why should he kill himself?' I asked. 'Was he ill?'

'Not as far as I know.' She told me several stories about Uncle James, none of which had any relevance to the question of the suicide, but that made it clear to me that he was quite capable of enjoying life.

While she washed her hair, she told me to go and read. I sat in front of the fire and thought about Uncle James and about suicide in general. It had never been a subject that had interested me, and I had never heard of anyone I knew committing suicide. It seemed extraordinary to me that a man should decide that life is not worth living because he had a few debts. Finally, having nothing else to do, I looked through the bookshelves. They were all book-club editions, and although they looked very impressive I could not understand the principle of selection that had brought them together. I picked out a biography of Friedrich Engels – it seemed about the least boring book there – and glanced through it. A photograph of Karl Marx's daughter Eleanor attracted me; the caption mentioned that she had committed suicide. I was struck by the coincidence, and read the chapter dealing with this. I was still reading it when Patricia came in, rubbing her hair. She lay down on the rug, her head on a leather foot-rest and her hair close to the fire, and continued to dry it. She said: 'Read to me,' so I read her the two pages dealing with Edward Aveling's desertion of Eleanor Marx, and how he had written the prescription for the poison that killed her. Patricia said: 'Can you believe that a man could be such a swine?'

'Can you believe that a woman could be such a fool?' I said.

'Oh, I can understand her. She only wanted to be happy.'

Now I was no longer reading, I could watch Patricia stretched out on the rug, her stockinged feet on the settee between my knees. Without thinking about it, I leaned forward over her and kissed her. She said: 'Careful, you'll make me burn myself,' but after a moment removed the foot-rest from under her head, changed her position on the rug and allowed me to lie beside her. She had never looked so attractive, with her hair uncombed and spread around her, and small splashes of dried mud on her stockings from the rain and passing traffic. She also had no make-up on, and her uncoloured lips somehow seemed more sensual and soft. My excitement kept pace with hers this time. When she drew up her knees, her wide skirt dropped round her waist. I was feverish with desire, but nervous in case anyone interrupted us or the phone rang. Her eyes were closed, but her lips kept moving; she took my hand, which lay on her waist, and guided it to her thigh. When I said: 'Supposing someone comes,' she said: 'Never mind. It doesn't matter,' without opening her eyes. In spite of my desire, or perhaps because of it, I was clumsy; I was fully clothed, even to my jacket and shoes, and felt absurd; but when I tried to sit up to take off my jacket, she said: 'Don't stop,' and pressed against me. She removed none of her clothes; we went through the act of love-making as we were, with fire burning the right side of my face, and the foot-rest giving off a smell of hot leather. She seemed to become unconscious of everything but pleasure, and moaned as if I was hurting her. Even when most carried away with the warmth of her body, a part of myself was congratulating me for acquitting myself so well.

We seemed to reach a climax together. Then we lay side by side again; her eyes were still closed; she held my hand, and her face looked tired and ecstatic. I understood what Monty meant. She enjoyed sex in a way that overawed me. She allowed herself to plunge into it as a boat might be swept into the cave of some underground river. I felt that I had been de-personalized; it could be me or any other man.

The phone rang. She said: 'Damn', and stood up, smoothing down her dress as unconcernedly as if she had just been drinking tea with the vicar's wife. I took the opportunity of her absence to stand up and make myself decent. She came back a moment later, and said:

'How horrible. He cut his throat.'

She sat beside me on the settee and took my hand. Her mother had been able to tell her a few more details of the suicide; she seemed to have forgotten what had been happening a few minutes before, although she held my hand as though we were engaged. I was amazed by this capacity to change her mood. She said suddenly:

'I told mummy you were here. She said to make you a cup of tea.'

'When will they be back?'

'Not for hours yet.' She looked at me and smiled, and for the first time acknowledged what had happened between us. I pulled her down beside me; I could not believe it had really happened, and wanted to get accustomed to it by repetition. She said: 'No, please don't – not after the news about poor Uncle James.' But a few minutes later she was oblivious of it again, her eyes closed, her lips parted, in the stream of her own sensations. I still found it unbelievable that a girl could experience the same desires as a man; I had always suspected that girls allow themselves to be possessed only in order not to disappoint the man. Much later in the evening, I came to realize that there are times when a man has to go through the motions of love-making so as not to disappoint his partner.

It all felt strangely domestic. We made tea, and toasted crumpets at the fire in the other room. She sat at my feet and held the toasting-fork against the red coals. When she had finished toasting one of the crumpets she turned to me and said suddenly:

'Do you think I'm wicked?'

I felt that this was coquetry; even so, the question startled me.

'Why should I?'

She looked away, averting her face, then said:

'You know Monty made love to me.'

I wanted to laugh. The thought had never been far

from my mind for the past week, and now she was telling me as if she expected me to be surprised.

'I know,' I said.

'Don't you mind?'

'Not now,' I said truthfully. I had minded before, mainly because I often stared with longing at the shape of her breasts and the other secrets concealed by her dress, and envied Monty his knowledge of them. Now I knew them too, and I even felt friendly towards Monty.

'I didn't care about Monty.' I wanted to say: 'Then why did you go to bed with him?' but didn't. Perhaps she read my thoughts, for she said: 'He was like that man you've just been reading about – who made Eleanor Marx commit suicide. He didn't care about anyone but himself.'

We ate at the table, sitting on opposite sides; she poured the tea and handed it to me. She said:

'Don't you think it would be nice to be married?'

I nodded and said yes, feeling that this was what she wanted.

'I'd like to be married,' she said. I only nodded, my mouth full of crumpet.

Later, we went up to her bedroom; she wanted to show me her Swiss dolls. The inevitable happened; this time we undressed and climbed into bed. It was dangerous; her parents might return at any moment, and we would have no warning, as her room was at the back of the house and we could not hear the car. But I could see that it was important to her. And, after all, she risked more than I did; I could only be thrown out of the house; she had to live with her parents. But it was exciting, being completely naked. When it was over, she placed her lips close to my ear and said:

'That's the first time it ever happened in this bed.'

I said 'Good'.

'Why don't we get married? Then we could sleep together every night.'

I was taken aback, and said:

'Don't you think we're a bit young?'

'I know. I know it's impossible. Still, it's nice to think about it.'

I felt that I at last knew her well enough to ask her that question that had been in my mind for the past week.

'Why do you want to get married to me? Wouldn't it be more exciting with Monty?'

She misunderstood my question.

'Why? He's not all that exciting – even if he likes to boast that he is.'

'But after all – I'm only seventeen.' It was hard to say, but I got it out. 'Isn't that a bit of a . . . come-down?'

'Of course not. Age doesn't make any difference. Besides, Monty'd be a rotten husband. He'd always be off with other women. I don't think you would.'

This was not flattering, but I no longer cared. The truth was that, in the complete and sudden satisfaction of all my appetites, I suspected that I might be tired of her. This was not because I wanted to desert her; on the contrary, the idea would have made me feel like a murderer. But I suspected that when I came to examine my emotions my interest in her would have evaporated. I tried to make up for this by an excessive tenderness.

A false alarm scared us into dressing hastily, and we hurried down. But there was no one in the house; it had been a noise from next door. We both sighed with relief, and she pulled on her underwear, which she had been carrying screwed up in her hand. The next hour seemed an anti-climax; we sat and talked, and then listened to the radio. Finally, at half past nine, I suggested that perhaps I should not be there when her parents arrived, and was surprised at the readiness with which she agreed.

208

As I walked home, I wondered if Patricia felt as I did – drained of emotion, and slightly disappointed. It was not that I was disappointed with my first experience of sex; on the contrary, in certain ways it had exceeded my expectations. But it seemed to have left nothing behind. I felt that we were two hypnotized strangers who had just been dehypnotized and realized that they had nothing in common.

The following morning, this indifference had gone. All the events of yesterday left an after-taste of sweetness. Although I had gone over them in my mind half a dozen times, they still seemed incredible. Once in the night I woke up, dreaming of Patricia, but of Patricia as I had known her a week ago, a pretty and unattainable Patricia; it was hard to realize that this had changed. The old Patricia co-existed in my mind with the new one, as if they were two different girls. Occasionally they merged for a moment, and I felt delight and a longing to see her again immediately.

I rang her directly after breakfast. There was no reply. I tried half a dozen times over the next few hours, but still without result. I guessed that her family was probably at the home of her aunt. I hoped that she might ring me; but by eight o'clock in the evening this hope had vanished, and I was annoyed with myself for wasting a day thinking about her and waiting for the phone to ring. Finally at ten o'clock I rang again, and her mother answered. Patricia had just gone to bed. Her mother was friendly enough, and said that she would like to meet me because Patricia had talked about me. I felt guilty as I listened to her, remembering what had taken place in her house, and wondering if she could not guess that something of the sort might have happened. It seemed to me that anyone had only to look at Patricia, with her fully developed figure, to guess her sexual responsiveness. (I learned later that neither her mother nor her father suspected anything of the sort.)

The next morning, as I left for the office, a letter arrived for me. I read it on the bus. It was from Patricia, written in a neat, small hand with sky-blue ink. In it she said she could understand my doubts about her, since I knew about Monty. Perhaps I felt that she had given herself too quickly? But if I could not understand that I was unlike Monty in every way, then I had a low opinion of myself. I found it hard to believe that Patricia had written the letter. Somehow it was too intimate and not intimate enough. She talked about herself with a frankness that startled me, admitting that there had been a lover before Monty, and remarking that Monty had once told her she was a nymphomaniac. (I had to look that up when I got to the office.) But she was sure that he could never understand her. She also suspected that I could not understand how a woman feels; my comments about Eleanor Marx showed that I underestimated a woman's need for security.

All this seemed to be leading logically to the assertion that she would like to entrust her future security to me; but if this is what she meant she swerved aside from it, and ended by saying only that she thought we could mean a great deal to one another. She signed the letter: 'love from Patricia' in her neat, very legible hand, and followed her signature with half a dozen demure little x's, which seemed absurd when I remembered her actual kisses.

This letter, which I read half a dozen times, at last allowed me some detachment from my emotions. The conflict of desire and satiation, longing and disillusion, now vanished; it seemed to me that I had satisfied my curiosity about Patricia and no longer wanted her. I had never been emotionally involved with her, only dazzled. I wondered whether men marry because women are sensible enough to refuse to satisfy their curiosity, and whether the whole idea of love is an illusion. At the same time, I was grateful to Patricia for giving me back something that had been lost for a long time – my intellectual enthusiasm. My mind was in a strangely pure and receptive state; it was as if this emotional shower had settled all the dust, and left me feeling like a spring morning. I could think about mathematics with all the old devotion, the certainty that it was man's road to the godlike. It was a pity that I no longer cared in the least about Patricia; but we have to take our revelations where we can get them. I suppose it was a silly and smug state of mind in some ways, but I can still remember its exhilaration. I can remember sitting in the office and looking at Marion and feeling free of all desire or curiosity. There was a kind of vengeful pleasure in this, because she knew she was attractive, and there was a slight coquettishness in her manner; it was pleasant to feel that I was now beyond its influence.

But at lunch-time, as usual, I went to meet Patricia out of work, and was dazzled when I saw her, and felt my possessiveness returning. She looked happy and vital, and I felt drab beside her. And I found myself wondering how she could care about me, and wanting her – irrationally – to care.

We had lunch in a café, and she told me that Monty had rung her at work that morning.

'What did he want?'

'He asked me to go out with him.'

'What did you say?'

'That I couldn't – that I was seeing you.'

'And what did he say to that?'

'To ring him up if I changed my mind.'

I was astonished at Monty's audacity; and he pretended he was a friend!

Patricia wanted to do some shopping, and I went with her. She asked me if I'd received her letter; I said yes; then we both felt embarrassed. Luckily, we bumped into Gerald Sutton at this point, and the subject was dropped.

Gerald looked at Patricia with open admiration. I understood why. As I looked at her, I was now sure I was in love with her. I listened to her voice, watched the way she smiled, and told myself that these were the things that made her unique. I introduced her to Gerald and told her that he was a member of the pistol-club.

'Are you interested in guns?' he asked her.

'I don't know. I've never had much to do with them.'

'Ah, you ought to try shooting. You'd enjoy it.'

'She might,' I said, 'but she's not allowed in the club, so . . .'

'She is! Why shouldn't she be allowed in?'

'As a guest?'

'Yes. Provided you notify the secretary two days before, and don't do it more than once a month.'

'Would you like to go?' I asked Patricia.

'I don't think so. I wouldn't like the noise. I hate bangs.'

Gerald immediately assured her that she would find it easy to get used to the noise. He said to me:

'Persuade her to come along. We need something pleasant to look at in the club.'

Gerald was no manufacturer of compliments, and I could see that this one was sincere. Besides, I was flattered by his obvious interest in Patricia. So as we walked back to work I was persuasive, and she finally agreed to come to the club on Wednesday.

Monday was overtime night; at seven o'clock I left the office and went to the Open Air Club for tea. I wanted to kill time until about nine o'clock, and then walk past the Palais. I felt that it was time to find out whether the 'leather-jacket' crowd were always to be found there when there was a dance. I sat in a quiet corner of the café, with a bi-lingual edition of Riemann open in front of me; but it was impossible to concentrate. I now began to wish that I had taken Monty into my confidence about my plan; I needed someone to talk to; the alternative was to write it down in a diary. I had occasionally wondered why murderers sometimes keep incriminating diaries that can be used against them by the police; now I understood.

In the past week, I had abandoned the idea of the shooting a dozen times, and then taken it up again. Why? I have tried to define my reasons many times since then; but I always know that I have left something out. I know that it was something to do with Patricia and with Monty; but it was also something to do with Uncle Nick and Garvin's hollow earth theory. If what I have written so far has not explained it, then I doubt whether I shall ever explain it fully. If I look inside myself, I can see the reasons clearly enough. Violence, the fear of violence, the carcasses in the butcher's shop, the Eagle in the burning church, the possibility that the world is like a malevolent giant swatting flies – this was one half of the story. And on the other side: mathematics – which is still for me one of the most beautiful words in the language. Man is like an animal trapped in the bottom of a pit, waiting for the hunters; yet he is not trapped in the same way as animals; his intellect has provided him with a ladder. As a child I had a book with a coloured picture of cave-men, crouching behind a rock waiting to attack a sabre-toothed tiger; on the other side of the page was a picture of a poet – obviously based on Shelley – sitting at his writing-desk and staring in front of him with a rapt expression. And underneath was a caption that said: 'The greatest power on this earth is not electricity or dynamite or even the earthquake – it is the spirit of man.' I wanted to believe this. I wanted to believe that I was not at the mercy of stupidity, like Archimedes. How was this possible when one blow from a crowd of mindless thugs could extinguish my 'spirit'?

As I sat there, planning my counter-attack on stupidity and brutality, I no longer felt helpless. I felt like the judge, the avenger. And this enabled me to feel, for the first time in my life, a sense of inner unity, a complete certainty of power and development.

On the other hand, there was no real danger to me in the enterprise. Nature provides most animals with weapons of defence; the snake, the scorpion, the bee, have their sting. A few hundred years ago, most men also carried a sting in a scabbard. I also had my sting, and I had as much right to use it in my defence as a bee or a snake.

The idea that I might be punished did not strike me as probable. Everything would be in my favour. No one could call me a 'young thug'; I was known to be a peaceable and studious young man, and I had every right to be carrying a pistol. It should not, of course, be loaded; I would no doubt be expelled from the club for this breach of the rules . . .

But then, the whole plan might collapse. It was unlikely that the Teddy-boys would be standing outside the dance hall on a winter evening. This was what I wanted to find out.

I had been sitting there for about ten minutes, pretending to read but thinking about the Palais de Danse, when someone sat down at my table; it was a boy I had known at school, and he had come in to play a table-tennis match. After five minutes of his conversation I made an excuse and left.

Outside, I wondered what to do for the next hour. If I went to the pistol-club, it would mean going home to collect my gun; but the idea of more shooting bored me. I intended to call in at the club before I went home, to ask permission to bring Patricia on Wednesday, but I would not stay.

I walked down to the Palais de Danse. It looked deserted. But then, it was only half past seven. The dance was advertised to start at eight-thirty. I decided to call on Monty. He came to the door in his shirt-sleeves, a pipe in his mouth. I said:

'I wondered if you felt like coming out for a drink?'

'Yes, I suppose so. Come on in for a moment.'

I stood in the kitchen while he shaved. He said:

'What did you think of old Nigel?'

'A nice type,' I said non-committally.

'Do you think so?'

It was evident that he did not. I asked why.

'I think he's a criminal type without the courage to be a criminal.'

I told him what Gerald Sutton had said about people who take up shooting for 'morbid' reasons.

'Your friend's right. Nigel won't be satisfied until he's shot a man – or better still, a girl.'

'But why?'

'How do I know? I suspect he's impotent. Perhaps he's afraid of women.'

As we were leaving the house he looked at me in a sly way, and asked:

'How are you getting on with Patricia?'

'Very well.'

'Are you still just friends?'

I wondered if Patricia had said something to him over the phone, then thought it unlikely.

'Of course,' I said.

He grinned, and I was aware of the malice.

'It's hard lines not having a room of your own, isn't it?'

215

We went into the pub where Monty had got into the quarrel with the Teddy-boys. It was not crowded. I ordered the drinks, and we sat in a corner. Two men came in and stood at the bar; I thought I recognized one of them. Then it came to me; I had seen his face in the book of photographs at the police-station. When I told Monty about this, he said:

'That's Joe Murphy. He does a bit of sharp business at the racecourse.'

'Why should the police have his photograph?'

'Probably for receiving stolen goods. I don't know whether he has any other side lines.'

'Do many crooks come in here?'

'Not many. Do you want to see a place that's full of 'em?'

'Yes,' I said dubiously.

'Come on then.'

We finished our beers and went out. We walked through the centre of town, and passed close to the Palais. I saw, with a tightening around the heart, that half a dozen youths were standing outside. To divert Monty, who was about to turn into a side street, I said:

'I think that's the gang who beat up that boy last week.'

'Where?' He was interested immediately. I pointed them out, adding: 'I'm not sure though.'

'Let's take a look.'

I realized that I felt more confident walking with Monty. As we came closer, I realized that I had never seen any of them before. We stopped in front of the dance hall and pretended to be looking inside. Out of the corner of my eye I saw that the youths had stopped talking and were watching us. Sounds of music came from inside. Then a man and a girl walked past us to the ticket office. The youths whistled and made comments; one of them called: 'Cor, I bet she sucks you dry.' The man, who was well dressed, pretended not to hear, but he looked embarrassed. The girl said something irritable to him, but she did not look round. The commissionaire came from inside the box-office, and the man said something to him. He came out of the door, and said:

'What do you lot want? Clear off.'

'Want to make something of it?' one of the youths said.

'You've got no right to stand there. Get outside.'

'Want to come and throw us out?'

Monty said to me: 'Come on.' We walked past the group, and as we did so one of them spat; it hit the pavement in front of us. Monty stopped, and turned; I saw his fists clenched. For a moment, I cursed myself for not having my pistol. I was certain this meant a fight. But the youth who had spat was looking in the opposite direction with a preoccupied expression; all the others were still looking at the commissionaire. Then Monty shrugged and walked on. I followed him with relief. When we were a few feet away, he said:

'What's the use? We need a couple more of us. But I'd like to get those yobbos.'

We turned down a side street and cut across the bus station. I said:

'But we wouldn't have stood a chance.'

'Oh, I don't know. I had this.' From his pocket he took a small jack-knife. 'It's surprising how much damage you can do. And they're all cowards. It's a pity you didn't have your gun.'

I murmured something non-committal, and wondered again whether I should tell him. But before I could decide, we stopped outside a café. I had expected that we were going to a pub; I said: 'What's this place?'

'You'll see.'

We went inside. It looked very much like the place

where I bought the office tea, except that it was darker and slightly larger. It was crowded. Monty said: 'Hello Charles.' I thought I recognized the man he spoke to – a short, yellow-faced little man with stained teeth.

We asked for sausage sandwiches and tea. The man who took the order had a big stomach, fat hairy arms, and a hairy chest that showed through an open shirt. I thought he looked unfriendly.

I glanced round the room as we went towards a table, and came close to spilling my tea. Sitting in the corner was the youth I had seen at the cattle-market – Patricia's burglar and my 'sex maniac'. He was reading a newspaper. I sat beside Monty at the same table as his friend. Monty was introducing me to the man, but I paid little attention to what he said. From where I was sitting I could see the 'burglar', half concealed by his newspaper. Then, as I watched him out of the corner of my eye, he folded the paper, stood up and went out. I asked Monty:

'Do you know that man?'

'I've seen him somewhere. Why?'

The little man said: 'Do *you* know him?'

'I've seen him around. I used to know him as a child.'

Now I looked at him closer, I felt sure that I had seen him before. Monty had introduced him as Charles Hassett; the name meant nothing to me. Monty now said:

'Hugh is a mathematical genius, Charles.'

'Are you?' the little man said.

'I must be if Monty says so.'

'Here's a little problem for you then. All right? You've got a sheet of paper – any sheet of paper – it can be as big as you like – hundred miles square if you like, OK? Now then, you fold it in half – right? Then you fold it in quarters. Go on doing that fifty times. How thick is it by the time you've finished?'

'That's a stinker,' Monty said.

218

'How thick is the paper?' I asked.

'Oh, I dunno. A thousandth of an inch if you like.'

Monty said: 'It'd be more than a mile thick, wouldn't it?'

I had worked it out by this time – it is elementary enough – and said: 'It would be about seventeen million miles thick.'

Monty said: 'Are you serious?' and the little man said: – 'He's right, y'know.' He asked me: 'How'd you do it?' I explained simply; if the paper is a thousandth of an inch thick, then it will have to be folded ten times to make it about an inch thick; fifty times will bring it up to a billion inches; divide by sixty thousand to get it into miles, and the answer is approximately seventeen million.

I was amused that they were so easily impressed. The little man tried me with a few more problems of the same type – none of them presented any difficulties, and in one case I gave the answer in five seconds. (He timed me with my watch.)

'You orter be on the stage,' the little man said. 'I used to know a bloke who made his living like that, but he wasn't half as fast as you.'

'Charles used to be on the stage,' Monty said.

'Hypnotist,' the little man said modestly.

Immediately it came back to me; he was 'the Great Kaspar'. But he now looked even more tired, small and withered.

'I knew I'd seen you,' I said. 'Don't you remember the time you tried to hypnotize me at the Palace?'

I described the incident to him, but he obviously had no memory of it. He said sadly:

'I expect I wasn't in very good condition that night.'

Monty said: 'Cheer up, Charles. Come and have a drink.'

'Don't mind if I do.'

We went to the nearest pub, and under the stimulus of a large whisky 'Kaspar' cheered up and became lively and talkative. He acknowledged candidly that he had ceased to work in the theatre because he was never sober. He now lived off occasional contributions from some benevolent society for theatre people, and 'small jobs'. He was not explicit about the nature of the latter, and I didn't press him; the café where we had found him supplied some clue.

Monty and I drank beer. I had not enough money to buy rounds of whisky, and I wanted to conserve the little I had for taking Patricia out. Although I was interested to meet Kaspar again I observed the rate of his whisky consumption with dismay, and wondered how soon I could leave. But he became very happy and confidential as he drank, and there seemed no prospect of a quick escape. At one point, Monty asked him:

'How could you hypnotize people when you're drunk? Surely you need all your will-power to do it?'

'No. That's a fallacy. People hypnotize themselves if they're that type. All you have to do is let 'em. Of course, a lot of people just aren't the type, and it'd take days to hypnotize them. But I reckon that about fifty per cent of people can be hypnotized.'

Monty asked – characteristically – if a virtuous girl could be hypnotized into allowing sexual intercourse. I expected Kaspar to say no, having read somewhere that no one can be hypnotized into committing an act that is contrary to their ideals. But he said:

'Of course, if she's suggestible enough.'

'You mean she'd just take off her pants and lie down?'

'Yes.'

'Is there any proof of this?' I asked.

Kaspar grinned, showing teeth that should have been extracted wholesale.

'I've seen plenty of evidence. But you won't find it in print.'

'You mean that a person could be made to commit a crime under hypnosis?'

'Certainly. And a lot of people have.'

As he talked, I suddenly became aware of someone behind me; I looked up, and was startled to find a greenish, diseased-looking face above my head. The man said:

'Could I have a word with you, Charles?'

Kaspar said: 'Headache again?'

'Something like that.'

Kaspar went out. I looked at the man as they went out, and found him unaccountably repulsive. Everything about him suggested something sub-human, a reptile or a spider. He even seemed to move as a snake moves, with a suggestion of economy of energy. He had a broad face that tapered to a kind of blunt point, so that it might have been carved from some yellowish vegetable – a marrow, perhaps. His voice had also struck me as oddly non-human; it was soft and throaty, but it might have been produced by some mechanical means. For the first time, I suddenly felt as if I was in contact with something criminal.

'Do you know him?' I asked Monty.

'Only by sight. He's a pimp.'

We both went out to find the gents; this was in a small backyard. Along the corridor we passed a door that stood slightly ajar; I glanced in and saw Kaspar, who was looking down at a woman sitting in a chair. The man with the green face was also there, and he pushed the door to as he saw us.

When we returned down the corridor, a few minutes later, the door opened again, and Kaspar came out, followed by the man, who said 'Thank you, Charles'. Kaspar said: 'That's all right, Dime.'

We went back into the bar. Kaspar said:

'His girl-friend's not too well. She gets nervous and depressed. But she's a good subject.'

'What did you do?' Monty asked.

'Just told her that she hadn't got a headache and that rain's good for her complexion.'

'Rain?' I asked, puzzled.

'He makes her work in the rain.'

'I still don't understand.'

'It's very simple. She's an easy subject, and I've often hypnotized her before. It only takes a few passes and she's asleep. Then I tell her that when she wakes up she'll want to walk about in the rain. She won't know why she wants to walk about – she just can't bear the stuffiness indoors, and she feels healthier outside. Then I bring her round again, and off she goes.'

'Won't she *know* you've hypnotized her?' Monty asked.

'Yes. But she won't know what I've told her to do.'

Under the stimulus of another whisky – bought by me – Kaspar told us the theory of post-hypnotic suggestion: that the subject feels a sudden compulsion to do something, but has no idea why. If asked, he will rationalize it.

'Could you hypnotize me?' Monty asked.

'If you wanted me to.'

Kaspar went on to tell us a curious story about a man who came to him for hypnosis. He was an odd-job man in a circus with which Kaspar was performing, and he seemed to be fascinated by the subject. He asked Kaspar to hypnotize him to make him give up smoking. Kaspar did this successfully; but the man seemed to resent the success of the experiment. He deliberately began to

222

smoke again, although it made him sick at first. After this, he often took the opportunity to say sneering things to Kaspar in public. Finally, Kaspar decided to teach him a lesson. One day, pretending to be friendly, he invited the man into his caravan and gave him several drinks, then suggested to him that he had a headache, and that he, Kaspar, should make it disappear by hypnotism. As soon as he had the man in a trance, Kaspar told him that he would find it impossible to urinate; the more he tried, the more he would feel a nervous tension that would make it impossible.

Twenty-four hours later, the man came to Kaspar to beg him to help him; he was obviously in agony. Having made him promise future politeness, Kaspar put him into a trance and released the inhibition.

Kaspar explained that these physical inhibitions are very easy to create. All our basic physical functions – breathing, digesting, excreting, sexual response – depend upon delicate subconscious mechanisms; any *conscious* interference with the function impairs its efficiency. For example if you think hard about your breathing it immediately becomes unrhythmical; thinking hard about your digestion will produce indigestion. It is a kind of 'stage fright'; the instincts resent being 'watched'. Kaspar was able to inhibit the man's natural functions by suggesting that he'd become extremely self-conscious when about to discharge them.

I found all this so absorbing that I forgot my anxiety to go home; I even forgot that I had to see the secretary of the pistol-club. Towards ten o'clock Kaspar's discourse became hard to follow; he tended to slur words and hiccough. I drank very little, for the reason I have mentioned. Monty bought Kaspar at least half a dozen whiskies. Finally, when the publican called time, we had to help Kaspar out of the pub. He insisted that he had a man to see, and went back to the café; we left him at the door. Near the top of the street, a girl came out of a doorway and said: 'Doin' anything?' Monty said: 'Not tonight, dear.' I recognized her as the girl I had seen in the pub with Kaspar and 'Dime'.

Monty was in a talkative mood, and suggested that I should go back home with him. He said:

'Fancy, a man with all that talent, who spends half his time drunk. Isn't it pathetic? He can hypnotize people into doing what he wants, and yet he has no will of his own.'

I pointed out that this was probably unimportant. Kaspar's story about the circus hand suggested that it was only a matter of 'throwing a spanner in the works'. This requires no particular will-power, only a knowledge of how to get at the works. The girl whose headache he cured, for example, could probably have cured her own headache by auto-suggestion.

Monty asked: 'And so you think Charles could cure himself of drinking by auto-suggestion?'

'I'm sure he could, if he wanted to. That's the whole point – he has no reason to want to. What would he do with himself if he didn't drink? Imagine him sitting in that café all day, looking at newspapers . . .'

At this point I remembered about the 'burglar' who had been sitting in the corner as we came into the café. I told Monty about him. 'What do you think I should do?' I asked.

'Nothing. He hasn't done anything as far as you know. I suppose the police could get their hands on him if they wanted.'

We dropped the subject. Back in Monty's room, we drank iced beer. He seemed very cheerful. As he drank, he said: 'Well, here's to Patricia.'

'She mentioned that you'd phoned,' I said.

This startled him. 'Oh, she did.' He was obviously at a loss for something to say; so I helped him by saying:

'I wonder what's happened to Jeremy?'

'He phoned again tonight. He's pretty annoyed about you.'

'Why?'

'I don't know. I can guess.'

'All right – guess.'

'I suppose he doesn't like losing his influence over you. He's not very fond of me. And he certainly doesn't like Patricia.'

'There's no reason why he should.'

He looked at me cunningly over the top of his glass, and said:

'Tell me the truth about Patricia.'

'What do you want to know?'

'I can guess something's happened. That's why I rang her – curiosity.'

I'd have found it difficult to describe to him what had happened in Patricia's house on Saturday; although I felt friendly enough towards him, a part of me resented his curiosity. However, I allowed him to get all the details by questioning me. He was obviously delighted; and yet I felt that his attitude to me was changing; I observed a will-to-power element, a sense of rivalry; some of his questions were deliberately blunt, a kind of sword-thrust, a deliberate invasion of privacy. But I have never been quick to resentment, so I answered him frankly.

The result was that he insisted on bringing out more beer, and talking for the next two hours. Although I was sleepy I found a curious kind of interest in his talk. He simply wanted to talk about women – about all the women he had ever seduced – about mistresses in Germany, in Paris, in Stockholm – and a great many in our town. If it was all true, it was as remarkable as

Leporello's catalogue aria. At first I was amused; then I began to look at Monty as though he was a total stranger. It suddenly seemed preposterous. Seduction after seduction was described in detail; the details were interesting, but the end was always the same. It struck me that Monty was like a bibliophile who buys a library of rare books; then looks through them and discovers that he simply has a thousand copies of the same volume. I said finally:

'Don't you ever feel like forgetting sex and studying mathematics?'

He said good-humouredly – acknowledging the irony: 'I'm no good at maths. And sex never ceases to fascinate me, just as butterflies fascinate a lepidopterist, although he doesn't do anything with them except stick a pin through them. It's the chase that's important. It's a sport, not a study.'

'In that case,' I said, 'I'm afraid I'm no sportsman.'

'No? Then why have you joined the pistol-club?'

'Even that begins to bore me,' I said. 'It seems to me there's an indignity about these unending seductions. I know that men like to flatter themselves that they're the pursuers. But supposing they're really the dupes?'

'Of women? Of course they are.'

He was now smiling patronizingly. But I was thinking of Kaspar and his explanation about post-hypnotic suggestion. I tried to explain this to Monty. Kaspar had mentioned a case in which a man under hypnosis was told that ten minutes after he came out of the trance he would approach a doctor in the room and begin asking him personal questions. He did this according to his instructions; then the hypnotist asked him why he had done it. He said that he thought it must be interesting to be a doctor, and simply wanted to learn more about it. He believed that he had asked the questions of his own free will. But supposing all human beings are in a state of

226

post-hypnotic suggestion? Some of us feel the impulse to benefit humanity, others to commit murder or rape. And how is it possible to explain the actions of politicians except as a kind of post-hypnotic suggestion? Who would willingly waste his life in the drudgery of public office if some hypnotist had not ordered him to do so? Monty was obviously interested. He said:

'You know, Hugh, you're always coming out with interesting ideas. If I understand you, you believe that people are subjected to hypnotic suggestion before they're born?'

'You can refuse to be hypnotized,' I said, remembering my first experience with Kaspar.

'What's the point? What would you do instead?'

I thought about this, then admitted: 'I don't know.'

'Quite. Neither do I. We've got to accept what we've got. We're alive – that's about the only thing we can be sure about. Except that we die. Does it really matter what we do in between?'

This subject also carried him away; he talked very well about the futility of human life, about the deaths he had seen in the army, about a sailor whose throat had been cut in a brothel in Hamburg, and how he and another officer had talked philosophy while they waited for the German police to come and remove the body. He finished:

'But it was all words. All the time I was talking I kept looking down at the sailor, with his head almost off his body, and thinking: We all end like him. But do you know what I did when we'd given our depositions and watched them move the body? I went back to the brothel and went to bed with a pretty little blonde girl who'd been out with the sailor. And before I fell asleep, I remember looking at the ceiling and thinking: the philosophy might be balls, but this is real, anyway.'

It struck me that, in spite of all their differences of temperament, Monty and Jeremy were very much alike. They both seemed to hold this tragic view of human life: it goes up like a rocket, but, no matter how high it soars, the stick has to fall back to earth.

After another half-hour, the fire was out. I was very cold, and Monty was talking about opening more beer. So I went home. It was a damp November night, and the fog made me cough. But I decided that I would ring Jeremy the next day, and go out and see him the following evening, with or without Patricia. After Monty's talk, I suddenly felt more sympathy for Jeremy. It was not that I was prudish about his talk of seduction – only that I felt there was a kind of indignity in this endless sexual itch, and a basic defeatism in his acceptance of it.

Before I fell asleep I suddenly felt miserable and exhausted, and a little frightened. Perhaps too much had happened to me too quickly, and the world seemed alien. I felt like a sleep-walker who wakes up to find himself balanced on top of a high wall, with no way of getting down . . . except falling.

Then an idea occurred to me that made me feel happier. It may be that Jeremy and Monty were right in accepting the basic defeat of being human, for it seems obvious enough that the rocket that goes up must come down again. And yet if a rocket could go high enough, it might escape the pull of gravity and fall into orbit outside the earth. If it could go high enough, if the sense of urgency was great enough . . . The last thought in my mind as I fell asleep was of a silvery ball out in space.

7

I did not see Jeremy the following evening; instead, Patricia and I went to a sentimental film. It ended with the death of the hero – a white-moustached, soldierly-looking man – whose spirit rose out of his body towards the sunset, and was met by the spirit of his childhood sweetheart, who had died earlier in the film; then the camera went beyond the lovers and focused on the Technicolor sunset as the film ended with full orchestra playing the theme-tune. Patricia clasped my hand very tightly, and when I glanced sideways I saw tears on her cheeks. Luckily, this was followed by the news, so my irritation had time to evaporate before we went out into the November rain. We then went back to my house, where everyone had gone to bed, made cocoa, and lay on the settee for an hour, until it was time for her last bus. As I walked back home, after midnight, I tried to analyse my mixed feelings. My body was still aware of her warmth, which had left its impression on it as an animal leaves its impression on the grass where it has slept. Her whole ambience was one of warmth – physical and emotional. The physical warmth was important; in fact, it seemed as necessary to me as food and drink. The emotional warmth was as uncongenial as hot water to a fish.

When I got home, I spent an hour cleaning the Biretta. I felt no desire for sleep; now it looked as though my plans might be put into effect sooner than I expected, and sleep seemed a waste of time. Patricia was to come to the club; Gerald Sutton had arranged this and phoned me at the office to tell me. Then my mother had mentioned that she would be out the following evening – she was taking my sister to a jumble sale and then to see Aunt Dinah. When I asked her if I could bring Patricia home with me for tea, she said of course. I had already checked and discovered that there would be a dance at the Palais on the following evening, with a famous London band. It began at eight o'clock. It seemed as though everything had been arranged for a crisis. I told myself that it would probably come to nothing – that the evening would be rainy, that Patricia and I would see no one outside the Palais – and yet every time I imagined the scene I saw the gang waiting there, the same gang that had forced John Duncan to walk in the road and that had beaten up the youth called Johnny.

I was also aware that I could simply forget the whole thing – drop everything. But I knew that I wouldn't. Something inside me told me that if I wanted to escape my own limitations I had to prove that I was not a weakling.

I find all this very hard to write, even though I feel a certain amount of sympathy for that self of fifteen years ago. I shall try to describe the events of the next few days as concisely and accurately as possible.

At lunch-time the following day I saw Patricia, and she told me that she had been to the police-station that morning. Scottie Gibbs had asked her to come to an identity parade. I asked her what had happened.

'I saw him, but I wasn't sure . . . so I said I didn't recognize any of them.'

'Why?'

'I don't know. It didn't seem fair . . .'

This puzzled me. If I had been asked to point out the man who had taken my sister into the spinney I wouldn't have hesitated, even if it meant sending him to the gallows. He was a dangerous man; he should be behind bars.

'Are you sure he was there?' I asked her.

'Oh yes.'

'And what did Scottie say when you refused to identify the man?'

'I didn't refuse. I said that several men looked rather like him. That was true anyway. They were all rough-looking types.'

I said: 'I don't suppose he'll be pleased to see you this evening.'

'In that case I won't come.'

I told her that I was joking, and we dropped the matter.

That afternoon was very busy, and it went by quickly. I was surprised at my own calm. Shortly after five I met Patricia, and we took the bus back to my home. She asked me once: 'Are you worried about something?' I said: 'Of course not.' I suppose I looked preoccupied.

My mother had left the table set for tea. I had also taken the precaution of buying a small bottle of whisky, which we drank in the tea; I thought I might need it to 'steady my nerves'. Patricia seemed very happy, and some of her feeling communicated itself to me. We made up the fire so that it lit up the room, and turned off the light. Patricia toasted muffins, and we ate a great number between us. My father was not due home until late; he was going to play billiards in his club after work; so we locked the back door, and lay on the settee. But for the first time since I had known her I felt no interest in love-making. We finished the whisky, then lay there looking at the firelight on the ceiling. Patricia said: 'It feels like Christmas.' She started to talk about Christmases in her childhood, and made me feel nostalgic. She said that a Sunday-school teacher had once told her that Christmas was a 'season of grace'. This meant that, no matter what worries you had on your mind, you were bound to feel happy and relaxed at Christmas. And all through her childhood she continued to believe that Christmas was happy because of some special magic engineered by Jesus – and only incidentally because of the food and the presents and party games. Something she said struck me as unusually perceptive for Patricia:

'After all, it's funny that the Christmas magic always seems to work. There are lots of times when we *ought* to be happy for all kinds of reasons, yet somehow it doesn't work. I'm always looking forward to things and being disappointed.'

This made her seem of the same flesh and spirit as myself; I could no longer resent her going to bed with Monty or previous lovers. Besides, I saw very clearly what she meant. All our emotions are unstable. Human beings are so unaccountable that you could imagine a man in the condemned cell dancing for joy, or a general who has just won a battle committing suicide in despair; there seems to be almost no relation between our emotions and the things that cause them. And yet it seemed to me that I was about to strike a blow against this absurdity by loading my pistol. I cannot explain this; I can see that I might just as well have felt that I was only increasing the absurdity.

At seven o'clock we switched on the light and put our shoes on; my mother might be home at any moment. Then I brought my Biretta out of my bedroom, and showed it to Patricia. She took it and looked at it, turned it over in her hand, and said: 'How does it work?' I took it to pieces for her, and filled the magazine with bullets. As I was doing this, she suddenly asked me:

'Why do you like guns?'

'I don't. But I enjoy shooting. You'll see why when we get there.'

'I hope the bangs aren't too loud.'

'That's part of the fun.' I tried to explain to her about the feeling of health that comes from learning to hit a target, to control the nerves, to overcome the tendency to pull the trigger or jerk the barrel of the pistol. She said:

'It seems to me that you could get the same effect by jumping in the river on a cold night.'

'I agree. But this is a more comfortable way of doing it.'

She was brushing her hair in the bathroom when my mother came in, loaded up with all kinds of useless odds and ends that she had bought at the jumble sale. I was sorry about this, but there was nothing for it, so I introduced Patricia, and she and my mother immediately went all through the objects – various woollen items of clothing, old books, a china dog – and began talking like old friends. My sister Anne was curious about my pistol, so I loaded it and unloaded it several times for her. Anne showed Patricia a golliwog she had found at the sale, and Patricia said all the right things about it. Finally, when Patricia went out to get her coat Anne said: 'When are you going to marry her? I like her.' My mother also said: 'That's one of the nicest girls I've met for a long time. Make sure you don't lose her.' I felt embarrassed, and unaccountably upset. For the first time I felt miserable and worried about my plan.

When Patricia and I got outside, she said: 'I think your mother's wonderful', and I wondered whether this was a female conspiracy to get me married. And when we arrived at the bus-stop I found Gerald Sutton there, and it seemed that fate was working against my plan. I decided to accept whatever should come. But I was glad

233

that Gerald and Patricia talked together all the way into town; it relieved me of the necessity of talking, and allowed me time to think. Gerald's presence would complicate things. To begin with, I had no reason for getting off the bus near the Palais, for the bus-terminus was within a hundred yards of the pistol-club. Alone with Patricia, it would have been easy enough to get off the bus at the earlier stop; but Gerald would be suspicious.

Before the bus arrived in town, I had decided that, if necessary, I would forget the whole thing. It was the easy way out – but I had tried hard all the same.

I had a book in my brief-case – it was a cheap edition of the notebooks of Leonardo da Vinci – and I tried to read this so as to avoid taking part in the conversation. Ever since Jeremy had introduced me to his work, I had admired Leonardo as an ideal of the man of intellect – scientist and artist, soldier and inventor, mathematician and man of action. Yet now, the 'notebooks' only added another touch of absurdity to the situation; they were ironically irrelevant.

The next stop was the Palais; I looked up from my book and started to my feet. Still talking, the other two followed me. Gerald did not even notice that we were at the wrong stop until we were standing on the pavement. He said:

'Here, we should have stayed on.'

'Sorry,' I said, 'I was reading and I thought we'd arrived.'

Patricia took my arm. I looked towards the Palais, and my stomach felt leaden. It was eight o'clock, and there were about a dozen youths standing outside, half blocking the pavement. Gerald also saw them, and said:

'Let's walk on the other side.'

'Why?' I said. He made no reply; probably he was ashamed to admit the reason in front of Patricia. So the three of us walked towards the gang. They were not actually blocking the pavement – only spread out loosely so that it was difficult to see a way through. As we came closer, a big youth in a black leather jerkin saw Patricia, and nudged the youth with him. Gerald was looking nervous. My brief-case was open; through its imitation leather I could feel the outline of the gun, and knew how I would reach in for it with the other hand. Then Patricia, her hand on my arm, began to steer me round the Teddy-boys towards the edge of the pavement. When I resisted she said quietly: 'Come on.' Gerald obviously had no intention of getting mixed up with them; he was already on the edge of the pavement. I ignored Patricia's pressure and walked straight for the centre of the group; at the last moment she gave way and walked with me. To my astonishment, the group opened up politely and let us through. The youth with the black jerkin whistled admiringly after Patricia. Gerald rejoined us and said:

'Blimey, you were asking for trouble.'

'Why?' I said innocently. I was still dazed with what had happened. I could not make up my mind what it meant. Patricia said:

'I didn't like the look of them at all.'

'Neither did I,' I said. 'That's why I wasn't going to walk in the road.'

'You're just as bad as Monty,' Patricia said. But she was not angry.

Gerald said: 'I thought they were going to knock you down.'

We arrived at the pistol-club. Before we went in, I excused myself and locked myself in the lavatory. There I unloaded the Biretta. I suspected that Scottie Gibbs would check to see whether it was loaded, for I was sure that I had aroused his suspicions last week. But I was wrong; he hardly paid me any attention. I had also been

wrong in thinking that he would not be glad to see
Patricia; he introduced her to the members as though she
was his guest, and offered to let her fire his pistol.

I hardly noticed this. I kept thinking: 'Nothing happened.' They had let me through politely. I did not know
what to feel. A part of me felt relieved; another part felt
cheated. I went into the shooting-gallery, found an empty
place, and fired a dozen rounds at the target. Then I went
back into the ante room, and found myself thinking: 'All
right, you don't have to do it. What now?' And I looked
across at Patricia – who was being a great success, at the
centre of a group of members – and felt simultaneously
pleased and irritated.

Scottie Gibbs took her into the shooting-gallery and
showed her how to hold the gun. Then the man standing
next to her fired, and she dropped the gun. Everybody
laughed. She said: 'I don't think I want to shoot.' Scottie
persuaded her. She fired one shot and almost dropped
the gun again. She said: 'I hate it,' and handed the pistol
back to Scottie. After that she went back into the ante-
room and talked to Gerald and his father. I joined them,
and found Gerald telling Mr Sutton about the incident
outside the Palais. Gerald said admiringly:

'Hugh just walked straight through them, and they
were so surprised they didn't try to stop him.'

Mr Sutton said: 'You want to steer clear of those lads.
They're no good. They'll break both your legs for
sixpence.'

As soon as we were alone for a moment, Patricia
whispered: 'Can we go now? I hate those guns.'

I looked at my watch. We had only been there twenty
minutes. I said:

'I'd like to, but I don't think they'd like it. I missed the
meeting on Monday. Besides, Gerald got special permission for you to come. He might be offended if we
walked out as early as this.'

236

I persuaded her to come back into the shooting-gallery. Bob Salomons, the secretary, and Ernie Timson, a scrawny youth with adenoids, were having a friendly match. They were both excellent shots, and I enjoyed watching them. But after ten minutes Patricia said: 'I've got an awful headache. I think I'd better leave you here.'

I thought quickly of the alternatives: if I left with her, we could go and have some tea in the Open Air Club, or I had enough money to buy us both a drink; but I felt too much on edge to go to cafés or pubs. There was no point in returning either to my home or hers, because our parents were in. On the other hand I would like to call in and see Monty later on, and I could hardly do this with Patricia. She saw my hesitation and said:

'Perhaps I'd better go anyway. I'd like to wash my hair.'

So I let her go, feeling a brute. She insisted that she would walk to her bus alone. I went upstairs with her, and then watched her walk away into the crowd. I now regretted not going with her, but it was too late to run after her. A sense of nostalgia and foreboding came over me; it seemed to me that I was somehow alienating the luck that had been with me for the past few weeks.

For the next half-hour I talked aimlessly with another new member about our respective pistols, then Bob Salomons came and talked to us, putting himself out to be entertaining with stories of shooting-matches. Then, at half past nine, Ewen Waite arrived, dressed in a dinner-jacket with silk lapels; he explained that he had been making an after-dinner speech. He and Scottie Gibbs shot together, and the rest of us watched them. Neither shot as well as Bob Salomons, but they were better than most of us. Ewen Waite used a Biretta that looked very similar to my own.

At a quarter to ten, Gerald said: 'We're going next

door for a drink. Do you want to come?' I said I would rather watch the rest of the match between the mayor and chief constable, so they went without me. Myself and Bob Salomons were the only spectators left; everyone else had gone up to the pub.

I was cleaning my gun in the corner of the ante-room when Ewen Waite came in, saying: 'We've just got time for a quick drink if we hurry.' He buttoned his pistol into a leather holster, and pushed it into the bottom of the ammunition-cupboard. Then he saw me, and said: 'You still here? Do you want a shandy before you go?'

I said yes. Then I asked: 'Could I leave my pistol in there?' I am not sure why I asked this, except that it seemed a sensible thing to do instead of carrying it back and forth to the club. A psychologist would probably recognize subconscious guilt-motivation in the request, a desire to leave behind a weapon that I identified with violence.

Ewen Waite raised his finger to his lips (the other two were still talking in the gallery).

'That's illegal, you know. I'm going to a party after-wards – that's why I don't want to carry it with me.'

'So am I.' This was not strictly a lie; I intended calling on Monty.

'All right. Shove it in. But don't let Bob see you. We'll both get thrown out.'

(This was the characteristic that made Ewen Waite so popular in the club – his assumption of equality.) He explained that all firearms must be kept constantly under lock and key and in the possession of the owner. I already knew this – it was at the head of the sheet of rules I had been given – but I had forgotten it.

'Still, I can't take a gun to a party with me, and it'd be just as dangerous to leave it in my car – more dangerous, in fact, because anybody could break in and steal it.'

He locked the cupboard – it was made of metal – and dropped the key into a drawer. Then we went out, with the other two close behind us. I noticed that Scottie Gibbs dropped the door-key into a bucket of sand, and covered it over. (This was because the caretaker lived on the top floor; he was supposed to collect it when he locked up, but he often forgot, so that members who arrived early always looked in the sand-bucket before tramping up ten flights of stairs.)

As soon as we walked into the pub I regretted leaving the pistol behind. A youth with a leather jacket was standing at the serving-hatch in the passage-way, buying drinks. The door of the back room stood open behind him, and I could see more black leather jackets.

Gerald Sutton's first remark was: 'Your pals have found you.' I asked what he meant, although I knew. 'Those boys from outside the Palais – they're outside in the corridor. They've been asking after you.'

'Have they?' For a moment I believed him.

'No, I was joking.' But as he said it I saw two of them looking at me from the other side of the hatch; I recognized the tall youth who had whistled after Patricia. He was staring at me as he talked to the other.

I was angry with myself for the emptiness in my stomach and for my feeling of helplessness. I glared back at them with hostility, and saw the tall youth smile. It seemed absurd, to be in this room full of people, with the chief constable only a few feet away, and to feel like a hypnotized bird. I took the shandy that Ewen Waite put into my hand, and said thank you. It seemed that he was a thousand miles away.

I put the shandy on the table in front of Gerald, and said: 'I shan't be a moment. Forgotten something.' All that was important was to get back to the Biretta. But as I moved towards the door the youth moved away from the hatch; when I got out into the passage-way he was blocking the door. He said: 'You going somewhere?' Then a man and a woman came up behind me. I jumped forward and pushed through the door. He stuck out his foot, and I tripped over it, but recovered.

The building next door seemed locked; I felt the taste of despair in my throat, then it changed to pleasure when the door opened as I pushed it. I groped my way downstairs – the light was off – and found the sand-bucket. After a moment's fumbling I was back in the room, and switched on the light. For a moment, I thought that Ewen Waite had played some trick with the key of the cupboard. It turned loosely in the lock, and nothing happened. Then I jerked the door, and it flew open.

I had used all my own ammunition, but I knew where it was kept. As I loaded the gun, the fear vanished; instead I found myself smiling. I can understand how the possession of a gun can turn a neurotic coward into a dangerous criminal, and why American gangsters call them 'equalizers'. Instead of feeling hunted I now felt myself the hunter. My only fear was that the caretaker would come down and interrupt me. When I finished loading, I opened the case of Ewen Waite's pistol, and loaded this too.

I know exactly why I did this, although I feel reluctant to admit it. The gun in my hand gave me a sense of power. Holding two guns doubled the power. I saw myself facing the gang of ruffians with a gun in each hand, and the fear and dismay on their faces.

I fumbled everything in my excitement, but somehow I relocked the cupboard and got out of the room. Somewhere upstairs I could hear the sound of footsteps. I started to tiptoe up, then realized that it was almost impossible to get out without being seen. Lights came on above, and the steps came slowly down the stairs. My

240

next thought was whether I could return Ewen Waite's gun before he arrived in the basement; after all, I had a right to be carrying my own. While I was still hesitating the steps crossed to the door upstairs, and I heard it close. Then the steps went away again, across the hall. Another door closed.

I ran up the stairs two at a time and let myself out, too anxious to get clear of the building to worry whether anyone saw me. It was a stupid thing to do; I might have walked into any member of the club, since it was closing-time in the pub. Luckily, I saw no one I recognized, and no one paid any attention to me. Then I saw the black-jacketed youth. He was still standing in the doorway of the pub, looking out. He looked surprised when I walked straight towards him, and I was pleased. I pushed past him, grinning at him, my brief-case pressed tight into my side. Some people came out of the main bar, and I had to let them pass. I now realized that it would not be wise to walk back into the bar carrying my brief-case. If Ewen Waite saw it he would immediately know what I had done. I took what seemed the only alternative – walked down the passage-way to the door labelled 'Gents'. As I passed the hatch I saw Gerald Sutton in the bar, and waved to him. He pointed to my shandy glass on the table, and I nodded.

The gents was situated in a small yard, with no exit. Standing at the urinal gave me time to think. Now my only regret was bringing Ewen Waite's pistol; it would be an embarrassment whatever happened, and I cursed the impulse that had made me bring it. The simplest thing would be to return to the bar, and leave the pub with as many people as possible.

The door from the pub opened; one of the youths was peering out into the yard. I heard someone say: 'He's gone over the wall.' I waited, and the door closed again.

This seemed a good idea. The wall was not high – about eight feet – and there were two dustbins standing in the corner. I ran to the corner of the yard, threw my brief-case over the wall, and then scrambled on to the dustbin. But as soon as I sat on top of the wall I saw my mistake. There was an entry below, with small gates leading into backyards. One end of the entry ended in darkness and the shape of a factory against the sky. At the other end, lighted by a street-lamp, stood two youths in leather jackets. My brief-case was below, so there was no alternative to dropping down after it. I grabbed it as soon as I landed, and started to run down the entry towards the factory. I knew I had been tricked; they wanted to get me in the entry and away from the pub; otherwise, why had they simply not attacked me in the pub yard?

Someone jumped out of the darkness ahead of me, and a voice said: 'Get him.' My knees struck a crouching man; I staggered, and ran on. Somebody hit me on the side of the head, but the blow was not heavy. I decided to get against the wall at the far end, and then fire a couple of shots at them. I was still not frightened – only a little exhilarated. The knowledge that I had a loaded gun made me confident.

I was wrong about the factory; it was not at the end of the entry. There was a piece of waste ground in front of it, and I was able to turn left and blunder through the darkness towards the light of street-lamps. The footsteps were still close behind me, but I was not worried. Two more turns, and I could be back on the main road, among people.

Then I tripped and fell; an empty oil-drum rolled under my shins, and my brief-case flew out of my hand. A piece of glass – probably a broken bottle – sliced into the palm of my left hand. As I started to pull myself to my feet, two knees landed in the small of my back, and I went down again, the breath knocked out of me. Someone shouted: 'I've got him.' When I struggled and tried to get up, a blow knocked my face against the ground. The youth sitting on me said: 'Come on, Jinner, he's yours.' They hauled me to my feet, and the youth behind me bent back my arm in a half-nelson. Then the tall youth came up and said: 'Now, what's it all about? What's your game?' The others laughed. Then someone said: 'Here's his bag.' I struggled, and the youth behind me said: 'Here, quit that.' He grabbed my hair with his other hand and pulled back my head. Then I heard one of them say in a startled voice: 'He's got a gun here.' The others said: 'What? Let's see,' and the youth behind me relaxed his grip. I managed to twist free. They were all looking at the gun in the light of the lamp, and one of them said: 'This is useful,' as I jumped forward and tried to grab it. Someone held me, and I missed the gun; then my hand encountered the brief-case, and I grabbed it and jerked hard. Someone was on my back, with both arms round my neck, and someone else was trying to kick my feet from under me. As I went down I groped in the bag, and found the second gun. It was wrapped in cleaning-rag, which was probably why they had missed it. I pulled the trigger as the gun came out of the case; it clicked harmlessly; the safety catch was on. Someone saw it and said: 'Look out, he's got another.' Then I got the catch off, and fired again. It seemed to explode in my face, and the youth on my back let go. I was on my knees, and they had backed away in a semi-circle. I pointed the gun at the black-haired youth, and said: 'Give that back to me.' As I spoke, I heard the other gun click, and knew he had tried to fire it at me. Shooting low, I fired again. This time they all scattered, except the youth with the gun, who yelled, staggered two paces, then fell down. I pulled myself to my feet, and went over to him. My foot kicked something; I bent down and found the other gun. As I put it back into the brief-case, he began to moan: 'Jack, he's killed me.' I made sure that both guns and my books were in the case, feeling with my right hand, then started to run back towards the entry. The others had scattered towards the street-lamps in the opposite direction. My shin was painful, and I had to limp. My whole body felt bruised. When I found myself in the darkness of the entry I stopped for a while and sat down against the wall. From where I was resting, I could see across the waste ground. At least one of the youths was coming back, calling: 'Jinner, you all right?' but no one replied. I wondered if Jinner could be dead. I had the impression that I had shot low – I had intended to hit his thigh – but it might have gone into his abdomen from the angle at which I'd fired.

After a few minutes I felt cold, and limped away down the entry. The street at the other end was empty. I decided against walking back to the main road; it was not yet half past ten – everything had taken place in a few minutes – and I might bump into someone from the pistol-club. So I turned off down another side-alley, and went on walking. Finally, I stopped under a lamp and bound my handkerchief round the palm of my hand. It was badly cut. I also pulled up my trouser-leg, and discovered that the shin was also cut, but was no longer bleeding. I began to shiver. The night was cold and misty, but I think it was nervous reaction. Someone walked down the street from the opposite end, and I walked on; as I drew near, I saw that it was a policeman. He passed me without even looking at me.

My chief regret at this point was that the pubs were closed, and that I had emptied the whisky I kept at home. Then I remembered that I was within a few hundred yards of Monty's, and decided to go and see him. I had no doubt that I could trust him, and that he would sympathize with what had happened. As I walked there, I rehearsed the story in my mind. It was not very creditable. I had achieved my purpose – defending myself against the young thugs – but it was not what I had set out to do. It all seemed pointless and accidental. And then there was the other problem – Ewen Waite's gun. I would now have no alternative but to admit that I had taken it; when the youths told their story to the police, they would mention two guns. I wondered if I could somehow get round this problem – replace Ewen Waite's pistol, and claim that the other gun had been a toy. Or perhaps that it had been one of Monty's guns.

After all the excitement I was feeling another pressing necessity – the relief of my bowels. I turned into Monty's street, and decided to approach the house from the rear instead of going to the front door. There would be less chance of being seen, and Monty had a lavatory in the yard there. His back gate was approached along an entry. When I opened it I felt exhaustion and disappointment. The house was in darkness. All the same I went into the lavatory, and sat there in the darkness, breathing in the smell of disinfectant and flaking whitewash and damp. In spite of the cold I could have fallen asleep. One thing was obvious to me: I had to return Ewen Waite's gun; this thought kept running in my head. I even cursed myself for closing the door behind me when I left the building with the guns; otherwise, I could return and replace it now.

As I came out of the lavatory a light came on in Monty's kitchen. I was already halfway to the back door when I saw Patricia approaching the kitchen-sink. She was wearing Monty's dressing-gown. I stepped back into the shadows and watched her fill the kettle, put it on the stove, then go out again, switching off the light. I stood there for five minutes longer in the darkness, unsure of what to do next. I felt no jealousy or anger about Patricia; only irritation at being thwarted in my design to see Monty. Even the thought that she was probably now removing the dressing-gown and climbing back into bed failed to touch my emotions. I felt drained of feeling, and perhaps secretly pleased with myself for being indifferent to what she was doing.

Finally I decided to go home. But first I wanted to wash my hands. I walked down to the bus station, but found the washroom closed. It had started to rain. On my way to the bus-stop I passed the café where I had been with Monty two days before. It looked warm and comfortable; but this was not the reason that made me go in. On Monday I had been fascinated to think that many of these people were criminals, and had looked at them as dangerous freaks. Now I saw them as a community who had chosen to be outcasts. This was no closer to reality than my earlier view, but it made me cease to feel completely alone.

Sitting in the corner, near the window, was the man I knew as Kaspar. I bought tea and went across to his table. He looked a great deal more weary – and sober – than the last time I'd seen him. He said: 'Hello, lad. What are you doing here?'

In the warm steamy atmosphere I felt tired, and almost sick. I said: 'Nothing. Just passing by.'

'Hurt your hand?' I noticed that the blood had soaked through the handkerchief.

'I tripped and scratched it.'

'Where's your pal tonight? Monty?'

This brought back a picture of Patricia in the dressing-gown, a surge of desire, and a sense of grief and frustration. I said I didn't know. The conversation stopped for a few minutes while I drank my tea. I kept wanting to

246

yawn, but shrank from lifting my grimy hands to my face. Finally I asked him if there was a lavatory in the café and he directed me upstairs. There I found a small and very dirty bathroom, with a heap of clothes in the bath. But there was a geyser above the bath, and I was able to fill the wash-basin with hot water. The sense of relief as I soaked my hands was enormous, although there was no soap and no towel. I dried my hands on the handkerchief as I went downstairs. Halfway down I remembered that I had left the brief-case under the table, and went hot and cold with fear. I took the remaining stairs two at a time, and pushed open the door to the café. It looked the same as before; Kaspar was sitting there, staring into space above his cold tea. But as I came in he said something, and I realized that someone on the far side of the table was bending down and looking at something under the table. He straightened up as I walked across the room. It was Patricia's 'burglar'. For a moment I was sure this was a trick, and could feel my face betraying me as I stared at them. Then Kaspar winked at me, as if to an old friend, and for some reason I felt a fool. As I sat down again Kaspar said:

'Was it all right?' (meaning the bathroom).

I said it was, but was afraid to try and lift my tea, because I was aware that my hands were trembling.

'You don't know Jed, do you?' said Kaspar. He obviously said it to fill in an awkward pause; he made no mention of my own name, or of 'Jed's' surname. I said 'how do you do?' awkwardly, but he was ignoring me and drinking his tea. I now raised both my hands carefully, lifting my cup between them – hoping that Kaspar would not notice the effort it was costing me – and drank from it. I stared at Jed as I did so. My first impression was indefinably unpleasant – or perhaps unpleasant is the wrong word. I felt exactly as if Jed was a wolf or some

247

other wild animal: not that he was 'criminal', but that he would do things as a matter of course that were dangerous to human beings. This impression may have been gained from the angle at which I was looking at his face, which turned it into a blunt triangle. His ears gave an impression of being pointed, or slightly so. His forehead was not low, but it had a deep crease across the middle that looked like a crease in the bone, and somehow made it seem low. When he looked up I saw that he had a slight cast in one eye – although again, when I looked closely, this seemed an illusion. His skin was dark, but not with the brownness of warm countries; it looked as if coal dust had been absorbed in all its pores. Looked at directly, his face was not as pointed as it seemed from above, and the alien effect was weaker. His expression was not sinister; on the contrary, it was friendly in a casual sort of way, as if he was good-natured but was thinking of something else. I remembered how he had turned and waved at me as he walked away from the spinney, and the memory was so clear that it was as if he had done it five minutes before. When he spoke, his voice (as I might have guessed) had our local accent – blunt and ugly, less broad than the North and as utilitarian as an earthenware chamber pot. He ignored me, and said to Kaspar:

'There's bin a bit o' trouble up be'ind Commercial.'

I knew that he meant the shooting, and again felt certain that he was out to trip me. Kaspar said casually:

'Oh, yes.'

'I was jus' coomin' pas' there an' I saw the amberlance.'

My cup slipped, and I caught hold of it by the handle, spilling tea down my sleeve. I had no handkerchief to mop up with – it was bound round my hand. I said: 'Damn', trying to sound only mildly irritated, and groping

248

in my pocket. Then, as if still searching for a handkerchief, I bent down, opened my brief-case, and looked
inside. Both guns were there, but they were unwrapped,
and the rag was lying at the bottom of the case. This
might have happened as I carried the brief-case. I closed
it and pushed it back under my chair. I rubbed my wet
wrist against my trousers. Only then did I meet Kaspar's
eyes, and found him looking at me with mild irony. I felt
confused and angry; this evening was obviously intended
to be a series of defeats and mortifications. I was tempted
to hurry out of the café, but I wanted to hear the news
about the shooting. But Jed seemed to have dropped the
subject. He drank his tea in big gulps, then stood up and
went out without saying goodnight. I finished the dregs
of my tea, then said, for something to say:

'What does he do?'

'That's a question I've never asked,' Kaspar said. His
tone made it clear that he thought it a silly question.

I sat there for a few minutes longer, then went out. I
found Jed still standing outside the café; he was talking
to the prostitute whose headache Kaspar had cured. She
looked even tireder, and her coat was wet. I stood in the
doorway for a moment to button my overcoat, and
overheard him saying:

'I could manage a quid for half an hour.'

She replied:

'No thanks. Not your way. That's too hard.'

He stood there looking at her, although neither of
them said anything more. She could see me, but he had
his back to me. I turned away from them and walked
across the bus station. The conversation did not strike me
as having any special significance.

When I got home I took both pistols out of the brief-
case and examined them. They looked very much alike,

and I was not sure which was mine. Then I remembered the firearms certificate, and looked up its number. I discovered then that I had fired Ewen Waite's gun. My own still had the safety catch on.

8

I now come to what is by far the most difficult part of my story, although for me it is also the most important. In writing earlier chapters, I have noticed that I often seem to lose the essence of an event by describing it precisely. If I think, for example, about my first evening with Patricia at Jeremy's it means certain things for me, it makes me remember something as unique as a particular piece of music. When I re-read what I have written about it, all this has gone; it is no more like the event than a monochrome photograph could be like the Blackpool illuminations. There actually seems to be an irrelevancy about the events as though a man should describe to you the most tragic event in his life while performing a series of handstands and cartwheels. But now it seems almost impossible to describe the events after the shooting without losing everything they meant to me.

I slept badly, to begin with. Finally, towards four in the morning, I felt queasy, and deliberately made myself sick to get it over with. I slept for a short time after this, then woke up in the dawn with a feeling of absurdity. The first thought in my mind, of course, was the shooting, and the various problems connected with it: returning Ewen Waite's gun, discovering whether Kaspar suspected me, and whether he would talk about it; I also had to decide what story to tell if the police questioned me. All this came quickly into my head; at the same time it seemed to have no connexion with me, as if it was all part of a film I had just seen. And then my mind seemed to reach out towards the question: 'But why is it irrelevant?'

If you are running to catch a train, and someone asks you the time, this is irrelevant because it has nothing to do with your immediate objective. I suppose what suddenly presented itself to me was the question: 'If the shooting is irrelevant, what purpose is it interrupting?' At the same time I remembered Uncle Sam's comments about all men being incapable of feeling. And suddenly I felt dizzy, as if falling backwards into a pit, and afraid for my life. This was not ordinary fear – fear of being caught by the police, for example, but a kind of fear that seemed to grope for a foothold among all my usual certainties, and to find none.

Since then I have sometimes managed to rationalize the sensation, and would explain it like this: I am suffering from amnesia. A man who has received a blow on the head may forget his identity and what happened the day before yesterday. A part of his life is missing. But at least he knows that he has a past; a part of the jigsaw puzzle is missing, but it must exist somewhere. What suddenly terrified me was the feeling that we are all suffering from a kind of amnesia. The area of all our certainties suddenly comes to a halt, and there is nothing beyond it.

But here is the problem – and the terror. If a piece is missing from a jigsaw puzzle we know that it is a piece like all the others, only different in shape and colour. But there is no conceivable 'something' beyond that unknowingness that could somehow complete this human jigsaw puzzle and make it complete. When the jigsaw is complete, when every piece has been fitted in, there is still empty space around it. The jigsaw puzzle is existence itself. If we keep on finding new pieces for the next ten million years, extending the puzzle outwards into the emptiness, the problem is still untouched; there is emptiness beyond, however far it extends.

I felt like a man who knows that some danger may lie behind him, but can never look round because he has no muscles for the purpose; he can only look in front.

At eight o'clock I went down for my breakfast; my father had called me twice, and he sounded irritated. Again, the glutinous absurdity surrounded me. His irritation was irrelevant. It was as if I was being forced to act my role in a play after receiving some bad news that left me numb; it was a mystery to watch my hands washing themselves at the bathroom basin, to look at my face in the mirror and find intelligence in the eyes looking back at me, like another being.

I sat at the breakfast table, trying to eat a piece of bacon and fried bread. The morning newspaper was propped up against the sauce bottle, where my father had left it. The headline was about a millionaire who had committed suicide by walking into the sea. For a while I forgot myself, reading about this man who owned shipping companies and newspapers, and could exert a strong influence on two governments. The article did not state openly that it was suicide, but talked about the 'mysterious death', and then quoted a man who had seen the millionaire walk into the sea from the beach in Jamaica, until his head simply vanished under the water.

It came to me: He has done something honest and sensible. When he added up the pros and cons of his life he was not deceived by his riches and influence into imagining that he was happy. He saw that human life is a farce, and that we are kept happy by incredible blindness. (In fact, when the full story came out a few days later, it was revealed that his wife had deceived him, and he suspected that he had lung-cancer.) At the same time I imagined myself walking into the sea like that, and the horror increased, for I became aware that I would be exchanging a stupid and meaningless existence for an equally stupid and meaningless non-existence.

My mother said: 'Do you feel all right this morning?' I said that I felt tired. She immediately began to lecture me about coming in late. Then she asked me what time I had taken Patricia home; to save trouble, I said 'About ten o'clock.' My mind formed a picture of Patricia filling the kettle, wearing Monty's dressing-gown, then of returning to his bedroom, flinging it off, and standing there with nothing on before she slipped back to bed. I felt no jealousy, no irritation; only, perhaps, a kind of pity for them, a feeling that they were going through an absurd ritual, like a condemned man eating his supper as if it matters whether he dies with a full or empty stomach.

I left for work twenty minutes earlier than usual; I wanted to see if there was a chance of returning the Biretta before I went to the office. On the bus I sat opposite two women, both holding young children. One was an exceptionally pretty fair-haired girl of about three or four who looked – as children of that age sometimes do – like an angel or a fairy; she had obviously inherited her looks from her mother, who was also pretty and fair-skinned. The child was clutching a gollywog; she kept looking across at me and smiling, then looking away quickly, as if she was very shy. I found myself feeling happy about her; but in a way this only made things worse. Her mother was chattering brainlessly with her companion, a fat woman with very plain features, and explaining how she cooked cheese fritters; there was something silly and complacent about her look and the way she referred to 'my husband', and I realized that the child would be like this in another twenty years, unless she inherited some intelligence from her father. But of what use would it be to her except to make life difficult?

As a child, I once saw a juggler who balanced a pencil on his nose, then balanced a chair on the pencil, then kept throwing up various objects until he had a column about six feet high above his face; he had to keep moving to prevent them all from falling, and every additional object had to be thrown a dozen times before it would lodge on top of the pile. It seemed to me that human attainments are like this; every new piece of knowledge is another plate or Indian club balanced on top of a wobbling pile. Once in a thousand years one man may have the knack of balancing his pile of objects perfectly; his knowledge does not threaten to overbalance and fall on him; every new piece of knowledge settles firmly on the one before, and a Plato or a Newton is produced. And some have no faculty for balance at all; the pile collapses before it is more than a few feet high; we call the result insanity, or nervous breakdown.

I thought of all this as I looked at the child, realizing that to wish her intelligent was only to condemn her to a lifetime of effort to balance the absurd column of pencils and chairs on her nose. Then I stood up to get off the bus, and my vision clouded for a moment with fatigue, so that I had to sit down again. I was aware as this happened that the link between my body and my consciousness had weakened for a moment, and again I felt fear, anger and futility.

I walked to the building that housed our pistol-club, without any real hope of being able to get in unobserved. I was right. The caretaker – a tall old man – was standing on the doorstep, his hands resting on a broom, talking to the char-lady. I waited for five minutes, standing at a bus-stop, then decided to go to the office. For a moment I considered walking in boldly, explaining that I had left my pistol downstairs, and demanding the key; but the caretaker would probably come down with me and it was not worth risking. On the other hand, it was important to get the gun back in the cupboard before long; it had not been cleaned, which almost certainly meant that Ewen Waite would call in for it at an early opportunity.

My chance came sooner than I had expected. I had only just finished my filing when the chief of another department came down to ask if I could collect some papers from the Water Board offices – their office boy was away. It was just after ten. My route to the Water Board offices would pass the pistol-club building.

To my annoyance, the caretaker was still in the hall, visible from the doorway. Then I saw a big car parked nearby that looked like Ewen Waite's, and my stomach contracted. I hurried to the Water Board offices, collected the folder, declined a cup of tea, and went back. A man came out of the building as I approached, but I could no longer see the caretaker. There was no way of finding out whether he was still downstairs except to go into the building, so that is what I did. No one was visible. I hurried down the stairs, which were badly lighted since no windows opened directly on to them. Then, to my dismay, I saw that the door of the club was already open. I stood there for a few moments, listening; there was no sound from inside. The only sound came from below – in the boiler-room – where someone was shovelling coal. I went forward cautiously and looked into the room; there was no one there; there was a bucket of steaming water and a mop in the middle of the room, and a smell of disinfectant. I decided that it was time to do things openly. If anyone came in now I would have to claim that I was there to collect my own pistol. So I switched on the light, closed the door, and got the key out of the drawer. In a few moments I had replaced Ewen Waite's Biretta in the cupboard. Then came a problem I had not considered. Should I leave my own gun or take it? Both courses were risky. If I took it away with me I could later claim that this was why I had been in the building. But it would also mean admitting that I had been in the building. If I left it, and had been seen entering the place, then I would no longer have any excuse for having come; otherwise, why should I go without the thing I had called for?

There was no time for hesitation. I thrust my own gun into the cupboard and locked it. I heard a sound of a key in a lock behind me, and turned quickly; but it came from outside the door. I dropped the key of the cupboard back in the drawer and hurried out. On my way up the stairs I met the char-lady; but she paid me no attention. Outside again, I felt suddenly pleased with myself for what seemed the first time in weeks, and started to whistle as I walked back to the office. Then I remembered that I had forgotten to wear gloves, and had probably left my fingerprints all over the cupboard and the key. Luckily I had not handled Ewen Waite's gun since I had wiped it clean the night before and wrapped it in cloth; even so, I had probably left a fingerprint somewhere on the handle.

It struck me that everything I was doing now was calculated to get me into more trouble. If I had fired the shot with my own gun and then owned up to it, I might at least have claimed self-defence; but all this subterfuge would make it seem planned. There was only one thing on my side – how could I have known that I might be attacked by a gang? I could hardly have planned it.

The worst of it was that I did not care. I knew I was in danger, that I might even end in a reform school for the next few years; but it seemed unimportant. As I walked back to the office I thought about the millionaire's suicide, and wondered if it would not be a sensible thing to kill myself. But it would be no answer to my complete boredom. Then I thought of Uncle Sam, and it seemed to me that I at least knew exactly why he had retired to his bedroom for twenty years. What could be more obvious? If life was as completely empty and meaningless as it seemed to me, then suicide was also pointless, for it would only be a doorway from one futility into another. What other way out could there be? Why not simply *refuse* to live? Sit in a room, have the window bricked up, and stare into space. Uncomfortable, of course, but more logical than suicide. Its only trouble as a solution: it depended on fate allowing you to retire from the world.

The office was intolerable to me; I was tired and irritable. When I had finished typing envelopes for court summonses I pretended to be searching the files, in order to be allowed to sit and do nothing. And I thought that it would be a fine thing if a man could somehow register his dissent to life, express total disgust. Unfortunately this is almost impossible. A few poets have tried it – but the very action of writing a poem, no matter how blasphemous, is a kind of affirmation.

Midday came at last. I hurried to the newspaper-seller outside Woolworth's to get the early edition of the evening paper; to my annoyance, it was still not out. I started to walk back towards the office of the *Daily Chronicle*, then remembered that I might meet Patricia and stopped. I felt no desire to 'have things out' with her – only never to see her again. While I was standing outside Woolworth's, hesitating about what to do, I saw Jeremy coming towards me. He seemed to be in a good mood. He told me that he had checked in three local libraries, and that his book was out from all of them; the bookseller in the market-place mentioned that he had sold three copies in the past week. Jeremy suggested that we should go and have lunch together, but I felt too sick and excited to eat, so I said, What about a beer? Jeremy must have felt unusually elated; he agreed without hesitation.

Seated in a corner of the bar, with half-pints of mild ale, I regretted being there. Then, like a fool, I overturned my beer in the act of picking it up; Jeremy had to borrow a cloth from the barman, and I bought another half-pint. When we were seated again, he asked, with unusual sympathy:

'What is it? You look depressed.'

I decided on a partial truth. I told him about Patricia, and that she had gone back to Monty.

'You mean she was actually wearing his dressing-gown, with nothing underneath it?'

I said I didn't know what she was wearing underneath it, but could guess. I began to feel that my information cheered him as much as the news from the libraries, although he looked sympathetic enough. He said:

'I'm sorry about that, but it's probably just as well. She'd have you married in no time.'

I drained my beer and stood up. Jeremy said:

'I suppose you want to rush home.'

'No. As a matter of fact, I wanted to buy a paper.'

As soon as I said this I cursed myself for letting it out, and cursed myself more for looking confused about it. Jeremy's sympathy had thrown me off my guard. He said:

'Ah. I suppose you want to read about this sex crime?'

'Sex crime?'

'Didn't you?'

'What sex crime?'

'The man in the library told me about it. Some girl was murdered.'

He said this as if he thought it was the girl's own fault.

'Where?'

'Oh, I don't know. Out Culverstone way somewhere.'

By now we were back at the news-stand; the vendor

was just untying a parcel of papers. I bought one and looked at the front page, no longer bothering that Jeremy was watching me. The headline was about a bus overturning in a field, but the second headline said: 'Girl Strangled at Culverstone.' The story had evidently come in late, for it occupied a few lines on the front page, and was continued inside. There was no mention of the shooting incident. Jeremy asked me:

'What *did* you want to read about?'

'The football results,' I said.

He took me seriously, and said: 'Good god, you're getting worse.'

I looked quickly through the newspaper; there was no sign of a story about shooting. I was impatient of having Jeremy standing beside me, so I said that I intended to catch a bus home. (It was actually too late to get home for lunch now.) So Jeremy came with me as far as the bus-stop, then went off to his own bus. I promised to come and see him the same evening.

I searched the paper a second time to make sure that I had not missed it, then, for want of anything better to do, read the story about the murder. The girl, who was not yet identified, had been found on a piece of waste ground just beyond the city boundaries, strangled with her own headscarf. Although the body was naked, the police surgeon said that there was apparently no evidence of sexual assault. Her clothes had been folded neatly and left beside the body. It was assumed that she had travelled on the last bus – the conductor remembered her – and had met her murderer on her way home. Since her handbag was missing, the police suspected that robbery might be the motive.

I now began to feel hungry. I ate a cheese-roll in a coffee-bar, then walked back to the office.

The afternoon went by quickly. I now felt in a dream-like state, only half awake, and yet not sleepy. At four o'clock Mr Coles sent for me. As soon as I saw his face I felt that he was going to say something unpleasant; it had the gloating, hostile look that occasionally replaced the look of permanent indigestion.

'You're wanted at the police-station, Greene.' (He was the only person on the staff who called me Greene.)

My dream-like state remained unaltered. I said:

'Police-station?'

'Yes, the central one. You'd better go now. Have you finished your work?'

'I haven't done the post yet.'

'The others will have to do it then. Go now.'

As I walked through the streets I wondered why I felt so detached. Perhaps it was because I felt sure they could not intend to arrest me if they sent for me like this. But apart from this I felt a positive elation about something happening at last. The waiting had oppressed me more than I had realized. On my way to the station I wondered what Scottie Gibbs could know about the shooting. Had the boys described me? If so, there was nothing for it but to be frank, and plead self-defence. The main point was: Would they realize that the bullet had not been fired from my gun? And if they did find out, could I convince them that I had taken Ewen Waite's gun in mistake for my own?

The police-station seemed very crowded; constables and men in plain clothes kept going in and out. The desk-sergeant ignored me for at least ten minutes. Finally he asked me what I wanted, and I explained that I had been sent for.

'Who sent for you?'

'I don't know.'

'That's useful,' he said irritably. 'Well you'll have to wait while I find out. Sit down over there.'

I sat down for another ten minutes. Although the sergeant took several phone calls, and talked to half a dozen policemen, he apparently made no effort to find out who wanted me. I began to wonder if this was part of a plan – to make me wait to increase my apprehension and uncertainty. If so, it was not working: I waited as indifferently as if I was in a bus-queue. Two old ladies sitting beside me complained to one another about lost dogs and police incompetence.

Suddenly, Scottie Gibbs came out of his office, and went over to the sergeant. He said something in an aggrieved voice. The sergeant looked guilty and glanced across at me. I stood up.

'There you are, lad!' Scottie said. His manner was not exactly welcoming – it was too irritable for that – but he seemed glad I'd come. 'Come on in here, would you?'

As I went into his office he asked me:

'How long have you been here?' When I told him he swore. He said: 'Now, you can guess what it's all about, I suppose?'

'My firearms permit?'

'No. Not that. That's all in order. No, it's this murder case.'

For the first time I went cold. So the youth was dead. But his next words undeceived me.

'It's this girl. You've read about it, I suppose?'

I nodded, unable to trust my voice. My heart was still pounding, and my face had turned hot.

'We're not sure whether it's a sex crime – she wasn't touched – but we've got to make a check on all sex criminals. We've roped in this bloke you claim you saw with your sister. I want you to tell us if you identify him.'

'Him? You think it might be him?'

'It could be.'

'But I thought you said he had no record for sex crime?'

'He hasn't. Your report was the first I'd heard of it. But a man of his description was seen getting off a bus near the scene of the murder last night.'

'The newspaper said they thought the motive was robbery.'

'I know. But we found the handbag, and nothing's missing. There's still a few pounds in it.'

I nodded. It was hard to repress the thought that was at the front of my mind: I was still not suspected of the shooting.

'Would you like to come out here now?'

I followed him out of his office. I asked:

'Is that what all the excitement's about?'

He nodded. We went into a large room with only a few chairs in it. Scottie Gibbs switched on the lights: they illuminated only the far end of the room. Scottie called: 'All right.' A door at the far end opened, and a policeman came out, followed by a dozen men. All were dressed like workmen. The last out of the door was the youth 'Jed'. They lined up across the end of the room, blinking towards us (although I doubt whether they could see us, since the lights were in their eyes). Scottie said:

'Can you see him?'

I looked along the line for a few minutes. I remembered Jed looking into my brief-case the night before. If I possessed some evidence against him, he also possessed some against me. I said:

'I'm sorry, but I'm not sure. Several of them look a bit like him. My memory's very bad for faces.'

'That's not what you said last Saturday.'

'I'm sorry,' I said.

He sighed. 'All right.' He called to the policeman: 'Take them out. Thank you, gentlemen.'

I felt sorry for disappointing him. I said:

'But what's the good of me identifying him if you haven't any evidence anyway?'

'Not much,' he said wearily.

He did not even say goodbye as I went out.

It was nearly five o'clock. There was no point in returning to the office. But outside, among the lights and evening traffic, I realized that I still knew nothing about the shooting – nothing except that the youth had been taken away in an ambulance. I decided to go to the café again.

There was no sign of Kaspar. Once inside, I regretted coming. I felt exhausted and depressed; I looked at the large, thick cup and the strong tea with disgust. The place was fairly crowded; most of them seemed to be workmen. There were very few seats; I had to sit at a table at which three men were already sitting. The men at the table were not workmen, although they were shabbily dressed; they sat there, hardly talking. I pretended to look at my pocket-copy of Diophantus, but this was only to avoid embarrassment. I wanted to leave, but felt no particular desire to go home. I cleared a small circle from the mist on the window and looked out into the street, and wondered what had happened to my springs of motive.

A newsboy came into the café calling 'Racing extra'. One of the men at my table jumped up and bought one. They turned to the back page, and then suddenly began to laugh and beat one another on the back. Workmen at other tables turned around to stare at them. One of the men, who had a high squeaking laugh, said: 'Five hundred nicker apiece. I told you it'd come up.' From sitting gloomy and silent, they now all began to talk together. At first I was irritated; then, in spite of myself,

I began to listen to their conversation. It was not particularly enlightening. They mentioned women and a woman called 'Aggie', of whom they all seemed to be in terror; then they began to remind one another of a day at Wolverhampton (I gathered that their horse had won at Wolverhampton) and to talk about a party at which one of them had playfully stolen Aggie's bra when she was drunk.

I mention all this because I experienced a curious effect of double exposure as I listened. It was like watching a film in a foreign language and listening to a conversation in English going on behind you. Every one of their sentences had an effect of the unexpected, the absurd. They might have been Martians twittering at one another in bird language. I felt a little afraid; I could not tell what was happening inside me. This meaninglessness was a new sensation. On the counter a portable radio was playing a symphony that sounded like Haydn or Mozart; this came in faint bursts between the conversation, and was mixed up with sentences from Diophantus: 'Hence if a pair of simultaneous equations exists, then there exists a pair of equations of the same form in which no two of the numbers x, y, z, t, have a common factor other than unity . . .' And it seemed that the Mozart, the arithmetic, the conversation, were all fragmentary and meaningless, all futile.

One of the men looked at his watch and said: 'Half past five. Pub's open.' They got up and went out. I was about to do the same when Kaspar came in. He looked worried. He came across to me – my table was the only empty one in the room – and said: 'Hello, young 'un.' Then he sat there, glancing at the newspaper that had been left behind. He obviously felt no desire for conversation, and no more appetite for the soup-like tea than I did. Finally he said: 'You waiting for somebody?' 'Not really,' I said, but he was obviously not interested. To attract his attention I said: 'I spent this afternoon at the police-station.' He looked up with interest, but only said 'Yes?'

'They wanted me to identify someone.'

This time there was no doubt about the interest; but I also noticed something more, an anxiety about what was coming next. I said:

'It was that boy we were talking to last night – Jed.'

I was surprised by the effect of my words. He became so pale that it was as if I had hit him in the stomach. He seemed to collapse in his chair, to deflate. Then he looked at me very tiredly, and said: 'So?'

'I didn't identify him.'

He looked unbelieving.

'You didn't?'

I was puzzled by this display of emotion, but not displeased. I had come to see Kaspar because I was worried about the pistol and wanted to know how much he knew, and it was obvious that I had somehow reversed our positions.

Kaspar said: 'We can't talk here. Come on over the road.'

I saw no reason why we should not talk there; the babble of voices was so noisy that there was no chance of being overheard; but I followed him across the road and into the pub where I had been with Kaspar and Monty. He said: 'What you going to have?' I asked for beer, and sat in a corner. It seemed significant that he had asked me to drink; somehow, I didn't think of Kaspar as a man who paid for drinks. He went to the bar, and I saw why he had brought me to the pub. He ordered a whisky, drained it standing at the bar, then had his glass refilled before he returned across the room. He took another large gulp from his glass as soon as he sat down. Then he said:

'All right. So where's Jed now?'

'I don't know.'

'How did you get mixed up in this?'

As I told him – about the episode in the spinney with my sister – he seemed to relax. When I mentioned about going to the police-station with Patricia, he became tense again. He said:

'Why'd you want to do that?'

I tried to explain that I had no special motive. I bore Jed no grudge for his unsuccessful attempt on Anne. I had mentioned it to Scottie Gibbs merely because he was in the pistol-club. I realized that I could not disclose the real motive – my nervousness about my loaded gun and desire to change the subject of conversation.

Kaspar bought himself another whisky – without, however, offering me more beer. When he sat down again, he seemed less nervous, altogether more in control. He said:

'Look, there's one thing I don't understand about all this. Where do you come in?'

'I've told you.'

'Why didn't you identify Jed?'

'Why should I? It wouldn't have made any difference anyway.'

He stared at me, and I realized that he was now trying to force me into retreat. But having seen him restore his courage with whisky I felt slightly contemptuous. So I met his stare for a few moments, then asked:

'Do *you* think that Jed killed that girl?'

From the way his face tensed, I knew he was jarred. He drank more whisky, then stared back at me in a quite different manner, as if he was talking to me – perhaps saying: 'You ought to know better than to ask questions like that.' But what he said finally was:

'I still don't see where you come in. Why do you want to tell me about it?'

I saw that he had gone to the heart of the matter, and remained silent. Then he said:

'Why were you carrying a gun in your bag last night?'

'I always carry a gun,' I said jokingly.

'Why?'

'I had two more in there. Didn't Jed look in the bottom of the brief-case?'

'Why?' he repeated. I had been trying to find out if he knew there were two guns in the case. I said:

'Because I'm a member of the local pistol-club. That's where I talked to Scottie Gibbs about Jed.'

I realized now that, to some extent, we were fencing. Kaspar knew I had a gun; but Ewen Waite had seen me leave my gun in the cupboard. So long as Kaspar didn't know this, however, I felt that I held the upper hand.

For a moment I thought he looked completely defeated. Then suddenly he smiled.

'I know why you want to talk to me. You shot that man on the waste ground behind the Commercial last night, didn't you?'

I wanted to deny this; but I hate lying pointlessly. So I said nothing – borrowing Kaspar's tactics – but simply stared at him for a moment, then drank my beer. He said:

'You came in there last night with your hand bleeding and looking as if you'd been in a fight.'

I stared back at him. Unexpectedly, he became friendly.

'Listen, son, you help me and I'll help you. You don't want to get me into trouble, do you?'

'No,' I said truthfully.

'Right. And it's the same here. Why did you shoot the bloke anyway?'

I suddenly decided that there was no point in lying. I realized that I might be making a mistake, but I said:

'It was nothing to do with me. A mob of Teddy-boys set on me. They didn't realize I was carrying a gun.'

'Set on you, did they?' He obviously thought I was lying. 'Why?'

I decided to tell the partial truth. I told him that they always blocked the pavement outside the Palais, and that this irritated me. I told him about pushing my way through them. It was evident that he now believed me. He chuckled and said:

'That was a silly thing to do. You can't mess with those lads.'

I shrugged, and he said:

'But of course you'd got your gun with you. But it wouldn't have been any use if it wasn't loaded . . .'

I shrugged. He was sharper than I had thought.

'So it must have been loaded, eh? I didn't know you were allowed to carry a loaded gun.'

'You're not,' I said.

'I see.' He began to pick his teeth. Then he said:

'Well, that's all right. You've got nothing to worry about. It was self-defence. Of course they're bound to catch you. If you take my advice, you'll go and see your friend Gibbs and tell him the whole story.'

'Why?'

'They'll check on the bullet. How many did you fire? One? Well, they'll dig it out. It might have got flattened if it hit a bone, but the chances are that it's still all right. So they'll be able to tell that it came from your gun. That's all right. You can plead self-defence. When did you load the gun?'

'Out in the lavatory at the Commercial,' I said. I felt that it was time to stretch the story.

'Well, that's all right. You knew these boys were waiting for you outside – you needed some kind of self-defence. You haven't got a record, have you? Haven't been nicked for anything? No, I didn't think you were the type. And you're under eighteen. So what you worried about? You're laughing. Judges don't like the Teddy-boys anyway. They'll tell you to be more careful next time and let you off. You might get thrown out of your shooting-club, that's all . . .'

I said: 'Do you know anything about the shooting? Do you know if I killed him?

'No. I haven't seen anything in the paper.'

'It's not in the paper. I looked.'

'Hmmm.' He began to pick his teeth again. 'That might be serious. They don't usually keep things dark unless they've got a reason.'

'What sort of a reason?'

'I don't know . . . Depends what they know. Have you been home yet?'

'Today? No. Why?'

'They might be waiting there for you.'

This thought jarred me. I said:

'What would you advise me to do?'

'I'd advise you to go and see Gibbs and tell him everything. Tell him you've been trying to make up your mind all day.'

I thought about this for a while. This was an inviting idea; but I had been to the police-station once today without saying anything, and I would have to explain why. This made me less certain that Kaspar's advice was good. Besides, how could the police connect it with me unless the boys themselves had described me? And if they had, then I would be forced to admit that I had used

270

Ewen Waite's gun, and the whole story would be out. I might as well keep silent until they found out for themselves. I asked him:

'Have *you* got any way of finding out what happened to the boy?'

He thought about this for a moment.

'Where did the bullet hit him?'

'I don't know. Fairly low down. It was all dark.'

'All right. I'll try and find out what I can. See me in the café the same time tomorrow.'

He seemed anxious to go. The door behind him opened, and Jed looked in. He saw me and stopped. I said:

'Here's your friend.'

Kaspar looked around, and said irritably: 'What do you want?' Jed came slowly across to us, and sat down. He seemed to have no self-confidence left. As Kaspar glared at him he cringed. He started to say: 'I'm sorry, but they don't know anything. They . . .' Kaspar said: 'Shut up. Tell me outside.' He stood up and said to me: 'Tomorrow, over the road.' Then he grabbed Jed's arm and pushed him towards the door. Something about this surprised me. From the little I had seen of Jed, he had not struck me as the sort of person who could be bullied.

I sat there for another ten minutes, and it struck me that I might have blundered into a position of considerable danger. Jed and Kaspar were criminals; there could be no doubt about that. And Kaspar was not the worn-out dipsomaniac I had taken him for; he had somehow succeeded in getting me to tell him everything, and had told me nothing. And here I sat, holding a dangerous piece of information: that Jed was a sex killer. Strangely enough, this thought left me untouched. Probably it seemed too remote; I could not imagine Jed strangling a girl and then stripping her. Besides, there was something

271

oddly indefinite about the case itself; the girl had not been raped or robbed. I remembered the words the prostitute had spoken to Jed the night before: 'Not your way; it's too hard.' What could she mean? That Jed wanted to practise some perversion on her?

I thought about these problems all the way home, although my attention was divided by the question of whether I would find detectives waiting for me. My thoughts were unsatisfactory; everything seemed so indeterminate. When I thought back over the conversation with Kaspar I could not imagine why he was worried. I had no evidence that Jed was the killer, and nothing I had to say would interest the police. So why had he been so afraid? The explanation I hit upon was probably the right one: I had caught him off balance, before he had been drinking, and for a moment he thought I knew more than I actually did. But what could I know? This was the thing that puzzled me. Why should Kaspar be so anxious on Jed's account? What was the connection between the two?

Deep inside me, I did not expect to find detectives waiting at home for me, and I was right. I ate some tea – kippers on toast – and as I did so the phone rang. My sister called 'Hugh, it's Patricia.' I cursed and went on eating. When Anne came in to repeat her message I told her to say that I was not at home. 'But she heard me call you.' 'Then tell her you made a mistake.' Anne went and delivered the message, and my mother started asking me questions – why had I quarrelled, etc. I sat there sullenly, refusing to answer. So much had happened in the past twenty-four hours that I no longer felt any regret about Patricia. A part of me was pleased about this: I realized that if I had nothing else to think about, I would be tormented by the thought of her infidelity. This only made me aware that human beings waste their lives on emotions that don't deserve attention, out of sheer empty-headedness. I thought of the men in the café and their pleasure about winning on a horse, and the aimless conversation that followed: it struck me that human life is all freedom, far too much freedom. And we destroy ourselves with freedom.

To avoid my mother's questions, I went up to my room afterwards. The phone rang twice – both times for my sister – and I realized that I was waiting in a state of tension for something to happen. I remembered my promise to Jeremy and decided to go, although I felt no desire to see him. It had turned into a wet and windy night, and when I got off the bus in Cranthorpe square I was tempted to get on again and simply return home. I have never felt so completely devoid of motive as that evening; every step I took towards Jeremy's cottage was an effort, requiring an inner dialogue: 'Why are you doing this when you don't want to go? Because I don't want to go back either.'

I found Jeremy looking depressed. As soon as I came in he said: 'Something's going to happen.' I asked what he meant. 'As soon as I came in this afternoon, I saw the gardener.'

'You mean the ghost?'

'Yes. But he was in here. He was like a shadow as I came through the door. I thought someone had got into the cottage. Then he just vanished – he wasn't there.'

'But you've seen him before. Why should you be worried?'

'I know. But he's never been visible in the house before.'

'Perhaps he doesn't like the cold,' I said.

The rest of the evening was a failure. I had hoped – without any real conviction – that Jeremy might talk to me, cheer me up. But he remained depressed. At one

273

point, after we had listened to a movement of the Franck sonata, he turned from the record player suddenly and asked: 'Do you think I'm going to die?' I said I didn't, and we dropped the subject; but we both felt that the music was just an irritating noise. I realized that I was hoping for someone I could turn to, to restore to me a sense of human warmth. But there was no one: neither my parents, nor Jeremy, nor Monty, nor Patricia. I felt like a man who wants to fall down and go to sleep, but is forced to keep on walking. Jeremy's room seemed a mockery of my feelings; with its albums of music, the Hammond organ, the books, it implied that there is another life besides the aimless stupidity of human 'normality', the absurd, repetitious chatter of everyday life. I had spent my life pursuing this reality because, for some reason, I had been born lucky; I had always had mathematics and ideas. Consequently I had never been forced to search for meaning in trivial repetition; my meaning arrived concentrated and airtight, between the covers of a book. But this had only increased the irony, delayed the recognition of futility.

This was one of my worst moments. I felt that I was falling, and there was nothing to stop me. The question of whether the police caught me ceased to be important. A feeling of evil pressed on me, an inescapable evil, *with no alternative*. Everything became meaningless. Bach, who was now dinning in my ears, was a stupid, fat old organist with a huge family and a naïve faith in Christianity. I felt as if I was vomiting, but vomiting up ideas. And just as a man who is racked with nausea cannot understand why people thrust food into their mouths and swallow it, so I could not understand why people smiled and expressed emotions. The thought of the men in the café came back to me, but its last level of meaninglessness was now revealed. They were grimacing and laughing;

274

but they had no idea that *everything* in life is deception; there are no values connected with the things we accept as meaningful.

I felt that I was stifling, and that my body would disintegrate with the horror. It was a sharp pain, as real as if I had gripped the edge of a sticking-plaster that covered a burn, and ripped it away, exposing the raw flesh. I saw that I had been mistaken in believing that Uncle Nick was mad. He was neither more nor less mad than anyone in the world. It is only that the rest of the world has come to a general agreement to accept a certain kind of madness as sanity, as normality. It is like a colony of lepers deciding that a certain stage of the disease shall be accepted as total health.

There was no point in sitting there any longer. I told Jeremy that I felt ill, and left. He made no attempt to stop me; it was obvious that he was also full of apprehension. I wondered if his 'ghost' had been a presage of this revelation that had come to me. Our human delusions are like a house, enclosing us on all sides, keeping out the cold of reality. It seemed that I had torn a hole in the fabric, and the cold was blowing through. Was this why Jeremy looked so tired and depressed? The cold was coming into his room.

It was a bad night; the rain was so violent that I could hardly see. I made no attempt to cover myself against it. It seemed absurd that the world should still keep on demanding reactions of me when I felt that everything was meaningless. But at one point I slipped on some mud and skidded into the ditch. I reacted automatically, trying to balance myself, and scrambling out, my shoes full of water, I found myself smiling. The force of habit, at least, is strong. In the village, I went into the pub and ordered a whisky. The owner looked at me very hard – he knew I was under age – but he served me. I drank it quickly, disliking the noise of people, and feeling again a return of the horror of futility, and feeling that they might as well vanish into nothingness since everything they did was already nothing.

But as I sat in the front of the bus, travelling back into town, it came to me that there was an element I had left out of my calculations. If all men are futile, why had I been given a perception of the futility? If all men are equally diseased, how had I managed to recognize it, if not from some intuitive idea of health?

But what puzzled me most was the question: How had I got into this condition? I was like a man who wakes one morning to find himself covered with scales of dead flesh and no knowledge of how it had come about. I had always been happy enough in the past; I had eaten my meals and talked to relatives and studied my chosen subject, all with a sense that it was meaningful. How, then, had I failed to notice that it was entirely deception? And how had Uncle Sam managed to see a half of the truth and not the other half? He knew that human beings are inefficient machines, incapable of feeling, dragging around a body as heavy as a mountain. And yet he did not seem to feel that the whole of human life is a monstrous joke – worse than that, a horror, a dead end, with nothing beyond it.

I was frozen and wet to the skin when I got off the bus. It was still not ten o'clock, which probably meant that my parents would not yet be in bed. I decided to walk across the park; then I noticed that the light in Aunt Bertha's kitchen was still on, and decided to gain more time by going to see her. Any other relative would have been unbearable; but Aunt Bertha expected nothing; she would not have been surprised if I had sat there without talking for half an hour and then walked off without saying goodnight.

There was a big fire burning. Aunt Bertha looked up from her rug-making to say, 'Hello, dear,' and then went on working. I poured myself tea – there was nearly always a pot on the table, more or less warm – and stood in front of the fire to drink it. She asked: 'Have you come to see your Uncle Sam?' I had not, but could hardly say so. I said: 'Won't he be asleep?' 'He might be. I'll go and see in a moment.' 'Don't bother.' 'No bother.' So ten minutes later I found myself following her up the stairs. I should have preferred to avoid Uncle Sam; I could not talk to him about what was on my mind. There was no point in talking to anybody. What did it matter if Uncle Sam had experienced this same insight of total and universal futility? It had no relevance for me.

There was something about Uncle Sam's presence that was an antidote to depression. No mediocrity seemed to hang in the air around him. I do not know how he maintained this sense of alertness when he lay there for sixteen hours of every day, staring into the darkness. I felt this tension of his consciousness as soon as I spoke to him, and was grateful for it.

'Well, boy, what have you come to tell me?'

'Nothing, I'm afraid.' It sounded feeble, vapid.

'You look tired. Have you been overworking?'

I said no. I sat there for another five minutes. Neither of us spoke. Then he said:

'That's one of the things I like about you. Most people of your age seem to be ashamed or afraid of silence.'

In spite of my gloom I felt flattered. I said:

'I suppose they don't realize the impossibility of saying anything that matters.' I felt ashamed of this as soon as I'd said it; it sounded pompous.

He took a long time about replying – as always – then said:

'That's meaningless. Anything's worth saying if you feel a need to say it.'

'Supposing you feel no need?'

'Supposing you don't want to live at all?'

'Is that why you're in here?' I asked him. I had always been afraid to ask this question; it seemed too personal; but now it was the obvious question.

'Because I don't want to live? Good heavens no, boy. On the contrary. I'm here because I want to live, and because I'm tired of the poor imitation of life that most people accept.'

This came out so readily that it sounded rehearsed. He stared at me after he said it, as if to see whether it had been worth saying. I said finally:

'Is there any other kind?'

'There could be.'

'Are you sure? Wouldn't that be just another delusion?'

'What do you mean, a delusion? There's only one thing you can know for certain – that you exist. And if you sit on a pin and it hurts, then you know it hurts because it hurts your existence. That can't be a delusion.'

I had not intended to talk to him, but I now found myself expressing the total nihilism that was in me, even though it seemed pointless to express it. I cannot remember the words I used. Probably they seemed clearer to me than they actually were. When I had finished I felt a certain curiosity. I was certain that he would say nothing that was relevant to the ideas I had expressed, yet somehow I believed that he might. What he said was:

'If there's no such thing as truth, then everything you've said is meaningless. You've been going round in a circle.'

'Unless the truth is that there is no truth.'

'That's meaningless too. Listen, boy. The one thing of

which I'm fairly certain is my own existence. Man is surrounded by darkness. This wouldn't matter if he had just one certainty to fall back on – if his own existence was a final certainty. But it's not. His existence is also full of darkness. There's darkness outside and darkness inside. He's like a circular band of light, with darkness inside and out. Do you see what I mean?'

I did.

He went on: 'Now you're telling me that you've found another certainty – that the whole thing's meaningless. Now I agree that this is one possibility of many. But why should you be so dogmatic about being right?'

I was astonished. I should have thought it impossible for any impression to be made on my self-enclosed circuit of nihilism, but he had somehow broken in. And yet I saw his point very clearly as he explained it more fully. I had recognized that human beings impose their own meanings on the world, as any religious crank can read his own meanings into the Bible. And because I saw that most of these meanings are delusions. I was imposing my own meaning on it – the idea of total futility and meaninglessness.

Aunt Bertha interrupted us with his bed-time drink. When she had gone out, he said: 'I think I'd better sleep now. All this talking tires me.' Before I went out, I turned to ask him:

'Have *you* got any idea of the reality behind it all?'

'Only one. It's power. That's why I know you're mistaken. If you think you've seen truth, and it's dull and disillusioning, then you haven't seen it.'

'Have you seen it?'

'No, not steadily. I've seen it in flashes – like all of us. Read Blake.'

I walked back across the park – walking cautiously because it was still raining and the ground was slippery.

The fatigue was still there, and what he had said made no difference to the sense of futility. For I asked myself: 'If the reality of the world is power then why am I incapable of seeing it?' The answer was obvious enough: Because human beings are incapable of feeling. In that case, the question of the world's reality was irrelevant to me. All that mattered was the human reality – futility and weakness.

And yet Uncle Sam's words fermented inside me. I was still aware of their presence, as a kind of excitement.

It came to me, before I fell asleep, that a certain phase of my life had come to an end. Ever since Uncle Nick taught me about the hollow earth and his secret enemies, I had been looking for a belief that would not collapse, for a truth 'out there'. Mathematics became the symbol of that truth. Now I knew there was no truth 'out there'. But I possessed no mathematic capable of surveying the inner darkness.

9

I experienced a curious feeling of foreboding as I left the house the following morning. The weather was cold. There was frost on the pavement, and on the leaves of the hedges. Before I went to the bus-stop, I bought a morning paper, and glanced quickly through it, in case the news of the shooting had somehow reached the national newspapers. There was nothing although I noticed that several papers carried front-page stories about the murdered girl. She had been identified as a typist called Moira Page, who lived about half a mile from the spot where her body was found.

As I stood at the bus-stop, reading about the murder, a throaty voice said in my ear: 'Lookin' for news, are you?' I turned, smiling, thinking that it was some local acquaintance, then felt a chill as I looked into the yellow, reptilian face of the man called Dime. He was heavily muffled in a black overcoat, and was wearing a checked cap – a cheerful-looking object that was completely unsuited to the wax-like face. At this point I felt no alarm; after all, he might also be on his way to work. But a moment later he said:

'Where can we go where we can talk quietly?'

He was gripping my elbow in a way that hurt it, although his face looked casual and friendly enough. There were several other people around us, but no one seemed curious; no doubt it looked like two acquaintances chattering. I said:

'We could walk up there.'

We left the stop and walked up towards the recreation-ground. At this time of the morning it was closed. Beyond the recreation-ground was a spinney with a small pond in it; we walked towards this. It was now, for the first time, that I felt some intimation of danger. How had he found me? What did he want? He walked without talking, his hands in the overcoat pockets. I said, trying to sound casual: 'I can't spare much time. I'll be late for the office.' Without looking at me he said: 'You'll find some excuse.' The tone of this was peremptory, domineering; he was telling me that I would do what he wanted, and like it.

At the edge of the spinney, in a clear space, stood a corporation cart, covered with heavy tarpaulin. He said: 'This'll do.' We stopped behind this cart; where we were standing we were invisible to the road, although our legs could be seen under the cart. He turned to face me and looked down at his shoes, as if he was looking for the right words to begin. Then he said, in the same level, neutral voice:

'Now I hear you're acquainted with Jerry Pierce.'

'Who?'

'You know,' he said, his voice immediately taking on the irritable, bullying tone, 'Jed Pierce.'

'I didn't know his name was Pierce,' I said.

'Didn't you?' He looked at me as if he disbelieved me.

He frightened me, but I was determined not to show it, either by talking nervously or going to the opposite extreme and pretending to be eager to be friendly. I waited for him to go on. At close quarters he no longer produced in me the same sense of evil power; the way in which he made a casual pretence of disguising his threatening tone might have been learned from any gangster film; there was something vulgar about it. Finally he said:

'Charley tells me you didn't identify Jerry yesterday.'

I remembered that Kaspar's name was Charles. I said:

282

'That's right.'

'That was kind of you. I just wanted to say thank you for that.'

I looked at him with surprise. 'Why?'

'It was a friendly act. Of course, Jerry didn't 'ave nothing to do with that girl who got strangled, of course.'

I said nothing. He added:

'He was with Doris at the time . . . Doris, my . . . girl-friend.'

I knew this to be untrue; I had been behind him when she refused to let him go back home with her. Naturally, I said nothing of this. I was a little reassured by this time; it seemed plain that he only wanted to talk. People walked fairly close to us every few minutes, and any one of them would have heard me if I had shouted, so it was unlikely that he wanted to attack me.

'Still,' he went on, 'Jerry's had a little trouble with the police before now, and they might like an opportunity to put him inside.'

While he was saying this I was trying hard to decide why he wanted to talk to me, and what connection he had with Kaspar and 'Jerry'. He went on smoothly:

'Now I gather you're in a spot of trouble yourself.' He looked at me as he said this; so far, he had kept his eyes elsewhere.

'Am I?' I said.

'Course, I know it was self-defence. Still, if he dies, you might be in a bit of a mess.'

As he said this he took his hand out of his overcoat pocket, and I saw that he was holding a thin and ugly-looking knife. He began idly chipping at the edge of the cart with it. It was razor-sharp; the lightest touch peeled off thin slivers of wood. Then he began using its point to clean dirt from under his nails. He said:

'Right. Well, that's all I wanted to say.' He looked full

at me, and his smile was entirely cold. 'You help us and we'll help you. Right?'

'Right,' I said automatically.

'Because,' he said, pointing at me with the knife as if it was his finger, 'we know how to stand by our friends. And we don't like people who talk to the police.' As he said this, his smile became definitely unpleasant. I remembered that I had told Kaspar that I had identified Jed's photograph in the police-station, and I read a threat into his words. As he went on smiling, he drew the point of his knife very lightly along the cloth of my coat, and the fibres parted. It was a shallow cut, but it revealed that his knife was kept very sharp indeed. He looked at the cut and smiled again, this time making no pretence of hiding the threat.

I decided to try asking the question that troubled me.

'How did you find out where I lived?'

'Oh, that was easy enough.' He started to chip at the cart again, and said: 'Nice little house, that is. I saw your sister too. Was that the one Jerry made a pass at?' He had cut a long, deep splinter from the cart; now he grasped this with his hand, and wrenched it off, with a tearing of wood. The gesture was unmistakably intended to convey violence. Then he said: 'Yes, a nice-looking girl, your sister.' I knew that he was lying about having seen Anne; she was still in bed when I left the house. But I sensed the seriousness of his threat for all that.

He was so preoccupied at playing the gangster that he failed to notice the group of workmen who came towards us. Before he could put the knife away, one of them had walked round the cart, and stared at the long splinter of wood in his hand, then at the side of the cart. He was a fat, red-faced man, and I presume he was the foreman. Then he said, in an outraged voice: ''Ere, what you think's goin' on 'ere?' The knife disappeared as if by a conjuring trick, but the foreman was not impressed. 'It's no use hidin' it. I saw that knife. What you think you're up to, eh?' Dime, scowling and looking oddly guilty, turned away and started to walk off. But the foreman was in a bad mood. He said: 'No you don't,' then shouted to the men: 'Come on here.' Then, as Dime started to walk away: 'Stop him. Let's have his name and address.' The men moved across Dime's path, and the foreman followed him, saying: 'That's corporation property. We could 'ave you in court for that.' Dime looked round, and his face was malevolent. I was amused and delighted by this baiting, and was smiling; but my smile disappeared as I caught his savage glare. His hand moved in his pocket, and I suspected that he was going to use the knife. Instead, he marched straight at the men, said something in a snarling voice, and was allowed to go on. At this point I saw a bus at a stop a few hundred yards away, and knew I could intercept it by running. No one tried to stop me. As I climbed on to the platform, I saw Dime's black shoulders, and the festive-looking check cap, disappearing into a side street.

When I sat down and thought about it I felt less complacent. Dime's discomfiture was no victory for me. Boaster or not, he was undoubtedly dangerous. And he knew where I lived – or at least, would obviously have no difficulty finding out. But *why* did he want to threaten me? What could I tell the police?

Another question troubled me; he had said: 'If the boy dies . . .' He might be bluffing, of course. But what other explanation accounted for this silence about the shooting? If the youth had been badly injured – too badly injured to talk – then the police would have to wait until he could be interrogated. Perhaps the other boy had run away – the one who must have phoned for the ambulance, or summoned a passer-by to help. But why should it not appear in the newspapers? This was what baffled me.

Throughout the morning I found it difficult to concentrate. The whole business produced a curious feeling of inner conflict that was almost completely unrelated to fear. I was somehow irritated by the *irrelevance* of these complications. At the same time, I realized that it was my own fault for getting involved in the pistol-club and the idea of administering 'justice' to the Teddy-boys. Why had I done this? I knew the answer. It was an attempt to prove to myself that I was more than an ineffectual thinker. And what *had* I proved? This was what troubled me. The whole thing had dissolved into meaninglessness – or into such a tangle of meanings that I was lost in them.

When I walked out of the building at lunch-time I found Patricia waiting for me. She was another irrelevancy. I noticed irritably that she blushed and looked unsure of herself. Yet I was not angry with her; in a way, I felt sorry for her. She was caught in the same meaninglessness as the rest of us, and this explained why she had been to bed with Monty after leaving me. I understood her too well to resent her; I forgave her as I forgave myself.

I said: 'Hello'; then, as she stood looking uncertain of what to say, I suggested that we should walk towards her bus-stop. She asked finally:

'Why have you been avoiding me?'

I was in no mood for evasion. I said: 'Because I know where you went after you left me on Wednesday.'

'I went home . . .'

I did not even bother to look at her to see how she was carrying off the lie.

'I know you didn't because I saw you with Monty.'

'But I was waiting for you. Let me explain . . .'

She claimed that she had met Monty and Nigel on her way through the town; Monty had told her that I would probably go there later, and invited her to go back and wait for me. She said that she left Monty's at eleven o'clock – with Nigel.

'Why were you wearing his dressing-gown?'

'Because his room was freezing. His fire had gone out, and I sat there shivering. So he told me to put his dressing-gown on . . .'

I felt baffled by this. I thought it was probably untrue; but it hardly mattered to me whether it was true or not. We had reached her bus-stop. I said:

'Look, this is stupid. I don't know whether you're telling the truth or not . . .'

'Ask Monty . . .'

'That wouldn't prove anything.'

She said, with sudden exasperation:

'Why do you think I'm here now if I've been sleeping with Monty?'

'Why are you?'

'Because I don't want to quarrel.'

All this struck me as tiresome; perhaps, also, I felt some embarrassment, the possibility of being in the wrong. I said awkwardly:

'Look, I've got to go home now. Meet me at five this evening . . .'

I walked off quickly, wondering what motive the fates had in flinging this new development at my head.

All the way home I tried to concentrate on the problem. At one point I made up my mind to go and talk to Uncle Sam and ask his advice; I thought I would do it immediately, in the lunch-hour. Then I changed my mind, realizing that he could do nothing to help. I considered going to Scottie Gibbs and talking to him frankly. But what could I say? That I thought that Kaspar, Jed and

Dime were partners in a burgling gang, and that Jed had killed the girl called Moira Page? He would ask me if I had any evidence. On the other hand, perhaps Scottie Gibbs might be holding a missing piece of the jigsaw. Otherwise, why were Kaspar and Dime so afraid that I might talk to the police about them? I toyed with this idea until I got home, then dismissed it.

An incident in the lunch-hour intensified the uncertainty. My mother said casually:

'By the way, Hugh, someone rang you half an hour ago.'

'Who?'

'He had an odd name. I've written it down somewhere.' She found an envelope on the shelf and read out the name: 'Dime'. She said vaguely: 'He didn't sound a very nice man. I hope he's not really a friend of yours.'

'What did he say?'

'Oh, nothing. He just asked me if you were home, and asked me to say that Dime had rung, and he'd see you later.'

That was all. Dime evidently wanted me to know that he knew where I lived. I looked at Anne – cheerfully eating her soup with sucking noises – and wondered if she could really be in any danger. Again, I thought of talking to Scottie, then decided to wait and see what happened.

I was so absorbed in these problems that I forgot about Patricia, and was surprised to see her waiting when I came out of the office. We walked along in silence for a while, then she asked:

'Do you believe what I told you?'

I said something non-committal. Finally she asked:

'Do you want to quarrel with me?'

This was difficult to answer honestly; I had to say no. She said: 'I'm sorry. Perhaps I shouldn't have gone back to Monty's. But it was a misunderstanding. If you saw me wearing his dressing-gown, you must have seen that I had my shoes and stockings on.'

I had to admit that I had not looked that closely. We walked on again in silence for a while, then she said:

'Won't you please tell me what's the matter?'

I overcame a reluctance to speak, and said: 'Look here, it's nothing to do with you. I've got another worry on my mind.'

'Can't you tell me about it?'

'No.'

'But you're not still angry with me?'

I said no. This was true enough; it was also true that I now felt completely indifferent about her. Perhaps she sensed this, for she asked:

'Do you want to go on seeing me?'

It is almost impossible to answer this question with a flat negative. I hesitated, and she said: 'If you don't, I'll go home now.' I said hastily:

'No, no, that's all right.' Then, realizing that we were near the café where I was supposed to see Kaspar, I added: 'You'd better go home, though. I've something to do.'

'What?'

'See a man . . .'

'Can't I come?' I think she believed I was lying. So I said unwillingly: 'All right. But I shall have to speak to him alone for a few minutes.'

Kaspar was already there in the café. He looked surprised when he saw Patricia. I bought teas, asked Patricia to sit at another table for a moment, and went across to Kaspar. He asked immediately:

'Who's she?'

'Just a girl-friend.'

'How much does she know?'

289

'Nothing.'

'Is she the one who saw Jed?'

'Yes.' I had forgotten that I had told him about this.

He made an uncertain, muttering noise, and passed his hand over his eyes. He looked very tired and strained. We sat there without speaking for a moment; then he said:

'I hear Dime came and talked to you.'

'Didn't you send him?'

'No, young 'un, I didn't. What's more, I'm sorry he came. Just you forget all about it. He always tries to do things the rough way. I try to tell him it won't work, and that you're not likely to go talking to the police anyway . . .'

He took a long sip of his tea, rubbed his eyes again, and said:

'Now, your bit o' business.'

'Have you discovered anything?'

'Not much. I've got a friend in the infirmary who says that some lad was brought in on Friday night and had an urgent operation. But he doesn't know anything else. He doesn't even know whether it's the same lad.'

'Does he know what kind of an operation it was?'

'Lower abdomen, he thought. But he's not sure.' He leaned over to me and I noticed that there was whisky on his breath. 'Now my opinion's this: for some reason they're keeping it very dark.'

'Why should they?'

'That I don't know. I could have one or two guesses. For example, you say the mayor and chief constable are members of this shooting-club? Well, I suppose they might find it a bit embarrassing if one of their members had done it, eh? If it gets into the papers, they'd get a lot of unwelcome publicity. Whereas if they can nab you without anybody hearing about it . . .'

For a moment I felt hopeful.

'You mean they might simply drop the whole thing?'

'Oh no. They couldn't do that. You'd have to appear in a juvenile court. But it'd be easy enough to keep the Press away. You'd get a couple of years in a reformatory, and no one'd ever know why . . .'

This all sounded horribly plausible. I said finally:

'Is there nothing I can do?'

'Not a thing.'

'Is there anything *you* can do?' It was obvious, from his manner, that this was what he wanted me to ask. He wanted to drive a bargain, and I had to propose it.

'Well, there's one possibility. It's my belief the police are looking for the other lads in the gang. If they find 'em, you've had it. They'll describe you, and the coppers'll have you like that. But if I should use a bit of my influence to talk with some of these lads before the police get to 'em . . .'

'They might have found them already.'

'They might. You'll soon know, if there's a copper waiting to see you at home. But if they haven't we might be able to swing something. Jed knows a lot of these lads. It wouldn't take him long to find out who they were.' He looked up and said: 'Well, here's Jed.' It was evident that Jed's appearance had been prearranged. I felt strongly that Kaspar was trying to trick me, but could not see how. Jed came and sat next to me. His eyes were on Patricia, sitting at the next table and pretending to be absorbed in a copy of *Vogue*. Patricia glanced up, saw him and went pale. Jed's big, loose hands were on the table top; they were ugly hands with chilblained knuckles, and as I looked at them I imagined them choking the life out of Moira Page. Then, to my surprise, Kaspar's papery-white hands approached them across the table top; his nails dug into Jed's flesh as he pinched the back

291

of his hand. Jed's eyes left Patricia slowly, and settled on Kaspar with a blank, incurious look. I glanced down at his hand. One of Kaspar's nails had broken the flesh, and blood was welling out of the tiny cut. 'Pay attention Jed,' Kaspar said sarcastically. I expected to see Jed look angry, but he only looked blank. Kaspar said softly:

'Now, Jed, our friend here wants a little help from you. You'd like to help him, wouldn't you?'

Jed nodded. It crossed my mind to wonder if he was hypnotized, but the idea seemed too romantic. He was only stupid and bovine.

'Now,' Kaspar said, 'you'll have to try and find some boys . . .'

'What boys?' Jed asked. It was the first time he had spoken.

'That's what we've got to find out.' He asked me: 'Can you tell us anything about them? Can you describe any of them?'

I thought hard, but could think of nothing distinctive.

'How about names? You must have heard them use some names?'

I shook my head.

'That's not very helpful,' Kaspar said. 'Still, we'll do our best.' He began to pick his teeth with a bitten matchstick; this gave him a rat-like appearance. 'The main thing is not to worry. You've helped Jed, and Jed'll help you. And you needn't worry about Dime either. He's a bit too eager to use that knife of his . . .'

Jed's eyes had gone back to Patricia. I could understand why; she was sitting with her legs crossed, the book propped on her knees, and the top of one stocking just showing under the edge of the dress. Kaspar was consulting a notebook that he had taken from his pocket and did not notice that Jed's attention had strayed again. Jed's face was as impassive as an Egyptian statue. Then as I looked, something altered in his eyes; they widened, and his mouth set into a line. What surprised me was that he was oblivious of me and of Kaspar; he was watching Patricia with the look of a hunter, with an almost happy gleam in his eyes. Kaspar was saying:

'Here's a couple of lads you could start with – Terry Brown of the Metcalf Hill gang – he knows everything that goes on – and Sandy Moran of the Wood Lane boys. They're both regulars at the Palais as well . . .'

I was fascinated by Jed's stare – and also because he had lowered his clenched hands into his lap, and was pressing them into his thighs. Kaspar looked up then snarled irritably:

'Jed!' Jed ignored him. I expected Kaspar to repeat the word in a more menacing tone. Instead, he said with a deceptively calm, almost cooing voice: 'Jerry, look at me.' Immediately Jed's eyes swung back to him, with the same blank, obedient look. In that moment I was certain that I was not mistaken in thinking that Jed had been hypnotized – or at least, that he was completely under Kaspar's sway. Kaspar put a piece of paper in front of Jed, and said: 'Take that with you. Go and see Terry Brown and find out if he can help us. Come back to me afterwards. Go now.' Jed stood up, took the paper and walked out, without another glance at Patricia. Kaspar's parchment face cracked into an oily smile. He said:

'Your young lady's very attractive. Can't you ask her to come and sit here, now we've done talking?'

I did as he asked – out of curiosity. I wanted to see her reaction to him. Kaspar was charming to her. He said: 'May I look at your hand?' All women are eager to have their palms read. She extended both her hands, and he took them in his and studied them. Then he told her that she had a vital, passionate nature, and a hasty temper, but that she would make an excellent housewife. He kept looking at her as he spoke, and I am certain that he guessed the kind of thing she enjoyed hearing from her expression. I cannot remember everything he told her, but it was all flattering; at one point he implied she would marry me, or someone like me. Then he looked at his watch and asked us if we would like to come and look at his room. I found these tactics puzzling. 'Yes, come and talk to me,' Kaspar said, pressing Patricia's hand. So finally we followed him out of the café. His room was only a few yards away, and it was at the top of the house; it was small, untidy, had a sloping roof, and dozens of yellow-brown photographs on the walls. He produced a full bottle of gin from a cupboard and poured three large helpings, asking simply: 'Do you take orange or tonic?' I was unwilling to drink – I had an absurd idea that they might be drugged – but I decided that a tonic water should be safe enough. A tiny gas-fire with broken elements soon had the room stiflingly hot. Patricia and I sat on the unmade bed and listened to Kaspar talking. I remembered how he had talked in the theatre – making the audience forget his failure to hypnotize the girl by giving them a brief history of hypnotism – and I was aware that he was doing this now. Ten minutes before I had thought of him as an enemy – or at least, a man who wanted to trap and deceive me; now I found myself liking him. He took down photographs, most of them of women in theatrical costumes, and reminisced about them. He showed us a picture of a strong man, dressed in a lion skin, and explained that this was his brother. He then told us his brother's history, and we found it hilariously funny: how his brother had been walking round a circus when the manager approached him and asked him if he would take the place of the lion-tamer for an evening, the lion-tamer having had his leg broken by one of the trapeze artists when he tried to seduce the artist's wife;

Kaspar's brother – whom he called Midge – had been introduced to an ancient and sleepy lion, who was guaranteed to obey anybody who cracked a whip at him, and agreed to act as temporary lion-tamer. Unfortunately, the lion detested cats, and on Midge's first night in the ring a small girl brought her kitten to the ringside . . .

I am certain that Kaspar improvised the whole story; it went on for a long time, and when we got tired of laughing at Midge's exploits Kaspar switched to another picture, which he said was his mother, who cut short her career as an opera singer to marry a snake-swallower. The father had died – absurdly enough, of a sore throat – and Kaspar talked of his mother's struggles to support three children. One of his stories was about how they were all stranded on the west coast of Ireland in the middle of a plague that killed off whole towns. This was almost the only one of his stories that struck me as true, although I cannot explain why.

He had refilled our glasses as he talked, and at one point Patricia said she wanted to go to the bathroom. Having shown her the way, he came and sat down again and said:

'It's a hard life, Hughie.' (He had started to call me this as soon as Patricia joined us, he also insisted that we call him Charles.) 'I sometimes wonder why I carry on at all.'

Since I was feeling friendly, I asked:

'But why do you get mixed up in all this semi-crooked stuff? Surely you don't have to associate with people like Dime?'

'Dime's a roughneck – a nasty, unpleasant man. Still, he's not really what you'd call a friend of mine. We just have . . . er . . . business interests in common. He *likes* living on the wrong side of the law. I never did. But after all, when you've worked like me for forty years and you find yourself at sixty without a penny, what can you do? Starve?'

I wondered how far Kaspar had convinced himself that he was sincere about all this. He certainly seemed to be speaking with complete frankness. I began to feel sorry for him; he was a pathetic old man, friendly, needing to talk to other human beings, slightly crooked, perhaps, but in a frank and humorous way. Patricia came back; he poured more drinks – although by this time I was hungry and wanted no more to drink – and when Patricia observed shyly that he seemed to drink very quickly, he went on to tell us about how he had lost several good jobs – on the stage – through this fondness for gin or whisky. Some of these stories were also very funny. I suppose we were both flattered at having an old man treating us as equals. Patricia began to ask him about hypnotism and how it worked. He said that three-quarters of it was nonsense – for example, the idea that anyone could be made to do things against his will. It struck me that some of this conflicted with what he had told me and Monty two weeks ago, but I said nothing. I suspected that he had completely forgotten this conversation.

'The thing is,' Kaspar said, 'the person who's being hypnotized has to do three-quarters of the work.' He glanced at me and grinned: 'Shall we try and hypnotize her?'

'Could you?' Patricia said, fascinated.

'I don't know. See, it's not like on the stage. Then you've got a kind of mass hysteria, if you see what I mean. It'd be more difficult in a room like this . . .'

As he spoke I thought I could see what he was trying to do. However, I had no reason to object, so I said:

'Yes, why don't you try and hypnotize her?'

'We could try.' He went to a drawer and took out a

296

small metal object, the kind of mirror suspended in bird-cages. He then turned on a desk lamp with an adjustable shade – it was the kind of lamp that is fixed over drawing-boards – and turned it so that it shone on the mirror, and across Patricia's face. He then went through the procedure I had already seen on the stage – asking her to look at the mirror, which he swung, talking softly – mostly telling her that she could relax and not be afraid – and occasionally making passes in front of her face. 'Your eyes are closing against your will. You find it difficult to keep them open. The eyelids feel heavy. You are very tired . . .' I found my own eyelids starting to close, and jerked them open. When I looked at Patricia, her eyes were shut. He turned to me and said: 'She's an excellent subject.' He said to her: 'Your left cheek itches slightly. Would you like to scratch it?' Patricia immediately scratched her cheek with the nail of her index-finger. Kaspar said: 'The itch has moved to the back of your head.' Patricia immediately scratched the back of her head. This did not surprise me; I found myself itching in response to his suggestion, although not on the face. I cautiously scratched my left shoulder. Kaspar said: 'Are you afraid of spiders?'

'I'm afraid of big spiders,' Patricia said.

'But not of little ones?'

'No.'

'That's good, because there's a little spider walking on your left knee. Brush it off.'

Patricia obediently made a brushing movement, but on her right knee. I had noticed several times that she confused left and right.

'That's the wrong knee,' Kaspar said. 'Now the spider's underneath your dress. Knock it down.'

Patricia pulled back her dress to her waist, and brushed her hand all the way along the thigh. Kaspar turned and winked at me. He said: 'She's a very shapely young lady.' Patricia pulled down her dress again, and sat with her hands on her knees. Kaspar told her to open her eyes. I noticed they looked blank, like Jed's. Kaspar said:

'Now, I'm going to wake you up. When I snap my fingers twice, like this, you'll wake up. But if I snap my fingers only once, you'll fall asleep again. You'll find your eyelids getting heavy. Do you understand?' Then he snapped his fingers twice, and Patricia opened her eyes. She evidently knew that she had been hypnotized, and could remember Kaspar telling her that she had a spider on her leg.

As I expected, Patricia suggested that Kaspar should try to hypnotize me. He pretended to be unwilling, and I said I was a bad hypnotic subject. But I knew this was probably untrue. The way my eyelids had closed, and my shoulder started to itch, proved to me that I was almost as suggestible as Patricia. I shrugged and said: 'All right, go ahead.' I was aware that the heat of the room and the effect of the gin would make it easier for Kaspar, but I felt a perverse desire to accept his challenge.

He swung the mirror in front of my eyes, and I found its glittering arc fascinating, and the way it turned and reflected the light in different ways. As he talked to me my mind became receptive, and my attention concentrated on the mirror. Then I remembered what had happened last time Kaspar tried to hypnotize me, and I deliberately thought of a problem that had been occupying my mind earlier in the day – Diophantus's 'three square' problem from Book Five.* This is a simple enough problem with the aid of functional analysis, but one that I had not looked at for several years. As soon as

---

* To find three squares such that the product of any two of them, added to the sum of those two or to the remaining one, gives a square.

I thought about it my mind proceeded to work at it automatically, and I became unaware of the moving mirror or of Kaspar's voice. Kaspar must have taken my abstraction for a trance state, because he said after a moment: 'You will now close your eyes.' I closed my eyes. I heard Patricia gasp with admiration, and Kaspar said: 'I didn't expect him to respond so easily.' He said to me: 'Now I want you to resist any orders I give you with all your force. Resist them as hard as you can, but you will find yourself carrying them out all the same. Now, you will stand up and raise your arms above your head.' At this point I solved my problem in Diophantus – which was one of the reasons that I preferred to keep my eyes closed – and there seemed no point in sitting there, so I opened my eyes and grinned at him. For a moment, he looked confounded, and Patricia said: 'Oh, he was only pretending.' 'Sorry,' I said, 'I was working out a problem of my own.' I caught the look of irritation on his face, but this vanished immediately, and he smiled.

'I didn't think you'd be as easy as that. Not like this young lady.' As he said this, he turned to Patricia and snapped his fingers in front of her face. She looked surprised, then stared at him blankly, her eyes gradually closing. But it was obvious that she was struggling against it, and that the effort worked. A moment later she said: 'Oh, I nearly went off again.' She shook her head and rubbed her eyes. I expected Kaspar to be disconcerted by this double failure, but he looked pleased. He said to me: 'She's a good subject, that girl.'

By this time I was feeling a strong desire to visit the lavatory, having drunk about half a pint of gin and tonic; but I was unwilling to leave Patricia alone with him. So I looked at my watch and said I ought to be going. Kaspar said pleasantly: 'Oh, all right,' and as he saw us out of the door said that it was good of us to come and talk to a

299

lonely old man. From Patricia's friendly smile I saw that she was touched by this; to me, it sounded like a line out of a Drury Lane melodrama. We went down the stairs, and I tried the door of the lavatory, and found it closed. A moment later it opened, and the girl I knew as Doris – Dime's 'girl-friend' – came out wearing a gaudy dressing-gown. She said hello to Kaspar, and went into the nearest room. As her door opened, I caught a glimpse of a man lying in bed; it was not Dime.

As Patricia and I walked along the street, through a cold fog, she said: 'He's a fascinating man, isn't he? Where did you meet him?'

'In the café where we met him tonight.'

It was now half past seven. Patricia said:

'What are you doing now?'

'Going home to get something to eat.'

'Would you like to come to my place instead?'

'How about your parents?'

'It's their bridge night. They'll be out by the time we get home.'

This was how it came about that, an hour and a half later, I found myself back in Patricia's bed, feeling enveloped by her nakedness, and willing to agree that our 'misunderstanding' had been largely my own fault. I accepted her assurance that she had not been to bed with Monty that night, and never had the curiosity to find out. It hardly seemed important.

Looking back on it, I suspect there may have been an almost superstitious motive in my reconciliation with Patricia. Things had started to go wrong from the moment I suspected her of infidelity with Monty, and although I had thought the break with her was a matter of indifference to me, it may have oppressed me more than I realized. It is certainly true that my natural optimism began to re-form during the course of that evening. As I lay beside her, I suddenly saw clearly what Uncle Sam meant when he accused me of imposing my own judgements on the world. I had been bundling up all my perceptions and emotions, and declaring that the result was true of 'life in general': Patricia's betrayal, my own cowardice, the indifference of nature, the human capacity for self-delusion, the failure of mathematics to help me in living my life; all these had got stirred up together into a kind of grey paint, with which I painted the universe. The sight of Patricia unhooking her suspender belt was like flinging some brighter colour over everything. And later, feeling a pleasant exhaustion and the warmth of her body, it seemed obvious to me that no philosopher has ever glimpsed the true nature of 'the universe'; it may be brighter than any fire known to man.

It was inevitable that I should tell her everything; she was curious, and I no longer felt mistrust of her. Even so, I did not tell her that this idea of shooting had come to me many weeks before, and was my true motive in joining the pistol-club. But I told her about leaving my gun behind in the cupboard, and about returning for it and taking Ewen Waite's gun as well. When I'd finished she said:

'So what you really want to know is whether this boy is seriously injured?'

'Yes. Have you got any ideas for finding out?'

'I might. I've got a friend who works in the infirmary. She's a trainee nurse.'

We decided that it could do no harm to get in touch with the nurse – a girl named Miranda. Patricia phoned the infirmary; after five minutes, she came in and said: 'She's not on duty. I'll try her again in the morning.'

'If it's not too late,' I said; but I sounded more pessimistic than I felt.

At ten o'clock, I left her and walked home. I wanted

301

to find out if there had been any more phone calls, and my mother would probably still be awake. But when I tried the back door, I found it locked. I rang, and after a few minutes my sister asked from an upstairs window: 'Who is it?' She came down and let me in. She said in a whisper:

'We had to lock it. We heard somebody in the garden.'

'When?'

'About an hour ago. I went out to get some washing that mummy had left on the line, and I heard someone at the bottom of the garden.' She took my Biretta from the pocket of her dressing-gown. 'I got this, just in case, but I didn't know how to put the bullets in it.'

I was inclined to laugh at her. She insisted on talking in a whisper, and was obviously not really frightened. All the same, it *was* remotely possible that Dime might be hanging around.

'Another thing,' Anne said. 'Someone rang up, but when I lifted the phone I got no reply.'

'I suppose the caller forgot to press button A.'

'I don't think so. I could hear breathing.'

This struck me as serious. It looked as if Dime was trying to frighten me by upsetting my family. I took the gun from her, loaded it and went out into the garden with a torch. I walked all round the house, shining the torch, which was as powerful as a car headlight, but saw nothing. I told her that she was imagining things, and that the phone call had probably been one of her school-friends playing a joke. This seemed to reassure her, and she went off to bed again.

I made myself tea, then sat in the kitchen, staring at the fire, with the curtains drawn. I kept the Biretta on the table. I was tempted to go out immediately and find Kaspar, to ask him why Dime was behaving like this; but I did not like to leave the house again. My tiredness had vanished. For a while I was unable to read, think, or sit quietly; then I thought about Patricia and felt better. I tried to recapture the insight that had come to me as I lay beside her, and became so absorbed in the thought that I forgot my nervousness and began to hum to myself – a habit of mine when thinking. There was a knock at the door, and I jumped to my feet, my heart pounding. For a few moments, I was too breathless to ask: 'Who is it?', but when I did there was no reply. I picked up the Biretta, pulled back the safety catch, and immediately felt less nervous. The thought went through my head: 'If that's Dime, I shall shoot him. I'd rather kill him now and have done with it.' I concealed the gun by my side, unlocked the door and pulled it open. There was no one there. I was afraid of waking Anne, who slept above, so I did not call again, but stood there, peering into the darkness. Then I turned back into the room and picked up the torch. As I did so someone came in; I turned and levelled the gun. It was Jed, and he looked more frightened than I felt. Neither of us spoke, until I said finally: 'What do you want?' For a moment, I was certain that he was there to kill me; but his obvious fear was reassuring. He stood there, shaking his head and staring at me, very pale. I pointed to the armchair – which was very low, for its springs were broken – and ordered him to sit in it. He did so, moving slowly. Then I backed to the kitchen door and closed it. I knew the armchair well enough to realize that it would cost him a considerable effort to get out of it, so I was in no immediate danger; I sat down, the gun on my knees, watching him. I repeated: 'What do you want?'

'Just to talk to you.'

'Are you armed?' He looked at me stupidly, and I said: 'Have you got a gun?' He shook his head. 'Knife?' He nodded. 'Give it to me.' He fumbled in his pocket and pulled out an ordinary jack-knife. I laughed and told him to put it back. By this time it was fairly plain to me that he was harmless, although I still wondered whether Dime was hiding outside, waiting to take me off my guard. But I had locked the door, and was fairly certain I was safe. I pulled on the safety catch and placed the Biretta on the table, where I could reach it. I started to drink my tea and offered him a cup. He nodded, and I poured some for him. When he had taken it, I sat down again and said: 'Now, what did you want to talk to me about?'

He looked at me in an odd, cunning way, and the look made him seem harmless, somehow like a country poacher, shabby, dishonest and humorous. He said:

'You can tell him to let me alone.'

'Who, Kaspar?'

'No, Dime.'

'Why shouldn't he let you alone? Doesn't he like you?'

'He wants to kill me.'

'Why?'

He shrugged and went on drinking his tea. I decided to try and jar him into openness.

'Did you kill that girl the other night?'

It had the effect I expected; he choked on the tea and stared at me. He put the cup down, rubbed his watering eyes. I repeated the question. Then he said:

'No, I didn't.'

His face had gone very red, and a vein bulged across his forehead. His eyes glanced at the door, then at the gun, and it was obvious he was judging his chances of getting out of the room before I could shoot. I said:

'Look, I can't help you if you run away, can I?'

He started to drink his tea again, and sat there, breathing heavily but not looking at me.

'How can I help you?'

He looked up at me, and my doubts about his sincerity vanished. It was obvious that he was terrified.

'I've got to get away from them.'

'Why?'

'Dime wants to kill me.'

'Why?'

His eyes bulged, and the vein throbbed. He said: 'I can't tell you that.'

I decided to try a different line.

'Why do you come to me? What makes you think I want to help you?'

'You didn't tell the cops about me, did you?'

By this time I felt confident. Nothing was more obvious than his fear. My suspicions that he had been hypnotized returned. I knew enough about hypnotism to realize that, if this was true, then Jed would not be able to answer certain questions. If I pressed him too far, he might even feel a compulsion to attack me, to escape the questions. And yet I felt that I was now within reach of the truth – about the shooting, about Kaspar, about the murdered girl, and I decided to try once more. I said:

'Listen, Jed, I know you killed that girl. All I want to know is whether Dime helped you?'

The fear came back. Finally he lowered his face and shook his head. My suspicion that he had been hypnotized returned.

'Why did you kill her, Jed?'

He looked up, and said: 'Why should I tell you?'

'If you want me to help you.'

He stared down at his hands. I said:

'Look, I won't ask you any more questions about Kaspar or Dime. I don't want to get them into trouble.'

He looked up. 'You don't?'

'No. I don't want to get you into trouble either. I want to help you. Now tell me why you killed her.'

He smiled, and said in a matter-of-fact voice:

'Because I wanted her.'

I had got used to the idea that he had killed her, and yet his admission came as a shock. I felt myself going pale. It suddenly came to me that I was now in possession of a dangerous piece of knowledge – a piece of knowledge that would make me worth killing. But my curiosity overcame the fear. I said:

'But why did you strip her and then leave her? Did you get frightened?'

'How do you know I did?'

'The police report says she wasn't assaulted.'

He grinned. 'Perhaps they looked in the wrong place.'

He now began to talk freely. As he talked, I saw on his face the expression I had noticed earlier as he looked at Patricia. He told me how he had waited in a front garden near the bus terminus until the last bus came in, and only one girl dismounted from it: of how he had taken off his shoes, and walked after her. She had turned and seen him, then hurried on more quickly; at this point he ran at her and knocked her down, then beat her into unconsciousness with a piece of wood.

I listened, frightened and revolted, but he talked as if he had forgotten me. He explained that he had no intention of killing the girl – only of preventing her from resisting. But she had wakened up at one point and started to scream, and he grabbed her throat.

What struck me as most strange was his admission that he had not wanted to assault the girl in the normal way. It was obviously important for him that sex should remain entirely mental. He reminded me of certain boys I had known at school, who talked gloatingly and minutely about sex; the sexual act became an immense number of small steps, of gloating at every stage, so that the final act became relatively unimportant, in that it could hardly

306

intensify an excitement that was already a fever. Jed admitted that he had undressed completely, and remained like that for more than half an hour. I asked if he did not feel the cold. 'Only afterwards.'

It came to me later that Jed's type of sexuality was less perversion than a kind of excessive worship of the feminine, a morbid intensification of the normal male feeling of feminine separateness. In his own twisted way, Jed possessed powers of concentration, of single-mindedness, that a Newton might envy. With most of us, the sexual emotions of early adolescence are weakened, or vanish entirely, in contact with real women; they are replaced by a less morbid, more personal response. Jed's sexual development – criminal and furtive at every stage – had intensified these emotions until they achieved a power that made 'normal' sexual response impossible. This still seems strange to me, for I think of the 'morbid' adolescent emotions as a kind of shadow of real sexuality, essentially unreal themselves; somehow, Jed had 'thought' it into a reality that made personal contact with a woman impossible; even a conscious woman became an object.

I listened to this for three hours, until it seemed that the rest of my life was remote. The fire went out; I was unwilling to go outside to get more coal; although I no longer suspected Jed of wanting to attack me, it seemed stupid to take more risks. The strangest thing was to think of my mother and sister above us, while this curious flood of foulness poured out in the kitchen, and of Anne's 'murderer' being in the house while they slept. (My family had felt sure that she would have been murdered if it had not been for my intervention, and always referred to Jed as 'the murderer'.)

I cannot write of all that he told me; it was too long and confused, and I would hesitate to set some of the

307

details on paper. I did not encourage him; it was obvious that he wanted to talk, and once he was started he went on like the ancient mariner. At one point I asked him if he had ever been to bed with Doris, Dime's 'girl-friend'; when he said no I began to suspect his truthfulness, and asked him what, in that case, she had meant when she said that she didn't want it 'his way'. He seemed puzzled by this; then admitted that he had been to bed with one of Doris's professional colleagues, and that no doubt the two had talked about it. Even this explained nothing, because he flatly denied having attempted an 'abnormality' with the girl. It was only later, when he was describing to me the details of his first assault – he had been fourteen at the time – and I observed again the concentration of his stare, the minute memory for detail, that I understood what Doris had meant by 'his way'. It was the way of total negation of his partner. Sexual murder was the natural conclusion of his attitude to women, even if he seemed singularly free of any taint of sadism, or even of masculine aggressiveness. His total concentration reduced the woman to an object, to a nothingness suspended at the other end of his stare. The woman would feel herself a dummy, an object with a number of casual sexual qualities.

It struck me then that, in spite of his lurid sexual history, Jed might have been easier to cure than most 'sex maniacs'. Any continuous relationship with a girl would obviously have weakened that morbid concentration, which, even more obviously, could hardly have survived marriage. The question I wanted answered was: why had he developed in this way, when he seemed, on the whole, a reasonably pleasant human being, who might be expected to attract a woman. Only one explanation seemed to me likely. When he paused to drink more tea (I made several lots before he left) I asked casually:

'By the way, how long have you known Kaspar?'

The suspicion and tension returned, but he evidently saw no harm in answering, and said briefly: 'A long time.'

'Years?'

'Yes.' His sullenness had returned, so I dropped the subject.

At four in the morning my father went to the bathroom, then called downstairs: 'What's going on down there?' This gave me an excuse to say that I wanted to go to bed. I asked Jed where he would go; he said he would walk home; 'home' was about seven miles away, on the other side of town. I could see that he had forgotten about asking me to help him; the talk had relieved his mind. As he left I said: 'Come back to me if you need help,' and he looked slightly surprised. Then he said: 'OK. Thanks,' and left. As he walked away he called back: 'I'll be seeing you,' and the gesture reminded me of the time I had seen him walking away from the spinney. I said aloud: 'I hope not,' and locked the door.

I had no expectation that the wish would become an actuality.

10

I woke at seven the next morning with a sense of danger;
then I heard my father poking out the ashes in the fire
downstairs, and Anne's voice talking to my mother in the
next room (she always climbed into mother's bed as soon
as my father got up). With the realization that there
could be no immediate danger came the memory of what
Jed had told me; I was inclined to treat it as a bad dream.

Strangely enough, I was not particularly concerned
with the question of whether I should go to the police.
At seventeen, I suppose my sense of social responsibility
was not well developed; I should have felt it a betrayal of
Jed to report his 'confessions' to Scottie Gibbs. Besides,
I no longer felt that criminals were somehow on the
'other side of the fence'. I had plotted and carried out a
criminal act that was far more premeditated than any of
Jed's assaults. What interested me mainly was the question of the nature of Kaspar's hold over Jed. I knew very
little about hypnotism, but I knew the Freudians treated
the whole Svengali legend with contempt; it was supposed
to be impossible for a hypnotist to gain power over
another person, and to force him, or her, to commit 'anti-
social acts'. (I knew nothing, at the time, of the Swedish
Sala case of 1929, or the even stranger Heidelberg case
of 1936, where a woman was hypnotized without her
knowledge and made to commit criminal acts.) What
seemed fairly obvious was that Jed had been induced to
commit burglaries for Kaspar, who probably took most
of the proceeds. By means of 'locking mechanisms'
Kaspar made it almost impossible for Jed to betray him;

this explained why Jed began to show signs of strain when I tried to get him to talk of Kaspar. But now Jed suspected Kaspar of wanting him killed. This seemed probable enough; since the murder of the girl, Jed was a dangerous ally, a Frankenstein's monster out of control.

At breakfast my mother said:

'Have you quarrelled with that nice girl Patricia?'

I said sullenly that I had seen her the day before.

'Good. She's a nicely brought up girl, anybody can see that. She looks a bit like Anne, don't you think?'

It had not struck me before, but it was true; and this led further to the thought that Patricia might also be in danger from Dime and Jed; without thinking, I had involved her in a situation that might become violent at any moment. I remembered the way Jed had looked at her in the café last night. This decided me; I rang her up, catching her a few minutes before she left the house, and told her to meet me at the bus-stop in a quarter of an hour. She said: •

'Is anything wrong?'

'No.'

'Has anything happened?'

'Yes, I'll tell you when I see you.'

'All right. I'll try and ring Miranda in the hospital again. She should be on duty by now.'

When I arrived at the bus-stop near her home Patricia had not yet arrived; I waited for ten minutes, getting more impatient; then I heard her footsteps and saw her running towards me, clutching her handbag against her chest, her face pink. For a moment, she was too breathless to speak, then she got out:

'Sorry I'm late . . . but . . . rang the infirmary and found out about the shooting. He's all right. He went out two days ago. It was only a flesh wound through here' – she indicated the inside of her thigh.

311

'Are you sure?' Already, the surge of relief made me feel drunk.

'Quite sure. She says he was brought in on Friday night, and they let him out again on Sunday. His name was Roy Coleman.'

The bus arrived and we climbed to the top deck. She explained that her friend had been unable to give many details – she had only heard gossip from the other nurses. Patricia had been cautious; she had rung her friend on the pretext of inviting her to the office Christmas party, then had casually turned the conversation to the topic of the shooting, explaining that she had seen the boy taken away in the ambulance. When Patricia had asked 'Who shot him?' Miranda had said vaguely: 'I don't know – it was some gang.' Patricia had changed the subject, afraid that Miranda might become suspicious.

When she had finished telling me this, she asked:

'What did you want to tell me?'

I had already decided what to tell her about Jed. I could not admit that Jed was a murderer. She would insist that I should go to the police; she would point out that, if I hesitated, he might murder other girls. And plainly she would be right. I wanted time to decide for myself. What I hoped, of course, was that events would decide for me – as they did.

I told her that Jed had been to see me, and that I thought that he might be the sex murderer. I said that I was not certain, that I had no definite evidence – but from the way he talked about sex, and the way he had been looking at her the previous evening, I had a 'feeling' that it was probable. When she mentioned the police, I pointed out that they could do nothing on a mere suspicion – that they could do nothing even if Jed had openly confessed his guilt to me, because it would be my word against his. (In this way, I rationalized to myself my decision to do nothing.) I said that I might mention my suspicion to Scottie Gibbs at the pistol-club.

'You're not going there again, are you?' she asked with astonishment.

'I have to. If I simply stopped going they might suspect something . . .'

I walked as far as her office, although I was late, and explained that I thought she might be in danger. This did not appear to worry her; she obviously felt I was exaggerating for dramatic effect. All the same, I made her promise not to go out alone in the evenings. Then I went to the office.

The day started badly; Mr Coles was standing by my desk as I came in. He said: 'You're late.' I said 'Am I?' and sat down. His triviality was suddenly unbearable. He asked me where I had been. I said: 'Getting here.' He bristled, thumped the desk, and said: 'Young man, your manners are getting very bad. Look at me when I talk to you.' I looked at him, suddenly felt a contempt that made me want to hit him, and said: 'Oh, go away and don't be a fool.' This staggered him; he went purple, then began to yell: 'I will not be talked to like that in my own office . . .' I ignored him and began taking things out of my drawer, scowling; finally, his shouting so irritated me that I was tempted to throw something at him; I looked up at him, and he must have seen how I felt, because he suddenly turned and walked out. Miss Roberts said: 'Now you've done it!' and John Duncan came in to ask me what it was all about. They told me I should apologize to Mr Coles; I refused, and began to feel the same irritation with all of them; I went sullenly on with my work. Later, I talked to John Duncan about it, standing in the accounts department where no one could hear us. I said that I didn't care if Coles sacked me; John replied that he probably wouldn't sack me, but that he could make life

313

very unpleasant. I said I didn't care, and went back to my work. I was beginning to calculate how soon I could leave the office for good. I even found myself feeling a certain sympathy for Kaspar. He might be a drunken old has-been, but he didn't have to endure people like Coles and Miss Roberts. The life of crime seemed to have distinct advantages.

Towards midday the girl on the switchboard told me there was a phone call for me. It was my mother, and she told me that Uncle Sam was ill. He wanted to see me immediately; I promised to go straight to Aunt Bertha's when I left the office.

Half an hour later, on my way there, I wondered how I would feel if Uncle Sam died, and realized that the answer was probably: indifference. I liked him; I could talk to him more frankly than I could talk to anyone else, including Jeremy; he was the only member of the family with whom I had any real kinship since Uncle Nick. And yet he was sixty years my senior, and this meant that a profound indifference was bound to exist between us, as far as I was concerned.

Aunt Bertha was crying. The doctor had just left, and he said that he thought Uncle Sam might not have more than a few days – or even hours – to live. (He was wrong; Uncle Sam lived for three more years.) Uncle Sam had been taking his exercises that morning – he used to bend and stretch a few times every day – when he had collapsed. Unfortunately he had fallen with his head in a large bowl that he used as a chamber pot, and had almost drowned in his own urine while he was 'blacked out'.

He looked worse than I had ever seen him, his breath-ing fast and shallow, and his skin so loose that it gave the impression that his skeleton must have shrunk suddenly. Aunt Bertha left us alone. He opened his eyes, and said: 'Hello m'boy. Sit here.' I sat on the edge of the bed, as he indicated. He smiled feebly and said: 'Bloody stupid thing, the human body. A bad joke.'

There was the usual long silence, then he said:

'Listen, Hugh, they seem to think I might die. I don't think they're right. Why should I die? I'm not eighty yet. I just lie here all day. My brain's all right . . .' All this was said very slowly, between wheezes; yet I had a feeling that he was not trying to 'act' in any way; he meant precisely what he said. He took some time to work up more energy, than said:

'But just in case something trips me up . . . I want to talk to you. I want to say just one thing. You've got a good brain, Hugh.'

I said: 'I know.'

He opened his eyes, and said slowly:

'Well, *don't waste it on mathematics*.'

The violence with which he spat out these words appeared to tire him; he leaned back and seemed to fall asleep. I waited for a while, then said:

'I don't quite understand. What's wrong with mathematics?'

'Nothing wrong with it.' He talked again with his eyes closed, in a low voice. 'But I've spent a part of my life fighting a battle. There aren't many people who are born to fight that kind of battle. You're one of them. Some people think that life's wonderful. Some people think it's so stupid that they can't bear to live. That's you and me . . .'

I could now see what he was getting at, but only partly.

'What battle?' I asked.

He ignored me. Finally, he went on:

'Hugh, there are about three ways open to people like us. The simplest is to die. Commit suicide. Somehow, I don't think you'll do that . . .' His eyes opened, and he smiled. 'Even if you feel like it sometimes. Another way is to become a man of action . . . like George Fox, General Gordon . . . start a new religion, a new political party . . .'

He paused, and I said: 'I don't think I'll do that either.'

'No. Well, there's a third way. That's to go it alone, as I've done.'

I said: 'But to what purpose? Who knows about it? Who cares? Do you think God cares?'

'I don't know. I don't even know if God exists; that's no concern of mine. But I've done something, lying here. I've tried to extend the powers of human beings. To some extent I've succeeded . . .'

'Your own powers, you mean?'

'It's the same thing.'

We sat in silence for a while, then he said:

'You'd better go now. Just think about what I've said. Don't waste your brain on mathematics. Get down to the real problems . . .'

I said, laughing: 'You mean like how to get away from home?'

He looked at me again.

'Yes, that's true. You ought to get away from your parents. They're fools. Do you need money? I'll give you money. We'll talk about that later. Go and think about what I've said.'

When I went down again Aunt Bertha was still crying. She asked: 'Do you think he'll live?'

'I think so.'

'Why?' She looked hopeful.

'Because he's got no reason to die.'

'People don't need a reason to die.'

'Oh yes they do,' I said. I walked home across the park. It was a damp December day, the sky low and smoky, the wind cutting; the trees were bare, black ghosts streaming with cold moisture. The grass of the park

316

seemed to be mostly churned-up mud. And yet, as I walked across it, a bubble of happiness surprised me; it seemed to come from deep inside me, as if energies in my interior were circling and growling actively, like an upset stomach, and the happiness was some gaseous release. It was still obscure, but it felt like the awakening of energies in spring.

It soon vanished when I got home. The first thing my mother said to me was: 'Your friend Mr Gibbs rang up. He wants you to go to the police-station on your way back to work.'

'Did he say why?' I asked, startled into showing my anxiety.

My father said irritably: 'I'd like to know the truth of all this. Why should the police want to see you?'

I tried to eat my meal, my stomach tight with apprehension. Luckily, my mother changed the subject to Uncle Sam's health, which was agreeable to both my parents. They were pleased that I was one of Uncle Sam's favourites; they were certain that he would leave me money in his will. It also pleased them that our other relatives were aware of this favouritism, and were maliciously but impotently jealous. I told them of the doctor's opinion, but not of my own, and they were obviously pleased; they would have been inhuman not to be pleased, even if they had known and liked Uncle Sam ten times as well as they did. My father said ruminatively: 'It's funny how our Hughie always attracts the daft 'uns like Nick and your Dinah.' For them, Uncle Sam was an insane old man.

I could not eat, and although I tried to shut out their voices it was probably just as well that they distracted me; I was prepared to plunge into a bitter meditation on the irony and malice of fate. I was certain that Scottie Gibbs had found out about the shooting. The only astonishing thing was that he had not found out before, since there were about a dozen youths who had seen me and could describe me. I had to make up my mind whether to 'make a clean breast' about Ewen Waite's gun, or hope to confuse them with the problem.

My mother said: 'You've hardly touched your food. I'd better pack you some sandwiches.' I told her not to bother – that I could buy buns or sandwiches at work. I left the house a quarter of an hour earlier than usual, pretending that I wanted to avoid being late at the office. In fact, I did not want to sit there looking at them, and wondering how they would take the 'scandal'.

I was afraid that Scottie Gibbs might be out at lunch, and I would be forced to hang about, indulging in gloomy anticipations. But the sergeant on duty picked up a phone, and within half a minute I was in his office. He looked more cordial than I had expected. He said: 'Ah, Hugh. Sit down.' His fatherly smile baffled me.

'Now, Hugh, I want you to be perfectly frank with me.'

I said: 'Certainly,' and tried to guess what he had in mind.

'I've got a suspicion you weren't quite . . . open the other day. Were you?'

'About what?'

'About the identity of that man we pulled in. Jerry Pierce.'

I felt like laughing aloud when I realized that he wanted to talk to me about Jed again. He said, still smiling at me pleasantly:

'We've had him in here all morning. He's in there now.' He indicated another door. 'And he's mentioned your name twice. How did you get to know him?'

I had to think hard. This was probably the perfect opportunity for repeating Jed's confession to him. If I did not repeat it, and he found out about it later, I might be accused of being an accessory after the fact. But Jed also knew that I had shot the youth called Roy Coleman; if I became a witness against him, he might also become a witness against me. Admittedly, he might already have done so. I felt like a man trying to walk over ice in shoes made of glass. I said:

'I wouldn't say I know him. I've talked to him . . .'

'How did you meet him?'

I told him, quite truthfully, about going to the café with Monty, and of how I had seen him there. It was necessary to speak of Kaspar, and Scottie interrupted me immediately.

'What do you think of this Kaspar? Do you think this man Jerry knows him well?'

'I don't know. I've seen them talking together.'

He asked me why I went to the café, which was known to the police as a hive of racing touts and petty crooks. I think he ended with the impression that I thought it somehow 'romantic' to go to such a place. He shook his head at me and warned me to avoid it in future. Suddenly, he fired at me:

'Why did you tell me you couldn't identify Jerry Pierce when you knew him all the time?'

'Because I couldn't. You asked me if I could identify the man who took my sister into the spinney. I didn't think it was the same man.'

'Did you think so when you first saw him in the café?'

'Yes, for a moment. Then, when I saw him at close quarters, it didn't look like him.'

This seemed to satisfy him. He asked me one more question:

'Why does he seem to feel that you're his friend?'

I shrugged, and said that I thought Jed was simple-minded.

319

'You can say that again,' he said. 'He's as daft as a brush.'

I was told I could go. As I stood up I asked:

'Do you think he is the murderer?'

He looked at me and smiled, and for a moment I felt embarrassed for asking the question. Then he shrugged:

'I think he might be. He's the type. But we need some evidence . . . either that, or a confession.'

Before I went, he asked me:

'Do you still stand by your statement that you don't think he's the man who went off with your sister?'

'I don't think so. It's so long ago. He's *like* him. But at close quarters there's not so much resemblance.'

He let it go at that, and I went out. My first impulse of self-congratulation faded when I realized that Jed might confess, and then admit that he had also confessed to me. I started to walk towards the office, then changed my mind and decided to take the rest of the afternoon off. I drifted towards the café, hoping vaguely to see Kaspar, then realized that it might be under police observation, and my conduct would seem even more suspicious. Since I was, by now, within a hundred yards of the bus station I had an impulse to take a bus out of town for the afternoon. As I stood there, a bus came round the corner; its destination indicator said Moorley Glen, a small village on the edge of the coal-mining belt, about twelve miles out of town; as it slowed at the corner I jumped on the platform.

My spirits revived as we drew out into the countryside, then dropped again as I began to feel hungry. I was thinking seriously of Uncle Sam's suggestion of leaving home – going, perhaps, to London, or even to Cambridge. At first the idea was exciting; then, in the depression of my hunger, it deflated slowly. After all, every town was like every other town; and while undergraduate life might be more amusing than living in a provincial town, could I stand undergraduate stupidity?

In Moorley Glen I looked around for a shop where I could buy chocolate, but everywhere was closed. It was not an attractive village; there were two rows of grey-looking houses on either side of the wide main street; it might have been a suburb in East London. I knew there were some woods to the north of the village, with old slate-quarries, and I walked towards these. About five hundred yards out of the village I found a small house with a notice: Afternoon teas. The doors were all closed, and there was no light, but I knocked on the door. A dog barked, then a bad-tempered-looking old man opened the door, and asked me what I wanted. A big Alsatian growled behind him. When I mentioned tea, he said: 'It's a bit early, isn't it?' and took out a thick watch from his waistcoat. It was not yet three o'clock. An old woman's voice asked who it was, and when he told her she said: 'I'm not really ready yet. There's no fire.' I said it didn't matter and turned away, but she came to the door, and said: 'Come on in, we'll see what we can do for you.' The man led me into an icy little parlour, and the dog growled at me; I sat at the table, looking at a bowl of wax fruit on the sideboard, and cursing myself for wasting an afternoon like this, when the old woman came in and said: 'You can't stay in here. It's too cold. Come into the other room.' I was taken into a far pleasanter room that smelt strongly of apples; the hearthrug was covered with them. 'We're sorting them out for Christmas,' she said, and told me to sit down. She switched on a light and left me there. The old man and the dog must have retired to some other part of the house. Ten minutes later she brought me in a pot of tea, a plate of toast, and some jam. I was already feeling a great deal happier. Now, with the hot tea, all my fears about the police and Dime vanished. It was an irrational cheerfulness; but ever since Patricia had told me that the youth had been released from hospital I had felt an obscure conviction that fate intended to treat me well. Now it turned into a blaze of certainty. Then, my stomach full, and indisposed to move, I sat back and thought about Uncle Sam. What had he meant about not wasting my brain on mathematics? What did he call 'real' problems? Then I remembered what had happened to me at Jeremy's a few nights ago – the terror and sense of bewilderment, the feeling: 'What am I doing here?' and I suddenly felt I understood. But how could I tackle that kind of problem?

The thought made me restless; I paid for my tea – it was remarkably cheap – thanked the old woman, and left. It was now half past three, and already beginning to get dark. I walked along a footpath to the woods, and soon realized that I should have been wearing rubber boots; tractors had turned the road into a series of muddy puddles. But in the woods themselves the ground was thick with black dead leaves, and the air smelt of wet earth and wet tree-trunks. I stopped to look into one of the deserted quarries; they were fenced off, but school-boys had made holes in the fences. The water looked green and evil, and it reflected the steep sides and the dark sky. I remembered stories of bodies disappearing into these quarries and never being recovered. The curious thing was that I felt no depression about this; there was a warmth and vitality inside me that opposed the alienness of that dead water. This was not simply the warmth of the tea, although that was obviously one of its direct causes. As I walked out of the wood I pondered on the question of man's inner physics, the inexplicable changes from exhaustion to rising vitality. And again I became aware that this was what Uncle Sam had meant about 'real problems'.

It was growing dark as I walked into the village. I approached it down a hill that came in direct from the woods, and stopped on a bridge to look at a stream. It was mud-coloured and swollen; it tore at its banks, and tried to pull away grasses that streamed in the direction of the current. I knew the stream in summer; it was always icy, but it flowed gently, and you could gather watercress under the bridge. I stood looking at this for a long time, in spite of the cold and my wet socks, trying to concentrate the glow of exaltation inside me, which was somehow increased by the sight of all this roaring force attacking the supports of the bridge. Suddenly I remembered the phrase that had so excited me in Jeremy's book: 'Life is subsidized by a hidden power-house . . .' It was suddenly amazing to me that I had ever forgotten it; it was even more amazing that Jeremy had written it, and then turned back to his anti-human Manichaeism. This was a basic statement of the problem; not a solution, but the beginning of a clear statement. All the problem came after. As I walked down to the village in the darkness I was at once excited and irritated; excited by my mind's sudden agility and power, irritated by the feeling that I could not think everything at once. In a few hours' time this power would probably vanish, and I would not be able to return and explore all the alleyways of thought that I was now missing in my haste to try to see some general conclusion.

At the bus-stop, I checked with the time-table and discovered that I had ten minutes to wait. It was now very cold indeed, and I was shivering again. Further down the street, outside the church, some workmen were digging a trench, and there was a coke brazier outside their canvas hut; I walked towards the glow. The men were standing at the edge of the trench, which ran across the pavement and then along the wall of the churchyard, and I saw that it was half filled with water, which appeared to be seeping through a crack in the wall. I asked one of the men what had happened; he said that they had hit some kind of underground spring, or perhaps a water-main. The foreman was at the moment talking to the vicar. I warmed my hands at the brazier and watched them. Apparently they were supposed to be laying electric cables into the church, and this set-back seemed to promise a long delay. Finally one of the workmen accompanied the foreman to the crack in the church wall, and carefully inserted the end of his pick. He levered heavily, and a great section of the wall – about a yard square – fell out. They leapt back, and a sickening stench was blown towards me. It was unmistakably the smell of a decomposing body. I quickly moved away from the fire and to windward. The navvy with the pick – a youngish boy – turned towards the gutter and vomited. Nothing was visible in the dark cavity uncovered by the fragment of wall, but on the pavement among the scattered earth was a globular object that was obviously a skull, and an easily recognizable human forearm with a hand. One of the men lifted a lantern and shone it into the cavity; it caught the gleam of the eyes of a rat, which turned and disappeared into a hole. The vicar said mildly: 'Oh dear, I'm afraid you've hit a grave.'

I saw my bus approaching, and walked off to catch it. The fire had warmed me, and I felt the happiness inside me expanding. I thought about this as I sat staring out of the window into the darkness, aware of the wind that poured past the windows like icy water; I reflected on the absurdity of human responses. Three days ago this same event would have filled me with a sense of horror, with the conviction that life is a trap, an escape from torment into futility. And now . . . it would not be true to say that the sight of that decomposing arm had struck me as

324

pleasant; there was revulsion; but it was a revulsion counterweighted by its opposite affirmation. For about half an hour it seemed that my mind had become capable of grasping, in one single act of apprehension, all kinds of distant and unrelated aspects of life, seeing their essences. I was as aware of evil as of good, and I think it would be untrue to say that the evil outweighed the good. But the total effect made this unimportant. I think I had a sense of a meaning that was neither good nor evil, something of a different order. I suppose this is what a theologian would mean by 'good'; but it seemed to have little in common with normal ideas of good. It was a sense of power rather than of good, a kind of internal heat capable of transforming anything.

As I got off the bus I made a resolution not to allow this mood to disappear. Most moods change day by day; we see events through happiness or boredom or tension and attribute to the events some of the qualities of the mood. And we no more attempt to 'retain' a mood than we would try to hold back events. But I felt that this mood contained a far higher degree of 'truth' than my usual insights, and wanted to keep it intact.

Back at home, I ate a large tea and cleaned my pistol; then I walked across the park on my way to the shooting-club, and stopped at Aunt Bertha's. Uncle Sam was asleep; I said that I would return the next day.

I met Gerald Sutton on the bus, and told him that I was thinking of going to London. He was dismayed at first, then said that he would get a list of the London pistol-clubs for me. I had to turn away to avoid letting him see my smile. As the bus passed the Palais I looked out of the window; although the lights were on and the commissionaire stood outside, the usual gang of youths was not there. I asked Gerald:

'Incidentally, did you hear anything about a shooting last week?'

'Shooting? When?'

'After the club.'

I told him that Patricia had heard about it from a nurse at the hospital. It was obvious that Gerald knew nothing about it.

Scottie Gibbs was not there when we arrived. Gerald and I shot a friendly match, and he beat me. I began to wonder if Scottie was still interrogating Jed, and the thought of what Jed might tell him did not improve my aim. But at half past nine, he came in with Ewen Waite; the friendly way he nodded at me convinced me that nothing was wrong. At the first opportunity I asked him what had happened. He said:

'Oh, we let your friend go. For the time being . . .'

This was a relief. When I did a little more target-practice before we left, my shooting was more accurate.

As we went into the pub next door I felt a certain tension of the stomach, and it seemed to be justified when I saw a youth in a black leather jacket standing at the serving hatch in the passage-way. I did not recognize him, and he was not looking in my direction. Inside the pub Gerald and I sat in a corner; I determined not to budge from it until closing-time. I also made a resolution that, whether I went to London or stayed at home, I would not come into this pub again; it was stupid to risk meeting the louts who had attacked me.

Gerald and I drank our shandies. The rest talked about a forthcoming match. Someone asked Scottie Gibbs whether he had caught the murderer yet, but changed the subject when they saw him scowl.

Then, as I was emptying my shandy and watching the clock, Gerald suddenly said:

326

'Is it true there was some shooting incident last Wednesday, Mr Gibbs?'

My heart began to pound absurdly; I put my glass down in case my shaking hand betrayed me. I hoped that no one was observing my face. I heard Scottie Gibbs' voice say: 'Who told you that?'

'Hugh.'

'Did he! Where did you hear it, Hugh?'

Trying hard to control my voice, I said:

'From my girl-friend – the girl I brought last week.'

'And where did *she* hear it?'

'From a nurse in the infirmary.'

'Ah, I see,' Scottie said.

'Is it true?' Bob Salomons asked.

Scottie said in a bored voice:

'Oh, it wasn't much. Some kind of gang-fight. We couldn't get much truth out of them.'

By this time my heart had stopped pounding, and I was reasonably sure that my voice would not betray me, so I asked:

'What kind of gun was used?'

'I don't know. I suspect it was one of these home-made things. It couldn't have been very accurate, because the bullet went low – through the lad's thigh.'

'What kind of a bullet?' Bob Salomons asked.

'We don't know that either. It went in and out, and we couldn't find it. It was on that waste ground at the back thick with rubbish and weeds.'

The others pressed him for details. He said that one of the boys had stopped a passer-by and asked him to phone an ambulance for his friend, who'd been shot. A police-man found the boy groaning as if on the point of death. Unfortunately, he allowed the companion to go to the hospital with his friend before he tried to take a state-ment; he believed that the two youths decided on their 'story' in the ambulance. They had been walking along the street on the other side of the waste ground – just the two of them – when a man in a white raincoat approached them and asked for a light. While they were standing there, he pulled out a gun and ordered them to hand over any money they had. They tried to run away and he fired at them, bringing down Roy Coleman.

'That was a lie, to begin with,' Scottie Gibbs said. 'The doctor said the bullet entered the front of the thigh, not the back . . . Anyway it wasn't a serious wound, although he seemed to think he was dying.'

'What do you imagine really happened?' someone asked.

'I should say some rival gang set on them. Probably one of them had this gun – I wouldn't be surprised if it didn't belong to this Coleman lad. He was a nasty young lout. Someone twisted the gun away from him and shot him, that's all – then they all ran away.'

'That's a bit serious,' Mr Sutton said. 'These lads going around with guns.'

'Yes. But we know they exist. The elder brother brings one back out of the forces, and when he wants to hand it in at the amnesty it's disappeared . . . But they'll have a job to buy ammunition.'

'Why didn't it get into the papers?' I asked.

Scottie Gibbs grinned.

'Because we didn't want it in. We didn't want them to throw the gun into the canal. I was hoping we'd find out who'd got it. It'd mean checking around the street-gangs – finding out what gang they belong to and which are the rival gangs. It's a thankless job. Then this murder case blew up, so we had to drop it.'

Mr Sutton said: 'I still don't like the idea of one of these louts walking around with a gun.'

'Neither do I. And if I catch him with it he won't be walking around for a long time.'

The barman called time, and we all went out. I turned up the collar of my coat and kept between Ewen Waite and Mr Sutton; but the precaution was unnecessary; the 'leather jackets' had already left. A kind of morbid curiosity made me walk past the Palais on the other side of the road. The usual crowd was outside – half a dozen youths eating hot dogs. I thought I recognized some of them as youths who had attacked me, but I was not certain.

It was obvious that I would have to leave the town. Sooner or later I was bound to meet the same gang, even if I stopped going to the pistol-club. And next time I might not be armed.

An impulse made me turn towards the bus station; I wanted to see if Kaspar was in the café. Strangely enough, I felt no resentment against Kaspar. He had tried to deceive me, but it was understandable enough. Now I wanted to tell him that I was going away; I felt that it might set his mind at rest. At the same time I remembered that the police might be watching the place, and decided to approach it cautiously; if there was any sign of police observation I would sneak away.

The first thing I saw as I rounded the corner from the bus station was four policemen outside the café. A police-car was drawn up at the kerb. I stopped and watched. The usual curious bystanders were also watching from a distance, mostly on the opposite pavement. I crossed the road and asked one of them: 'What's happening?' He shrugged and said: 'I don't know. I suppose there's been a fight.' The café windows were steamy, but I could see more people inside. A few minutes later an ambulance arrived. Two men went into the café with a stretcher. The crowd became expectant, hoping to gain a clue now to what had happened; but ten minutes went by, and the stretcher-bearers stayed inside. Another police-car drew up behind the ambulance, and two men in plain clothes got out. I recognized one of them as Scottie Gibbs. I saw the opportunity to satisfy my curiosity; as he stood talking to a police sergeant I asked him:

'What happened?'

He snapped: 'Mind your own business,' then looked at me and said: 'Oh, it's you. What are you doing here?'

'I was just passing . . .'

'Were you? Well, it's your friend Jerry.'

'He hasn't . . .' I started to say. Luckily he interrupted me.

'He's dead.'

'Who did it?'

'A man called Ted Barston. Do you know him?'

I shook my head. He added:

'He's known as Dime.'

'Dime! Yes, I know him.'

'What about him?'

'He was a pimp. He lived off a woman called Doris.'

'We know that. Did he know Jerry Pierce?'

'Yes.'

He looked at me for a moment and said: 'You know a lot.' Then he turned to the sergeant and said: 'Let's go.' He left me standing there.

I felt dizzy; everything was happening too quickly. I was tempted to stay and try and find out what had happened, but the policemen were glaring at me irritably; perhaps, from Scottie Gibbs's closing remark, they assumed I was a petty crook. I walked towards my bus-stop, but felt so little like sitting down that I walked most of the way home.

I slept badly that night: the question kept running in my mind: Why had Dime killed Jed? To prevent him from talking? But that was hardly common sense; the cure was more serious than the disease.

I suppose I should have felt a certain exultancy at the thought that Dime was under arrest for murder (at least, I presumed he was). I detested the man; given sufficient provocation, I could have shot him without any compunction. And yet now I felt nothing – except a sense of having been somehow cheated.

I discovered the details next midday: both the local papers carried the story. Dime had strangled Jed in a room above the café – Dime's own room. According to Dime, he had strangled Jed in the course of a scuffle; he protested that Jed was insane and had attempted to assault 'my missus' – the latter being Doris.

Dime's trial took place when I was in London; I read about it in the newspapers. His defence was that he had invited Jed up to his room 'on business', and had left him in the room with Doris while he went out to buy a newspaper. When he returned he found Jed attempting to rape Doris, and choking her to prevent her from screaming. They fought, and he said that Jed behaved like a madman, foaming at the lips; he choked him to save himself, but with no intention of killing him. It turned out that Dime was actually married to Doris, and this was a point in his favour, even when the prosecution established that he was living off her immoral earnings.

The prosecuting counsel, Sir Kenneth Ramsay, pointed out that Dime had invited Jed into his room and then left him alone with his wife, knowing him, according to his own story, to be a 'sex maniac'. He also pointed out that Jed had a lump at the back of his skull: this might have been caused by the life-preserver that Dime was found to be carrying, and Jed might have been strangled when he was actually unconscious. On the third day of the trial Dime caused a sensation, and sent reporters scurrying to the telephones, when he declared that Jed was the murderer of Moira Page. The judge asked him whether he had any evidence for this: Dime became sullen, and said eventually that Jed's behaviour had been 'queer' the day after the murder. He was sentenced to two years for manslaughter.

A week after Dime's arrest I was in London. Uncle Sam had agreed to give me two hundred and fifty pounds with which to establish myself there. At first my parents refused to allow me to go; then Uncle Sam dropped hints of making changes in his will, and they gave way. During that last week I saw a great deal of Uncle Sam; he talked more than ever before. Later, when I was in London, he occasionally wrote me letters, and I continued to write to him, up to the time of his death, at least once a week.

I also saw a great deal of Patricia in London; she got herself a job as a model early in 1950, and moved to a room in Earl's Court exactly six weeks after I had myself found a room there. For about a year we were 'engaged'; then a rich young man with expectations of a title took her away to the south of France in his Jaguar and asked her to marry him. They lived together for a time and then, I believe, separated. But I never saw her after she had left. I was hurt and bewildered at the time – Patricia had come to represent for me almost everything I meant by sex and woman but there is no point in dwelling on that. At least she made my first year in London unexpectedly pleasant.

Epilogue

Epilogue

When Uncle Sam died in 1952 he left me twenty thousand pounds, a great many books (which I never knew he possessed) and the manuscript that I have already quoted, the 'Letter to My Nephew'. His fortune was larger than anyone suspected – even though families are liable to exaggerate these things – and my share was only about a tenth part of it; the rest was divided between Aunt Bertha and other relatives.

Although, as I have said, Uncle Sam talked to me a great deal in the week before I left for London, it was not until I read the 'Letter to My Nephew' that I grasped why he had spent half a lifetime in the dark. This was not because he'd tried to conceal his motives – he'd often attempted to enlighten me – but because, in some sense, I wasn't ready to understand them. The manuscript opens with the words: 'I have sat here for nearly twenty years, staring at the opposite wall, and I have created a certain power over my own stupidity.'

This manuscript makes it clear that he thought of me as the continuer of his work. He had already told me this before I came to London; but again I had failed to grasp what he meant. My chief difficulty was that I did not see how anyone could continue the 'work' of a man who had sat staring at a wall for twenty years. At first I thought I had a simple answer: he was 'meditating' after the manner of the Eastern sages – brooding on God and man and infinity. But he stated clearly in one of his letters: 'I do not meditate in the sense you mention.' This left me back where I was before. The answer came to me in 1955, when I was spending the winter months in a cottage near Lake Windermere, adding the finishing touches to my *Mathematics and Phenomenological Analysis*. I was expecting to be joined for Christmas by three friends – a man and two girls. (One of the girls was my assistant, Denise Frazer, who is now my wife.) But the snow was so heavy that I was 'cut off' for nearly two weeks. I was tired after my effort on the book; I had looked forward to the relaxation of long days of talking and Christmas festivity; then, to make things worse, I had a mild attack of flu. After a week in bed, with very little to read, I began to understand the true magnitude of the problem Uncle Sam had set himself; for I realized that six months of this would lead to total moral degeneration or to a mental breakdown. I always thought of myself as a fairly independent person, capable of amusing myself for hours with calculations and speculations. Now for the first time I recognized the basic bankruptcy of the human will. I had no artificial aids to make the time pass; time beat in my brain like a death-watch beetle, demanding an act of will. Uncle Sam's feat of will now seemed incredible; alone, with no kind of help, he had perfected a discipline for carrying the full burden of freedom on his own shoulders. But to anyone who understands the feebleness of the human will and the magnitude of man's freedom, this is as unbelievable as the notion of a man picking up a block of granite weighing fifty tons and walking away with it.

I recalled now the curious atmosphere of power and health that I had always noticed in his presence. I understood now the question that I should have asked while he was alive: How had he succeeded in living in a darkened room for twenty years without going insane, or showing any other sign of moral degeneration? What new 'muscles' of the brain had he discovered to combat the human tendency to drift? There is no clue to this in the 'Letter to My Nephew'.

But I should speak of what happened to me after I came to London.

My first act was to find a 'room of my own'. When I had moved in there (it was at the top of the building, with a view over the rooftops towards Fulham) I brooded on the problem of the best use I could make of my freedom. The idea of taking a job immediately seemed absurd; I still had £200 left of the money given me by Uncle Sam, and this seemed to represent years of working capital.

It was Jeremy who accidentally started me on the problems that have occupied me ever since. He came to stay with me in February 1950, and spent most of the week in the British Museum reading-room. There he fell into conversation with a young American, who had come to England to work with Professor Rivers Maclaine on the problem of laboratory verification of Einstein's general theory of relativity. Jeremy told him that he had a friend who was a mathematical genius, and ended by inviting the American – Peter Ruitenbeck – back for supper. We became friends immediately, and Ruitenbeck explained the problem to me – of treating matter as a concentrated 'field' and gravitation as a warp in space-time – and how the verification depends on reducing experimental error to one part in a million.

At first this excited me; I read through several books on the subject, paying particular attention to Milne's attempt to dispense entirely with general relativity. I met Professor Maclaine, and within twenty-four hours had been offered a post on his staff. I asked for a week to think this over. For already certain objections were beginning to trouble me like a toothache. These objections were of a kind that would never have struck me six months before. It was not that I disbelieved in the possibility of Maclaine's work; one-in-a-million accuracy is attainable by modern techniques. What troubled me was altogether vaguer and deeper. Ever since Newton, modern man has relied on science to 'illuminate the universe'; he is always discovering useful things that he did not know before. Einstein's special theory had been introduced to explain the failure of the Michelson–Morley experiment. But the later Einstein theories are attempts to embrace the universe in a mathematical theory – the unified field theory. And all these attempts to 'verify' it suddenly struck me as an absurdity. The scientists are faced with a riddle – and their answer is to demand one-in-a-million accuracy in their experiments!

But my own experience of a 'breakdown' was too close to allow me to forget that the problem of 'external reality' is only half the riddle. Besides, I remembered my speculations about Jeremy's ghost and my long discussions with Jeremy on apparitions, telepathy, etc., and our agreement that a great many 'objective phenomena' may actually be caused by the human mind, without human beings realizing it. I also remembered Uncle Sam's comment – that I was painting the universe grey because I happened to feel exhausted and depressed.

When I expressed these ideas to Jeremy he said: 'Ah, you're only saying what Bishop Berkeley said.' Now I had never read any philosophy except Nietzsche. I read Berkeley and Hume, and saw what Jeremy meant. But this only verified my feeling that my objection to Professor Maclaine's plan was a genuine one; I merely needed to find out how to express it. I wrote him a letter, trying to explain my reasons for deciding to decline his offer. From his reply it is evident that he failed to see what I was talking about. I spent the next three months in the British Museum reading steadily through Locke, Hume,

338

Kant, Hegel and William James. An accident put me on to the work of Husserl, and for the first time I understood clearly what I was trying to do: to ask how far human prejudices and preconceptions have managed to creep into our 'objective' scientific knowledge. It came to me that I had been preparing for this work all my life, ever since Uncle Nick introduced me to the 'hollow earth'. Because the question I had always been asking was: How can *I* decide what is true? Do 'true' beliefs carry a kind of mark on them, like a Hindu caste mark, to distinguish them from false beliefs? There was a time when scientists would have said: 'Yes. Simplicity.' Nowadays we know better. I had turned to mathematics as the home of the 'true'. Luckily, the world of violence always stood behind me, whispering doubt into my ear, like Alexander's slave whose job was to whisper 'Remember you are mortal'. And so one day I discovered that my world of mathematics was a half-world, and its truth a half-truth. And so it seemed to me that my whole life has been a training for the work I now chose: to discover a new scientific discipline capable at once of true objectivity and of recognizing that human beings and human life are themselves a part of the 'riddle'.

A medical friend recently told me about experiments to transplant organs from one body to another – so that a surgeon can replace damaged kidneys, eyes, etc. The main problem, apparently, is that the body has a defence system that immediately rejects anything that it recognizes as 'alien'. This is obviously necessary in order that the body should reject germs or poisons. Unfortunately, the body cannot distinguish between 'harmful aliens' and 'useful aliens', so that it rejects a transplanted kidney as ruthlessly as it rejects a germ – even though it kills itself in doing so. Doctors have to find a way of modifying this obsolete defence system.

339

Well, the problem in philosophy seemed to me to be exactly analogous. Why is human consciousness so absurdly limited? Obviously, it is a biological necessity. Because we cannot see beyond the present, we apply all our energies to the present. The result is that man has mounted the evolutionary ladder at a gallop and become the master of the earth. But a point has now come where this limitation of consciousness is obstructing any further progress and threatening everything we have gained. We are too narrow; we need a new breadth and depth of consciousness, a new wisdom, if we are to correlate everything we have learned and move to a higher stage. Doctors, psychologists and philosophers will have to unite to find the switch that keeps consciousness concentrated into a narrow beam; we have got to learn to broaden and narrow it at will. And it seemed obvious to me that this problem must be attacked by someone who is equally at home in the fields of mathematics, psychology and language. I decided that, since no one else seemed to be aware of the problem, I may as well make a start on it myself.

When I told Uncle Sam that I wanted to devote five years to writing a book that would probably never find a publisher, his response was to write me a cheque for a thousand pounds. But I was luckier than I expected. My *Critique of the Principia Mathematica* not only found a publisher; it brought me a generous grant from the Salzedo Foundation and another from the American Institute of Mathematical Studies. I owe the leisure to write my three-volume *Structure of Language* to their generous support. Its second volume is devoted to the analysis of the general theory of relativity that I had promised in the earlier book; so in a sense Professor Maclaine might be said to have 'started me in life' after all. Peter Ruitenbeck has become a frequent visitor to our house at Guildford. Last time he came he opened the third volume of *The Structure of Language* and said: 'You're lucky to be a mathematician. That means the professional thinkers will need a ten-year start to catch up on you. But when they realize what you're trying to do to philosophy, they'll try to carve you into pieces.' This, I believe, is true. I am only just becoming aware of the implications of the revolution I am proposing. It is not merely a new 'way of doing philosophy'. It might be called a new direction for human language and a new possibility of human effort. I believe that my method of mathematico-linguistic parallel may be regarded as an entirely original contribution.

I began to write this book six months ago, on the day after I saw Kaspar for the last time.

I was due to meet my wife for lunch. I sat in a small and not very sanitary café in Soho, reading the galleys of the last chapter of *Structure of Language*. My attention was distracted by the man at the counter, who was saying: 'Now look here, we're not a charitable institution. Go and try somewhere else.' I glanced at the bent shoulders of the old man who walked out of the café, and was struck by their familiarity. I walked after him and passed him, then glanced back. Sure enough, it was Kaspar, but looking about twenty years older and very ill. I stopped him; he continued to stare at the pavement, and said: 'C'n you spare half a dollar, guv'nor? Haven't eaten since yesterday.' When I spoke his name he looked up at me, and his eyes had become so pale that he seemed blind. Finally he said: 'Why, it's young Hugh, isn't it?' In spite of the cold (it was December) he was wearing a torn plastic raincoat, and I noticed he had no socks on. I asked him if he wanted a meal; he nodded, then looked at me cunningly: 'I could do with a drink to warm me up.' So I took him into the nearest pub, and watched him drink a large whisky in a way that carried my mind back fourteen years. Then I managed to persuade him to have a meal, and I left him with another whisky while I phoned my wife to cancel our lunch engagement. He toyed with the meat, ate a potato, then left it.

Like most old people, he was interested only in his own problems. He did not even ask me what I was doing for a living, but began to tell me about a quarrel with his landlord that seemed to revolve round the question of whether he used foreign coins in his gas meter. After his third whisky he became sentimental, talked about past glories, and started to cry. To distract him I asked him about Dime. He shrugged irritably and said: 'He's out. Didn't do more than six months. He's up north now.' He went on talking about his misfortunes, and finally I gave him five pounds. He began asking me questions that were plainly intended to find out where I lived, but I had no desire to find Kaspar on my doorstep every other day, so I refused to tell him. He seemed to have jumped to the conclusion that I was a writer of some kind, for he began to talk about a 'collaboration', and to offer to sell me the information that would enable me to write a best-seller about the life of a magician. It was so obvious that he had spent years like this, begging for half-crowns and quarrelling with landlords about foreign coins in the gas meter, that I suddenly had the impulse to offer him some real money. But it was clear that he would only dissipate a lump sum. On the other hand, I did not want to have to see him once a week to hand over an 'allowance'. Finally, I hit on the solution: I would give him a post-office savings-book, and I would agree to pay five pounds a week into a certain post-office, where he could draw it every Friday. He could keep in touch with me by writing letters to a *poste restante* address, but I would not give him my home address.

I put this idea to him, and for the first time he showed signs of understanding something I had said; he seemed to come to life, and the smile on his face was no longer a grimace that had no connection with what was happening inside. He stood up, grasped my hand over the table, and said: 'You was always a good lad,' as if he was my father. We went along to a post-office immediately and arranged it; he gave an address in Fulham to which his bank-book could be sent. After this we went to a small club for a 'final drink'. But my gesture seemed to have penetrated the shell of self-pity, and he began to talk to me in a way that reminded me of the evening Patricia and I had spent in his room. And for the first time I learned the full story of Jed Pierce, Dime and the 'burglaries'. He talked without inhibitions, evidently feeling that, even if this ever came to the ears of the police, he could only spend his last years in a comfortable prison-hospital.

He verified my suspicion that Jed was under hypnosis. He told me that Jed was a 'simple-minded' type, easy-going and good-natured, who couldn't understand why anyone should object to his occasional sexual experiments on little girls. As soon as Kaspar met him he realized that here would be an ideal 'slave'. Jed was an exceptionally easy subject for Kaspar, who got him drunk one night and hypnotized him. After a few weeks Jed was so much under his influence that Kaspar could make him fall asleep by merely raising his hand, or repeating a key word. In these trances Jed talked about his enthusiasm for small girls, and Kaspar realized that he had caught the 'sex maniac' for whom the local police were searching.

At first Jed was only ordered to steal small sums of money from his parents. Kaspar was far too interested in drinking to plan more elaborate crimes. For nearly a year

Jed was not used for specifically criminal purposes. Under hypnosis, Kaspar tried to cure him of his sexual abnormality; he was afraid that Jed might be caught by the police, and he would lose a useful source of income.

One day Kaspar overheard Dime saying how easy it would be to burgle certain houses at Stoneyvale if a child could be found to scramble through pantry windows. Kaspar thought of Jed. And, in fact, Jed soon proved to be a naturally talented burglar. He was small (he was only fourteen at the time) and athletic, and he was accustomed to stealth and speed. So Dime planned the jobs, Jed carried them out (often with Dime's help), and Kaspar took a third of the proceeds. Kaspar took most of Jed's share too, and when Dime found out about this he insisted that his own share should be increased.

This continued for several years. The burglaries were infrequent, and Jed was never caught. But one night they planned to rob an old widow who lived in the village of Cawlstone, seven miles out of town, and ended by killing her. Dime (who was outside) heard her screaming, and saw her holding up Jed with a gun. He picked up a large stone and hurled it at her through the window. It cracked open her skull. They escaped, and the body was found the next morning.

I knew nothing of this burglary; I never read the newspapers. Consequently, I had no possible inkling of why Kaspar was so anxious to keep Jed quiet.

But soon Kaspar discovered that he had another problem on his hands. He had tried to 'uproot' Jed's sexual abnormality by hypnotic methods; the only result was that the abnormality found a different outlet. Jed's interest in small girls vanished, and re-formed on adult women. One night, in the course of a burglary, he discovered a sleeping girl; he knocked her unconscious and committed a form of assault on her – although his hypnotic inhibitions were still so strong that he was incapable of the act of rape. He also took away some of her clothes, which he kept for several months afterwards. Kaspar knew nothing about this; he had had no 'sexual trouble' with Jed for years, and did not suspect that it was breaking out again. The consequence was a series of minor assaults on girls – usually girls who were returning home alone late at night. These girls were never seriously hurt, and many of the cases were not even reported to the police, the girls being afraid of publicity.

When Kaspar found out, he again tried to implant hypnotic inhibitions in Jed, and for a while he was successful. But these assaults were the only outlet of Jed's erotic impulse; the hypnosis could restrain them only for a limited time. Finally came the murder of Moira Page. This happened a week after Jed had been interrogated by the police about the burglaries. (The police had interviewed Jed immediately after Patricia and I had reported him as the burglar and 'sex maniac'. They were looking for a burglar who had a tendency to sexual abnormality.) Kaspar was panic-stricken; he redoubled Jed's inhibitions about talking of the burglaries, but at the same time released the inhibitions about the sexual assaults. If Jed was caught, he would confess to the sexual assaults under pressure, but flatly deny the burglaries.

The rest of the story I knew. Dime was afraid for his neck; he did not trust Kaspar, and he trusted his hypnotism even less. If the inhibitions about sexual assault had collapsed, then the inhibitions about confessing to burglary might also collapse. Kaspar was only a receiver; Dime was a murderer. He decided to kill Jed.

Kaspar never knew the whole story about Jed's murder. Presumably Doris invited Jed up to Dime's room, perhaps with the promise of giving herself. There Dime knocked him unconscious, strangled him, then disarranged the room to support his story of a fight. Dime's statement, at the trial, that Jed was a sex maniac and the murderer of Moira Page lent colour to his story that he was defending his wife against a madman.

Kaspar left town immediately after the murder and went to Manchester. He was afraid that Dime might decide to kill the only remaining witness of the Cawlstone murder. Ever since then, Kaspar had made it his business to know where Dime was 'operating' – and to make sure that he never came closer than a hundred miles.

Kaspar's talk finally became incoherent, and he fell asleep at the table. I got his address from him, put him in a taxi, and paid the driver in advance. The taxi disappeared in the fog along Oxford Street; that was the last I ever saw of Kaspar.

But, to my surprise, he wrote to me – about once a fortnight. In his first letter he tried to persuade me to give him his 'allowance' for six months ahead; he explained that he wanted to go to Spain for the good of his health, and that he could live more cheaply there. I knew that, with a hundred and twenty pounds in his pocket, he would not get further than the nearest pub, so I wrote to him saying that this was impossible, alleging my own 'financial difficulties' as the cause. He never raised the subject again. But I continued to get the clumsily scrawled letters, often in pencil, with the address written in childish block capitals. He frequently returned to the project of a collaboration; it was evident that he had no idea of what I did for a living. For Kaspar, I was not really a person; only a human being who showed some concern about him – probably the only one in the world to do so.

When his letters stopped – less than six months later – I guessed that he might be ill and sent him a postcard with my address on it. A week later came a reply: 'Dear

Sir, Mr Weiss died a week ago after a lot of couging [*sic*]. Yrs sinc. E. Ladbroke, landlady.' I do not know whether Weiss was Kaspar's real name; he had been introduced to me as Hassett. I discovered a few days ago that Weiss was Houdini's real name, and am inclined to believe that Charles borrowed it for this reason.

I continue to see Jeremy periodically, although he has become more of a recluse than ever. His character and ideas have changed very little in fifteen years. A few months ago, I met a Benedictine monk whose interest in comparative religion immediately made me think of Jeremy. When he mentioned that he was about to launch a quarterly magazine devoted to religious studies, I told him about Jeremy and sent him a copy of *Old Truths With New Names*. The result was that Jeremy was asked to write for the magazine. He promptly dug out half a dozen vitriolic attacks on the Pope and the Catholic Church, and submitted them to the Benedictine, who was rather taken aback, and returned them with a tactful letter explaining that they were hardly suitable for his magazine. Jeremy sent me the articles, together with a letter in which he said: 'You see, it is useless for me to try to compromise with The World. My ideas are completely unpalatable to the spiritually corrupt West; my modes of thought are too alien, too oriental.' Nothing I could say would convince him that it was not his 'spiritual outlook' that was unacceptable, but only his peculiarly dogmatic way of expressing it.

Jeremy and Monty came to my wedding; immediately after this, Monty went to Kenya to join Nigel Lever as some sort of game warden. I heard later that Monty had married a nurse, but since he is still in South Africa I am unable to give further details. Jeremy has achieved a certain local success recently – as a composer rather than as a writer; I believe that one of his large-scale vocal compositions has been performed in the cathedral and was praised by competent critics. He has sent me two long-playing records – privately recorded – of his piano and organ music. In some ways they remind me of his prose: square, brilliant, driving, dogmatic. I find it hard to recognize in these Beethovenish statements the soul of the Proustian hermit of Cranthorpe; but then, the contradictions of the bundle of responses called a human being can never be resolved as simply as the contradictions of philosophy.